Nabokov's Mimicry of Freud

Dialog-on-Freud

Series Editor: M. Andrew Holowchak

The Dialog-on-Freud series invites authors to explore the history and practice of analytic therapies through critical analysis of and expatiation on the seminal work of Freud. It seeks books that critically scrutinize the numerous facets of Freud's work over the course of his life, that investigate how or to what extent Freud's thinking causally gave rise to the various sorts of therapies that currently exist, and that examine the relevance of Freud's thinking today for those therapies.

Titles in the Series

Freud's Theory of Culture: Eros, Loss, and Politics by Abraham Drassinower
The Unconscious without Freud by Rosemarie Sand
How Talking Cures: Revealing Freud's Contributions to All Psychotherapies by Lee Jaffe
Freud's Theory of Dreams: A Philosophico-Scientific Perspective by Michael T. Michael
Nabokov's Mimicry of Freud: Art as Science by Teckyoung Kwon

Nabokov's Mimicry of Freud

Art as Science

Teckyoung Kwon

LEXINGTON BOOKS
Lanham • Boulder • New York • London

Published by Lexington Books
An imprint of The Rowman & Littlefield Publishing Group, Inc.
4501 Forbes Boulevard, Suite 200, Lanham, Maryland 20706
www.rowman.com

Unit A, Whitacre Mews, 26-34 Stannary Street, London SE11 4AB

This work was supported by the National Research Foundation of Korea Grant funded by the Korean Government (NRF-2012S1A5B1016645)

British Library Cataloguing in Publication Information Available

Library of Congress Cataloging-in-Publication Data
The hardback edition of this book was previously catalogued by the Library of Congress as follows:

Names: Kwon, Teckyoung, 1947– author.
Title: Nabokov's mimicry of Freud : art as science / Teckyoung Kwon.
Description: Lanham, Maryland : Lexington Books, 2017. | Series: Dialog-on-Freud | Includes biblio-
    graphical references and index.
Identifiers: LCCN 2017006391 (print) | LCCN 2017006713 (ebook)
Subjects: LCSH: Nabokov, Vladimir Vladimirovich, 1899–1977—Criticism and interpretation. |
    Freud, Sigmund, 1856–1939—Influence. | Psychology and literature. | Literature and science. |
    Imitation in literature.
Classification: LCC PS3527 .A15 Z748 2017 (print) | LCC PS3527 .A15 (ebook) | DDC 818/.5209—
    dc23 LC record available at http://lccn.loc.gov/2017006391

ISBN 978-1-4985-5760-3 (cloth)
ISBN 978-1-4985-5762-7 (pbk.)
ISBN 978-1-4985-5761-0 (electronic)

For Charles Mignon

Contents

Acknowledgments

When reflecting on the many people who made this book possible, I am especially grateful to Professor M. Andrew Holowchak, editor of the Dialog-on-Freud Series, who encouraged me to pursue this project after a chance reading of my essay, "Nabokov's Memory War against Freud." The essay, composed during a period of severe depression, represented a hard-won victory over my longtime fear of writing in English. I also owe a debt of gratitude to Professor Peter Rudnytsky, who published that essay in *American Imago* and, sometime later, introduced me to the impressive Butterfly Rain Forest in Gainesville, Florida. At that time, I was preoccupied with two distinct types of butterflies that are mentioned in the works of both Vladimir Nabokov and Sigmund Freud. Furthermore, I would like to thank Professors Jeffrey Berman and Mark Bracher, who provided me with helpful advice regarding an essay on *Lolita* that I presented at the Annual Conference for Psychoanalysis and Culture at Santa Barbara in 2000.

My affection for Nabokov and his novel, *Lolita,* can be traced back to my years as a graduate student in the United States, where I benefited from Professor Norman Hostettler's course on the twentieth-century American novel. At the end of the semester, after reading representative works of fifteen different writers, I was asked, "Which one is the most favorable to you?" Without hesitation, I expressed my admiration for *Lolita,* which struck me as a haunting examination of the mysteries of love. Many years later, in 1997, I was privileged to translate the novel into Korean, although I regret to note that this particular translation has been out of print since 2010. When I look back on my fruitful years in the United States, I am thankful for the assistance of Professor Charles M. Mignon, of the University of Nebraska-Lincoln, who helped me to obtain a doctoral degree and encouraged what has proven to be an enduring love of literature.

I would be remiss if I failed to express my warm appreciation to Ralph Cohen and Rita Felski, editor of *New Literary History,* who published my essay on Freud's memory systems, and Professor Susan Griffin, who affirmed my passion for William James when she published an article I submitted to *The Henry James Review.* I am deeply indebted to Kyung-Hee University, which provided me with the fellow grant and leave that enabled me to pursue this project. In addition, I would like to express my appreciation to my graduate students for their support and affection.

During the 1990s, their passionate response to my lectures on Freud resulted in three consecutive semesters that were devoted to readings of his work. Looking back, I will always cherish the assistance of Jung Gyu-woong, a fine journalist who helped me to promote my research during my formative years as a scholar.

This study would not have been possible without the generous support of the National Research Foundation of Korea (NRF), which awarded me their Fellow for Excellence Scholarship in Humanities. I am deeply grateful to my publisher, Rowman & Littlefield, whose acceptance of this manuscript marked the realization of a longstanding dream. Finally, I would like to thank my dear friend and editor, Dr. Thomas Welsh, who has reviewed a number of my published works. Last but not least, I want to thank my family, Changkook Shin and Hyewon. Without their love and support, I would not have been able to accomplish what I have today.

It is important to note that chapter 6, "Nabokov's Memory War against Freud," originally appeared as an article in *American Imago* 68.1 (Spring 2011): 67–91.

Abbreviations

ABBREVIATIONS OF WORKS BY NABOKOV

Full details of the items listed will be found in the references.

AD *Ada, or Ardor*
BS *Bend Sinister*
DP *Despair*
LL *Lectures on Literature*
LO *Lolita*
LD *The Luzhin Defense*
PF *Pale Fire*
SO *Strong Opinions*
SM *Speak, Memory: An Autobiography Revisited*
SL *Vladimir Nabokov: Selected Letters 1940–1977*
PN *The Portable Nabokov*

ABBREVIATIONS OF WORKS BY FREUD

SE Volume number and pages *The Standard Edition of the Complete Psychological Works of Sigmund Freud.*

Introduction

In 1959, film director Stanley Kubrick invited Russian-born author Vladimir Nabokov to produce a screenplay for the film adaptation of his novel *Lolita*. While Nabokov initially declined, he ultimately agreed to Kubrick's request. In time, however, Nabokov found that his role in the project was unexpectedly restricted. According to a letter written by Vera, the author's wife, editor and translator, Nabokov struggled to locate "an artistic solution" that would balance Kubrick's needs with his own vision of the novel. After a yearlong delay, Nabokov forwarded, in sequential order, the various acts of his screenplay. Moreover, in response to Kubrick's recommendations, he shortened the first draft of the screenplay by half. Yet, despite these cooperative efforts, he was systematically denied information on the film's production. To make matters worse, when the film was screened, Nabokov was not among the first to view it. This unhappy state of affairs culminated in the author's measured criticism of the film after its 1962 release. Although he acknowledged Kubrick's gifts as a director, Nabokov indicated he was not entirely satisfied with the film adaptation of his novel, noting that "only ragged odds and ends of my script had been used" (Nabokov, 1997, xii). As Nabokov later revealed in a 1967 interview, his reservations extended to Kubrick's failure to follow his lead on the pivotal role of dreams in the development of the narrative (Gold, 2003, 205). While it is unsurprising that two gifted artists would find themselves at odds in the course of a creative collaboration, the nature of their disagreement is worth exploring. Fortunately, clues abound, due in part to the 1974 publication of Nabokov's revised screenplay, replete with the author's wry observation that the document had "remained intact in its folder."[1]

The published screenplay opens with a dramatic, vaguely surrealistic scene in which the protagonist, Humbert Humbert, dispatches his archenemy, Clare Quilty, with several gunshots. At that point, we are introduced to the narrator, psychiatrist John Ray, who claims to have edited Humbert's confessional manuscript. Neither scene contributes in obvious ways toward the narrative's development in the original novel. Nor are these scenes presented in a manner that would be likely to capture the attention of readers—or ultimately, viewers. However, in accordance with Nabokov's meticulously organized plot, the reader eventually grasps that the murder is the culmination of years of conflict between the story's two "literary rivals," Humbert and Quilty. In the novel itself,

1

Ray's preface may hold little interest for the casual reader, but some Nabokov scholars treat it as a rich vein of clues regarding the author's intentions. Through a series of flashbacks, the reader learns that Quilty's murder is linked to the protagonist's relationship with Lolita. During the pair's travels, which are punctuated by hasty retreats from the potential intervention of neighbors and colleagues, they are shadowed by a stranger whose obsession with Lolita matches Humbert's own. In the end, the stalker makes off with Lolita, with her evident complicity.

One could argue that the artistry Nabokov displays in the composition of his tragi-comic novel (a work that moves seamlessly from suspense to nostalgia to humor) has been diminished, even displaced, because of his decision, in the screenplay, to foreground the rivalry between Humbert and Quilty. From its abrupt opening to its disturbing conclusion, the screenplay concentrates on the two characters' battle for possession of Lolita, who stands firmly on the side of Quilty. Overall, the rivalry appears to function as an allegory for the larger conflict involving critics and proponents of Freudian psychology. Indeed, the extent to which Quilty serves as a stand-in for Freud, while Humbert represents the author's position, makes it difficult to interpret the narrative as one that deals with the mere confession of a murderer. Significantly, the novel unfolds as a scandalous tale of prohibited love, prompting literary critic Lionel Trilling to comment that *Lolita* is not about sex, but about love. Yet, the text of the screenplay is dominated by the confrontation between the two rivals, which leads the reader to wonder if they are competing for possession of the text itself, as opposed to the girl. Their competition is sustained, even escalated, by the periodic intrusions of Ray, who is implacably committed to his belief in the efficacy of a psychoanalytic cure. The psychiatrist outlines his evaluation of the murderer's confession, which stands in clear opposition to Nabokov's view of art. Interestingly, one scene indicates that Nabokov himself would appear in a cameo role as a butterfly hunter, a comic figure that Lolita dismisses as "that nut with the net over there," as though she were resisting the inept psychiatrist's naïveté (Nabokov, 1997, 127).

Apparently, Nabokov has invited the reader to engage with his screenplay as an extension of his ongoing battle against psychoanalysis, rather than as a tragi-comedy whose wistful and nostalgic tone points to something deeper. Not only does Quilty repeatedly urge Humbert to receive treatment from a therapist, but Ray also reveals his identity as a psychiatrist with comments such as "my patient is flabbergasted," or "woe to him who gets stuck in his own quilt complex" (12). The screenplay concludes with Humbert's announcement that he has triumphed through an appeal to the ultimate refuge of art, thereby securing a means to guarantee the immortality of love. Kubrick's reputation as an experimental director notwithstanding, it would be difficult to imagine him embracing Nabokov's screenplay, which pits the claims of Freudian stand-ins against those of the author's creative vision. How could one reconcile the audience's expectations of an adapted bestseller with the strange, enigmatic dialogue that characterizes Nabokov's screenplay? It is hard to imagine how viewers would have responded were Ray to discuss "the sexual symbolism of golf" (15), or Humbert to refer dismissively to a "Freudian nursery-school of thought" (70).

Late in life, Nabokov appeared determined to highlight the prevalence of Freudian traces within his work. In retrospect, it seems surprising that he should have felt the need to do so. Freud's shadow looms large across Nabokov's body of work, and this might have been discerned by any astute critic, even if it eluded general readers. Yet, it was not until the 1980s, some time after the author's death in 1977, that critics came to regard Freud as Nabokov's "constant companion"—a phrase that, in the author's screenplay, Quilty directs toward Vivian Darkbloom, an anagram of "Vladimir Nabokov" (145). Indeed, prior to the 1980s, critics devoted far less attention to Freud than did the author himself. A close reading of Nabokov's texts—not only *Lolita*—yields myriad traces of Freud's influence. Not surprisingly, the author was impatient with critics' apparent failure to grasp this influence when they interpreted English translations of his early work that were published in the 1960s. In time, we see increasing references to Freud in Nabokov's prefaces and interviews, although the psychologist's work is routinely "mocked and ridiculed until the aversion to Freud becomes itself a thing Nobokovian," as Geoffrey Green observes (Green 1989, 373). A description of several examples will shed light on the author's urgent desire to highlight the ways in which he responded to psychoanalytical traces in his work. This trend intensified as Nabokov approached the end of his life.

Among the first of Nabokov's early novels to appear in English was *The Luzhin Defense*, which he wrote in 1930, during his residence in Berlin. Significantly, the author himself translated the Russian-language work into English, along with several other early novels, in the wake of *Lolita*'s critical and commercial triumph in the United States. When the English translation of the novel appeared in 1964, its preface observed that Nabokov would make it "a rule to address a few words of encouragement to the Viennese delegation" (Nabokov, 1990, 10). Furthermore, the author suggests that his protagonist's mental breakdown was inspired by details culled from a number of biographical sources. The narrative can be read as a parody of the psychoanalytic cure, a project that lurks beneath the surface of a story dealing with the life of a mysterious chess player. Subsequent translations of the novel also include prefaces that feature an ironic nod to "the Viennese delegation." Likewise, the forward to the English translation of *The Eye* (1965) contains a sarcastic reference to Freudian therapists. While he asserts that his book is devoid of elements that could be interpreted from sociological or mythological perspectives, Nabokov nevertheless contends that "Freudians flutter around them avidly, approach with itching oviducts, stop, sniff, and recoil" (iii). In addition, the work includes an overt parody of the Freudian primal scene, which unfolds in a passage in which the narrator attempts to commit suicide, only to be saved by chance. Meanwhile, a sendup of psychoanalytical theory surfaces in the foreward to the English translation of *King, Queen, Knave* (1968), in which Nabokov's antipathy toward Freud is no less evident. After rescinding an invitation to the Viennese delegation to review his text, the author warns any Freudians who manage to slip in that "a number of cruel traps have been set here and there in the novel"(x). Similarly, in his foreward to *Bend Sinister* (1974), Nabokov announces that his books should be stamped with a special message to Freudians: "Keep Out"(xii).

What was behind the author's apparent hostility to the analytic cure? And what elements of Freud's discourse did Nabokov find particularly offensive? Given that the author left behind no clear or coherent theoretical examination of psychoanalysis, readers may find themselves somewhat bewildered by the gleeful manner in which Nabokov pillories all things Freudian. His motivations remain, to some extent, obscure. However, some critics, including Jenefer Shute, have attempted to discern his motives through close examination of his texts. Such critics are apt to conclude that Nabokov's antipathy was a product of his long-running discursive battle with Freud, or that it reflected his hatred of *the double*, or the other self. In this vein, Leland de la Durantaye's argument features a markedly different perspective. He calls attention to a final irony brought on, in equal measure, by Nabokov's advocacy of *the detail* and his relentless attacks on Freud as an advocate of *the general*: "In vilifying Freud, Nabokov followed only the most general lines of attack" (de la Durantaye, 2005, 69).

One is inclined to ask, why has a consensus on this issue proved so elusive? A clue can be found in the fact that Nabokov's motives are formally embedded within the text itself, serving as its underlying structure. Given that this structure is an essential element of the author's aesthetic approach, it is difficult for the reader to identify. Indeed, Nabokov's skill at concealing his motives is a vital component of his artistry: one that transforms his novels into an intellectual contest between author and reader, as though the two are involved in a literary game of chess. While the author's antipathy toward Freud is conveyed in fragmentary, sporadic comments, it also serves as a key element of his complex narrative strategy, which often involves skirting his motives, while distracting the reader with humor. Critics have found this quality impressive and bedeviling, in equal measure.

Would it be too much to suggest that the leitmotif that recurs throughout Nabokov's works of fiction (with its continual reference to the Freudian delegation) also serves as the foundation upon which his narratives are constructed? If so, would it be imprudent to further surmise that his works of fiction would barely hold up in the absence of this leitmotif? This may be an unfair assessment, and one that would undoubtedly prove distasteful to Nabokov's admirers. Perhaps it would be more accurate to suggest that Nabokov's response to Freud reflects his "resentment of the precursor who may already have written all one's best lines," as Richard Rorty puts it (Rorty, 1989, 154). In any event, there appears to be more involved here than a simple case of territorial rivalry. Indeed, Shute notes that, given Nabokov's relentless effort to compete with Freud's discourse, he must have viewed the stakes as extraordinarily high (Shute 1995, 413). Without revisiting the subject of the two men's similarities, I would like to pose a simple question: In what way did Nabokov absorb the Freudian method or concept, only to actively resist it and, at the same time, sharply differentiate it from his own worldview? The strategy involved must have been related, in certain respects, to the concept of *resemblance with difference*, which is equivalent to playing a game that involves both protection and subversion, as in the case of animal *mimicry*. Before I develop this hypothesis, however, I would like to continue my examination of established views regarding the source of Nabokov's hostility to Freud as well as the context in which he rejected the therapist's school of thought.

While attacks on Freud appear in his earliest work (and would remain a constant throughout his forty-five year writing career), Nabokov tended to express his criticism in sardonic asides, many of which featured pejorative terms such as "Viennese quack," "Viennese witch doctor," or the more generally applied "humbugs." Nevertheless, a pattern emerges in which several Freudian concepts are roundly rejected—a pattern that de la Durantaye identifies as Nabokov's general lines of attack. During his 1966 interview with Robert Hughes, appropriately titled "Why Nabokov Detests Freud," the Russian-born author, in typical fashion, placed writers into two categories: those he liked and those he didn't. In general, Nabokov indicated that he preferred those writers that he regarded as anti-realist, whose styles he deemed playful, comic, deceptive, and above all, experimental. Writers in this category include Joyce, Kafka, Bely, Dickens (in snatches), and Proust (if one limited oneself to the first half of *In Search of Lost Time*). Meanwhile, he held a less favorable view of serious writers such as Dreiser, Mann, Henry James, Faulkner, and Pasternak, whose work actively engages with social and political issues. This distaste prevailed despite the fact that some of these writers employed styles that could easily be described as experimental. Taken together, these lists may provide clues to Nabokov's much-vaunted disdain for Freudians.

Interestingly, some writers he included in the latter category operated with a clear sense of social purpose, while others apparently embraced the idea that an individual's mental problems could be resolved through a confession that relied on human memory. Nabokov, of course, enjoyed nothing more than usurping the classic form of the confession and turning it to his own artistic purposes, as he does in *Lolita*. Likewise, in *The Luzhin Defense*, he employs the format of the case study to develop a novel characterized by mimicry (resemblance with a difference) of the therapist's discourse. In contrast to the demands of the "talking cure," however, Nabokov posits the creative artist as an exile from society, insisting that he be alone in his room. A writer is expected to maintain a cautious distance from others in order to avoid revealing his secrets, for in Nabokov's literary world, there is little room for the general public, or an "average" reality shared with others. Reality, for him, is too fluid, subtle, and complicated to be grasped as a general concept.

In this vein, Nabokov views Freud as crude and medieval, given that he demands that we accept an interpretation of dreams that is based on the ancient myth of Oedipus, that family triangle of love and hate. Likewise, he rejects the Freudian concept of a libido based on infantile sexuality, or childhood sexuality, a position conveyed through Humbert's voice in *Lolita*.[2] Accordingly, he repudiates any symbols, including sexual symbols, configured in the interpretations of dreams, commenting humorously that he does not see *umbrellas* in his dreams. Along with his repudiation of such symbols and metaphors, he denies the shared (and average) reality of the general public.

Indeed, Nabokov's responses in the 1966 interview echo sentiments expressed in his fictional biography, *Speak, Memory*, in which he indicates that he ransacked his dreams for keys and clues to sexual symbols and rejects "completely the vulgar, shabby, fundamentally medieval world of Freud, with its crankish quest for sexual symbols" (1989, 20). On the same page, he denies the Freudian concept of *Primal Scene*, dismissing what he describes as "its bitter little embryos spying, from their natural nooks, upon the love life of their parents" (SM, 20). Any observer familiar with Freud's analysis of the Wolf Man would readily discern the meaning of these lines. In *Pale Fire*, Nabokov's resentment toward the concept of the primal scene is suggested, on a surface level, in the work of the poet, John Shade, who hints at a very different kind of primal scene in the last segment of his poem.[3] While such examples reveal the *generalized* essence of Nabokov's distaste for Freud, Jeffrey Berman has gone further by listing the concepts the writer appears to have found particularly offensive: the Oedipus complex, unconscious motivation, dream interpretation, and biological drives (Jeffrey Berman, 1987). Indeed, Berman was the first critic to interpret Nabokov's war on Freud as a battle waged against a literary rival, a view that he outlined in his essay, "Nabokov and the Viennese Witch Doctor," when critics largely ignored it.

RESEMBLANCE WITH A DIFFERENCE: TOWARD MIMICRY

Before Berman called attention to the ubiquitous presence of Freud in Nabokov's fiction, most critics of the 1970s focused on two issues: the morality of Nabokov's work and the formal innovations contained therein. Douglas Fowler, for instance, concentrated on Humbert's transgressions against the established moral order, observing that the protagonist neither kills Charlotte nor stops loving Lolita. Moreover, he added, Humbert sets out to purify his soul by dedicating his life to a love that yields no reward beyond the immortality inherent in the creation of art. True, he murders Quilty, but the slain pornographer is an emblem of evil, and his death seeks of poetic justice (1974, 147–175). Meanwhile, explorations of Nabokov's formal innovations routinely focused on those artistic devices that were consistent with, or reflected the influence of, postmodernism. Placing his work within the context of a larger literary trend toward anti-realism, Albert J. Guerard identified several distinctive devices that were clearly inconsistent with a realist approach (1974, 3–50), while Robert Detweiler analyzed 60 works of fiction, including collections of short stories that were published after 1965, and postulated that their underlying structure is closely related to the strategies involved in games and play. In Nabokov's case, the game involving author and reader is a salient feature of his work (1976, 44–62). Paul Bruss referred to the author's open-ended and puzzling style as *textuality*, differentiating it from the traditional style of a closed *text*. He indicated that this style was characteristic of postmodernism, insofar as the narrative authority had been transferred from the creator to his or her creation, thereby placing special demands upon the reader (1981, 30). Further, there was a visible tendency on the part of critics, at that time, to place his work within the category of metafiction. In *The Metafictional Muse*, for instance, Larry McCaffery persuasively argues that, among writers of the self-reflexive novel, Nabokov's work exemplifies how metafiction can effectively address the human emotions of love, pain, and mental suffering, while employing an innovative, anti-realistic style (1982, 21).

During a period when critics focused overwhelmingly on Nabokov's anti-realistic, metafictional approach (which they compared to—or contrasted with—other postmodern narrative techniques), Berman's decision to examine the author's work in the context of the "Viennese Witch Doctor" constituted a bold departure. Yet he was not entirely alone. By the mid-1980s, a move in this direction had been initiated in Claude Mouchard's short essay, "Doctor Froid." In his groundbreaking essay, the critic stresses that Nabokov himself raises the issue of Freud in his preface to *Lolita*, which Mouchard describes as "almost an obligatory rite of passage" (1984, 131). Moreover, Mouchard identifies several characters as avatars of Freud, notably Dr. Heiler and Dr. Sig Froid, who are linked by their desire to plumb the secrets of a patient's mind through psychoanalysis. He concludes his brief but impressive essay with a question, "Can psychoanalysis be the death of literature?" Mouchard then goes on to analyze the death of Shade at the hands of Gradus, a disguised therapist, in *Pale Fire* (132). While Mouchard's essay sparked a smattering of interest in Nabokov's anti-Freudianism, it was some time before readers would encounter an exhaustive examination of the author's complex rivalry with Freud. Indeed, it would take Berman to shed new light on the nature of this contest.

Armed with an expertise in the interpretation of literature from a psychoanalytical perspective, Berman contends that Nabokov's extraordinary (even unprecedented) aversion to the therapist produces an ironic situation in which Freud emerges as a central figure in the author's text. Indeed, Freud looms so large in Nabokov's work that Berman is led to conclude: "If Freud had not existed, Nabokov would have had to invent him" (1987, 213). For Berman, the former is the latter's shadow, or alter ego, whom the novelist felt compelled to challenge and defeat repeatedly. By analyzing Nabokov's comments on Freud—in the context of novels, essays, and interviews—Berman attempts to identify the source of his hostility. He concludes that the author's reality was "generated and sustained by the artist, not the reality unlocked by the analyst" (229). Notably, Berman's attempt to differentiate the artist's reality from that of the analyst has facilitated a greater understanding of Nabokov's literary output, particularly his most celebrated novel, *Lolita*, where the disguised Freudian, Quilty, is finally trapped through Humbert's stratagem. In the end, Humbert succeeds in producing a great work of art in the form of a confession, which would have been impossible without Quilty's richly deserved destruction.

Yet, as Berman observes, the relationship between Nabokov and Freud is far more complex than it appears to be at first glance: "Given their differences over sex, love, psychoanalysis, and art, it is impossible to believe that Freud and Nabokov could ever agree on anything; yet, in the final analysis, there are surprising similarities between the two" (236). These similarities, despite Nabokov's outspoken criticism of Freud, constitute a crucial element in the author's work that has drawn the attention of critics like Berman. Hence, in an ironic twist, the rivalry between the author and therapist has encouraged us to read Nabokov's work from the perspective of Freudian psychoanalysis. Despite the author's passionate repudiation of Freudianism, articulated mostly through his denial of the efficacy of therapy, critics have discerned something akin to the ideas of psychoanalysis within Nabokov's work. Moreover, experts in psychoanalytical theory, including Green, have found ways to examine these similarities in the face of Nabokov's disdain for all things Freudian.

If one considers the atmosphere of the 1960s, a period during which a shrinking pool of influential writers and critics appeared willing to accept the theories of Freud at face value, Nabokov's truculent demeanor seems odd, as though some unstated motive were operating beneath the surface. One might ask, why did Nabokov feel the need, at that time, to passionately condemn Freudian ideas and practices in each and every forward to his translated works, while duplicating these sentiments in essays and interviews? (This trend was evident even in his later years.) Interestingly, one discerns the absence of crucial elements in this apparent literary rivalry, components that might have contributed to an impression that such a conflict was inevitable. Instead, we find ourselves drawn to the arresting similarities between these figures. At the risk of returning to my starting point by engaging in a psychoanalytic reading of Nabokov's work, I would like to pose a question: Is it possible to move in the direction of accepting the differences that the author himself so passionately outlined? What I am suggesting is an approach that would take into consideration the strategy of mimicry, thereby enabling us to move in a direction that permits us to affirm the resemblance without minimizing the differences. Perhaps this approach would involve investigating similarities for the sake of differentiation. Before going further, however, it is important to examine the perspectives of other critics who identified these similarities, and in some cases, set out to defend Freud from Nabokov's attacks by psychoanalyzing his own characters.

Geoffrey Green's *Freud and Nabokov* was perhaps the first book to highlight the similarities between the literary rivals. As the title suggests, Green devotes an equal amount of space and analytical energy to both camps, and he goes on to observe that "psychoanalysis, as exemplified by Freud, has become more subjective and literary, subject to critical interpretation, while fiction as exemplified by Nabokov, has become more theoretical" (1988, 6). Armed with a conviction that hatred is little more than the other side of love, Green focuses on Nabokov's tendency as a writer to engage in doubling, and this approach enables him to analyze Nabokov's work in light of the Freudian concept of the double. With his vast knowledge of the two writers' oeuvres, he sets out to draw parallels between the fictional characters in Nabokov's work and the real-life individuals documented in Freud's case studies. He points out, for instance, that Humbert suffers from an obsessional neurosis, much like the Rat Man, while the symptoms of Kinbote, like those of Dr. Schreber, reflect a condition of paranoia (102–105). Overall, Green's work demonstrates the efficacious manner in which psychoanalytical theory can be applied to a range of literature; and in his masterful hands, Nabokov's antipathy toward all things Freudian appears to conceal a tortured sympathy. While Green is not the only critic to achieve this effect through a psychoanalytic approach, his analysis counts as a significant contribution to our understanding of Nabokov.[4]

Perhaps the most interesting point that Green raises in his essays on the topic, notably in "Splitting of the ego: Freudian doubles, Nabokovian doubles" (1989), is a concept he shares with Berman: Nabokov, in the absence of his hatred of Freud, is not Nabokov (375, 377). This observation, which (in my view) mirrors the essence of Nabokov's art, suggests an entirely new approach to the situation. Rather than positing envy as the double, we can examine the manner in which emulation, as a strategy of resistance, serves as the inspiration for his literary work. To put it differently, Nabokov's excessive aversion to Freud is neither the product of envy nor of the concept of the double; instead, it flows from a strategy of mimicry in which he dons the opponent's mask, only to react against him. Given that the following chapter deals in depth with the literary strategy of mimicry, there is no need to elaborate here. At this point, however, it is worth noting that mimicry is a significant human strategy: one shared with plants and other aninals. Furthermore, it arises naturally, as a means of protection from predators. Yet, for Nabokov, it has another vital purpose, which is reflected in so-called non-utilitarian mimicry. The author appears to borrow Nature's survival technique in order to facilitate his own artistic creativity. While Green does not go this far, he outlines certain features associated with a strategy of mimicry, including Nabokov's tendency to introduce disguised characters, and to construct his narratives as a veritable contest between author and reader: "the clash is not between characters (as it would be between people in the real world) since characters are the mere fabrications of their creator, the author" (1988, 7). To this insightful observation I would add that Nabokov goes on to disguise his *bête noir*. In other words, his characters are not mere fabrications of the author alone, but also of his rival, Freud. As Nabokov observes in *Strong Opinions*, "the *Doppelgänger* subject is a frightful bore" (83), unless, of course, as the conflict unfolds, the resemblance proves to be insignificant. Since the author evidently believes that differentiation is as important as resemblance, I would suggest that Nabokov's art should be treated not as a Freudian cure, but rather as mimicry of Freud.

The fact that Nabokov's protagonists and antagonists often serve as mirror images of each other has arisen as a topic of interest within the literary community. Yet, many readers are largely unaware of the author's complicated relationship with Freud. Nabokov's literature, of course, can be enjoyed when the reader is entirely ignorant of psychoanalysis, as the popular success of *Lolita* shows. That being said, if we do not understand that Freud and Nabokov lurk behind the author's various characters and thereby lend them force and energy, we would miss a good deal of the playful interaction among these characters. We also would fail to grasp the author's motive when he entreats the reader to participate in what is essentially a literary game. Those hostile to Freudian thought might be inclined to accept the author's attacks on Freud as valid, thereby assenting to characterizations of the psychologist as a false prophet, a witch doctor, a "Viennese quack." Those who are sympathetic to Freudian thought, on the other hand, would tend to resent such caricatures and might be inclined to resist them. Either way, we find ourselves engaged with the material, and we are virtually compelled to reread even those passages that give offense.

Jenefer Shute, in "Nabokov and Freud" (1995), exemplifies this tendency as she carefully rereads the author's work, selects passages, and calls attention to the enemies that lurk within the background of Nabokov's major works of fiction. Shute then poses a rather perplexing question: "Nabokov evidently believes that he has engaged such a strategy against Freud—but has his endless scorn served to dominate and displace Psychoanalytic discourse, or has it, on the contrary, only confirmed Freud's omnipresence?" (1995, 414). Her conclusion that Freud functions for Nabokov as an emblem of totalitarianism seems reasonable, but one question remains unanswered: Why should Nabokov choose to target Freud alone, given that he identifies Marx, Lenin, and Darwin as other thinkers that are aligned with totalitarianism?[5] The most obvious response lies in Nabokov's own comment that his novels' themes overlap with the concerns of psychology. If this is so, however, why should he focus so insistently on Freud, who is by no means the only relevant figure in the history of modern psychology? Perhaps Nabokov was seeking to divert his critics' gaze from his extreme discomfort with Lenin and Marx, while at the same time proposing an alternative aesthetic, one that was not so dependant on sociopolitical depictions of the real world and real people. However, before I set out to outline this alternative psychology (which is coupled with an alternative aesthetic), I would like to refer to Richard Rorty's essays on the two rivals, in which he grants them equal weight, as a great artist and a great philosopher, respectively.

This approach inspires yet another question: What happens to those readers who find themselves simultaneously enthralled by Nabokov and Freud? Not surprisingly, there is a quality of perplexity in David Andrews's examination of Rorty's essays, "The barber of Kasbeam: Nabokov on cruelty" (1989), and "Freud and moral reflection" (1991). While Rorty interprets Nabokov's hostile attitude toward Freud as a reflection of the younger man's envy for a predecessor who had already written his best lines, he makes a variety of observations that illuminate aspects of Nabokov's life and work, especially his novel *Lolita*. At the same time, Rorty draws upon Freud's philosopy in a manner that reflects his admiration for the psychologist. Thus, if one were to read the two essays separately, one could conclude that each was an excellent source that demonstrates a deep knowledge of its subject. A comparative reading of the two essays, however, highlights Rorty's ambivalence toward Nabokov's "war" with Freud. While Rorty offers a perceptive overview of the two writers and their works, he appears to gloss over Nabokov's criticism of Freud and his proponents. This is not altogether surprising. Indeed, one might ask, how could Rorty deny the narrative power and perceptiveness of one or the other of these two figures, given his appreciation for both? Andrews concludes that while both essays are impressive, Rorty's seemingly even-handed praise for both of the two men is misleading (2000/2001, 31).

In contrast to readings in which Nabokov and Freud are accorded equal praise, other critics have elected to grapple with the Russian-born author's disdain for psychoanalysis. This approach is exemplified by the work of Leland de la Durantaye, who latches on to the term *generalization* (one Nabokov employs in his criticism of Freudian ideas) and applies it to the artist himself. De la Durantaye observes that Nabokov, who relished terms such as *details* and *particularities*, repudiates any attempt to generalize the human condition or the human mind. In a bold reversal, de la Durantaye argues that Nabokov fails to describe *specifically* his motives for rejecting Freud. He goes on to contend that the author, ironically enough, follows Freud's lead when he pursues "the most general lines of attack" (2005, 69). In this engaging and intuitive essay, de la Durantaye suggests the possibility of dealing with both camps in a manner that is irreverent and refreshing. He also makes us aware of the need for a new approach: one that includes elements of a game of hide and seek. This proposal is based on de la Durantaye's understanding that Nabokov wanted readers to engage with his texts in order to uncover those elements buried within.

Nabokov did not seek to convince his readers with generalized, rational explanations. On the contrary, he preferred that readers participate in a game in which a close rereading of the text yielded the Freudian components inherent within. A considerable challenge lies in the fact that the game is demanding and requires the reader's full intellectual engagement. It is a game riddled with traps that are buried here and there, often in the form of tangled plot developments and camouflaged characters. Perhaps *Lolita* stands as the single work in which these elements are sucessfully intertwined without sacrificing poetic justice, probability, and artistic finality in the form of fantasy. Perhaps this is the only way in which Nabokov could have resisted deceptive generalization and totality without falling into the trap of producing a sociopolitical grand narrative. The fact that he is a demanding writer is clearly reflected in the variety of directions that criticism of his work has taken.

Before going further, it seems important to examine Nabokov's pattern of *mimicry* in the context of his integrity as an artist and amateur scientist. It is widely known that the author possessed two chief passions: butterfly hunting and fiction writing. Nabokov himself hinted at the complimentary relationship between the two when he stated that there is no science without fancy and no art without fact (LL 6). A critical step toward the merging of the precision of poetry with the intuition of science was taken at the end of the twentieth centrury, when almost twenty years had passed since the author's death in 1977. As de la Durantaye notes, recent trends within Nabokov studies include a tendency to evaluate the author's scientific interests, along with efforts to draw a parallel between the development of a work of art and the creation of the world (2009, 63). This approach reflects the clear influence of phenomenology, given that art and natural phenomena are inseparable according to the writings of Heidegger and Merleau-Ponty—and this concept owes much to the psychological theories of William James as well.[6] Perhaps the key to grasping the leitmotif of Nabokov's aversion to Freud can be found through a new approach, one that assumes that the camouflage techniques found in art mirror the strategies of nature. For Nabokov, "science" refers to natural science and natural phenomena that exist beyond the boundaries of race and culture, beyond any social or political ideologies. The natural things are those infinities that, as an exile, he could appreciate in different countries. As he often recalled, beneath the immigrant sky, he longed for one locality in Russia, *Vyra*, in his "hypertrophied sense of lost childhood" (SM 73). (Interestingly, the name *Vyra* puts one in mind of his wife's name, *Véra*, a woman to whom he dedicated each one of his manuscripts.)

LITERARY RIVALS, INCLUDING THE ALMIGHTY

Born in St. Petersburg in 1899, into one of Imperial Russia's minor noble families, Nabokov benefited from an exclusive intellectual training. In addition, every summer, the family relocated to their country estate, Vyra, where the young Nabokov was exposed to the exquisite beauty of the natural world. The blissful experiences of his childhood and adolescence came to an abrupt halt in 1919, when the family was forced to flee to Crimea in the wake of the Bolshevik Revolution. Uprooted and dispossessed, they entered upon an impoverished exile in Western Europe. As Nabokov observes in his autobiography, *Speak, Memory*, he continued to cherish impressions of his idyllic upbringing at Vyra, and these were an important source of his emotional endurance and creativity. The author seems to have inherited a taste for the sensual from this mother, Elena, who advised him "to love with all one's soul and leave the rest to fate" (SM, 40). In later years, he recalled that she often drew his attention to the smallest, most delicate details of nature, such as a mushroom flourishing beneath a tree, the colorful wings of a butterfly, a lark in full flight, maple leaves scattered on brown sand, or the footprints of a tiny bird on newly fallen snow. When he was seven years old, his mother's decision to establish a library in his bedroom that included numerous volumes on butterflies sparked a passionate interest in butterfly hunting, and he remained enamored of the delicate designs of their wings. He was no less entranced by the butterfly's ability to fly around the world, as well as its capacity for self-transformation, moving from an unsightly pupa into a graceful creature with delicate wings. His autobiography indicates that, by 1908, he had obtained "absolute control over the European lepidoptera as known to Hofmann" (123). Amid the confusion, adversity, and tedium of immigrant society, Nabokov evidently drew comfort from his memories and impressions of a sensual world in which insects lived in harmony with sun and stone. This obsession with his childhood may well have provided him with the inner strength to survive the painful years of loss that came in the wake of his family's exile from Russia. Indeed, Nabokov, in *Speak, Memory*, equated the loss of his country with the loss of his love (245). Given that his memories of the past focused on the beauty of the natural world, it is not surprising that he should dismiss symbols and grand narratives as crude, vulgar devices that undermined the uniqueness and delicacy of individual experience. His commitment to particularities would emerge as one of his most enduring traits.

At Cambridge, Nabokov entered Trinity College, where he studied French and Russian literature. In time, his wistful longing for his homeland was replaced by a determination to continue to speak the Russian language and to function as a Russian writer, even though his work would most likely be banned in Soviet Russia. Unsettled by the wide-ranging political assertions of immigrant society and depressed by the precribed ideologies that held sway in Europe, he resolved to turn away from politics and focus on literature alone—in the same manner that his protagonist, Luzhin, concentrates on the game of chess in *The Luzhin Defense*. Published in Berlin in 1930, this early work of fiction featured the type of Nabokovian protagonist who is devoted to one activity—in this case, the game of chess, which is played according to detailed, accurate, and empirical rules, unlike the generalized rules employed by the Viennese therapy group. The story not only sheds light on the young Nabokov's artistic temperament; it also offers clues to his distaste for Freud, which was already evident.

His attachment to the natural world apparently fueled his disdain for the concepts of psychoanalysis, which he considered inconsistent with the diversity inherent in nature. This impression was compounded by the blind faith and dogmatic attitudes shown by many of Freud's followers, a phenomenon that Nabokov witnessed firsthand during his years at Cambridge. It was Freud's treatment of childhood, in particular, with its supposedly universal stages of development, that Nabokov found odious. After all, he would be haunted and inspired by his childhood experiences for the remainder of his life. The allure of these childhood memories, along with the pleasure he took in nature's smallest details, held a deceptive power over him that led him to reject even the possibility of an objective reality. Not surprisingly, the idea of the "talking cure," in which a patient's psychological issues were resolved through a detailed confession of his or her past, struck Nabokov as ridiculous. Decades later, in the course of a 1967 interview, he responded to a query on *reality* by posing his own question: "Whose reality?" For Nabokov, the very term *everyday reality* was static and meaningless, given that it presupposes a situation that is essentially objective and unchangeable—one that, in his view, could never possibly exists (Gold, 2003,197).

One of the short stories Nabokov produced during his years in Europe exemplifies his obsession with details. In "Cloud, Castle, Lake," his protagonist Vasili Ivanovich wins a pleasure trip through a contest sponsored by a society of Russian refugees. Ivanovich is a mild, modest bachelor whose gaze reflects a combination of compassion and intelligence. His sensitive and poetic nature is shown by his refusal to relinquish his hopeless love for another man's wife, a situation that has haunted him for seven years. Uncomfortable in social situations, he is marginalized by his traveling companions. In the regimented atmosphere fostered by the trip's organizers, his discomfort with group activities and impatience with bureaucratic exercises mark him as uncooperative. During the second day of his trip, Ivanovich engages in a hike that leads him to an idyllic spot in the countryside. There he encounters the kind of pastoral scene of which he had dreamed: a pristine blue lake whose surface reflects a large, billowing cloud. Above the lake, on a hillside covered with trees, looms an ancient black castle. Without hesitating, he abandons his traveling companion and makes his way to the enchanted spot, where he happens upon an inn that offers rooms to travelers. Shortly after the trip, he quits his job and takes up residence at the idyllic locale that has captured his imagination. The story, with its juxtaposition of the oppressive atmosphere of the organized trip and the solitude the protagonist enjoys in the countryside, moves seamlessly like a river, devoid of either symbols or riddles and depending heavily upon Nabokov's descriptive powers. Written in 1937, "Cloud, Castle, Lake" highlights the backdrop of perfect happiness of which Nabokov dreamed. This became clear after the enormous success of *Lolita*, which enabled him to leave his professorship at Cornell and relocate to a pastoral spot in Montreux, Switzerland, one that resembled the locale that figured in one of his earliest literary efforts.

It is tempting to wonder how Nabokov experienced the influence of the Viennese delegation during his years at Cambridge, the place where he first resolved to be a writer. While he later indicated that his knowledge of Freud was limited at that time, he could not have been insulated from the trends that swept European intellectual society between 1914 and 1918. Carl Pletsch observes that, by the time Freud published his analysis of the Wolf Man, the psychoanalytic movement was firmly entrenched as an academic discipline as well as a specific kind of knowledge: the case study was established "as the methodological anchor which united psychoanalysts in their scientific community" (1981, 116). It is well known that Freud had been disappointed over the Wolf Man's sudden departure, which prevented him from conducting further analysis. Indeed, he was so dissatisfied with the truncated analysis that pro-

duced the concept of *the primal scene* that he waited four years before
publishing it in 1918. There is no doubt that Freud's analysis of the Wolf
Man had a considerable impact on Nabokov, as a number of critics, including de la Durantaye, have observed.[7] Among other things, Nabokov
shared with the Wolf Man a similar background as well as the experience
of extreme personal loss. Both were the sons of privileged Russian families that had been forced into exile after the Bolshevik Revolution. Indeed, the influence of the Wolf Man case as well as Freud's theory of the
primal scene are relatively easy to detect in Nabokov's work. In the case
of *Pale Fire*, the primal scene (in contrast to Freud's) is shrewdly concealed in the final section of Shade's poem. Meanwhile, in *The Luzhin
Defense*, the protagonist's real name is concealed until the story's closing
line, at which point the reader learns that he is known as "Aleksandr
Ivanovich." Again, this details appears to mimic the case study of the
Wolf Man, given that the patient's real name, Sergei Pankejeff, was hard-
ly known among members of the general public. Most did not appear to
care who he was, and Nabokov pokes fun at this situation even as he calls
attention to it.

Perhaps additional historical context is needed to secure a better
understanding of Nabokov's encounter with psychoanalysis at Cambridge. Such material could also help to explain the author's deep antipathy toward Freudian approaches to therapy, which he nevertheless continued to mimic throughout his literary career. John Forrester's essay,
"Freud in Cambridge," is especially illuminating on this subject. Forrester points out that, by 1922, Freud enjoyed fame throughout Europe and
America as "a scientific media star on a par with Einstein and Marie
Curie," while the influence of psychoanalysis was so far-reaching that it
became "a required part of the training for the police officers of Calcutta"
(2004, 1). Given this climate, it is difficult to imagine how Nabokov
would have felt had he had been confronted with the news that, in May
1921, the Moscow Institute of Psychoneurology had established the Children's Home, which was managed by former anarchist leader Vera
Schmidt "under the direct patronage of Leon Trotsky, who fancied himself a Freudian" (4).

Freud's apartment in Vienna was regularly crowded with international luminaries such as James Strachey who became the first translator of
Freud's complete works into English, and the Bloomsbury writer whose
faith in the efficacy of Freud's theories was reflected in the fact that he
began analysis with the master in October 1920 and completed it toward
the end of June 1922. Such well-known patients were the primary means
by which "psychoanalysis became disseminated as a theory, as a vision of
the world, as cocktail party chat, as a practice—and perhaps even as a
form of knowledge suitable for inclusion in the teaching and research of
an ancient university like Cambridge" (3). As Forrester writes,

The currents of interest in psychoanalysis in Britain were several, rang-
ing from sexology and medical psychology, to a literary strand, including not only Bloomsbury but also the efflorescence of the psychological
novels during the First World War, to progressive education and to a
more general philosophical interest. Many of these came together in
Cambridge, particularly with the First World War: Bertrand Russell's
students in logic, such as Susan Isaacs, Dorothy Wrinch and Karin
Stephen; the enormous impetus given to psychoanalysis in Britain on
account of the experience of 'shell-shock' during the war, including the
influential adaptation of Freud's concept of repression, trauma and the
cathartic cure by W. H. R. Rivers, physiologist, anthropologist, and
psychologist, Director of Studies in Natural Sciences at St John's College, Cambridge, after the war. (Forrester, 2004, 3–4)

Given that Freud's theories and case studies were prevalent in Europe
during the time that Nabokov was a university student, his characterization of them as totaritarian and Boshevik is not altogether surprising.
Freud's influence in England was precipitated, in part, by the Cambridge
academic network, along with a host of field scientists who disseminated
his theories. As late as 1925, controversy erupted when Sir Arthur Tansley commented publicly on the value of Freud's case histories: "Case
histories are of special value to students because every psychoanalysis is,
or should be, an organic whole, a definite development of the patient's
mind in relation to the analyst" (Cameron and Forrester, 2000, 245). Nabokov himself felt revulsion at Freud's analysis of the Wolf Man, a response that informed his subsequent literary works. For the time being,
however, he chose to focus on other matters.[8] The young Nabokov
avoided university libraries, skipped lectures, and concentrated almost
exclusively on Russian language and literature, as though determined
that Cambridge would leave no imprint on his soul. At the same time, he
recognized that Cambridge had supplied "not only the causal frame but
the very colors and inner rhythms" for his special brand of Russian
thought (SM 269). His ambivalent position at the university gave rise to a
creative force that manifested itself as an artistic strategy of mimicry, in
which resemblance and difference were melded into a single entity. One
is inclined to wonder about the ways in which this force was utilized.
There is little doubt that it functioned, in part, as a means of protection, as
so-called *protective mimicry*. In addition, it functioned as a kind of game in
which the more deceptive player was bound to vanquish his less deceptive opponent.

Along with the relatively idyllic memories of his childhood, Nabokov
harbored painful memories of his family's escape from Russia and their
lives as refugees in Western Europe. In the wake of the Bolshevik Revolution, the First World War, and the rise of Nazism, Nabokov was forced to
adopt the *nom de plume*, V. Sirin. His close relatives would fare poorly
amid the political turmoil that followed. Nabokov's father was killed

mistakenly by Russian right-wingers, and his brother, Sergei, accused of homosexuality, starved to death in a Nazi concentration camp. For Nabokov, life was essentially absurd. It was informed by errors, deception, and chance, a perspective given voice through the lips of the narrator of his novella, *The Eye*, written in 1930. At that time, Nabokov lived in constant fear that he was being watched by agents, like one of the refugees that figured in his works of fiction.[9] Later on, in America, he recalled a host of harrowing experiences, including his family's narrow escape from Crimea to Western Europe. He noted that, in order to protect themselves from the Bolsheviks, his relatives adopted false identities. Agents of the Bolshevik government routinely assassinated people they identified as unsympathetic, and his father, a prominent politician, had adopted the mimetic disguise of a doctor without changing his name. Consequently, for Nabokov, mimicry was not only an essential gift of the *Almighty*, of Nature; it was also a tool of survival amid upheaval and uncertainty. Enchanted by the intricate deception exemplified by the dead-leaf butterfly, Nabokov found inspiration for his own art. As he noted, protective mimicry lulls us into "the state of torpid security which an insect experiences when mimicking a dead leaf" (SO 96).

In a telling comment, Nabokov revealed that, if there had been no revolution in his homeland, he would have devoted his life to lepidopterology and never written a single novel. Apparently, his sole means of revisiting his lost country was to engage in a detour that involved hunting butterflies and producing works of fiction. In the process, he combined the precision of poetry and the enthusiasm of pure science to create a uniquely artistic form of deceptive mimicry. For Nabokov, the artist's responsibility was not to attempt a depiction of reality *per se*, but rather to blend a variety of episodes and experiences in a magical act of deception. He contended, after all, that there was no objective, unchangeable reality, in the same way that there is no such thing as a perfect resemblance. Given that art is produced by a conjuror who disguises characters and sets out to deceive his or her reader, it has much in common with a game of chess. Interestingly, Nabokov went through scores of index cards as he developed his works of art, in a manner resembling a scientist who is engaged in research, or a chess player designing an intricate play. For the author, nature, like art, is informed by deception, from the insect that mimics a dead leaf to the human being engaged in the construction of "facts," so that even "terminology between any branch of science and raceme of art" is interchangeable (SO 79). In Nabokov's fiction, Freud is a subject to be examined carefully. The same is true of Nature, for as the author once stated, a creative writer must study the work of his rivals, including the Almighty. If indeed Nabokov viewed Freud as a rival (and there is little doubt that he did), a question remains: Did he have a card up his sleeve that enabled him to suggest an alternative to Freud, given that he described his own novels as "psychological"?

WILLIAM JAMES: DECEPTION IN MEMORY AND COGNITION

When Nabokov speaks of science, he is referring to natural science; and biology, like psychology, is a branch of that field. It is worth noting that, in his complicated work of fiction, *Ada,* the sciences and the humanities are linked together in a metaphor of incest. In what appears to be a commentary on Freud's concept of incest (which involves mother and son), the author introduces Van Veen, a psychologist and philosopher who falls passionately in love with his sister, Ada, an insect lover. After an extended period of suffering in which their love endures, they consummate their relationship. In much the same way that a violation of the boundary between author and character permeates Nabokov's fiction, the incestuous relationship between Van and Ada appears to reflect the merging of two individuals into one: a disguised Nabokov. In this way, the disciplines of art and sience are blended in an act of deceptive mimicry. While the character of Van is by no means a perfect match for the author, he functions as a camouflaged Nabokov, in a manner that calls to mind the narrator V and character Sebastian in another work, *The Real Life of Sebastian Knight.* Overall, Nabokov presents an image of psychology that has little to do with group therapy; nor can it be described as a cultural phenomenon. Instead, psychology is presented as a philosophy of the individual mind. Moreover, as a natural phenomenon, it should be analyzed as such.

Yet, if Nabokov rejects Freud, he is practically compelled to advocate an alternative approach to psychology, one that focuses on memory and cognition, along with our sensual perception of the details of nature. As noted, however, a close review of the author's interviews, memoirs, lectures, and works of fiction yields little in the way of definite clues. This should not be surprising, given that the game of deception the author plays with readers and critics alike is not designed to provide easy answers. During a 1991 interview, Nabokov's son, Dmitri, provided a list of books his father had urged him to read when he was a young. Not surprisingly, the list included the works of Poe, Shakespeare, Pushkin, and a smattering of Dickens. It also featured a number of specific works, including *War and Peace, Anna Karenina,* and *Mimicry in the Animal World* (Johnson and Proffer, 1991, 74). During the interview, Dmitri added the names of other authors that his father had read during his years in Berlin—including Blok, Bergson, Joyce, Proust—and mentioned several German entomological texts (78). When reviewing this list, one is struck by the number of books that deal with entomology and mimicry, while the vast majority of the literary works also surface in his lectures and interviews. Meanwhile, the absence of texts dealing with the subject of psychology is startling. For Nabokov, the subject of psychology appears to have been closely linked to philosophy.

For Nabokov, *reality* cannot be reduced to an objective, static entity. On the contrary, it is inherently subjective and can only be adduced through a gradual accumulation of information that is absorbed in the context of specialization. A butterfly, for instance, is likely to be more real to a lepidopterist than to an ordinary person. Since the concept of general reality is a phantom entity for Nabokov, he is compelled to limit the object of writing mainly to the concerns of the writer himself, with a focus on the multiplicity of ways in which the writer views those around him. Consequently, any form of writing, or other practice, designed for certain groups, or for society at large, strikes him as no less farcical than Freud's concept of the primal scene. When we examine memory and other cognitive processes, as Nabokov would observe, it becomes clear that our psyche tends to deceive itself in proportion to the experiences we have accumulated over time. The passage of time becomes a resource for creativity, even fantasy; and time itself often functions as a magician of sorts that weaves fairy tales in its wake. Creativity does not emerge from external facts alone. Nor is it the sole byproduct of the unconscious. Indeed, it is consciousness itself, which flows ceaselessly and continually transforms itself. In this fictional world, God (as McFate) is a deceptive component, a contingency of our memory and cognition.

This approach to psychology appears to have much in common with phenomenology. Significantly, we have two clues to Nabokov's motivations, both of which can be found in his surviving texts. The first surfaces in his autobiography while the second can be found in a personal letter that he wrote to Edmund Wilson. In the "Foreword" of *Speak, Memory*, Nabokov sheepishly refers to sections of the manuscript that his readers should review carefully. He makes particular reference to a "vicious snap" at Freud in the first paragraph of chapter 8, in section two, as well as the last sentence of section two of chapter 11 (SM, 15). Yet, when we refer to pages 156 and 219, we find something beyond mere jibes at Freud. The former includes a reference to an incident in which a practical joke was apparently inspired by the primal scene in Freud's analysis of the Wolf Man, while the latter contains a significant passage on the stream of thought. After acknowledging his strong interest in consciousness and time, Nabokov contends that human thoughts invariably emerge in the present moment, as a synthesis of various thoughts that have already been experienced, a process which enables us to recognize elements of the present in the past and to recall the past in the context of the present moment. This passage becomes more intriguing when we refer to Stephen Blackwell's notes on a significant component of Nabokov's intellectual heritage (2009, 101).

As Blackwell points out, it was common in the decades before the twentieth century to place psychology in the same general category as philosophy, a practice evident at the prominent Moscow Psychological Society. Interestingly, members of this society were close to both Nabokov and his father, and Nabokov would later establish a friendship with a former member who had once served as the organization's research secretary. This tantalizing information suggests that the author was well acquainted with the tradition of psychology that developed into European phenomenology, a school of thought associated with William James. Notably, in 1957, immediately after the publication of *Lolita* in the United States, Billy James, an American painter and art teacher who was the second son of William James, contacted Edmund Wilson and asked him to pass on his regards to Nabokov. After receiving Wilson's letter, Nabokov responded with a warm note stating that "my father considered his father's works as one of the greatest and most brilliant contributions to psychology and had me read him when I was twelve or thirteen" (Karlinsky, 1979, 311). It may be that James's psychological theories served as a leitmotif of Nabokov's literary devices, no less than the author's strategy of mimicry.

Significantly, James began his career as a biologist whose primary focus was the animal brain, including the human brain. As a disciple of Darwin, his research included a range of experiments on animal brains, given that technology had not advanced to the point that it could accommodate the study of human brains. James tended to focus on the ways in which bodily habits are formed as tools of survival. At the same time, he set out to examine the qualities that distinguished human beings from other animals in the scale of evolution. He determined that, among animals (including humans), survival mechanisms develop as habits which, in turn, are the product of repeated acts. His research led him to conclude that only humans, owing to the evolution of consciousness, possess a type of memory known as *episodic memory*, which transcends the habitual memory that we share with other animals. For James, consciousness is the fundamental agency responsible for thinking and remembering, processes which gave rise to cultures and societies. Significantly, in order to bear these seemingly infinite potentialities, consciousness requires the primary memories that are formed by bodily experiences. This is true, whether consciousness functions at the lower level of basic habits or at the higher level of remembering and cognition. To put it another way, in the absence of sensual habits (the domain of the lower part of our brain that is shared with other animals), consciousness fails to function. This assumption, of course, stands in stark opposition to Cartesian cogito. Given the primarily sensual, material basis of consciousness, human memory and cognition are inevitably in the process of changing with a person's experiences over time. This topic will be explored further in chapter 2, which examines the ways in which Nabokov adapted James's psychological theories to his own artistic purposes.

TO MIMIC FREUD

It wasn't until the last decade of the twentieth century, almost twenty years after the author's death, that critics began to evaluate Nabokov as both a scientist and writer. A few years earlier, Philip Zaleski initiated the trend with his essay, "Nabokov's Blue Period," which appeared in *Harvard Magazine* (1986, 34–38). Holding up Nabokov as a paradigm of the writer who deftly combines his artistic and scientific interests, Zaleski explored the author's six-year experience at the Harvard Museum of Comparative Zoology, from 1942 to 1948. Zaleski's early attempt to analyze Nabokov's life as a serious scientist who was also a well-known novelist was eventually overshadowed by Kurt Johnson and Steve Coates' groundbreaking book, *Nabokov's Blues: The Scientific Odyssey of a Literary Genius* (1999). This was followed, a decade later, by Stephen H. Blackwell's *The Quill and the Scalpel: Nabokov's Art and the Worlds of Science* (2009), which was the next major work to reflect a spirit of consilience. In the wake of these earlier efforts to explore Nabokov's scientific passion, the next step would appear to be a project that examines the ways in which these apparently divergent interests combined to form a single literary device, namely the artistic dimension of mimicry. To put it another way, there is a need to explore the manner in which Nabokov sought to integrate his knowledge of biological phenomena with his formidable skills as an artist in an effort to demonstrate the ways in which memory and mimicry converge in a single work of art. (I will explore this topic further in chapter 1.)

The overall purpose of this book, however, is to show how Nabokov mimics Freud in the medium of dialogue, thereby integrating resemblance and difference. Among other things, I will examine the ways in which he uses Freud as a foil in order to develop his own art, with a focus on the artistic devices that characterize his major works of fiction. As part of this analysis, I will examine Nabokov's largely reductive interpretation of Freud's work, which is especially evident in his treatment of *remembering*. In the process, I hope to shed light on Nabokov's primary arguments against Freudian ideas. It is quite possible, of course, that Nabokov chose to mimic Freud in order to cement his own position as an artistic innovator: a strategy that would have enabled him to resist Realism (or Absolutism), while at the same time subverting many of Freud's key concepts. To illustrate this point, I will provide a brief overview of some of Nabokov's major works.

The Luzhin Defense is the first of Nabokov's major works in which the author mimics Freud's interpretations of dreams. We are introduced to a young chess player, Luzhin (a name that sounds like "illusion") who is so absorbed in a chess game that he withdraws from the routine of everyday life. For Luzhin, the fantasy world of the chess game is more compelling, more rational, and more real than the outside world that he shuns. Consequently, people begin to treat him as though he were mentally ill. Through his clever juxtaposition of the real and the unreal, Nabokov offers a wonderful mimicry of the Freudian approach to dreams. Interestingly, a similar act of mimicry can be seen in *Despair*, where the protagonist, Hermann (a stand-in for Freud), concocts a perfect plan at the very moment he chances upon a perfect double. As with the case of Humbert in *Lolita*, a criminal's confession serves as the reader's entry into a world of magic and deception that reflects the process of remembering the past. In this way, Nabokov presents a fine example of *contingency* in human consciousness: a stick. Even as he analyzes Freud, who famously interpreted a stick as a phallic symbol, the author goes out of his way to subvert him.

In *Lolita* this deceptive style reaches its summit, as reflected in his treatment of a battle involving a disguised Freud and a disguised Nabokov. While his use of camouflage is most evident in the characters of Quilty and Humbert, it can also be detected in the figure of John Ray, the supposed author of the "foreword" as well as Nabokov himself, the composer of the "afterword." This battle for narrative authority is artful and witty, and it underscores the fact that Humbert views Quilty as a literary rival. In a protective mode of mimicry that involves a departure from Freud, who describes childhood as a stage of *infantile sexuality*, Nabokov interprets the nymphet as a deceptive childhood memory, while at the same time, he transforms the object into the substance of immortal art.

In *Pale Fire*, the primal scene implied in Shade's poem stands in stark contrast to Freud's counterpart, as formulated in his analysis of the Wolf Man. The story comprises two distinct parts: the poems by John Shade and Kinbote's considerably lengthier commentaries. In an apparent effort to imitate the process of psychoanalytic discourse, the two sections are fused into a single work of fiction when the bungling Gradus inadvertently murders the wrong person, Shade. The role of Gradus, the poet killer, is essentially twofold. On the one hand, his presence facilitates the passage of time, thereby making possible the *magic* of memory. On the other, he provides the contingency that links the seemingly disparate elements of the story into a single work of fiction. In the same way that most of Nabokov's fiction deals with his own art, *Pale Fire* serves as a humorous commentary on Nabokov's artistic idiosyncrasies. Meanwhile, in *Ada*, the integrity of art and science achieves its culmination through the incestuous love of two siblings: an insect scientist, Ada, and a philosopher and psychotherapist, Van. The story involves two worlds: *Terra*, the Freudian world, in which incest is taboo; and *Anti-Terra* (a sister planet of *Terra*), Ada's world of incest (as well as of insects). The pattern of incest differs from that described by Freud. The relationship between father and son differs substantially from the model presented in Freud's *Oedipus complex*. (Significantly, Nabokov himself remained deeply respectful of Russia and its literary icons; and his relationships with his father and other family members were informed by affection.)

Overall, Nabokov's revulsion for Freud is coupled with a passionate disdain for any *objective* approach to politics and society. Despite his reservations about Freud and the literary byproducts of his theories, one thing seems clear: Nabokov and Freud are literary siblings, in the manner of Ada and Van. Indeed, the artistic merit of Nabokov's work depends largely upon Freud, whom he imitates, borrows from, and ultimately repudiates. As noted, Nabokov is strongly opposed to the generalization of all human behaviors and pathologies that are part of an attempt to explain causality. For him, human memory and cognition are too elusive to be grasped through static concepts, whether they happen to be myths, symbols, or theories on the underlying factors in sexuality. This begs a question: Are we to accept Nabokov's suggestion that Freud himself was so naïve? Indeed, based on everything we know, does this seem plausible?

NOTES

1. Regarding the exchange of letters between Nabokov and Kubrick, please see pp. 296, 313-320, 333 in *Vladimir Nabokov: Selected Letters 1940-1977*. Nabokov's *Lolita: A Screen Play* was originally published in 1974 at McGraw-Hill International, however, the text used here is from the 1997 Vintage International edition.

2. In the first part of *Lolita*, Humbert mimics Freud's infantile sexuality by disguising himself as a pervert criminal who is sexually involved with a nymphet, but in later part, he exposes himself as author Nabokov who tries to represent his childhood as a deceptive and playful game of memory and art.

3. In Canto Three of *Pale Fire*, Shade discovered a misspelling of "mountain" as "fountain," and commented, "Life Everlasting—based on a misprint!" (See lines from 803 to 815.) This particular passage will be discussed further in chapter 4.

4. Alan C. Elms, in his chapter, "Cloud, Castle, Claustrum: Nabokov as a Freudian in spite of himself," in *Russian Literature and Psychoanalysis* (1989), interpets Nabokov's short story, "Cloud, Castle, and Lake," in the context of womb imagery. He goes on to connect these images with the landscape as dream symbols for the female body, as suggested by Freud: "I shall take it for the rest of my life"(359). See pages 353-368.

5. In 1962, in a BBC television interview, Nabokov indicated that he loathed Freud, Marx, and regarded them as false thinkers (SO 18); in a 1968 interview with BBC-2, he also referred to four doctors whom he despised: Dr. Freud, Dr. Zhivago, Dr. Castro, etc. (SO 115). Nabokov often condemned realists, idealists, absolutists, group workers, social workers, Darwin, Lenin, and, most of all, dictators of every kind.

6. About the concept of art in line with phenomenology, we can think of James's idea of stream of thought, Heidegger's postulation of the origin of art as the emptiness inside of a jug, and Merleau-Ponty's concept of gaze between the eye and mind.

7. Leland de la Durantaye remarks that "there are a number of reasons to suggest that the text was known to Nabokov." For more of this, see his essay, "Nabokov and Freud, or a Particular Problem" (2005, 62-63).

8. According to Steven H. Blackwell, the Freudian movement was entered its international heyday when Nabokov entered Cambridge University, in October of 1919. By 1920, practical application of its method, along with apparent clinical successes, produced "a cultural maelstrom," in short an industry (Blackwell, 2009,102). Blackwell refers to three notes related to Nabokov's early exposure to these cultural phenomena,

"Quacks in our midst" (*The Cambridge Reviews*, 28, Nov. 1919); "A Student's Hoax"(*The Times*, London, Dec. 12, 1921); "A Useful Hoax" (*The Times*, London, Dec. 17, 1921) (Blackwell, 2009, 228, note 19).

9. For instance, in *The Eye*, Weinstock felt that not only was he regularly watched by agents, but there was a blacklist. See p. 26.

ONE

Mimicry as a Form of Art

This chapter opens with the assumption that Vladimir Nabokov's unique approach to the writing of fiction was inspired, in part, by the mimicry of a creature with which he was well-acquainted, the "dead leaf butterfly," a species known to subtly camouflage itself amid fallen leaves. Nabokov's artistic adaptation of mimicry that is found in the natural world is intrinsically *theatrical*, as P. D. Ouspensky (1931) and Nicholas Evreinoff (1927) have observed. Yet, the author's technique also appears to stem from a political, even subversive, motive, as though he anticipated the postmodern subject later proposed by Jacques Lacan, or the postcolonial political perspective reflected in Homi Bhabha's *The Location of Culture* (1994). To an extent, an application of the psychological term mimicry to Nabokov and his work echoes the manner in which Bhabha has applied Lacan's concept of mimicry to colonized people. As Bhabha observes, colonized populations imitate the practices of the imperial culture, though they are destined to betray this "disguise" and reveal their native identity. Since the mimic's imitation of the model is strategic, she or he can never be a pure simulant. Similarly, when Nabokov set out to become a psychological novelist, he chose his literary rival (Freud, among others) as a model. Freudian psychiatry was at the peak of its popularity in Europe when Nabokov was at Cambridge, and despite the almost imperial breadth of its influence, many regarded it as a relatively benign model of totality and generalization. Not only was Freudianism a branch of psychology, but it could also serve, for Nabokov, as a suitable model for subversion just like the most authoritarian ideologies, including Soviet communism and Nazism.

When Nabokov adapted the concept of mimicry to his own artistic purposes, his concerns may have included his awareness of readers' ignorance of the new spirit of consilience, which was not prevalent during his lifetime. Such concerns would have been well-grounded, given that few critics reviewed Nabokov's work from the vantage point of consilience until the end of the last century, decades after the author's death. Moreover, despite Nabokov's repeated references to Freud in his forwards and introductions, most critics and readers failed to recognize that his argument with the "Viennese quack" had crystallized as a uniquely artistic form of mimicry. This oversight owes much to the author's complex narrative style. Indeed, readers often overlook or misunderstand Nabokov's riddles and word games because they are apt to interpret his narratives from the perspective of traditional realism. At the same time, Nabokov faced the challenge of many authors, given that he was limited to communicating his ideas through his work, as opposed to well-delineated theories or explanations. His awareness of the reader's ignorance made him anxious, even as it granted him a perverse pleasure. In the interest of shedding additional light on Nabokov's challenging body of work, I would like to describe the origin and nature of scientific mimicry. From there, I will move on to investigate several techniques that characterize his texts, with an eye toward the manner in which they give artistic form to scientific notions.

Notably, Philip Zaleski observes that, during Nabokov's Blue Period at the Harvard Museum of Comparative Zoology, the author was anxious to build a bridge that linked his overriding passions: the production of fiction and the study of butterflies (1986, 37). This goal is reflected in the rather hefty novel, *Ada*, where a symbolic merging of art and science is achieved through the incestuous love of two siblings. One of the siblings is a scientist, while the other is a writer of psychological fiction. Their attempt to produce a joint memoir forms the basis of the novel itself. As though to highlight the links between art and science, Nabokov's research method for the novel involved the use of index cards, and the work itself features an astonishing number of taxonomical details. Curiously, though, for a man so passionately interested in mimicry, Nabokov failed to leave behind a single article or creative work that focuses directly on the topic. Indeed, little survives, beyond sporadic observations in his memoir and offhand comments made during interviews. We know that the author attended regular meetings of the Cambridge Entomological Club, and reports indicate that, on April 12, 1943, he presented a chapter titled, "Mimicry in Theory and Practice," which was described as part of an unpublished book (Boyd and Pyle, 2000, 277–78). The book, however, was never published, and the chapter has long since disappeared. Almost a decade later, Nabokov was invited to write a book on the theme of mimicry by Edmund Wilson's daughter, Rosalind, who was then employed at Houghton Mifflin Publishing. Yet, again, all traces of the project have disappeared, with the exception of a letter written by Vera that confirms her husband's interest in the offer. The letter, dated July 24, 1952, states that "the question of mimicry is one that has passionately interested him all his life and one of his pet projects has always been the compilation of a work that would comprise all known examples of mimicry in the animal kingdom. This would make a voluminous work and the research alone would take two or three years" (SL 134).

Based on this evidence, it would appear that Nabokov's silence on this matter was intentional, even tactical, as though he were determined to be remembered as a writer of fiction alone, not as a theorist. Hence, any interpretation of his work is the province of the reader, not that of the author. Given that Nabokov's primary tool of deception was mimicry, it is not surprising that he should set out to conceal this fact from his readers. Indeed, the author's narratives not only comprise a game of hide and seek involving two rival characters operating within the text, but they also involve a game that pits the author against the reader. It is not enough for Nabokov to hide his intentions in order to deceive his readers; it is also necessary to increase the subtlety and complexity of this deception with each consecutive work: the pattern becomes more and more complex, by internal chemical and mechanical constraint (Alexander, 2002/2003, 186). Therefore, *Pale Fire* is more complex and deceptive than *Lolita*, and *Ada* is arguably the most challenging work of his oeuvre. In this vein, it should not be surprising to find that *The Luzhin Defense* is far less challenging than, say, *Despair*.

Aristotle contends that art does not imitate natural things but instead mirrors nature's design. For Nabokov, a pattern of observable nature serves as the primary inspiration for his increasingly deceptive narratives. Without exception, his works reflect his fascination with the phenomenon of mimicry, or resemblance with a difference. Unlike Freud's libido, which refers to infantile sexuality, or the death drive beyond the pleasure principle, mimicry (or deception) is a phenomenon of nature that is not associated with humans alone. Given that the design of Nabokov's work mirrors the existential and ontological mysteries of nature, it is not surprising to learn that he was impatient with any interpretation that included references to supposed symbols or allegories. This became apparent when he repudiated Diana Butler's interpretation of *Lolita* in 1960, employing such language as "complete ignorance and muddle of terms" (SO 96). Perhaps, Nabokov's condemnation of Butler's interpretation reflected his concern that her persuasive entomological symbols would blind readers to his true intentions.

Meanwhile, he might have felt a certain affinity with Alfred Appel, Jr., who was able to discern the broader pattern of deception that characterizes his fiction. In "Nabokov's Puppet Show-II," Appel identifies a number of important features of the author's work. He indicates that his characters function as the author's puppets, for they are basically disguised aspects of Nabokov himself; and he goes on to argue that the cycle of insect metamorphosis serves as the dominant pattern of his fictional narratives (1967, 25–32). One senses that Nabokov would have been sur-

prised, and not entirely pleased, to find his underlying strategy of mimicry revealed in such a manner. After all, one of his creative goals was to
engage in an intellectual contest with the reader, a battle he stood to lose
once his secrets were exposed. For Nabokov, this situation presented a
dilemma. On the one hand, he was delighted at the prospect of a reader
with an intuitive understanding of his hidden strategy. On the other
hand, he was determined to win the game at all costs. Therefore, it seems
prudent to examine the origins and significations of mimicry within the
field of science before engaging in further exploration of the manner in
which Nabokov turned this phenomenon toward his own creative purposes.

MIMICRY IN SCIENCE

Mimicry among butterflies was discovered early in the mid-nineteenth
century, when a great number of plants and animals were also found to
be mimetic. Since then, scientists have debated the aim and typology of
deception, and numerous classifications abound. Despite a divergence of
scientific approaches to mimicry, three basic components are generally
accepted: the mimic, the model, and the predator. Wolfgang Wickler has
defined the biological dimension of mimicry as follows: "two or more
organisms, usually biologically unrelated, or only distantly related, resemble each other closely, the resemblance itself conferring advantage
upon one or both of them" (1998, 109). For the most part, the advantages
of mimicry accrue on the mimic, whose resemblance to the model usually
ensures a degree of protection from a potential predator. In other cases,
however, it is the predator who gains the advantage through a resemblance to its prey, a phenomenon known as *aggressive mimicry*. Indeed, a
variety of possibilities exist: the model may be duped by the mimic, or a
third party; and the predator or signal-receiver may be fooled. Of the
various forms of mimicry, two are distinctively classified as typical forms
related to evolution. The first type was discovered by the English naturalist Henry W. Bates, who noted, in an 1862 report to Darwin, that an
edible insect may secure protection from predators because of its resemblance to an inedible species. Darwin swiftly accepted Bates' discovery
and he referred to specific cases involving moths or butterflies that had
taken on the appearance of a less palatable species in order to gain a
measure of protection. He identified the agent of this process as natural
selection. For Darwin, the phenomenon of mimicry served as proof of
evolution and adaptation, given that its development over time contributed to the survival of individual species; and this was the origin of what
became known as *Batesian Mimicry* (Wickler, 1998, 110; Forbes, 2009, 26).

    This phenomenon raised the question of whether, for example, the
swallowtail butterfly's uncanny resemblance to a more threatening spe-

cies reflected the presence of an intelligent motive. Ultimately, biologists dismissed the idea that one species consciously emulates another, and Bates himself discerned in mimicry a positive motivation lying beyond individual contention. Nevertheless, he found it difficult to explain the reason that a certain species of butterfly known as Heliconidae mimics a less palatable type of Heliconidae in order to gain protection from predators. This question led researchers to explore the issue of *palatability*, as reflected in the system of classifications developed by John R. G. Turner (1984, 141–161). A possible answer to Bates's query surfaced in the research of the German zoologist Fritz Müller (1821–97), who, in 1878, discovered another kind of mimicry. Muller discerned a striking physical resemblance among several unrelated types of butterflies, all of which were known to be inedible. The researcher posed this question: Why do certain caterpillars and butterflies possess such beautiful and elaborate patterns of color? What advantage is to be gained through the presence of such bright patterns and warm coloration? The principles of *Mullerian mimicry* suggest that butterflies endowed with a highly developed sense of color find colorful males or females of another species more to their taste than drab members of their own species. It would appear that the incentive for an insect to join such a "club" is irresistible. Therefore, unpalatable species band together, wear the same "masks," and establish a united front against a potential predator (Forbes, 2009, 36).

Notably, there are forms of mimicry that do not fit easily into the categories mentioned above, and they feature a range of differences.[1] However, a more detailed introduction and overview of the various definitions would prove a "trivial hair-splitting" task, as R. I. Vane-Wright observes, in "On the Definition of Mimicry" (1980, 4). In light of this wide diversity, let us simply explore the ways in which biological treatments of mimicry have influenced the humanities. This will lead us to an examination of the ways in which the scholarly writings of Ouspensky and Evreinoff affected Nabokov in the 1920s and beyond. Before exploring this topic, however, I would like to provide an overview of the ways in which mimicry has been adapted by significant figures in art and literature. As Peter Forbes observes, this natural phenomenon has appealed to a dazzling variety of artists (2009, 133).

ARTISTIC ADAPTATIONS OF BIOLOGICAL MIMICRY

Darwin was the first biologist to highlight the phenomenon of mimicry, which he quickly presented as evidence of natural selection, thereby inspiring generations of researchers to examine this phenomenon. It is easy to grasp the attraction of deception (or camouflage) among members of the scientific community. At the same time, it is not entirely surprising that the phenomenon caught the attention of artists and philosophers as well. Human beings, after all, are no less mimetic than plants and animals. Furthermore, among all the animals, humans perceive themselves as the most detailed copy of the original, i.e., the closest imitation of God. Hence, we are the most ardent mimic of *the real*. If indeed human beings merit a preeminent position on the scale of evolution, Darwin is correct to present mimicry as proof of the theory of evolution. Meanwhile, if mimicry is an inherent impulse among humans, it is natural to connect this phenomenon to the fields of art and literature. Is not art the mirror of the deceptive mind, the duplication of reality? Although some scientists have taken exception to the extension of biological principles to art—notably Vane-Wright, who does not believe in mimicry "with human value judgments of deception" or artistic adventures (1991, 461)—the fact remains that a distinguished group of artists and theorists have been closely associated with psychology, phenomenology, and surrealism. They took note of biological mimicry and placed it at the core of their philosophy.

Indeed, Jacques Lacan, upon his return to Freudian principles, adopted mimicry as a basic component of the human psyche and identified its influence upon the visual arts. In his reformulation of Freudian dynamics between the unconscious and consciousness into that of the imaginary and the symbolic, Lacan is especially attentive to the partial drive in relation to the visual scope, namely the *gaze*. Given that he regards the dialectic between the eye and gaze as comparable to the dynamics between the imaginary and symbolic, he considers the chief function of art as the laying down of our gaze. To put it differently, he explores the process of constructing the subject of fantasy in the context of mimicry. If the unconscious is the primal narcissism upon which a secondary narcissism is constructed, the origin of the human subject turns out to be the unconscious, the repressed instinct. Human beings, as social animals, must continually seek a compromise with their other half, i.e., the animal self. On the side of the symbolic, the subject emerges when the imaginary self attempts to do its best to imitate its inseparable model, the social self. We might ask, "Why do so many failures, difficulties, and conflicts arise in the course of a human lifetime?" Here are two contributing factors: 1) the instinctive self is forced to imitate the social self, and 2) a pure imitation is essentially impossible, given that the former is the master of the latter. In other words, the unconscious is the basic libido, which is never relinquished but merely *disguised* and transformed, as Freud argues throughout his entire body of work.

Lacan frames the process of disguising the unconscious as the result of an emergency brought on by surplus *jouissance*, or the remains of symbolic mediation. The surplus of instinct that arises within the scope of the eye is referred to as the gaze, a beautiful act of mimicry that functions as a lure. Since the mimic is essentially the predator of its model, its purpose is not to be similar but rather to intimidate, as in the case of *aggressive mimicry*. Indeed, it continually threatens the subject with its drive to return to its true form, the origin of life, as Freud proposes through his concept of the death drive.

In this context, we can appreciate Lacan's following statement: "mimicry reveals something in so far as it is distinct from what might be called an *itself* that is behind. The effect of mimicry is camouflage, in the strictly technical sense. It is not a question of harmonizing with the background but, against a mottled background, of becoming mottled—exactly like the technique of camouflage practiced in human warfare" (Lacan, 1981, 99).[2] Significantly, Lacan does not view a picture as a reflection of reality, in the manner of the Realists. Instead, he discerns in that image a mimic of the original, in the form of the inscribed painter within the picture. Hence, the function of art is not necessarily to render the object realistically, but rather to encourage the viewer to share the real that lurks beyond its mask, its veil, in an effort to lay down one's gaze. The viewer (or reader), as if engaged in a game of hide and seek, attempts to uncover the mysteries of the double, the veil of Apollo that is manifested beyond the Dionysian real, which Nietzsche refers to in *The Birth of Tragedy*.

In his interpretation of the subject of fantasy as the double, or the resemblance between the mimic and the model, Lacan provides us with the insight needed to understand the nature of the psyche as aggressive mimicry, and he suggests that art alone is capable of minimizing that aggression. Moreover, he contends that only humans can play with the mimic, the mask of the animal self, without becoming caught up in the imaginary capture. Referring to Caillois's statement that "the facts of mimicry are similar at the animal level, to what, in the human being is manifested as art, or painting," Lacan goes on to persuasively characterize art as a manifestation of human mimicry that is based on its biological counterpart (1981, 100). Nabokov evidently takes a similar stance, for he also regards mimicry as a fundamental element of both art and Nature. As an exile whose nostalgia for his lost homeland would remain acute, Nabokov learned that his sole consolation lay in his effort to immortalize the lost subject in a form of art that utilized the magic of Nature.

Naturally, Caillois and Lacan were hostile to Realism and favored Surrealism or anti-realism. This was no less true of Nabokov. As Peter Forbes observes, mimicry in the arts is often characterized by a blurring of the line between fiction and mundane reality (2009, 135–136). Significantly, Nabokov had little interest in the kind of "average" reality that emerged as the focal point of social or political realists. Instead, he turned to a new strategy in which he combined his passion for butterfly hunting with his love of writing fiction, once boasting that "there is a butterfly in every one of my novels" (Berenbaum, 2000, 57). Not surprisingly, Nabokov admired Bates's book, *The Naturalist on the River Amazon*, and he inserted butterflies into his work with the same frequency with which he condemned Freud in his interviews of the 1960s. Nevertheless, such attention would have to wait for the publication of two groundbreaking books on his Blue Period, which, in turn, inspired a series of essays that appeared in journals, magazines, and book chapters. In "Nabokov's Dreams," an essay published in *The New Yorker*, a man is camouflaged in a manner comparable to that of a butterfly—an apparent attempt by the writer to suggest the literary device of a disguised author. Meanwhile, scores of well-regarded science journals featured stories on Nabokov's life-long scientific interests.[3] *Nature* shed light on the author's Blue Period, while *Science* published reviews of two books, *Nabokov's Butterflies* by Boyd and Pyle (2000), and *Nabokov's Blues* by Kurt Johnson and Steve Coates (1999). In her review of these works, titled "Blue Book Value," May Berenbaum acknowledges Nabokov's pioneering effort to merge two fields, while hailing the author as an outstanding literary interpreter of butterflies and moths. After noting how Johnson and his colleagues were inspired by Nabokov's sixty-page paper, "Notes on Neotropical Plebejinae," published in *Psyche* (1945, 52.1), Berenbaum describes in a tone of admiration an author whose achievements in the areas of both science and literature were remarkable. She concludes that, "with an eloquence borne of deep knowledge, he brought the excitement and wonder of insect lives to millions around the world" (2000, 58).

While this posthumous reevaluation owed much to the rise of the new intellectual paradigm of consilience, it was also facilitated by the intellectual contest that exists between Nabokov and Freud, given that clues to his motives abound in his often puzzling narratives. The author's adamant rejection of Freud, along with psychiatry as a whole, was bound to raise eyebrows among readers and critics alike. Among other things, his readers must have asked, "Why Freud?" In Nabokov's view, perhaps, Freud was a safe choice, given that he was a model that the mimic could imitate and simultaneously intimidate. Above all, Freud was the most suitable model to serve as a disguise for Nabokov and this disguise ultimately enabled him to shield himself from social and political attention, while positioning him to criticize generalization in favor of "divine" detail. During the chaotic period in which he lived as an exile in Western Europe, Nabokov employed a pen name, *Siren*: a natural move for the scion of a wealthy and noble family that had been dispossessed in the wake of the Bolshevik Revolution. Overnight, Nabokov and his family found themselves in a turbulent expatriate community that was fragmented along political lines. The assassination of his father clearly inspired the murder of one of his characters, John Shade, and many other characters in his early works seem paralyzed by the fear that they are being watched by spies. This is especially true of the unnamed narrator of *The Eye*. After an unsuccessful suicide attempt, the narrator develops a strategy to escape the gaze of others by distancing himself from them. Instead of merely allowing himself to be watched by others, he watches himself in relation to others, concluding that their knowledge of him is diverse, highly personal, and partial. Nabokov's treatment of mimicry in such stories reflects his rejection of the idea that this phenomenon is an exclusive byproduct of natural selection. The author's well-known distaste for absolute ideologies was obsessive, and for Nabokov, Darwinian evolution was another such ideology.

Lacan formulates the human subject in the context of a dialectic between the mimic and model, while extending it to the scope of the gaze and visual arts. Nabokov also explores mimicry and takes it well beyond biological boundaries in order to approach the essential nature of human psychology. There is a slight difference in their approach to mimicry, however, and it is most evident in their respective views of *sexuality*. Lacan—like Freud—regards sexuality as the product of mimicry (1981, 100), while Nabokov, who rejects this view, treats sexuality as an object of play. Yet, for both men, deception (whatever its uses) is an essential feature of human existence, as is Nature itself. For the author, the deceptive nature of the human being is nothing more than the design of God manifested in a work of art, which is our sole source of comfort and delight. This is the starting point of Nabokov's concept of aesthetic beauty, which he terms as "the immortality of art" in *Lolita*. For Nabokov, the creative impulse inherent in human works of art is no less evident in the acts of mimicry found in Nature. To put it another way, "a caterpillar or a spider that perfects a resemblance to bird-dung is like a Dutch still-life artist lovingly recreating the texture of folded velvet" (Forbes, 2009, 128).

BEYOND DARWINIAN MIMICRY: THEATRICALITY IN NATURE

In the 1800s, British naturalist Alfred Russel Wallace encountered the leaf butterfly, *Kallima*, a genus of the subfamily Nymphalinae, which is found throughout Southeast Asia. The butterfly bears an uncanny resemblance to a dead leaf, with its brownish hue, intricate veins, and markings that resemble fungus spots. Wallace concluded that, when the butterfly sought to escape from a predator such as a hungry bird, it employed an intricate form of camouflage that had been developed over time through a series of intermediate stages. While the naturalist interpreted his discovery as evidence of Darwinian evolution, he found one aspect of the phenomenon difficult to explain. Wallace was puzzled by the fact that the butterfly's camouflaged form featured a subtlety and perfection that transcended the practical need to deceive a predator. What accounted for an act of mimicry that was so stunningly accurate? Indeed, in its delicacy, the camouflage was capable of deceiving even the discerning eye of a human being. This mystery was at the center of a series of debates that would continue into the next century. In 1917, for instance, Richard Swann Lull argued that we cannot conceive of natural selection taking adaptation beyond the point of efficiency (Forbes, 2009, 47). Then, in the 1940s, the American geneticist Richard Goldschmidt rejected the possibility of a gradual change in the Kallima's adaptation. On the contrary, he argued, its camouflage may have developed suddenly, by chance, and without intermediate stages. This argument, which has raged for over a century, has yielded a wide array of assumptions, and the debate continues today.

Nabokov apparently regarded the dead-leaf butterfly as one of the most remarkable examples of mimicry found in Nature, for its purpose was twofold. The primal function of such mimicry, as the author noted in several interviews, was protection. As if to highlight the ways in which his own approach to writing paralleled the protective function of mimicry, he inserted phrases such as "a glaring disadvantage may turn out to be a subtle protective device" into the "Foreword" of *King, Queen, Knave* (1968, viii). Is it possible that such phrases shed light on his own response when he disguised himself as Humbert or insulated himself within the protective rhetoric of Freudian psychology? In the first portion of *Lolita*, the protagonist provides a remarkable imitation of Freudian sexuality, only to reject it in order to embark on his quest to become a true artist. Significantly, it was Nabokov's own disadvantage as an exile that provided him with the opportunity to develop into a writer. As he once acknowledged, without the Bolshevik Revolution, he might have been satisfied with the relatively stable life of a professional lepidopterist. Indeed, protection is seemingly the goal when the author takes on the appearance of a psychologist, in much the same way that certain moths take on the shape and color of a wasp, even moving their antennae in a manner characteristic of the wasp.

For Nabokov, however, the dead-leaf butterfly's significance transcended any proposed utilitarian goal of protection. In fact, he firmly rejected the idea that Darwin had told the entire story about mimicry, given that the refinement insects demonstrate far exceeds the requirements of survival. If we examine this issue from a strictly Darwinian perspective, how do we account for the fact that the beauty, mystery, and attention to detail inherent in camouflage far exceed what it necessary to deceive the primitive eye of an animal? What is the purpose of this luxurious beauty, which goes far beyond the rudimentary shapes and patterns required for protection? Doubtful that the purpose of mimicry was wholly utilitarian, Nabokov sensed the existence of an *other world*, one situated beyond the grasp of our consciousness.

Despite the assertions of theorists who contend that changes occur in a gradual and generalized manner, Nabokov suggests that we avoid judging everything in the world from a utilitarian perspective. His own experience of sudden, unpredictable change taught him that life involves mysteries, chance developments, and coincidences. Indeed, without reference to the invisible hand of McFate, or *Unknown Agent X*, Nabokov found his own personal experiences (as well as developments in the world at large) inexplicable. It is well known that his life was shaped by events that were harrowing in the extreme. During the weeks leading up to Nazi Germany's invasion of France, he struggled to secure visas and tickets for his family, which had taken refuge in Paris. Finally, the author and his family left Europe for the United States at the end of 1940, just three weeks before German bombs destroyed the building in which they had been living. Drawing on such experiences, Nabokov appears to conclude that we can neither estimate nor predict positive or negative developments by means of generalization or logic alone. Likewise, mimicry, one of Nature's most brilliant achievements, reflects the intervention of something beyond systematic causes, or symbolic significance.

In his story, "Signs and Symbols," Nabokov appears to argue for the concept of *contingency* in biology as well as art. Set during one of Europe's darkest periods, the story involves a husband and wife who discuss their plan to remove their son from a mental clinic and bring him home, despite the fact that he has attempted suicide twice since his institutionalization. The story ends, however, with a series of apparently mistaken phone calls, and the parents, like the reader, cannot guess at the significance of the final call. We are never told who is calling or what the message concerns, a conclusion that underscores Nabokov's central message: Life is inexplicable, unpredictable, and contingency will always overshadow rational regularities and symbols. Interestingly, this view is reflected in the work of Victoria N. Alexander, who questions traditional utilitarian interpretations of mimicry. In her examination of two groups of butterflies, the *viceroy* and the *monarch*, Alexander concludes that their resemblance to each other cannot be attributed to natural selection. Instead, she argues for the presence of an unknown element she describes as *agent* X. In some cases, the resemblance between different species emerges suddenly, often because of dramatic changes in climate (2002/ 2003, 201). For Nabokov, this unknown agent, which functions as chance or coincidence, is one of the three forces that mold a human being, along with heredity and environment (LL, 1982, 126). He contends that the *other* world, or unknown factor, is *already always* part of our consciousness and shapes reality in a manner that renders it ever elusive—a subject that I will explore further in the next chapter.

If we accept the *contingency* of our consciousness, we are also obliged to accept Nabokov's assertion of the primacy of *the divine details*. He discovered in nature the nonutilitarian delights that he sought in art. For him, both were a form of magic and at the same time, a game of intricate enchantment and deception. Indeed, the adroit hand of the artist bears more than a little resemblance to a butterfly's act of mimicry, or an opponent's elaborate chess move. Apparently, Nabokov regards the artist as a musician, or a chess player, who conceals his tricks in plain view. As shown in works like *The Luzhin Defense*, the relationship between a writer and his readers is not unlike the relationship between a conjurer and his audience. The reader is invited to discover the secret, or solve the riddle.

This theme is spelled out in *Bend Sinister*: "the glory of God is to hide a thing, and the glory of man is to find it" (BS 106). Given that art, nature, and humans are implicated in the act of mimicry, it is natural for us to view the writing and reading of fiction as processes that comprise a continual *masking* and *unmasking* that plays out as though upon a stage. Overall, Nabokov's concept of art is not unlike that of Lacan, given that both men viewed art as a mask that mimics *the real*, or *unknown* X. It is interesting to consider that Nabokov and his wife, Vera, occasionally worked as film extras during their challenging years in Berlin. After all, mimicry is essentially another name for *theatricality*, and the author treated it as little more than a literary device. This calls to mind the fact that, from 1912 to 1919, the Russian philosopher, P. D. Ouspensky produced essays on mimicry among insects that referred specifically to the theatricality of nature; and in 1931, these works were published in a collection of essays.

What Ouspensky explores in the phenomenon of insect mimicry is the subject's desire, or instinct, to become something other than itself—an impulse that goes beyond the need for protection. In other words, the practical outcome is a byproduct of an inherent need to become desirable and attractive. In a human context, this impulse helps us to understand the popularity of tattoos and cosmetic surgery, which once again, reflect a basic desire to be more beautiful and more conspicuous. Yet, these operations involve a degree of risk. Indeed, those who make themselves conspicuous are more likely to be targeted by predators. Therefore, the impulse toward mimicry cannot be understood entirely from a utilitarian perspective, and it becomes necessary to examine it within a broader, and distinctly philosophical, context. Notably, Ouspensky perceives in Nature a tendency toward decorativeness and theatricality. In other words, Nature continually seeks to adorn herself and *not to be herself*: "All the time she is dressing herself up, all the time changing her costumes, all the time turning before a mirror, looking at herself from all sides, admiring herself—then again undressing and dressing" (1997, 48). In the course of the seasons, Nature adopts a series of masks and dons an array of new attire, as if all of life unfolds upon a stage. The fundamental law of Nature is not to be itself, but to resemble something else, and such choices range from a dead leaf to a social icon. If an individual molds herself to the demands of society, for example, she will eventually embrace her mask as a fundamental reality, and the mask will become her. This fundamental emphasis on form is illustrated in a memorable scene from *Lolita* in which the girl expresses little interest in winning or losing. Instead, she focuses on the gracefulness of her movements, as though she is conscious of the fact that she is being watched: "Her form was, indeed, an absolutely perfect imitation of absolutely topnotch tennis—without any utilitarian results" (LO 211). In short, for Nabokov, the nymphet is an emblem of childhood, a playful, deceptive, and unreachable period in one's memory.

Nabokov, like Ouspensky, views mimicry as the product of *theatrical beings* on the earth. The two men also shared a similar view of Nature, insofar as they rejected the idea that its essence lies in utility, as opposed to fashion. For Nabokov and Ouspensky, Nature was a form of art that reflected the handiwork of God, the influence of the unknown X. This agent expresses itself in the form of coincidences that occur in the course of worldly developments, just as contingency arises in logic and consciousness. We are incurably devoted to the stage, in the same way that the stage-struck Lolita is obsessed with acting. The theatrical, after all, is the essence of reality. Lolita isn't alone in her obsession, given that Humbert takes his theatricality to an even higher level. Initially, he assumes the role of an enchanted fool who is trapped by a nymphet and victimized through a conspiracy involving Lolita and her counterpart, Quilty. Humbert then assumes the roles of pathetic lover and murderer, only to take his final bow as the author of an immortal love story, *Lolita*. His mimicry of a criminal is picture perfect. Like a wolf who dons sheep's clothing in order to deceive its prey, he mimics Freud—a strategy that conforms to the model of *aggressive mimicry*, given that he assumes the appearance of his prey. This situation raises questions about the way in which we should view Humbert. Is he a victim or a victimizer? Is he good or bad? Throughout the first part of the narrative, Humbert comes off as a veritable paradigm of Freudian infantile sexuality. However, in the wake of his defeat at the hands of the nymphet and Quilty, he doffs his mask, eliminates his rival, and reveals his true nature as an artist. For Humbert, it seems, "sex is but the ancilla of art" (LO 236). Meanwhile, we are left to wonder: Who is the predator and who is its prey?

Traditional boundaries, like common sense, are meaningless in the face of theatricality, which is invariably connected to trickery for the purpose of *transgression*. Moving beyond such boundaries is perhaps one of Nabokov's most unique literary devices. It is reflected not only in the nature of his characters, but also in the distinctive boundaries drawn between author and character. In Nabokov's work, the term author does not suggest an implied author but the real author, Nabokov himself. His own desires are reflected in the characters' actions. The evidence for this is overwhelming, and much of it is supplied by the author himself. In the "Afterword" of *Lolita*, for example, Nabokov hints that Humbert is the disguised author. Such camouflaged authors abound in his works. They include Ardalion in *Despair*, and Shade and Kinbote in *Pale Fire*, to name a few. Under these circumstances, it is not surprising that so many critics have focused on Nabokov's literary device of transgression. In some cases, critics have suggested that the author speaks through his characters, even though such characters are not always clearly identified (Forbes, 2009, 130). Others have described Nabokov's characters as the author's puppets, since they are essentially disguised authors (Appel, 1967, 28). One critic contends that the clash is not between characters "since characters are the mere fabrications of their creator, the author" (Green, 1988, 7). Traditionally, a reader engages with characters that reflect the author's ideas as well as his moral vision. In Nabokov's case, however, the boundary between the author and his characters is blurred, leaving readers with the unsettling impression that the real author's voice has been expressed through the characters' words and actions. Given that the narrative functions as an elaborate game of hide and seek between author and reader, the real conflict does not occur between the characters. Indeed, they are merely the shadows of Nabokov and Freud, or their *doubles*, that perform on a stage.

Interestingly, the literary device of transgression is closely related to the ideas of another Russian philosopher, Nicolas Evreinoff. In his 1927 book, *The Theatre in Life*, Evreinoff contends that theatre exists in nature in the form of mimicry (2013, 11). He goes on to suggest that the thousands of instances of masquerading in nature are the byproduct of an instinct among all organisms to become something other than oneself. Hence, transgression is inevitable, and it often takes the form of *transfiguring*, i.e., to recreate oneself as another being. In the work of Nabokov, this instinct is most evident in the author's tendency to reinvent himself in the form of a character. What is theatricality, after all, other than the essence of literature? To put it differently, the impulse to transfigure arises from a strong desire to sublimate oneself, to become better: "in this transfigured reality we remain the same as we were, and yet we become different, we see ourselves in a better, nobler, brighter light" (Evreinoff, 2013, 66). Indeed, one might go so far as to assert that sublimation through empathy is the main function of literature. Employing a model of play, Nabokov clearly aims to enlighten and liberate himself, even as he stimulates the reader's mind, in a manner that parallels his own father's efforts in the field of politics. This is Smurov's goal in *The Eye*. Like Evreinoff, he posits a higher form of play as a means to promote intelligence, to achieve *transformation*, and to increase one's happiness.

As Nabokov continually reminds us, however, the idea of transformation draws inspiration from biology. In this vein, one could refer to lepidoptera larvae, which undergo a complete metamorphosis from caterpillar to pupa, or chrysalis to adult, in what is perhaps the most astonishing transformation in Nature. Likewise, in fiction, transformation tends to occur, in tandem with the development of the narrative. Hence, a cruel, calculating, and immoral Humbert evolves into a repentant and sympathetic lover, only to emerge in the end as the author of an immortal love story. This is achieved, however, through the *author's interference of character*. Perhaps this is the reason Nabokov refers to fiction as a *combinational* concoction. He would argue that humans are essentially theatrical beings, and the essence of all theatrical art is transformation. As one distances oneself by taking the stage, the artistic devices of transgression and transformation become closely intertwined.

The transfiguration of biological mimicry into an artistic form involves numerous components, including puzzling, resemblance with a difference, contingency, the double, riddles, games, play, theatricality, transgression, metamorphosis, and combinational concoction. While these devices may appear unrelated, they are all closely connected to the concept of mimicry. When considering what might have been left out, it seems prudent to examine Nabokov's own views on the subject, as expressed in a passage from *The Gift* in which the narrator discusses insect science as a present from his father and, perhaps, part of the cultural heritage of Russia:

> He told me about the incredible artistic wit of mimetic disguise, which was not explainable by the struggle for existence (the rough haste of evolution's unskilled forces), was too refined for the mere deceiving of accidental predators, feathered, scaled and otherwise (not very fastidious, but then not too fond of butterflies), and seemed to have been invented by some waggish artist precisely for the intelligent eyes of man (a hypothesis that may lead far an evolutionist who observes apes feeding on butterflies); he told me about these magic masks of mimicry; about the enormous moth which in a state of repose assumes the image of a snake looking at you; of a tropical geometrid colored in perfect imitation of a species of butterfly infinitely removed from it in nature's system, the illusion of the orange underside possessed by one being humorously reproduced in the other by the orange-colored inner margins of the secondaries. (*The Gift*, 1963, 122–123)

One element that appears to be missing from my inventory is the capacity of the human consciousness to turn tragedy into comedy. In the above passage, Nabokov seems to suggest that mimetic disguise in Nature reflects the wit and inventiveness of a *waggish artist*, as though it were intended to be viewed by the perceptive eyes of a human being. Through Fyodor's voice, the author affirms the privilege of human consciousness, with an emphasis on the wit and humor that serve as powerful evidence of enlightenment. Only humans, after all, can be blissful spectators of the world, glorifying their humor and wit so as to transform nothing into a sublimated entity. Art alone makes this possible. Perhaps the celebration of humor and wit is the most basic tool of his mimic of Freud, whose concept of art is not so different than that of the "Viennese quack," as a close reading of such essays as "Creative Writers and Day-Dreaming," and "Humour" would suggest. As a psychological novelist, Nabokov adheres to the pattern of William James's consciousness, as opposed to the Freudian unconscious. Therefore, it is important to consider how these two psychologists differed in their approach, while also bearing in mind the ways in which they agreed. At the same time, we must consider the ways in which Nabokov adapted the concepts of Time, Memory, and Consciousness. Indeed, this will be the focus of the next section.

NOTES

1. Timo Maran, for instance, suggests four patterns of deceptive behavior in Nature, in "Semiotic Interpretations of biological mimicry" (2007, 228-229); Karel Kleisner and Anton Markoš reinterpret three different forms of mimicry (Batesian, Mullerian, Pouyannian) in terms of *semes*, an explanatory unit of resemblance: the genetic code, mobile cellular phones, fashion (2005, 209-222).

2. See Lacan's conceptualization of mimicry in his *Seminar XI*, pp. 73, 98-100, 107, 109.

3. One recommended way to confirm the transition of critics' concerns toward the end of the century is to search for critical notes published in magazines and first-rate science journals. Among others, I would suggest the following: Scrapbook, "N's Dreams," *The New Yorker*, Mar. 29, 75.5 (1999): 87-88; David B. Ritland and Lincoln P. Brower. "The viceroy butterfly is not a batesian mimic," *Nature*, 350, (April 1991): 497-498; Philip Zaleski, "Nabokov's Blue Period," *Harvard Magazine* 86.6 (1986): 34-38; May Berenbaum, "Blue Book Value," *Science* 290, no. 5489, (6 Oct. 2000): 57-58.

TWO
Memory as a Form of Fiction

Once Humbert abandons his search for Lolita and her supposed captor, he reassesses her as the sweetest and most mischievous of muses, *Mnemosyne*, and he produces an essay titled, "Mimir and Memory," which appears in a certain *Review*. In his essay, Humbert outlines a theory of perceptual time that involves "the mind's being conscious not only of matter but also of its own self, thus creating a continuous spanning of two points (the storable future and the stored past)" (LO 237). The details of the theory, delineated in five lines, may strike the reader as incongruous, since they originate with a character he or she has come to view as a ruthless and calculating pedophile. However, the voice that informs the essay should be regarded as that of the author, Nabokov. For it is at this point that the reader experiences the author's intervention into the novel as a character, in the manner of a metamorphosis from beast to artist. This begs a question: "Why does Nabokov transgress the boundary between author and character, to a degree rarely found in literature?" It is as though the mischievous goddess of memory were implicated in the literary device of transgression. This development inspires a series of related questions: "Is memory more deceptive when it takes the form of mimicry? How is remembering the past related to time? Is human consciousness, itself, combinational and puzzling?"

Perhaps Lolita, a female child, functions less as an object of sex than as an emblem of time. Is it possible she represents *the childhood* to which we can never return, that is, unless we seek to revisit it through a hypertrophied sense of recollection? The highly intellectual and complicated passage attributed to Humbert, while abrupt, will strike a familiar chord to any reader who is aware of the materiality of consciousness posited by psychology as well as phenomenology. Under these circumstances, it is prudent to be attentive to the manner in which the concepts of conscious-

ness, memory, and time are intertwined. Moreover, their role in Nabokov's fiction is no less significant than the concept of mimicry. As Zoran
Kuzmanovich observes, "there is no mimicry without vivid memory and
no vivid memory without rapt attention" (Kuzmanovich, 2002, 31).

In the course of his 1962 interview, Nabokov indicated that literature,
language, and childhood are the three main elements that he hoped to
contribute to his lost country, Russia. On yet another occasion, he referred to Proust as one of his favorite writers, although with one qualifi-
cation. He valued only the first part of *In Search of Lost Time,* citing its
fairy-tale qualities. Significantly, in remembering the past, Proust's narrator revisits the period spanning his early childhood and adulthood, moving in chronological order. Therefore, the first part of the book focuses on
his childhood. It is worth noting that for Nabokov, unlike Proust, duration of time plays a pivotal role in the development of fiction. The larger
the gap in time, the more fantasy and the magic of deception are likely to
become involved. Therefore, Humbert perceives the gap in age as a crucial condition for the emergence of a nymphet. When he developed a
relationship with the teenaged Anabel, who was the same age, she failed
to qualify as a nymphet. Twenty-nine years later, however, the adolescent Lolita serves as a fateful object for a bewitched exile. In order to be
trapped by the spell of a nymphet, the age gap should be no less than ten
years, he contends, but an age gap of thirty or forty years can be fatal (LO
19).

Not surprisingly, Nabokov adapts the perception of time in a manner
that distinguishes him from other modernists, including Kafka, Bergson,
and Proust. Above all, he utilizes the function of memory and cognition
that is associated with time, as formulated by William James. (The fact
that Nabokov rarely mentioned James helps to explain critics' failure to
comment on this influence until recently.) As Brian Boyd notes, Nabokov
thought of William James as "a dear soul with an admirable delicacy of
string-tone" (1991, 216). While Boyd fails to expand on this point, Stephen Blackwell devotes considerably more space to James's influence
upon Nabokov. Among the themes he attributes to this influence are the
following: the manner in which the mind can deceive itself; consciousness as a gift of nature; the error-prone nature of the mind's creations;
and the fact that life, at its core, is (or can be) driven by a higher law.
Blackwell's argument that these elements operate in tandem with mimicry also takes into account such literary devices as transgression: "images
of the author or his world regularly appear in what he called a demiurgic
capacity in relation to the created fiction" (2009, 8).[1] He goes on to describe characteristics such as accuracy, detail, and self-consciousness as
key components. While he merges James's psychology with literary adaptations, Blackwell's analysis takes the form of a general survey that
touches upon a variety of other influences.

Blackwell's insight on the essence of consciousness, in regard to inevitable distortions of objective narrative, sheds light on Nabokov's art of memory. Given Nabokov's passionate desire to turn the limitation, or lack of objectivity, within our consciousness into a creative force, he treated fiction as nothing less than a gift of nature. Indeed, Nabokov perceived memory as a tool of art, as did Proust. Yet, there is a crucial difference between the two authors. The former focuses on the past as a force that shapes the self and world at large within the flow of time, while the latter concentrates on perceptions of reality in retrospect. Nabokov enriches his memory for the purpose of developing what he might describe as an exile's literature. In the process, he conjures up memories of his homeland, his childhood, his native tongue, and the rich body of Russian literature. These elements are linked by the unifying theme of love. For Nabokov, memory is the sole means to voluntarily exile oneself within the deceptive, infinite land of fantasy, which he posits against the forced exile that was brought about by the Bolshevik Revolution. In a manner that distinguishes him from Proust and Joyce, Nabokov explores consciousness in a way that involves not only a negation of objectivity, but also a negation of time itself. In line with his approach to deceptive mimicry, the magic of recollection is linked inevitably to hostility that is directed against totalitarianism, absolutism, and among others, Freudian generalization.

Building on this proposition, this section will examine James's psychology in detail, with an emphasis on stream of thought, the materiality of consciousness, the empirical subject, and the concept of "the relations." Moreover, my exploration of these subjects will link them to Nabokov's literary adaptations. I will then compare James's structural model of memory to that of Freud, in a way that takes into account their similarities, while also shedding light on Nabokov's perception of the unbridgeable gap that separated them. A third section will focus on the creative function of memory and duration. In this section, I will pose the question: "Why does the highest state of consciousness involve feelings of emptiness and loss, which, in turn, give rise to feelings of love, as well as a desire for fantasy?" In my conclusion, I will demonstrate that the narrative strategies through which Nabokov focuses on the workings of memory correspond to the concept of mimicry.

CONSCIOUSNESS AND FRINGE: JAMES AND NABOKOV

As Erick R. Kandel and Gerald Edelman observe, modern neuroscientists repeatedly return to the seminal works of William James and Sigmund Freud (Kandel, 2012, 53; Edelman, 2004, 4–7, 82–84, 95). James's *The Principles of Psychology* (1890) and Freud's "The Project for a Scientific Psychology" (1895) are monumental works which heralded a new age in the study of the mind—and they remain startlingly relevant. While the two men gradually moved into diverse (often divergent) areas of research, their work on the human brain reflected a similar spirit. Both men, after all, were intellectual heirs of Darwin and started out as neuroscientists. It seems natural, therefore, that their work should agree on at least one point: the materiality of consciousness. The purpose of this section, however, is not to shed light on the two psychologists' similarities, which will be outlined in chapter 3. Instead, I will spotlight their differences, which Nabokov fully recognized. While he treated the one as a great favorite, he dismissed the other as a "Viennese quack"; and this dichotomy proved to be a major source of Nabokov's creative energy. Therefore, it seems appropriate to examine the novelty of James's thought.

William James, who rejected the Cartesian subject, denied that consciousness was a solid entity (stuff) and presented it as a flow, one that pertained to temporality. Thus, in his view, consciousness changes in ways that are transgressive and operates with contingency at its core. James stands with the Darwinians in his contention that the study of the animal brain is the gateway to any meaningful understanding of the human brain, since lower animals are the ancestors of humans on the evolutionary scale. Therefore, the difference between them and us is not a matter of kind but of degree. Yet, unlike animals, humans have developed a cerebral cortex, *consciousness*, the upper portion of the brain that is charged with direction, guidance, and the establishment of a sense of order. However, the upper portion of the brain cannot function without the lower portion. Hence, James contends that "a certain amount of brain-physiology must be presupposed or included in psychology" (2010, 9). Adapting Darwinism to the study of the brain, he proposes that the essence of the psyche is *transgression*, which accrues in the experience of the inner mind as it reacts to the external environment. Mental life cannot exist without bodily life, for prudence and learning arise from experiences stored in memories that have, in turn, been inscribed in neurons. Since the mind inhabits a particular environment, it both acts upon and reacts to that environment. The inter-subjectivity between action and reaction gives rise to voluntary and involuntary responses, such as reflexes and semi-reflexes, so that the boundary separating instinct and volition tends to blur. When compared to Freud's concept of instinct, James's concept of bodily transgression appears more radical. After all, Freud's postulation of the unconscious is presented as a tool of the practitioner, whose aim is to help a patient to adjust to his own specific society, based on the reality principle.

Since James was as much a philosopher as a psychologist, it is not surprising that his discovery served as the ground for American Pragmatism and European Phenomenology. He placed consciousness within the ceaseless flow and transgression that occurs not only between mind and body, but also between the inner and outer world. Through this process, the human mind is pressured to function as a limited entity; and yet, paradoxically, it is also directed toward infinite potentialities. For James, the basic structure of the brain is geared toward *habit*: Living creatures are bundles of habits (2010, 1: 74). Since the animal body comprises the plasticity of organic materials, its survival relies upon a strong sense of necessity, which is implanted at birth but expanded through learning. In order to overcome arising obstacles, it is vital to develop new habits, and such developments facilitate changes within the tissue of the brain. Unlike Freud, who strove to establish a new explanatory model of the human mind, one that relied heavily upon myth and archeological symbols, James, with his focus on the practical value of our lives, based his model on experimental science.

From this vantage point, a phrase like "learning by heart" no longer possesses an abstract, ideal connotation; it is imbued instead with materialistic precision. Learning involves repetition of the same action in order to perpetuate it, so that those actions are essentially *branded* upon the cerebrum. Significantly, the *traces* of this process are never wholly lost, even if our conscious memory of the process becomes faint, devoid of color. Again, James refers to this process as *habit*, and habits are fundamental resources for all creatures, no matter where they happen to fall on the evolutionary scale. Indeed, the bundle of neurons that is rooted and implanted through the process of repetition makes life possible. It functions automatically, in order to operate in a manner that is precise and accurate but nevertheless fails to produce fatigue: a quality that distinguishes it from neurons of a higher level. The term *habit* has its corollary in Freud's concept of *instinct,* or unconscious, and, when we refer to the system of memory, it virtually overlaps with his concept of memory-traces. However, while James's concept of habit arose in association with the phenomenology of memory and consciousness, Freud aimed for the more extended—and universal—concept of the unconscious, which can be altered to suit a variety of situations. In contrast to Freud's concept of consciousness, James's automatic habit is presented as a necessity, that is, if one is to maintain an ordinary life. As the neuroscientist Antonio Damasio has argued, in the absence of this second nature, consciousness is useless: "the apparatus of rationality, traditionally presumed to be *neo*cortical, does not seem to work without that of biological regulation, traditionally presumed to be *sub*cortical" (Damasio, 1994, 128).

What is *consciousness,* if it is not a sensation of conscious automata? As mind and body are two and one, much like a nail and a coat, so are the brain and the mind. They are different aspects of the same coin. When the rearrangement of molecules occurs in the higher regions of the brain, a change of consciousness simultaneously takes place (James, 2010, 1: 95). If this is so, consciousness is essentially an agency of selection that is directed by interests. Lower animals move regularly, and habitually, without experiencing much in the way of illusion. This is particularly obvious when they are compared to the most highly developed animal, whose nervous system is unpredictable and indeterminable. Given the instability of consciousness, our thoughts tend to be independent of objects themselves, for they are shaped by *personal experience*, which includes certain events and excludes others. For James, consciousness is synonymous with *feeling*, since it is personal and always changing, as a sequence of *differents* in time. Heraclitus once said that we cannot cross the same stream twice. Similarly, James said, "there is no proof that the same bodily sensation is ever got by us twice" (2010, 1: 154). A person's sensibility is altering constantly, adding new experiences to neurons, so that his brain is never under the same condition. It is consistently altering, and redistributing, implanted memories.

> He *remembers* his own states, while he only *conceives* Paul's. Remembrance is like direct feeling; its object is suffused with a warmth and intimacy to which no object of mere conception ever attains. This quality of warmth and intimacy is what Peter's *present* thought also processes for itself. So sure as this present is me, is mine, it says, so sure is anything else that comes with the same warmth and intimacy and immediacy, me and mine. What the qualities called warmth and intimacy may in themselves be will have to be matter for future consideration. (James, 2010, 1: 158–159)

This passage suggests why an isolated human is such a lonely creature. Since thought is personal, subjective, *mine*, it is extraordinarily difficult to communicate to others. Given that consciousness is time-bound, it cannot be chopped into segments, in spite of the time-gap. It flows like a stream. Perhaps the term, *stream of consciousness*, proved to be James's greatest contribution to Modernist literature, as utilized by figures such as Joyce and Proust. For Nabokov, however, James provided two other elements that became the basis of his art—a body of literature that stands apart from work that is generally associated with Modernism. First of all, like James, he believes in neither an objective reality nor an absolute ideology, given that our sensations are always fluid, personal, and temporary. Secondly, in recalling the past, Nabokov did not rely upon the device of the inner monologue. Instead, he regarded a magical evocation of the remote past as the essence of fiction, and he viewed the author as a conjurer, a magician.

Unlike Freud, who focused on the patient's past as remembered in the present, Nabokov was attentive to the deceptive memory, whose distortions reflect an individual's feelings of intimacy and affection—and which lend such power to his literature. This led him to the inter-subjectivity, *the relations*, which produced a groundbreaking narrative technique that involves a transgression between author and character: an approach that reflects his assumption that the author cannot depict characters objectively, i.e., independent of his feelings of affection and intimacy. Indeed, in Nabokov's epistemology, the knower inevitably becomes part of the object known, which James contends in "Does Consciousness Exist?" (1904). As a consequence of this feeling of *relations*, or relation-feelings (a product of the propinquity of ides, or associated ideas), we do not have isolated sensations. Notably, in his *Lectures on Literature*, Nabokov refers to this phenomenon as the *rainbow edge*, and indicates that, while the author and narrator may be different, the boundary separating them is blurry and indistinct, much like the borders that divide the colors of a rainbow:

> At this late point, then, one might be tempted to say that Proust *is* the narrator, that he *is* the eyes and ears of the book. But the answer is still no. The book that the narrator in Proust's book is supposed to write is still a book-within-the-book and is not quite *In Search of Lost Time*—just as the narrator is not quite Proust. There is a focal shift here which produces a rainbow edge: this is the special Proustian crystal through which we read the book. It is not a mirror of manners, not an autobiography, not a historical account. It is pure fantasy on Proust's part, just as *Anna Karenin* is a fantasy, just as Kafka's "The Metamorphosis" is fantasy—just as Cornell University will be a fantasy if I ever happen to write about it some day in retrospect. (LL 210)

A feeling of relations, referred to as *fringe*, serves as the aesthetic core of James's psychology, and it would emerge as the kernel of phenomenology. Significantly, however, it inspired a wide variety of terms: Husserl's *intentionality*, Merleau-Ponty's *chiasm* or *intertwining*, and Lacan's *intersubjectivity*. James argues that "as our sensations or perceptions are of various species, so are there various species of relations;—the number of relations, indeed, even of external things, being almost infinite, while the number of perceptions is, necessarily, limited by that of the objects which have the power of producing some affection of our organs of sensation" (2010, 1: 165). For better or worse, we are not aware of these feelings of relations, for they do not play an appreciable role in consciousness. Perhaps this is the reason Nabokov declares that "reality is an infinite succession of steps, levels of perception, false bottoms, and hence unquenchable, unattainable" (SO, 11). This may account for his utter denial of symbols and allegories, given that every definite image in the mind is steeped and dyed in the free water that flows around it. Interestingly, Freud's model of the apparatus of memory does not differ significantly from James's, given that he describes a brain comprising the mutually exclusive elements of consciousness and memory-traces. As consciousness moves forward to confront a new experience, it simultaneously moves backward to remember it. Therefore, the memory-trace is nothing but materiality, psychical origin in itself. This dual system would radically overturn traditional notions regarding time, memory, and cognition.

Nabokov appears to have been inspired by James's concept of fringe, which he adapts as one of his chief literary devices. Referred to as *superimposition*, it involves the overlapping of one image atop another. The author explicitly describes this key element of his art when he writes, "fold my magic carpet, after use, in such a way as to superimpose one part of the pattern upon another"(SM, 139). An example of how this device works can be found in *The Real Life of Sebastian Knight*, a novel in which there is no clear conflict between the main characters, narrator V and his brother, Sebastian. Indeed, the novel concludes with an ambiguity that allows for a range of possibilities. We might conclude that the narrator and Sebastian are not separate entities at all, but the same person. On the other hand, they may be another person altogether, whom they do not know. This playful ending suggests that the characters reflect different aspects of one person who has been altered over time; and they all bear a striking resemblance to one person: the author, Nabokov. To borrow Nabokov's expression, both characters are shadows of the author, himself, who is a most *obscure* figure. This pattern of superimposition is repeated in *Pale Fire*, where the poet, Shade, and the commentator, Kinbote, are evidently doubles of one person, Nabokov, who relates the story of his life. An important element in this phenomenon should not be overlooked, however. While the characters may resemble each other, they do not overlap precisely. While they function as doubles, they also differ in significant ways. Their resemblance inevitably contains an element of *contingency*, given that it reflects a loosening and renewal, in proportion to the ceaseless flow and change. The two characters are different aspects of the conjuror, Nabokov, and therefore they serve as shadows or *ghosts*, emblems of death, even though the author lives. The voices of the characters are diverse, but the reader is able to catch the overtones.

James defines the *fringe* as psychic overtones, which bear comparison to the overtones found in music. When different instruments offer up the same note, the various tones blend into a fundamental note and *suffuse* it, so they are not heard separately by the human ear (James 2010, 1: 171). Even though knowledge about a thing involves knowledge of its relations, we are exclusively aware of its unarticulated affinities. Our will to believe in that which consciousness designates tends to blind us to the sensual aspects of materiality, so that we are inclined to hear the sound of thunder without being aware of its inseparable relationship to its environment. Bearing this in mind, we can understand why Nabokov was so attentive to literary configurations that corresponded to the renovated concept of memory, along with time.

MEMORY AND TIME: JAMES AND FREUD

What is time, and why does our experience of it differ so dramatically from clock-time? Why do humans alone have a sense of history—a sense of the past, present, and future? These are among the enduring questions posed by the Phenomenologists, who, like Nabokov, were fascinated with deceptive memory. As noted, they were inspired by the ideas of their forerunner, William James. They recognized that, beyond habits, which are a primary resource for survival, humans possess a uniquely developed higher consciousness, which sets us apart from other species. As Nabokov puts it, man is "being aware of being aware of being," and this capacity for self-awareness accounts for a fundamental difference between an ape's memory and a human's memory, which can be understood as the difference between "an ampersand and the British Museum library" (SO 142). Of the two dimensions of memory, primary memory is charged primarily with bodily habits that are the result of practice, while secondary memory is related to consciousness's recollection of the past and anticipation of the future. Meanwhile, consciousness seeks to keep up with the present moment. While doing so, however, consciousness must also confront risks and develop solutions. In order to handle these tasks, consciousness must be continuously alert to the present moment, while sending each new experience to the other neurons, the cerebral cortex, in order to retain these experiences as memory-traces. If, for instance, we know how to ride a bicycle, this skill is a product of habit. However, if we remember the events that occurred on the day we set out to learn how to ride a bicycle, we engage in a process associated with secondary memory, which seeks to recall the past in the present moment.

These two forms of memory are not truly divisible, for the latter is feasible only when the former exists. Indeed, Philip Sicker has argued that "as memory evaporates so does identity, and consciousness" (1987, 257). In this sense, Bergson placed habit and image memory on an inseparable level situated beyond pure memory. The dynamic relationship between habit and image memory is fundamentally recognized today, although the terms applied to these phenomena have varied over time. Daniel L. Schacter (1996), for instance, employs the terms implicit and explicit memory, while Endel Tulving (1997) refers to semantic and episodic memory. Similarly, Gerald M. Edelman (2004) uses the terms primary consciousness and higher consciousness, while Antonio Damasio (1994) refers to core consciousness and extended consciousness. Awareness of the two forms of memory inspired enormous changes, giving rise to the perception of time and space. As James points out, this is the origin of our notion of past time, which has served as the foundation of culture and history: "to think a thing as past is to think it amongst the objects or in the direction of the objects which at the present moment appear affected by this quality" (2010, 1: 403).

Since pure memory is beyond our reach due to our successive states of consciousness, each of these momentary states comprises our whole being. As James notes, in the event of pure memory, "Our consciousness would be like a glow-worm spark, illuminating the point it immediately covered, but leaving all beyond in total darkness" (2010, 1: 404). Instead, our sense of the past surfaces when knowledge of some other part of the stream—past or future, near or remote—combines with our knowledge of the present. It is worth noting that Freud analyzed a patient's past in the context of her present desires. This suggests that the past, present, and future are not perceived in a linear manner. On the contrary, they are perceived in a stream that involves the lingering of old objects and the arrival of new ones; and these elements, together, facilitate our retrospective and prospective sense of time. Therefore, empirically, we perceive time only as *duration*, a situation that facilitates rational thinking. For Nabokov, duration is nothing less than the origin of the creative force, given that our capacity for fantasy relies upon the elapse of time. The longer the duration of time, the more fables are able to work their magic. Crucially, distortion of the past occurs in direct proportion to our feelings of affection and intimacy toward that past.

James's writing takes on a poetic and philosophical tone as he explores the implications of the limits of our lives and time itself. Nevertheless, his work depended upon the experimental science of biology. This rare combination of qualities helps to explain James's appeal to figures such as Husserl and Heidegger, not to mention Nabokov. In a manner that is precise, scientific, and yet aesthetically appealing, he explores two of the great mysteries of life: why we feel as though our lives are nothing, and why we experience time as emptiness:

> All consciousness is in the form of *time*, or that time is the form of feeling, the form of sensibility. Crudely and popularly we divide the course of time into past, present, and future; but strictly speaking, there is no present; it is composed of past and future divided by an indivisible point or instant. That instant, or time-point, is the strict present. What we call, loosely, the present, is an empirical portion of the course of time, containing at least a minimum of consciousness, in which the instant of change is the present time-point." (James, 2010, 1: 404–405)

In this way, James describes the intricate relationship between memory and time, and his approach is echoed in Heidegger's subsequent book, *What is Called Thinking?* Heidegger observes: "memory is the gathering of thought. Thought of what? Thought of what holds us, in that we give it thought precisely because it remains what must be thought about. Thought has the gift of thinking back, a gift given because we incline toward it" (2004, 3–4). For Heidegger, time is a passing away; it flows away in succession, with the emergence and fading of every *now* that rolls past, out of the *not yet now* and into the *no longer now* (2004, 97)

Hence, it is not plausible for us to demand that someone live fully within the present moment, to *seize the day*, for the present moment, in perceptive time, does not exist, except as duration. To grasp time objectively—as in the case of memory—is a feat that is beyond our grasp. James, who respected and understood the intricate details of cognition, notes: "The minimum of feeling contains two portions—a sub-feeling that goes and a sub-feeling that comes. One is remembered, the other is imagined. The limits of both are indefinite at the beginning and end of the minimum, and ready to melt into other minima, proceeding from other stimuli" (2010, 1: 405). If we are all in a state of transition, a flow, in which reality is beyond our grasp, what kinds of opportunities become available to a writer of fiction? Among others, this writer could feel challenged to depict deceptive reality as it is, to avoid *crude* generalization, and to place great value on *the details*. Not surprisingly, those components are the kernels of Nabokov's fiction. Yet, we are compelled to ask, "Was psychoanalysis the crude affair that Nabokov suggested it was, given that Freud laid out his own interpretation of the apparatus of memory?"

Freud's essay, "The Project for a Scientific Psychology" (1895), was written about five years after the publication of James's book. As Kandel notes, Freud's essay is rather difficult to read, given that it was "a bold but somewhat chaotic attempt to unify knowledge about the science of mind and the science of the brain," while James's parallel effort was "a clear, beautifully written treatise" (2012, 53). Significantly, Freud's essay did not become known to the general public until 1950, when it was published by Ernst Kris. Despite Kandel's disparaging assessment of the essay, and the document's lengthy obscurity, it appears to reflect Freud's passionate scientific curiosity regarding the apparatus of memory. In 1896, one year after he composed the essay, Freud explained in a letter to Wilhelm Fliess that "Neurons in which *perceptions* originate, to which consciousness attaches, but which in themselves retain no trace of what has happened. For *consciousness and memory are mutually exclusive*" (Freud, 1985, 207–208). The letter conveys the gist of Freud's dense scientific essay, since he describes the mutual and yet exclusive relationship between permeable and impermeable neurons. This piece of correspondence leaves no doubt that he remained fascinated with the process of remembering, even as he pursued seemingly unrelated research, including experiments associated with the *talking cure*. Thirty years later, the same content was expressed once again, though in a more refined form. This time, Freud compared the act of remembering to a technical device popularly known as a mystic writing-pad.

In "A Note upon the 'Mystic Writing-Pad'" (1925), Freud compared our perceptual system to a device consisting of three different layers: a surface layer of celluloid paper, a middle layer of waxed paper, and bottom level comprising a wax slab. He explains that, when we write upon the surface layer, it makes an impression upon the middle layer; and when we lift the two uppermost layers, a trace of the writing remains upon the wax slab. According to this model, the first layer serves as a shield that protects the mind from external stimuli, while the second layer functions as a receptor of such stimuli—in a manner strikingly similar to James's postulations. Meanwhile, the bottom layer functions as the memory-traces, a materialized portion of the mnemic apparatus. Freud's model was intended to explain that "an unlimited receptive capacity and a retention of permanent traces appear to be mutually exclusive properties in the apparatus which we use as substitutes for our memory" (1925, 227). Like James, he perceived consciousness as the other side of the memory-traces. Furthermore, in this short and precise article, Freud effectively summarizes the manner in which our perceptual and memory systems work together, based on the two forms of neurons. The mutually exclusive function that involves the two layers yields a huge difference, as reflected in the human concepts of culture, language, history, and time.

One might ask, "Did Freud concern himself with the concept of perceptual time?" This is not entirely clear. While James quietly, but persistently, proposed the radical concept of perceptual time, Freud only hinted at this possibility in a few terse comments, even though the implications of such a concept were groundbreaking. In line with the concept of perceptual time, consciousness, upon receiving external stimuli, *periodically* sends this stimuli to the memory-traces, while connecting and disconnecting with this layer of consciousness. Significantly, at the conclusion of his essay, Freud remarks, "I further had a suspicion that this discontinuous method of functioning of the system Pcpt-Cs., lies at the bottom of the origin of the concept of time" (SE 19: 231). In short, our perceptual consciousness routinely follows the track of the present time, while periodically making contact with the memory-traces. This process provides us with a sense of perceptive time that is associated with the past and future, but is actually formed in the present moment.

Freud perceived memory and perception in a manner largely consistent with that of James and Bergson, although each man employed his own terminology and adopted a somewhat different approach. Does Bergson sound so different than Freud when he argues that every perception fills a certain depth of duration, prolonging the past into the present, and thereby partaking of memory? (Bergson, 2004. 325). If the three men's theories featured more similarities than differences, however, why did Nabokov repeatedly dismiss Freud as a crude and vulgar fraud? A clue perhaps can be found in Freud's relationship with biology. According to Kandel, Freud abandoned biology because he questioned prevalent theories pointing to the localization of cognitive function, unlike James, who emphasized the importance of the localization of mental functions. Kandel goes on to suggest that "too little was known about the inner workings of the brain for him [Freud] to make a serious effort to cross" (2012, 58).

Beyond this, it seems likely that Freud gave up experimental psychology because it did not appear consistent with his revision of Breuer's method, i.e., the talking cure, a psychological treatment that involves transference between patient and doctor. Even in his 1895 scientific essay, Freud's attention is devoted to the traumatic incident that does not always register with the senses, but often does so later, when a similar action is repeated. He refers to this phenomenon as a *deferred effect*. In addition to this, he sensed the presence of infantile sexuality in his patients' transference of erotic desire. In cases where a patient projected her fantasies of seduction upon him, Freud concluded that sexual abuse experienced in childhood was the cause of hysteria and other mental maladjustments. In his view, the return of repressed memories needed to be treated seriously, given that early erotic wishes and desires are manifested in various disguised forms in adult life. Ultimately, these discoveries led Freud to conclude that "the erotic life of the adult invariably has its origin in childhood" (Kandel, 2012, 57).[2] Notably, this was an issue to which Nabokov returned repeatedly throughout his literary career. Given his conviction that childhood had no bearing on sexuality, he felt free to treat Freud's theory as an object of mimicry.

Nabokov's decision to take a different path in his pursuit of psychology was not precipitated entirely by his negative response to Freud's concept of infantile sexuality. Overall, he placed a radically different emphasis upon childhood. Among other things, Nabokov repeatedly questioned why certain memories reoccur naturally (even during difficult periods of an individual's life), while others do not. Furthermore, James tended to focus on positive memories that generated feelings of warmth and intimacy, while Freud concentrated on negative memories, traumas, to which his patients returned compulsively: a process that undermined their capacity to live normal lives. These divergent areas of concentration produced markedly different approaches to psychology. While the former promoted the capacity of memory (a quality of American Pragmatism), the function of consciousness, and above all, the creative force of memory, the latter focused on the talking cure as a means to expose repressed desires or traumas.

To Nabokov's horror and disappointment, the apotheosis of Freudian psychology produced a universal imperative that traced every symptom of the mind to the workings of the unconscious. This imperative was, in turn, applied to culture and the world in general. Through Freud's discovery of the unconscious, he laid the groundwork for a new field: psychoanalysis. In order to deliver a biological blow to human narcissism, he set out to prove that humans and animals are close relatives (as reflected in the return of the repressed impulses) and the unconscious (or memory-traces) is more powerful than either reason or consciousness.

This was the essence of his message, when he wrote, in "A difficulty in the Path of Psycho-Analysis" (1917), that "the Ego is not master in its own house." Significantly, this view is reflected in the work of recent neuroscientists such as Damasio. It is also consistent with the position of scores of contemporary neuro-psychoanalysts, who contend that emotion, or the primitive part of consciousness, plays a fundamental role in our feelings and thinking.[3]

In this vein, we can speculate upon some of the reasons Nabokov might have preferred James to Freud. First of all, it is likely that he sought to connect his own feelings of nostalgia for his lost homeland to James's concept of an intimate memory enriched by the magic of fantasy—an appealing alternative to Freud's proposal that childhood is the primary source of trauma. Secondly, as my previous survey indicates, Freud's celebrity status overlapped with Nabokov's period of exile at Cambridge: a situation that all but guaranteed that Freud would serve as an ideal model to mimic. By effectively disguising himself as Freud, Nabokov was able to ridicule his theories and call into question his influence. Notably, as a writer, Nabokov was devoted to the project of turning recollection of the past into an art form. Apart from his effort to recapture an elusive past, however, he also set out to prove that reality was the fictive construction that James described it as. He set out to show that the remote past was not so much perceived as conceived. Interestingly, we can discern the seeds of Nabokov's mimicry, *a resemblance with difference*, in James's argument that an attempt to recall the past cannot be described as a memory at all, but as "a duplicate, a second event, having absolutely no connection with the first event except that it happens to resemble it" (2010, 1: 435). For Nabokov, deceptive memory and time were equivalent to deceptive nature, which appeared as intricate mimicry.

Indeed, episodic memory is deceptive, for it is recall, reminiscence, and recollection that are conducted through the dynamics that occur between retention in the body and the retrieval of consciousness. Even though the image of the past is informed by the desires of the present, we are largely blind to this process. Therefore, we rarely treat these images as though they are the product of reminiscence. Instead, we routinely perceive them as direct experiences. This raises questions, once again, about our capacity to grasp the present moment. The fact is, when we realize *now*, that moment is already gone. This may help to explain why we can only experience time as *duration*, as Nabokov illustrates through Gradus in *Pale Fire*. In other words, we can only perceive time through "an immersion into empirical duration," as Christian Moraru observes (1995, 182). As noted, for Nabokov, duration was a major source of creativity. It afforded a feeling of freedom from the temporal order, a sense of regaining lost time. Duration permitted him to recreate reality as a magic carpet, to construct a narrative from combinations of index cards, and to superimpose one image over another. Relying on the duration of time,

Nabokov transforms the disadvantage of vagueness of recollection into the bliss of creation, which is reflected in his comment that "I am an obscure, doubly obscure, novelist with an unpronounceable name" (Gold 2003, 206). While he adapted James's interpretation of consciousness, he recreated it in his own way, moving beyond the Modernist's technique of *stream of consciousness*. For Nabokov, memory is an emblem of deception, mimicry, and above all, love.

MEMORY AS LOVE

In Part Two of *Lolita*, a careful reader will encounter a truly remarkable scene. Its unique qualities, however, will be available only to the *rereader*. They will go largely unnoticed by the inattentive reader, because it is only after we appreciate the way in which the author employs memory as a literary device that we can grasp the significance of the nymphet. During his second trip with Lolita, Humbert stops at a small town called Kasbeam, where he decides to purchase some fresh fruit for his languid lover. He recalls that, during his shopping, "a very old barber gave him a very mediocre haircut," while regaling him with stories about his baseball-playing son. The barber produces faded newspaper clippings and speaks so passionately about his son's exploits that he becomes somewhat careless with his scissors. After this rather harrowing experience, Humbert is stunned when he catches a glimpse of a framed photograph of a ballplayer who "had been dead for the last thirty years" (194–195). Richard Rorty refers to this scene as an example of Nabokov's empathy, as well as his distaste for totalitarianism and cruelty (1989, 146). The scene appears incidental, and yet it relates to the overall theme of *Lolita*. The barber, who has developed an overwhelming affection for "the old days," talks about his dead son's achievements as though they occurred yesterday. In a curious way, his situation bears comparison to that of Humbert, who is engaged in a reckless affair with his nymphet. The barber is a bewitched enchanter whose love of his son has grown exponentially over the duration of thirty years. Likewise, Humbert is obsessed by the nymphet, an emblem of his childhood. In a similar way, the author, Nabokov, was haunted by the memory of his Russian homeland, which he was forced to flee at least thirty years earlier.

Whether a good memory in connected to warm and intimate feelings or a trauma is associated with feelings of shame and disgrace, it is apparent that memory is inextricably related to emotions. As Singer and Salovey acknowledge, "the mechanism that prioritizes memory is emotion," although, at the same time, memory produces thought and action (1993, 122). During the last three decades, neurologists have found evidence to support the view that emotion and information influence each other: a process consistent with the ideas of both James and Freud. It is well known that the two psychologists assumed that, without memory, thinking and cognition are not feasible; and that without emotion, the encoding and retrieval of memories about oneself becomes all but impossible. This was certainly true of Nabokov, who once claimed that "the loss of my country was equated for me with the loss of my love" (SM 245). The only way to maintain a meaningful connection to his native country and his past, which included the Russian language and literature, was to achieve a feeling of oneness with Nature. Notably, this connection could not be secured through logic or theory. In his 1964 interview, Nabokov stated that time without consciousness was the province of the lower animals, while time with consciousness was the privilege of humans alone. Meanwhile, consciousness without time was reserved for a higher state (SO 30). He concluded that seeking to escape the tyranny of time by means of his imagination, which was equivalent to a form of memory, was the only means for him to regain time, a higher state of the timeless moment. Only art could save him in the wake of his staggering losses. Only art could free him from the prison of time, transfiguring nothing into immortality.

When we examine his aesthetic vision, it becomes easier for us to understand his longing for childhood, in the contexts of the combinations, the puzzles, and the riddles. The stronger one's love for the past, or a specific place lost to time, the stranger it is likely to appear. Nabokov would contend that the effectiveness of an image depends upon the power of association that is supplied and prompted by the degree of affection. Moreover, to recall vividly requires the presence of stored traces that can be employed when the writer sets out to assemble the puzzle pieces of his past. For Nabokov, index cards proved an excellent resource: He did not write from one page to the next in consecutive order. Instead, he picked out a bit here and a bit there till he had filled all the gaps on paper. When he wrote stories and novels which were based on index cards, every card was rewritten many times. Of all his literary works, *Pale Fire*, which consists of poems and attached commentaries, appears to be the purest example of this combinational style. In contrast to received wisdom, this eccentric approach to writing resembles the actual process of remembering and thinking. Hence, this strategy not only enabled him to achieve a feeling of oneness with the material parts of his mind, but it also helped him to experience a sense of harmony with Nature—and this was perhaps Nabokov's deepest desire. As Philip Sicker observes, "the juxtaposition and interplay of various bits of colored memory can produce a truer, more intensely felt past than photographic recall ever could" (1987, 265).

Significantly, an individual is the sum total of every single autobiographical trace that is stored in the course of one's lifetime, even if there are points at which they merge with the experience of others. This concept inspired Nabokov's idea of *multiplied authors*, which emerged as an aesthetic form of transgression between author and characters. He periodically insisted that he does not write for groups, nor approve of group therapy ("big scene in the Freudian Farce"); he only writes for himself in *multiplicate* (SO 114). For Nabokov, the moment in which he copied himself was the precise moment in which he felt the ecstasy of timelessness, as though he were standing among rare butterflies and their plant food. At that point, he became one with sun and stone, luxuriating in the highest state of freedom. We may ask, "What is the gist of the self?" Perhaps it is no more than a byproduct of the deception of memory, when it matches its natural surroundings. From this point of view, a deceptive butterfly is a deceptive self. To put it differently, one's effort to experience, and render, oneself should correspond precisely with one's effort to experience and depict Nature. Hence, when Nabokov explains how often he struggled to integrate the butterfly (his lost homeland of Russia) into his fiction, he also suggests the extent to which the outcome is pale and false. Indeed, he is discussing his own art of mimicry, which is also the magic of memory.[4]

In Nabokov's fictional world, deceptive nature is the handiwork of a transcendent maker, unknown X, the mysterious God, and that design is the model which the author *humorously* sets out to imitate. Brian Boyd describes an incident that evidently took place in October 1952, when Nabokov was inveighing against the "Viennese quack" in a Modernism class he was teaching. In the midst of his lecture, a female student rose to her feet and walked out of the classroom. In his response, Nabokov appeared "not so much offended or hurt as amused and even impressed by the student's courage in registering her protest on Freud's behalf" (1991, 221). The scene calls to mind Nabokov's observation that rare patterns of mimicry are purely coincidental, and they provide *humor and pleasure* to an intelligent consciousness.

Overall, Nabokov compares childhood to the dream of a playful poet, or to the sensual imaginary world that prevailed before the age of reason and the apotheosis of the crude concept. In this vein, he observes, "the world was made on a Sunday" (SM 298). If this is so, however, why should we discount Freud's sense of humor? Is there a more poignant human victory than the conquest of a disgraced, unloved, and aggressive self, which Freud describes in his 1927 essay, "Humour"? Nabokov evidently shared this perspective, as suggested by such heroic protagonists as Smurov, in *The Eye,* and Luzhin, in *Defense*—a topic that I will explore more fully in the next chapter. To regard the mind and the world as a memory, a dream, or an illusion is surely one way to be skeptical, while, at the same time, challenging the claims of totalitarianism and absolutism.

NOTES

1. Regarding William James's influence on Nabokov, see Blackwell (2009), pages: 19, 101, 104, 105, 128, 138. In this book, he outlines Goethe's influences on Nabokov (16), which seems a bit ironic, given that Freud, whom Nabokov perceived as an enemy, also regarded Goethe's natural science, along with Darwin's, as his precursor.

2. Kandel notes that, at the end of 1895, Freud abandoned his biological model. Yet, he remained a biologist, while waiting for mind and brain research to mature. He also regards Freud as a forerunner of cognitive psychology, noting that Ernest Kris and Ernest Gombrich, who believed in psychology as biology, continued to link art and science, an area where Freud was not fully appreciated in his time. See *The Age of Insight*, 2012, pp. 61-65.

3. To support Freud in this context, Theodor Reik's comment would be helpful. In his *Listening with the Third Ear* (1948), he argues that "memory-traces are of far greater importance than conscious knowledge," and furthermore "unconscious memories are the ruling factor, some of which may later become capable of conscious realization" (1998, 343-344).

4. Nabokov talks about a French governess who remembered her past, the time and place, long after she had lived in Russia: Her posthumous love for a remote and rather appalling country, which she never had really known, proves that "One is always at home in one's past" (SM 116).

THREE

A Dream Is Not for Analysis

The Luzhin Defense

In his foreword to the English-language version of *The Luzhin Defense* (1964), Nabokov compares his character's name, Luzhin, to the word *illusion*, drawing attention to the fact that it rhymes with this word and also sounds like it. Given the novel's thematic emphasis on deception, we can assume that the resemblance was intentional. Originally composed in Russian in 1930, while Nabokov was living in Berlin, *Defense* was eventually translated into English, in part, by the author himself. Not surprisingly, the English-language version featured an ironic nod to the "Viennese delegation," given that Luzhin is treated by a psychotherapist following an apparent nervous breakdown. As usual, the author provides a series of cryptic clues regarding his intentions. At one point, the narrator states, "I may as well confess that I gave Luzhin my French governess, my pocket chess set, my sweet temper, and the stone of the peach I plucked in my own walled garden" (LD, 10–11). This comment may prompt the reader to ask, "What do these four key words signify, and how are they related to Luzhin's treatment in the novel?" While it is clear that Nabokov takes issue with Freudian therapists, it is not so evident whether he is inclined to provide an alternative. Any clues to such an alternative would probably reside in the key elements that the author proposes. Taken as a whole, Nabokov's narrative appears to mimic a classic Freudian case study, and the four elements he describes are presumably intended to shed light on Luzhin's mental disorder.

In the narrative, Nabokov's French governess becomes the basis of fantasies that bear scant resemblance to the reality of his own childhood. In *Defense*, her role in Luzhin's mental life is unclear, and impressions of her are blurred with the protagonist's other childhood memories. Interestingly, the figure of the French governess emerges in some of Nabokov's other works of fiction. She makes a vivid appearance, for instance, in the fifth chapter of *Speak, Memory*, where she experiences hardship during her residence in Russia, but comes to miss it after returning to her native country. Her experience calls to mind that of the author, whose native language would prove useless in places of exile, while his nostalgia for a vanished homeland evolved into an obsession. Yet, Nabakov has a tool at his disposal which his governess does not. He is able to fashion the shadows of memory, as well as the tortured emotions of exile, into an immortal work of art. Nabokov acknowledges as much when he comments: "What bothers me is that a sense of misery, and nothing else, is not enough to make a permanent soul. My enormous and morose Mademoiselle is all right on earth but impossible in eternity"(SM 117). Nevertheless, Nabokov would concede that his governess played an important role in expanding his knowledge of literature. She not only exposed him to the beauty of the French language; she also read to him regularly, inspiring within him a love of the written word. Hence, her image stands in contrast to that of the English governess in Freud's case study of the Wolf Man, who is portrayed as a facilitator of early sexual instincts. Ultimately, these divergent images invite us to view the tragicomedy of Luzhin's life as Nabokov's response to the classic Freudian case study: an excellent example of resemblance with a difference.

However, what about the other three elements that Nabokov presents to Luzhin—his sweet temper, his pocket chess set, and the stone of peach that he has plucked from his garden? As though he were playing a game with the reader, Nabokov encourages us to examine the ways in which these three elements are compatible with the talking cure. Can it be that his pocket chess set bears some relation to the Freudian *primal scene*? Does Luzhin's breakdown, the seeming product of tension and self-deception, have something to do with his repressed sexual desires? Can Freud's Oedipus complex be applied appropriately when we examine Luzhin's recurring dream that involves the invention of a defensive chess strategy? Can his dream be analyzed in the same manner that Freud described in *The Interpretation of Dreams*? Above all, what parallels exist between the game of chess and literature? Why is Luzhin so intimidated by his rival chess player, Turati, while nevertheless taking desperate steps to defend him? What are the true faces that lurk behind these apparent masquerades? Equipped with Nabokov's four clues, I will embark on an adventure, in the company of a lonely player searching for a defensive move.

TO MIMIC THE FREUDIAN CASE STUDY

The novel begins with the protagonist's formative years in the countryside. Luzhin does not appear capable of vividly recollecting these experiences, given that they are limited to hazy impressions. He retains disconnected memories of summer days in the country with his parents, languid hours spent reading on the veranda, his family's annual migration from the country to the city, and his daily morning walk with his governess. Early in the narrative, we learn that the elder Luzhin is an author of instructional booklets. His own life is devoid of enthusiasm and creativity, and his enervated wife languishes in bed. The elder Luzhin had apparently hoped that his son would be exceptional and anticipated that he would do better in life than he had. Yet, he senses within his son a listlessness that appears to be the product of a tortured inner life. Indeed, his son's whole manner strikes him as enigmatic. With the departure of the French governess, no one in the household is able to determine what goes on in the protagonist's room. Unlike his father, who spends hours writing didactic books for children, the young Luzhin is alienated from his surroundings and devotes his time to the unraveling of a hidden pattern contained within a conjuror's book. He also derives a mysterious pleasure from the "harmonious simplicity" behind basic card tricks (LD 36). The youthful Luzhin appears to achieve a feeling of well-being by solving puzzles and participating in highly competitive games.

Given that the narrative opens with Luzhin's formative experiences and moves forward from there, we develop the feeling that we are reading the case study of a patient who, in some ways, is a stand-in for the author. Throughout, we have a sense that the author continually transgresses the boundaries of his protagonist: a sensation that becomes acute when we arrive at a crucial passage concerning the evening on which Luzhin is introduced to the game of chess by a visiting aunt. From that point on, he loses interest in school and derives a curious sense of freedom from playing chess. Then, in an instant, the story shifts to Luzhin's difficult years as an exile in Western Europe, in the wake of war and revolution. After his father's death, he is taken in and mentored by Valentinov, a highly imperfect father figure who raises him to become a professional chess player and sets up a series of international matches. Luzhin gains widespread fame, emerging victorious in each competition—that is, until he meets Turati, an Italian grandmaster who proves more resilient. When Valentinov abandons the young chess player to focus on his own business concerns, Luzhin embarks on a lonely, exhausting quest to develop the ultimate chess defense. During this time, he encounters a young woman who is drawn to him because of his fame but also pities him. In an effort to save Luzhin, she marries him, ignoring her own mother's antipathy for the chess player. Before long, however, her mother's reservations appear justified, for Luzhin seems incapable of leading an ordinary life; he is thoroughly absorbed in the intricacies of chess.

His monomaniacal focus on chess eventually contributes to a mental breakdown, and he is committed to a sanatorium and placed under the care of a psychotherapist. In the course of Luzhin's treatment, his doctor and wife discourage him from concentrating on anything related to chess and advise him to focus on painting instead. Yet, while Luzhin feigns an interest in landscape painting, he is by no means cured. This point is reminding the reader of a short story, "Signs and Symbols," in which a Jewish adolescent in wartime Berlin receives treatment at a mental clinic. The distraught boy had attempted to take his life on two occasions, jumping from a window in the sanatorium.[1] In an effort to alleviate his suffering, his parents secure his release from the sanatorium and attempt to care for him at home. The story concludes rather ambiguously with a series of mysterious phone calls. Unlike the boy in the story, Luzhin appears to escape those who seek to control him with questionable treatments. A pivotal development involves the arrival of a visitor from Russia who discusses the patient's aunt and reminds Luzhin who he is, thereby freeing his repressed instincts as a chess player. After drawing several items from his pocket, including the large *peach stone*, Luzhin places them on a desk and jumps out a bathroom window.

This scene puts the reader in mind of a Freudian case study, even though the narrator undermines the Viennese delegation by ridiculing its proposed treatments. After describing the patient's childhood memory of his aunt, his monomaniacal impulse to develop the ideal chess strategy, his nervous breakdown, the apparent failure of the talking cure to resolve his problems, and his successful escape, the narrative concludes with the following words: "the whole chasm was seen to divide into dark and pale squares," an image that calls to mind nothing so much as the chess board (LD 256). At this point, two fundamental questions arise, both of which involve the meaning of the aunt and the large peach stone. First, we must ask about the ways in which the image of the aunt is associated with the peach stone. Secondly, we should question whether these key elements stand in sharp contrast to Freud's interpretations. Significantly, the aunt and the peach stone appear to direct our attention to the Jamesian concept of memory, as well as the Nabokovian Primal Scene. For Freud, remembering the past—along with interpreting dreams—was the fastest route to the unconscious. We might ask, "How does Nabokov's view of memory differ from that of Freud, anyway?"

> The recollection was saturated with sunshine and the sweet, inky taste of the sticks of licorice, bits of which she used to hack off with blows of her pen-knife and persuade him to hold under his tongue. And the tacks he had once placed on the wickerwork seat croup were in retrospect equivalent with the sunshine and the sounds of the garden,

and the mosquito fastening onto his skinned knee and blissfully raising its rubescent abdomen. (LD 16)

In contrast to Freud's systematic tracking of a patient's past to determine the cause of his or her trauma, we find that Luzhin's recollection of the past resembles a fluid stream of thought. The past is composed of obscure and vague impressions, including fragmentary depictions of scenery, natural objects, and sensual phenomena. Images of Luzhin's father, mother, and governess appear and then retreat, without any reference to specific affinities and links. They are simply called forth, with no reference to cause and effect. Instead, they appear in the context of particular places, things, and scenes: the route to catch the train to St. Petersburg, the seat opposite his parents' in an open carriage, a bitterly cold day, a flowing river, a gust of wind, or the downy ripple in the gray bird's wing of a woman's hat. Like Impressionist paintings, the images reflect the fluid presence of the concrete and the sentient, while offering no generalized messages.

Michael Glynn discerned in Nabokov's poems a *thing*, an intensely vivid rendering of immediate physical reality that entails "a vindication of the material word and material worlds" (2006, 15). Notably, we cannot perceive or categorize phenomena in the absence of surplus, which enables us to experience them directly. This may help to explain why Nabokov luxuriates in the details. He understood that, without them, sensory communication is not feasible. Furthermore, in the absence of interaction with this sentient life, we may be susceptible to authoritarian ideologies, as well as the vulgar side of existence. This view seems compatible with James's concept of memory as the materiality, or memory-traces, contained within our brains. Yet, Nabokov was puzzled by the fact that we tend to remember more vividly certain places or things, as opposed to names or the content of particular events. In the novel, Luzhin's memories tend to consist of disconnected moments in time: "the village in the colorless sky a crow flew slowly over the stubble" (LD 19).

Unlike the Wolf Man analysis, where the subject's attitude toward his father is informed by fears of homosexuality while he is deeply jealous of his sister, Luzhin's childhood memories are devoid of such horrors. Furthermore, no particular fear is attached to other species such as wolves and butterflies. Far from being saturated with guilt arising from the incest taboo, Luzhin's memories are accompanied by warm feelings that border on nostalgia—a development in line with James's conception of memory as a phenomenon bounded by feelings of intimate affection. Images of a station platform where Luzhin stood alone or a train's puff of smoke are veiled by a mist of tears, obscured by longings for a time and place that will never return. As Richard C. Borden has argued, the childhood Luzhin recollects is not only dominated by personal phantasma, but it is also animated by the image of the sun (1995, 112). This has nothing to do with either mythology or the Oedipus complex. On the contrary, it is plausible to read the recurring image of the king or the kingdom in Nabokov's fiction as a metaphor for the phantasmal exaggeration of his childhood. Kinbote in *Pale Fire*, for instance, believes he is a king who escaped from Zembla, while Humbert in *Lolita* adores Poe's Annabel and muses about an ancient kingdom by the sea where he was a prince. Luzhin conforms to this pattern when he recalls "the time when he was quite small, playing all alone, and wrapping himself up in the tiger rug, to represent, rather forlornly, a king" (LD 70).

For James, memory is fabricated and essentially deceptive, for it relies upon one's experience of the present. At the same time, we are given to forgetfulness because of ongoing consciousness, even though memory is grounded on the value systems provided by history and society. In short, our memory of the past is fictive, subjective, and highly susceptible to change as time goes by. Significantly, cognition is no less deceptive than memory. Therefore, it is not surprising that Luzhin is skeptical about what he recalls, even though he elaborates upon sensual and concrete things without systematizing them. He seeks to relive the evening when he was first introduced to the game of chess. This functions as a primal scene, and we are compelled to ask about the manner in which the musician, father, and aunt are involved. While the narrative mimics a case study, Nabokov cunningly conceals the primal scene so that it can only be discerned by an attentive reader who treats the text as a game. In chapters 3 and 4, the narrative is so subtle and intricate that the deception involved in Luzhin's initiation is virtually obscured.

Unlike Freudian incest, which involves a mother and son, in this case an erotic relationship develops between Luzhin's father and aunt. Hence, the father is not involved in an erotic rivalry with the son over the mother. Instead, he serves as the facilitator for the moment in which his son discovers his vocation. At the same time, Nabokov's literary style ensures that the father's adulterous relationship with the aunt will be overshadowed by Luzhin's dramatic introduction to chess. The game of chess is an integral part of the *deception*—a secret love that is furtively described in the narrative.[2] Luzhin derives pleasure and a sense of freedom when playing chess with his aunt, who will never return to the house after that memorable evening. While the reader may pick up on hints of an erotic relationship between the father and aunt, the young Luzhin (at about eleven years of age) is too young to understand what is happening. Hence, the reader and narrator share knowledge that is denied the young protagonist. As the stealthy affair continues, however, it becomes evident to Luzhin's mother that her husband is cheating on her, and she bursts into tears. Yet, for the next two chapters, Luzhin appears blissfully unaware of the deception. When he catches his father with his aunt while making his way home one day, he is shocked and embarrassed.

If we place the protagonist's obsession with chess in the context of this deceptive affair, chapters 3 and 4 are analogous to Freud's primal scene in "From the History of an Infantile Neurosis" (1918). Freud, after all, concludes that the Wolf Man's trauma traced back to an incident that occurred when the subject was one-and-a-half years old. At that time, he contends, the patient gazed upon his parents as they performed *coitus a tergo*. He indentified this primal scene on the basis of the fact that the patient was infatuated with women he encountered who were posed in ways resembling that particular sexual position. Notably, Freud also connects the Wolf Man's recurring dream of white wolves to his memories of those experiences. He goes on to connect them to the patient's memory of a servant named Grusha, arguing that her position, when she scrubbed the floors of the family home, was the source of his passion for women posed in a similar way, as it called to mind the primal scene in which he witnessed his parents having sex. Freud linked this memory to that of the Wolf Man's fearful encounter with a large yellow butterfly, noting that "his fear of the butterfly was in every respect analogous to his fear of the wolf" (SE 17: 96).

Freud draws a strong parallel between dreams and memories in his groundbreaking case study: a revolutionary idea that dovetailed with James's approach. Yet, he was cautious in his interpretation, including such qualifications as, "perhaps what the child observed was not copulation between his parents but copulation between animals, which he then displaced on to his parents as though he had inferred that his parents did things in the same way" (SE 17: 57). Despite such qualifications, Freud viewed himself as a doctor who was bound by duty to treat his patient. Nevertheless, Nabokov dismisses the legions of therapists who came in his wake as apostles of generalization. His novel's skeptical view of the Vienna delegation is reflected in the fact that it features a scenario resembling Freud's primal scene. At the same time, the scene is carefully differentiated from that of the classic case study, as it involves an adulterous affair between the father and aunt. This raises a question: Why does Nabokov interpose the game of chess with this deceptive affair?

In the context of Nabokov's personal life, the development of chess strategies assumed a special position as early as 1917. As Brian Boyd notes, it was a hobby that consumed him almost as much as the writing of fiction: a pursuit he worked like a "valve for surplus creative energy, a training ground in artistic strategy" (1990, 137). His first work of fiction in English, *The Real Life of Sebastian Knight*, features characters analogous to chess pieces, each of which is controlled by the author. This underscores Nabokov's view that a work of art is basically a game of chess between author and reader. It would seem that Nabokov viewed the development of a chess strategy as comparable to the composition of a work of fiction. Both were a source of artistic delight. Indeed, he compared the sensation to the "twinge of mental pleasure" he experienced "as the bud of a chess problem burst open in my brain," and it satisfied his notion of strategy as "deceit, to the point of diabolism, and originality, verging upon the grotesque" (SM 289). In this case, however, the deception involved differs from the hypocrisy implicit in grand logic and ideology, where things assumed to be true may turn out to be false. Instead, the deception blends seamlessly with the larger narrative, not unlike a motif in a musical composition. In the narrative, the elder Luzhin regards his son's introduction to chess as the performance of a sacred rite, and the reader is left to conclude that chess occupies the same position in Luzhin's mental life that fiction-writing does in Nabokov's. In both cases, a creative obsession is intertwined with the deceptive memory of childhood: a never-never land which can be revisited only through the imagination, in a dreamlike form.

A DREAM IS NOT AN OBJECT OF ANALYSIS

As noted, the first part of *The Luzhin Defense* is characterized by renderings of vague, mysterious sentences—as though Nabokov were determined to deliver what he promised would resemble the absentminded recollections of a king. Throughout, the author presents an essentially phenomenological view of memory. With absolute lucidity he used to recall landscapes, gestures, intonations, a million sensuous details, not numbers and names. During his long exile, Luzhin pines for Russia, his family home, and his lost childhood, becoming lost in the sensual images of his memory. He eventually fantasizes that he is a drowsy king in exile. Such illusive memories of the past must be understood in the context of his nostalgia. At the same time, these deceptions are related to the game of chess, which is fraught with deception. For Luzhin, the deceptive *illusion* is treated as the real, while most people regard day-to-day reality as the real. Meanwhile, Luzhin's fiancée, her mother, and the team of psychotherapists view the realities of day-to-day life as the normal: a position the chess player regards as insane. He is especially impatient with arguments about political developments in his native Russia, as he treats social and political pronouncements as patently false, even though most people regard them as rooted in reality. He concedes that chess strategies are deceptive, but this deception is based on clear-cut rules. When he immerses himself in the development of such strategies, he feels as though something within him has been set free.

Interestingly, the narrator deals with the trangressive nature of illusion in such a way that it becomes clear he does not share Luzhin's point of view. On the contrary, the narrator shares the perspective of other characters in the novel, and Luzhin's condition is represented as a state of madness. We learn that Luzhin's fiancée was initially charmed by his gloomy, detached demeanor, as well as his absentmindedness. His focus on chess, to the exclusion of practical matters, struck her as evidence of potential greatness (LD 88). As the narrative continues, however, Luzhin's emotional unraveling is described to us largely from her mother's perspective. Fearing for her daughter's future, the mother advises her daughter against marrying Luzhin, insisting that he is incapable of living a normal life. She goes on to insist, rather excessively, that Luzhin is *not a real person*. As Luzhin continues his search for the ultimate chess defense, he becomes more disconnected from those around him. At various points, he tells his fiancée that *we're living in a fine dream*: "One should not scare off a dream, let them sit there, these people, for the time being" (LD 133). His dream of developing the ideal defensive strategy is related to his dreamlike obsession with his Russian homeland, and the process leaves him exhausted. As we examine Nabokov's narrative approach, we are left to wonder why he presents Luzhin as a madman while depicting those around him as relatively stable. Should we assume that the author accepts the "average" reality for which they advocate?

One thing is clear: the dream Luzhin harbors is not viable for those around him, and the energy required of him to keep it alive precipitates a complete breakdown. Perceived as a madman, he is committed to a sanatorium and placed under the care of so-called normal people, including therapists. Nabokov describes their ineffectual treatments in a narrative style that mimics the language and approach of Freudian psychology. By transgressing the boundary between the dream world and reality, Nabokov surreptitiously subverts Freudian postulation of the dream as an object for analysis. If our real life is a dream or an illusion, how can we hope to interpret it objectively? After all, does nocturnal dreaming differ so dramatically from day-dreaming? If our memory and cognition are both susceptible to constant change and myriad subjective influences, how then is it possible to interpret a dream based on mythology and thereby affect a cure? These seem to be fundamental questions that lurk beneath a superficially humorous tale of a madman.

In the phenomenological sensory experience of the world, communication is conveyed on a material, pre-logical basis, which ensures that the state of awakening is experienced like a dream. As the ancients contended, "Life is a dream." This old maxim, Sabine Metzger observes, becomes less mysterious when applied to Nabokov's work. She goes on to compare Nabokov and Freud, employing contrasting terms such as homo *poeticus* and homo *natura*. The former is the artist, who perceives "the simultaneous, reciprocal and mutual constitution of the sensing and the sensed," while the latter is the scientist, who perceives the mind in the context of natural science (2009, 13).[3] The division becomes blurred, however, when the poet's work is read in the context of natural science. If the ancients indicated our dream state is a state of being awake, their view would seem to overlap with the Jamesian contention that we experience the world in our corporeality. In this vein, we could argue that Nabokov focused more on corporeal *consciousness*, while Freud concentrated more on *the unconscious*.

When asked about the foreword to *Defense* in a 1964 interview, Nabokov stated: "One of the greatest pieces of charlatanic, and satanic, nonsense imposed on a gullible public is the Freudian interpretation of dreams. I take gleeful pleasure every morning in refuting the Viennese quack by recalling and explaining the details of my dreams without using one single reference to sexual symbols or mythical complexes" (SO 47). In the case of Luzhin, the dream of developing the ultimate chess defense appears compatible with his yearning for childhood. We must ask, though, whether Freud himself viewed dreaming as wholly incompatible with remembering. An examination of the 1918 Wolf Man case suggests this might not be the case. Much can be gleaned from *The Interpretation of Dreams* (1900), the work that secured Freud's place as a major figure in the emerging discipline of psychology, even though some critics found its claims arbitrary. Indeed, Freud's characterization of his interpretation of dreams lends weight to such claims of arbitrariness: "it made cleverer use of the actual facts in its construction, like a well-designed slander of the kind that makes people feel that 'there's something in it'" (SE 4: 140). Given that his scientific approach was less rigorous than it would prove to be in later years, responses to this early work were as varied as they were passionate. If Nabokov's critique of Freud seems to go too far, it is also true that Freud himself overreaches. His interpretations often seem as though they were predesigned to fit the dream by a seasoned rhetorician.

Freud postulates that dreams can be placed in several different categories: 1) a fulfillment of wishes, 2) a fulfillment of fears, 3) a response to some physiological need, and 4) a reproduction of a memory, like the residue of the day (SE 4: 123). Yet, he focuses primarily on wish-fulfillment in his analysis. Freud observes that each one of us has wishes that he or she would prefer to hide from others. In some cases, we do not even admit them to ourselves. We camouflage such unpleasant desires through dream distortions that undergo two basic steps of transformation. The first step involves condensation of the dream content into a metaphoric figure, while the next involves displacing it with some other thing that is related to it. Since distortion takes place in the wake of an act of censorship, the process by which a dream's meaning is ascertained resembles the act of interpreting literature. The two steps involved in distortion resemble the figurative system of language: the metaphor and the metonymy. In gradual steps, Freud narrows down several categories of dream genesis into one assumption: a dream is the disguised fulfillment of a suppressed or repressed wish. Acting on this assumption, he argues, it could lead us to the main road to the unconscious—and the disclosure of the patient's trauma. Hence, the physiological and corporeal elements within our thought are largely ignored, while an overwhelming emphasis is placed on the *talking cure*, entailing somewhat arbitrary interpretations. Yet, Freud was, above all, a practitioner who treated patients, and therefore samples and methods were required. Through an act of reduction, he generalized these interpretations; and for Nabokov, this generalization of interpretation was problematic. He was equally skeptical of Freud's tendency to draw upon myths in his interpretive process. (Freud, of course, contended that myths were stories that embodied the universal traits of human desire.)

For all their differences, though, Nabokov and Freud shared much in common *theoretically*. Their professions, however, were radically different. One was an artist whose respect for sentient life was coupled with an implacable hatred of totalitarianism, while the other was a doctor who sought to develop a method of treatment. To highlight their differences, we could examine the ways in which the doctor attempted to incorporate mythology into his treatment, while seeking to identify the point at which the artist became skeptical of this approach.

During his treatment of a young man who suffered from obsessive neuroses, Freud identified a pattern. While the young man felt an impulse to murder his disciplinarian father during his father's own lifetime, he fell into a pattern of obsessive self-reproach after his father's painful illness and death. The incident prompted Freud to reflect on his own formative years, during which he was in love with one parent and hated the other. He discerned a strikingly similar pattern in the myth of king Oedipus, as well as Shakespeare's *Hamlet*, which led him to conclude that patricide is "the essential constituent of the stock of psychical impulses" for both normal people and neurotics (SE 4: 260–261). The universal instinct to murder one's father and marry one's mother was the origin of Oedipus's tragedy, and the same was true of Shakespeare's Hamlet, he argued. Interestingly, generations of theatergoers have puzzled over Hamlet's tortured ambivalence as he plots to avenge his father's murder. One answer to this mystery could be that the young prince secretly identifies with his uncle, who has inadvertently fulfilled his own wish. Obviously, this desire to murder one's father and marry one's mother is so repellent to the normal person that it is deeply repressed, and he is entirely unaware of it. Freud contends that human egoism leads one to censor and repress this instinct so that it appears as a distorted image, even in dreams. Hence, the interpretation of dreams is aimed at uncovering the unconscious in order *to prevent generations of anxiety or other forms of distress*. In a further step, often described as *vulgar Freud*, he identified typical distortions: male organs represented by a stick, a hat, or tree; female organs by a landscape, water, or wood. Throughout his works of fiction, we find that Nabokov makes reference to these ideas, endlessly mimicking (and satirizing) the Oedipus complex and the distortions collectively known as vulgar Freud.

Nabokov's reservations about dream analysis appear to stem from its overwhelming emphasis on sexuality, along with its underlying contention that an impulse toward patricide is the basis of one's psychic constitution. No less repellant to Nabokov was Freud's proposal that dreams were objects of generalized interpretation. Given Nabokov's deep affection for his parents and nostalgic attachment to his country, it is not surprising that he rejected the sexual symbolism of Freudian psychology, as well as its insistence on generalization. Utilizing Freud's symbols and concepts as a springboard for his creative energy, the author drew upon the scientific phenomenon of mimicry to produce the aesthetic device of the *double* (resemblance with a difference), which he used as a weapon against the Vienna delegation.

It seems curious, though, that Nabokov chose to focus on Freud's earliest and most problematic work, while ignoring his later work. Perhaps the author determined that Freud's later writings did not serve as suitable objects of derision, as he set out to undercut what he saw as a blind allegiance to psychotherapists: a phenomenon he first experienced during his days at Cambridge. One might ask whether Freud himself was comfortable with his groundbreaking work. Significantly, there is evidence that he was aware of the arbitrariness of his method, and he was clearly uncomfortable with the public's response to it. Freud was especially sensitive to the criticism of colleagues, especially Wilhelm Fliess, who had been involved in the project. His ambivalence was expressed five years later, when he published *Jokes and their Relation to the Unconscious* (1905). In a section titled, "relation of Jokes to dreams and to the unconscious," he states, "I have an impression that my *Interpretation of Dreams*, published in 1900, provoked more 'bewilderment' than 'enlightenment' among my fellow-specialists; and I know that wider circles of readers have been content to reduce the contents of the book to a catchword ('wish-fulfilment') which can be easily remembered and conveniently misused" (SE 8: 159).

While reviewing the manuscript of *The Interpretation of Dreams*, Fliess expressed concern about the arbitrariness of Freud's approach, as well as his apparent overconfidence in the interpretation of dreams. He went on to observe that the dreamer seemed altogether too witty. Freud responded accordingly: "It is certainly true that the dreamer is too witty, but it is neither my fault nor does it contain a reproach. All dreamers are equally insufferably witty, and they need to be because they are under pressure and the direct route is barred to them" (1985, 371). There is no doubt, however, that Fliess's comments exposed *a methodological weakness*: one that Freud felt compelled to address repeatedly. As Brian Tucker notes, it was "this potential charge of arbitrariness, of excessive wit, that necessitates the joke book" (2011, 134). To deflect the criticism of arbitrariness, Freud set out to draw a parallel between the dream and the riddle, noting that the act of unraveling them requires significant intellectual labor, given that they both reflect strenuous attempts to detour and disguise the pleasure principle in order to avoid censorship. Meanwhile, in contrast to the obscurity of the dream and the riddle, the joke is designed for the attainment of pleasure by way of a sudden, clear revelation of unity. Its allusions are obvious, and the listener can easily fill in any omissions. Hence, it is grasped quickly by most listeners. The dream-picture, on the other hand, is largely inaccessible, since it is related to the repressed *cathexis*. Likewise, the riddle, as a game, involves obstacles that are intended to impede comprehension.

Overall, Freud appears to suggest that arbitrariness in dream analysis is unavoidable. He pushes the indirect expression and figurative language as characteristic of dreams beyond the boundaries and limits that are generally respected in the context of jokes. When he contends that a dream remains unintelligible to the subject himself, he is also suggesting that it is unreadable to the analyst: "Not only does it not need to set any store by intelligibility, it must actually avoid being understood, for otherwise it would be destroyed; it can only exist in masquerade" (SE 8: 179). Finally, Freud appears to conclude that a dream is not meant to be understood. If, however, a dream, like a riddle, is *an evanescent occurrence that expires as soon as its mask is lifted*, what then is the role of the analyst? We might also ask why Freud chooses to place so much emphasis on the obstacles, the bewilderment, the illumination, and the hermeneutic pleasure inherent in both the riddle and the dream. He energetically defends the dreamer's wit and emphasizes the analyst's challenge. In the end, however, Freud denies that the role of the analyst is to identify the correct answer or the absolute solution.

Comparing the manifest dream to a *picture-riddle*, Freud proposes that the impulse that drives one to solve riddles resembles the motivation behind psychoanalysis. In both cases, the final answer is deferred. Significantly, this approach overlaps with Nabokov's view of fiction, which he regarded as a game or a riddle. Yet, Freud's arguments regarding dream analysis also call to mind Theodor Reik's striking analogy in *Listening with the Third Ear* (1948), where he compares the interpretation of dreams to the excavation of ancient mummies. After being preserved for thousands of years, excavated mummies are suddenly exposed to the sun's rays, at which point they decay and crumble into dust: "Three thousand years of preservation in the dark and one moment of light and destruction!" (1998, 347). Reik describes this phenomenon in order to illustrate the fact that one cannot seek to restore the past without destroying it. This paradox is unavoidable, and the analyst should make no attempt to conceal it from the patient, thereby enabling him to escape confrontation with the traumatic event and to move on with his life. If, indeed, the analyst is unable to access the past as it truly was, it also seems likely that the version of the past we carry in our memory is not far removed from an illusion or a dream. In light of this phenomenon, we might ask, "Who wins the competition, Freud or Nabokov?" Before addressing that question, I would like to return to the game, with a focus on the defensive strategy employed by Luzhin.

WHO WINS? WHITE CHESSMAN VS. BLACK CHESSMAN

Catherine T. Nepomnyashchy observed that, in 1918, Lionel Penrose, who would go on to become a founding member of the British Chess Problem Association in London, delivered lectures on Freud's theory of dreams to Cambridge undergraduate societies. Significantly, he was one of the first psychoanalytic thinkers to draw a connection between the Freudian paradigm and the game of chess (2008, 10). Given the circumstances, it is quite possible that Nabokov, as a freshman at Cambridge, attended Penrose's lecture on the Oedipus complex and chess. Even if Nabokov disagreed with Penrose's premise, he may well have obtained new material to mimic in his fiction, in much the same way that Luzhin, as a writer, draws inspiration from Valentinov, a clear emblem of Freud. It took awhile for Nabokov to achieve a kind of *poetic justice* (not wit) in the form of fiction that reflected the application of renovated artistic devices: *fiction as a game*.[4] The competition is not between white and black players on a chessboard, but instead, between the composer and the hypothetical challenger. As Nabokov once argued, a first-rate work of fiction should not limit itself to the conflict among the characters; it should also function as a contest between the author and the reader. His work, therefore, is characterized by deceptive opening moves, as well as false lines of play that are evidently designed to mislead the reader (SM 290).

The contest, however, is not entirely between the author and reader. We could also interpret the two sides in the literary contest as comprising a disguised Nabokov and a disguised Freud. In any event, the ultimate purpose of the manuscript is to prevent the reader from easily discerning the author's intentions. For Nabokov, a satisfying work of fiction was brimming with cryptic clues and also featured a puzzling conclusion. He delivers such a conclusion in *The Luzhin Defense*, as a group of dinner guests at Luzhin's apartment bursts into the bathroom where the protagonist has retreated, shouting his name, "Aleksandr Ivanovich." We are left to assume that Luzhin has committed suicide by hurling himself out of the bathroom window, but the ending is typically ambiguous. Meanwhile, other questions arise. Is the last-minute reference to the hero's given name a reflection of the author's desire to highlight the case study of the Wolf Man, *Sergei Pankejeff*, whose name is rarely uttered within the psychoanalytic community? Who are those disguised chessmen from which the disguised author, Luzhin, appears so desperate to escape?

We can assume that the black chessmen that represent Freud include Valentinov, the protagonist's wife, and the psychiatrists who treat Luzhin in the sanatorium. (Interestingly, the group of psychiatrists includes one figure that sports a black Assyrian-style beard.) Meanwhile, the white chessmen include Luzhin, the protagonist's aunt, and the old man with flowers who proved to be a remarkable chess player. Overall, the contest seems a difficult one for Nabokov to win, in the same way that Luzhin appears outmatched by Turati, a stand-in for the reader. In every way, the opposition seems more powerful, since the characters who symbolize the black chessmen surround the protagonist. At the same time, those representing the white chessmen have been relegated to the past, though they remain vivid images in the protagonist's fantasy world, *the dream*. Which side is likely to prevail in the contest? Furthermore, if Nabokov were to defeat Freud, would this constitute poetic justice?[5]

What are we to make of Luzhin's patron and mentor, Valentinov, a man of undeniable talent who is nevertheless an enigmatic figure? He appears to care little for Luzhin as a person, treating him as an enchanting oddity, a view that is reflected in his comment, "Shine while you can, because you won't be a boy prodigy much longer." Valentinov's shrewdness is evident in his development of chess problems, but his true genius is reflected in his organization of widely celebrated amateur matches, in which Luzhin takes center stage as a freak of nature expected to entertain the upper classes. However, after organizing a series of tournaments, Valentinov grows weary of the enterprise and migrates to the motion picture industry. With his old mentor's departure, Luzhin experiences a rush of relief. At the same time, though, he is gripped by an enervating feeling of melancholy, as he reflects that not "a single, kind, humane word" had passed between them. Beyond Valentinov's largely negative impact on the protagonist, we encounter further evidence that he represents the black chessmen, which serve as emblems of Freud. We should recall that Valentinov has proposed an unusual theory in which Luzhin's talent for chess arose from the *sexual urge*. He goes on to suggest that the young prodigy's absorption in the game has enabled him to keep a distance from women and maintain a kind of morose chastity. In his view, Luzhin's obsession with chess is little more than a deflection of the sexual urge (LD 94). Given the author's continual repudiation of sexuality as the origin of energy, we can assume that he holds little sympathy for Valentinov's point of view.

Notably, when Valentinov reappears and attempts to bring Luzhin into a film project that is based on his match with Turati, the protagonist's wife barely remembers him, referring to him as "a Mr. Fa... Felt... Felty" (LD 232). Indeed, Valentinov comes off as a cold, distant, and frivolous father figure, standing in sharp contrast to the elder Luzhin, who appeared to care deeply for his son. At one point, Luzhin, as a writer, sets out to incorporate Valentinov into one of his stories, in the hope that it would infuse his narrative with an atmosphere of adventure. Ultimately, however, the elder Luzhin has little more than disconnected impressions of Valentinov, and he dies before he succeeds in cobbling these impressions together into a full-blown character. In many respects, Luzhin the writer appears to be a stand-in for Nabokov, who elects to incorporate Freud into his fiction. Luzhin, like Nabokov, is devastated by the loss of his father, and the resulting anguish helps to fuel his later achievements.

Meanwhile, it is telling that Mrs. Luzhin is given no name, as though she were simply a chess piece in the author's game. The daughter of a rich Russian émigré who resides in Berlin, she is so preoccupied with her social life that she seems incapable of reflecting on her actions. She does not even seem to grasp the nature of her attraction to Luzhin, who strikes her as a hapless genius incapable of managing his affairs. While she is warm and sympathetic to the distracted prodigy, she has no idea who he is or what he wants, and she shows little interest in his artistic aspirations. She is drawn to him mainly because of his novelty, and it becomes clear that her imagination is limited, while her affection for Luzhin is superficial. Proud of her family's economic status, she assumes that Luzhin is of peasant stock and dismisses his pursuits. Consequently, when her husband suffers a nervous breakdown, she is in no position to save him. She blindly follows the recommendations of the doctors at the sanatorium, discouraging Luzhin's passion for chess and urging him to focus on painting. For his part, Luzhin engages in a game of deception, concealing his interest in chess and pretending to share her interest in social and political issues. Overall, Mrs. Luzhin's personal qualities and opinions place her firmly on the side of the black chessmen.

Throughout the narrative, we gain the impression that no one loves Luzhin or fully understands him. The psychiatrists who set out to treat him seem incapable of understanding his loneliness, or appreciating the depths of his nostalgia for his homeland. Nor do they perceive the connection between these emotional conditions and Luzhin's overwhelming passion for chess. During his stay at the sanatorium, the protagonist engages in a long conversation with a famous psychiatrist with a black, Assyrian-style beard, who indicates that his condition is the result of the prolonged strain involved in playing chess (LD 157). To lead a normal life, the psychiatrist advises, Luzhin must abandon chess and get married, a situation that will provide him with the attention and diversion he needs. Naturally, the psychiatrist's reading of the situation turns out to be wrong. The reader will soon learn that the protagonist's breakdown has little to do with a "temporary clouding of the senses," and he is unlikely to experience a recovery after taking a prolonged rest. By presenting the bearded psychiatrist as a ridiculous fraud, the author takes clear aim at Freud, and his antipathy for the "Viennese quack" often appears to be the source of his creative vitality. If Luzhin's wife comes off as a simpleton, the celebrated psychiatrist is presented as a dangerous fraud. The reader has already gained insight into the source of the patient's nervous breakdown, and from this vantage point, the doctor's recommended treatment seems nonsensical. He misses the mark when he suggests that Luzhin's problems have arisen because of his obsession with chess (LD 162). Once again, Nabokov's comic mimicry of Freud is fully in evidence.

While the psychiatrist encourages Luzhin to talk about his childhood, the patient finds he has few words with which to describe the sensual images of his past, which have been softened by *the haze of time*. Once again, the past can be reached only by means of fantasy, which contributes to a *hypertrophied* sense of a lost childhood. As Nabokov observes, this fantasy life is "an amazingly safe spot, where he could take pleasant excursions that sometimes brought a piercing pleasure" (LD 164). Indeed, the narrator implies that a Freudian recovery of memory is less than feasible, while at the same time, insisting that childhood, far from being the origin of "dormant horrors and humiliating insults," is a source of wonder and delight.[6] Nabokov evidently hoped his novel would be read as a tragicomedy, informed by humor and the sweetness that infuses a peach from his old garden.

Notably, before jumping out of a window, Luzhin empties his pockets and places several items on a phonograph cabinet. These include a fountain pen, a crumpled handkerchief, a cigarette case, and a large peach stone (252). We might reflect on Nabokov's apparent desire to draw the reader's attention to the peach stone. In tandem with the sensual perception of consciousness, the peach stone appears to be analogous to the seed of memory and cognition. The sensual thing, or memory-trace, is at the core of consciousness, like the kernel of a missed heartbeat—the so-called *contingency* of life. In Nabokov's fiction, the metaphor of contingency emerges repeatedly, serving as an obstacle that thwarts perfect resemblance or generalization. In this vein, we find that the novel's ninth chapter is almost embarrassingly vague, especially the dream within a dream in which Luzhin is saved by strangers who encounter him in the street. Two intoxicated men, Kurt and Gunther, find a third man, Karl, lying in the street. Gunther and Kurt lead Karl to a taxi, but the driver mistakenly leaves Gunther standing in the street. When the taxi returns for Gunther, they are surprised to find someone else lying in the street, with his head resting against a curb. They take the man to his fiancée's house. With this dream sequence, the narrator illustrates that life and death are not controlled by logic, but instead by fate, or the hand of chance.

So, in the end, who wins? For the reader, it appears as though Nabokov has defeated Freud, even though the black chessmen in his camp do their best to promote a Freudian perspective. Meanwhile, the less numerous white chessmen take relatively passive roles, appearing mainly in dreams, memories, and fantasies. Still, they do help to fuel Luzhin's imaginative powers, enabling him to employ a final defense that takes him beyond the reach of his oppressors. Is the game truly over, though? Freud, after all, does not readily accept defeat. He is always prepared to present a metapsychology as a complement to his case study. In his "Creative Writers and Day-Dreaming," for instance, he presents childhood as the source of our creativity, proposing that "the child's best-loved and most intense occupation is with his play or games" (SE 9: 143). However, when the child becomes an adult, he ceases to play and therefore engages in *phantasies*, or day-dreaming. He conceals prohibited desires, disguising them as those that are permissible within society. While Freud never abandons his theory of wish-fulfillment, he does—at least in this essay—appear to share Nabokov's view of the creative significance of childhood, as well as the importance of play. It's worth noting that Nabokov's Luzhin appears to be nothing less than an artist who dreams in broad daylight. I believe that an especially compelling defense of Freud is offered by the aforementioned Theodor Reik:

> The founder of psychoanalysis was more modest. Freud never indulged in the belief that he had solved all the riddles of the inner life. A few years ago he likened his work to that of an archeologist who had rescued a few temples from the dark earth and brought them to light; but he had no doubt that great treasures still remained below, awaiting excavation. So much for what has already been disclosed and what still remains to be disclosed. For many of my colleagues psychoanalysis is a closed book, a book written by Freud. He would be the first to protest against such an idea. (1998, 442)

The ambivalence Reik describes calls to mind the two-headed monster in one of Nabokov's humorous stories. Joined together irrevocably, Lloyd and Floyd confront each other on a daily basis.[7] Yet, while they experience life together, only Floyd appears to recall the past with any veracity. In any event, Nabokov's lifelong battle with Freud would continue, exemplified by the next novel that we will examine, *Despair*. It will be up to us to discern who emerges victorious in this particular contest.

NOTES

1. Leona Toker also notes that this image calls to mind the troubled Jewish youth in "Signs and Symbols," though it may not correspond precisely to the failed treatments employed by the psychotherapist in *Defense*. See *The Mystery of Literary Structures*, p. 69.

2. In the course of this musical evening, young Luzhin makes his way to the quietude of his father's study, where he encounters a violinist who loves chess because of its various combinations, which resemble melodies. After his initiation into chess, he hears his mother's sobs and his father's voice indicating that she is "imagining things," as he passes along the corridor with his aunt (44).

3. See Sabine Metzger, "Beyond the Pleasure Principle: Nabokov's *Homo Poeticus*." *Nabokovian* 62 (2009): 2-25. She sheds light on Nabokov's poetics in a phenomenological context, our communication as sentient life, and suggests that, as an artist, Nabokov is compatible with the Freudian homo *natura*, a radically opposed concept of homo *poeticus*.

4. In the 1972 interview, Nabokov described the special characteristic of his fiction as "Schadenfreude," employing Wilson's word, which means "hatred of Freud." He added that it is not wit but poetic justice. See *Strong Opinions*, p. 220.

5. See Erick Naiman, "Litland: The Allegorical Poetics of *The Defense*," pp. 20, 24. He argues that the characters are chess pieces that are controlled by a mysterious, invisible manager, God, X, or the author. Naiman employs the French word, *souffler* which means *to blow*, "because the author may be seen as breathing a kind of limited life into his characters."

6. The words, "dormant horrors and humiliating insults" appear on page 164 in *The Luzhin Defense*, and they seem to describe the Wolf Man's childhood, as Freud interpreted it. Nabokov was highly skeptical of the Freudian primal scene, which he viewed in stark opposition to his own magical childhood memories. As Brian Boyd observes, Nabokov once asserted that "I am quite indecently optimistic and buoyant, whereas Bunin, as far as I know, is rather inclined to dejection and black thoughts" (1990, 343).

7. In "Scenes from the Life of a Double Monster," written in 1950, Floyd recalls his past during a conversation with one Dr. Fricke, a disguised Freud. The tone of this sad, complicated story is set by the narrator, who pines for a lost childhood and laments his current situation, in which he is an object of derision. The story calls to mind Nabokov's circumstances at that time.

FOUR

The Criminal as an Artist

Despair

If literary critics agree on nothing else, they concur that we are unlikely to plumb the depths of Vladimir Nabokov's fictional universe, with its myriad conspiracies and byzantine narratives. This view is often accompanied by the assumption that Nabokov's work offers little in the way of social or political commentary. Apart from the fact that the average reader is too distracted by the complex pattern of palimpsest to consider any political issues, we have the insistent denials of Nabokov himself that he espoused any social or political causes. While it may seem natural to place weight on the author's own words, we should not readily assume that Nabokov was apolitical. When we consider the manner in which he took issue with Freud, despite the fact that he shared many of the psychiatrist's views (and even used him as a doppelganger in his psychological novels), we must conclude that Nabokov was a masterful political writer who turned deception into a formidable weapon.

What the author rejected was not politics itself but the straightforward and naturalistic treatment of political issues, at the cost of a complicated and magical work of art. By means of a strategy of mimicry, in which he appears to mirror certain views and then repudiates them, he deftly undermines any ideology he regards as either authoritarian or wedded to the concept of generalization. During his lengthy exile in Western Europe, he often employed the penname *Sirin*, which exemplified his penchant for disguises. Masks and other forms of camouflage enabled him to veil his underlying attitudes toward anything that smacked of a political or ideological consensus, whether Communism or Nazism. In this sense, his self-identification as apolitical was no less a deception than his strategy of turning narratives into strategic contests with the reader. His repeated attacks on Freudian psychoanalysis serve as artistic devices that lend structure and vitality to his fiction, while politics enables him to detour artistic devices. Nabokov was quite political beneath his façade of political indifference, and nothing disturbed him more than the *naïve* realism that ensnares innocent people, in a manner not unlike Lydia in *Despair*, who is apparently blind to her husband's manipulations.

In truth, the difficulty of Nabokov's fiction arises from his effort to mimic (and amplify) what he regards as the lies and deceptive machinations of authoritarian ideologies—in an effort to expose their limitations. Yet, beneath his skepticism lies an assumption that we are all born liars, given that our memory and cognition invariably produce fiction amid the death and rebirth of memories. In a sense, we are also born artists. When we set out to recall past events, we unavoidably embellish them with material from the present. However, we could also be described as born criminals, a characterization that applies each time we set out to confess what we did in the past, as we conceal and reveal it, both inherently and intentionally. This should not be surprising, given that every moment a new experience is stored in our brain as an additional memory. From this vantage point, it appears plausible that resemblance with a difference in the name of mimicry is an essential part of humanity. For that matter, so is crime. Hence, when Nabokov claims that he seeks to produce "art not as a demonstration of topical ideas in a drizzle of politics, but Art with a capital A as big as the biggest Arch of Triumph," we should be careful not to be swept up in the trap that he has so carefully prepared for us. After all, he also states that the writer is a liar, while literature is a concoction of scientific passion and artistic precision, "burning the brow and cooling the brain."[1] For Nabokov, literature was born "not the day when a boy crying wolf, wolf came running out of the Neanderthal valley with a big gray wolf at this heels: literature was born on the day when a boy came crying wolf, wolf and there was no wolf behind him" (LL 5). In short, telling a lie to deceive the reader is the essence of art—and it is not far removed from the fabricated testimony of a criminal. For Nabokov, this impulse finds its parallel in Nature, when butterflies and birds protect themselves through mimicry or put on a display that is driven by an instinct for *theatricality*. Thus, the most valued quality of an artist also puts us in mind of the criminal, who draws lessons from the cunning and enchanting patterns of Nature.

Indeed, *Lolita* is the story of a criminal: Humbert Humbert, a pedophile who brutally murders his rival, Clare Quilty. His confession takes the form of a memoir that is addressed to legal authorities, as well as to the reader. *Despair* is also the story of a criminal, Hermann Karlovich, a sociopath who murders an innocent man as part of a plot to secure insurance money, given that the victim supposedly resembles him. In the foreword to the novel's 1966 English-language version, Nabokov takes a perfunctory jab at the "Viennese quack," observing that "the attractively shaped object or Wiener-schnitzel dream that the eager Freudian may think he distinguishes in the remoteness of my wastes will turn out to be on closer inspection a derisive mirage organized by my agents" (xii). He goes on to acknowledge that Hermann and Humbert resemble each other, since they are both neurotic scoundrels. There is a difference between them, however. There is a green lane in Paradise where Humbert is "permitted to wander at dusk once a year," whereas Hell shall never forgive Hermann (xiii). Yet, we should ask, what are the objects that the ardent Freudian might distinguish in the remoteness of Nabokov's wastes, and in what manner does Humbert differ from Hermann? Furthermore, we might inquire whether this difference sheds light on the qualities that distinguish Nabokov from Freud. Based on our reading of *Despair*, Humbert does seem to be a stand-in for Nabokov, while Hermann appears to represent Freud.

Overall, there is little doubt that *Despair* is Nabokov's most explicitly political novel. Therefore, we might be tempted to ask whether the author's playful and deceptive strategy of mimicry is compatible with a classic political critique. In what manner does Nabokov deal with this apparent dichotomy in the context of the narrative, and what clues are available to us as we seek to comprehend his strategy? In chapter 5, when Hermann tries to convince Felix to serve as his stand-in, stressing his future victim's role as a supposed doppelganger, Felix questions the closeness of their resemblance to each other. (Indeed, Hermann's premise proves to be totally inaccurate.) While sleeping at a hotel with Felix, Hermann dreams of "disgusting mimicry" in the form of "a triple ephialtes" (DP 96). In his dream, he encounters a small dog-like creature with the miniature black eyes of a *beetle's larva*. The creature is covered with the *fat of a white worm*, and reminds him of the Russian paschal lamb of butter served during the Easter holiday. The monstrous triple mimicry reflected in this image leads Hermann to briefly question his murderous plot. Interestingly, the image points to two possible motives that underlie Nabokov's narrative. First, the image highlights the fact that the work is structured along the lines of mimicry in Nature, where deceptive displays are related to either propagation or the need for protection. Secondly, it alerts the reader to the presence of three different levels of storytelling, even though the novel features a one-dimensional narrative voice. We are prompted to ask whose faces lurk behind those of the characters Hermann, Felix, Ardalion, and Lydia. Could they be those of the black and white chessmen that the author employs in his game with the reader?

For now, I will pursue my line of inquiry in three basic steps. First, I will acknowledge that, on the surface, this crime novel appears to be narrated by Hermann, whose memoir is periodically interrupted by Ardalion, a portrait painter who seems to be engaged in an affair with Hermann's wife. Secondly, I will consider another interpretation, in which two characters, Hermann and Ardalion, are engaged in a continual struggle for narrative authority. Third, I will examine the narrative as one in which the author's deep-seated opposition to Communism and other generalized ideologies inspires him to bring about their symbolic defeat in the context of the novel. Notably, one of the novel's most vivid examples of natural mimicry is the doppelganger Felix, whose walking *stick* is discovered in Hermann's car.

A PORTRAIT OF THE ARTIST AS A FOOL: HERMANN

Nabokov composed *Despair* in Russian during his exile in Berlin in the early 1930s, but it would not be published until 1936. Significantly, the novel's protagonist, Hermann Karlovich, is the son of a Russian-speaking German and a native Russian woman from the lower classes. We learn that Hermann has read *exactly* one-thousand and eighteen books between late 1914 and the middle of 1919. Given his belief that the world should be orderly, he is appalled by the slovenliness of his wife, Lydia. At the same time, he is mystified by her seeming lack of intellectual curiosity. Indeed, his love for her appears to be rooted almost exclusively in his belief that she loves him. Meanwhile, Hermann expresses a deep admiration for Germans, citing their musical ability and overall steadiness. He also takes a reverent attitude toward Communist Russia, contending that it is based on the concepts of collective well-being and the fundamental sameness of all humans. If Hermann has misgivings about Lydia, he harbors no doubts about her devotion to him, for he believes himself to be superbly gifted: intelligent, physically robust, and stylishly dressed. Over the years, he has told Lydia innumerable lies, but she seems to have forgotten all about them. Drawing on Hermann's description of himself, we can discern that he is intolerant of any confusion, disorder, or exception to the rule. Proud of his iron self-control, he voices a deep respect for general principles, and his belief in his own intellectual superiority rests largely on his disdain for anything that is contingent or disorganized. However, Hermann's unshakeable belief in himself is exposed as a delusion by the competing voice of Ardalion, not to mention the author's continual interference.

When the narrative opens, Hermann is thirty-five years old, and his chocolate company is on the verge of collapse. During a visit to Prague, he encounters a vagrant whom he believes to be a perfect physical replica of himself. Hermann's initial feelings of awe give way to an exploitative impulse, as he devises a plot that will capitalize on the supposed resemblance between the two men. Posing as a film actor, Hermann initially offers to hire Felix as a stunt double. Later on, he establishes a life-insurance policy, and persuades Felix to wear Hermann's clothes and drive his car to a spot on Ardalion's land that is marked by a yellow post.

Felix is told that he will provide Hermann with an alibi, but in reality, Hermann plans to murder Felix. Given Felix's supposed resemblance to Hermann, the protagonist believes that he can persuade his wife, Lydia, to identify Felix's corpse as his own. At that point, he predicts, the couple will flee to a distant land with the ill-gotten insurance money. Hermann regards his plan as flawless, and he encourages Lydia to follow his advice to the letter. With the precision of a stage manager, Hermann executes the murder, abandons the car with Felix's corpse inside, and flees to the French city of Pignan. Despite his unflappable self-regard, however, Hermann's decisions prove disastrous. Indeed, throughout the narrative, Felix's and Lydia's responses to aspects of Hermann's plot make them seem far more sensible than he. At one point, Lydia asks plaintively, "don't you think it's a swindle?" In response to news of the protagonist's faulty plan, another character states, "let him...do whatever he likes, it is his fate": a line in which we can clearly discern the author's voice (DP 149, 153). In the course of the story, Hermann continually reveals his foolishness, along with his cruelty and selfishness. Wedded to the concept of resemblance (or generalizing), he fails to apply the principle in a way that would further human equality. On the contrary, he exploits it for his own profit. He also suggests that his true motives are artistic, as opposed to materialistic, adding that an author does not show his first draft to the reader.

Predictably, Hermann's plan falls apart. Despite Hermann's insistence that Felix is his doppelganger, no one else discerns any physical resemblance between the two men. Hence, investigators conclude that the victim is an unknown male whose body has been placed in a stolen vehicle. Waiting for Lydia at a French hotel, Hermann receives this news with a sense of foreboding. His anxiety deepens when he learns that police investigators have also discovered a walking stick in the vehicle that is inscribed with Felix's name: a development that enables them to determine the identity of the victim beyond any doubt. Hermann is therefore deprived of the opportunity to assume Felix's identity. In an agitated state, he entitles his memoir as *Despair*. The unraveling of Hermann's plot is the result of two fundamental errors. First, Hermann mistakenly believes in the possibility of a perfect doppelganger, a flawless replica of himself. Secondly, he neglects to remove Felix's walking *stick* from his car. It seems safe to assume that Nabokov selected those errors as a means to highlight Hermann's weaknesses. We might ask, who is Hermann supposed to represent—and what is the significance of his errors, in light of the author's antipathy toward generalization? For the careful reader, clues abound regarding the protagonist's identity. As Hermann recalls his past, he reveals himself to be an aspiring artist, as opposed to a common criminal. He contends that his *impatient* memory should be regarded as the true author of his memoir: a claim that echoes Nabokov's contention that memory is a tool of art. Therefore, Hermann takes steps to ensure that his memoir will not degenerate into a common diary, although it may be a chronicle of failure. He concludes with a rhetorical speech that appears to prove that his failure as a criminal is paralleled by his failure as an artist. In this regard, *Despair* offers a portrait of the artist as a fool—the first stage of a humorous, satirical, and above all, political act of mimicry. Yet, the question remains: Why did he choose Ardalion's property, in general, and the yellow post, in particular, as the scene of the crime?

A PORTRAIT OF THE ARTIST AS A YOUNG CRIMINAL: ARDALION

Ardalion is not a criminal, that is, in the usual sense. Ultimately, he emerges as the novel's genuine deceptive artist, purporting to steal Hermann's wife, subtly undermining the fool's paradise, and gradually seizing control of the narrative. He functions as the second of the demons that appear in Hermann's dream. However, if Ardalion proves a formidable rival, Hermann seems to believe he can neutralize him. When he selects a spot on Ardalion's property as the scene of his crime, Hermann observes, "you smile, gentle reader?" Suddenly, it seems clear that Hermann's decision is part of a larger plan to undermine Ardalion, although anyone who rereads the novel is bound to treat the comment as ironic foreshadowing. Hermann, after all, will soon play the role of the fool in a drama of Ardalion's devising. Despite his modest circumstances, Ardalion has purchased a stretch of rural land whose chief landmark is a yellow signpost. Hermann selects this post as the place at which Felix will leave letters addressed to Ardalion, in what appears to be an attempt to implicate Ardalion in Felix's eventual murder. Thus, beneath the surface of his plot to secure insurance money is another plot to destroy Ardalion. As Hermann comments, "this meddlesome portrait-painter was the only person of whom I ought to beware" (DP 125).

Hermann's wariness regarding Ardalion stems partly from his rival's curious relationship with Lydia, who is actually Ardalion's cousin. On one occasion, Hermann discovers the pair in bed together. Later on, when Hermann returns from out-of-town business trips, he finds Ardalion lounging in his bathtub. Hermann is especially annoyed by an incident in which Lydia and Ardalion play the card game patience, the whole time pretending Hermann is not even in the room. As Ann Smock observes, "Ardalion is Hermann's rival in love, and in the art of making likenesses" (1985, 63). Smock adds that, when Hermann and Ardalion participate in a picnic with Lydia, Hermann leaves behind his chef-d'oeuvre, Ardalion's portrait of him, which suggests that Hermann is attempting to complete Ardalion's painting.[2] Hermann insists that the portrait does not resemble him at all; and despite the narrator's chronic unreliability, it is possible that Ardalion has projected his own image upon the supposed portrait of

Hermann, in much the same way that he inserts his ideas into Hermann's narrative. In his memoir, Hermann claims to have little faith in either God or man. Yet, as an aspiring poet and author, he voices a deep faith in major commercial enterprises. Beneath the surface of his boastful narrative, we sense that Hermann is intimidated by the raw sexuality and superior artistry of the passionate Ardalion. As Stephen Blackwell observes, Ardalion's very name has suggestive overtones relevant to the story. According to Farmer's *Vocabular amatoria*, "ardillon" refers to the "penis," or "the unruly member." In French and Latin, "ardalion" refers to a troublesome or unruly person, a meddler. Furthermore, John Rea cites the work of D'Ouville and Baron Wodel, who assign the same meanings to the word "ardilion" (2002/2003, 145).

Significantly, Hermann fully embraces the concept of resemblance, and he goes so far as to place fashion, lifestyles, and professions into basic categories: the rat type, the ape type, and so on. In stark contrast to Hermann's reliance on generalization (without contingency), Ardalion lacks confidence in typecasting. For him, each face is unique, and the role of the artist is to perceive the differences between things: "it is the vulgar who note their resemblance" (DP 41). Hermann's awareness of this divergent perspective may contribute to his desire to get rid of Ardalion. He hopes to achieve this by planting the victim's letters on Ardalion's property in order to frame him for the murder. To make it easier for him to persuade Lydia to participate in a proposed insurance scam, Hermann arranges for Ardalion to be away in Italy. During his conversation with Lydia, Hermann grossly misrepresents Felix, describing him as a chemically dependent younger brother who is prepared to sacrifice his life for his older brother's financial gain. Hermann then sets out to establish an alibi. He tells an acquaintance, Orlovius, that he is being stalked by a sociopath who has written a letter claiming to have stolen his money and slept with his wife. The motive behind this deception is obvious: Hermann wants people to believe that he is in fear of being harmed by the man who stole his property and coveted his wife. Hence, Hermann's means of deception is limited to a calculated lie, whereas Ardalion's approach is humorous, complicated, and subtle. This approach is exemplified in the fuss that he makes during the departure scene, which leaves Hermann thoroughly exasperated. For both characters, crime is a deceptive work of art, much like a masterful card trick. Hermann believes that, in Felix, he has the ideal pawn that will enable him to defeat his rival. His chance encounter with Felix—along with the vagrant's apparent willingness to do his bidding—leads Hermann to view his plan as providential. Yet, questions soon arise about Felix's suitability as Hermann's double in this game of mimicry. Interestingly, in Ardalion's portrait, Hermann is portrayed as blind: one of many factors that raises questions about Felix's resemblance to Hermann. While Hermann sees Felix as his double and concludes he is a pliable enough to manipulate, the truth will turn out to be different.

Hermann's shortcomings as a master of deception are highlighted by Ardalion. In a final letter, he ridicules Hermann's erroneous belief that Felix is his double, and he goes on to criticize his trivial alibi, commonplace lies, and banal aspirations (204–206). Hermann is obviously ignorant of the remains, or contingency, within his supposed double, Felix. He refuses to accept that two men cannot be entirely alike, no matter how well one may mimic the other. Moreover, his attempted insurance scam is a tired cliché, given that criminals have tried to pull off similar schemes for generations (205). Barton D. Johnson notes that cases of insurance fraud involving switched bodies were relatively common in the 1920s, and a particularly notorious incident involved a German criminal named Erich Kurt Tetzner, whose victim was a Czech laborer he picked up on the road. Emphasizing certain differences in the case (including Tetzner's burning of the car and mutilation of his victim's body), Johnson asserts that "the evidence linking Nabokov's *Despair* to the Tetzner case rests on a handful of details": the car; the vagrant as a substitute victim; the vagrant's nationality; the killer's hospitable purchase of food and drink; and the killer's flight to France to await his wife with the insurance money (Johnson, 2003, 13). The series of trials involving the murder were widely publicized in the German press between March and April of 1931, which makes it likely the case provided the inspiration for Hermann's plot. Moreover, Nabokov began writing *Despair* about a year later, on July 1, 1932. His decision to borrow details from a lurid crime that had dominated national headlines may have been intended to persuade readers that his novel had nothing to do with politics: a prudent move for a writer living in exile during a politically tumultuous era.

Interestingly, we can trace Nabokov's voice in Ardalion's letter: let her [Lydia] go free from your complicity (DP 205). If we interpret Hermann's crime as corresponding to the ideologies of Communism or Nazism, the author's voice calls for the release of the innocent people from *your* foolish, cruel, and selfish oppression. Ultimately, Ardalion—the criminal as artist—defeats the arrogant Hermann with a sophisticated bag of tricks. Serving as a proxy for the author, he employs a third level of deception; and at that point, the target appears to be Freud.

A PORTRAIT OF THE ARTIST AS AN EXILE: NABOKOV AGAINST FREUD

From Hermann's perspective, the materially challenged Ardalion is a cheerful but untalented hack. Yet, his love of nature has led him to purchase a countryside retreat comprising a small but pristine lake and a patch of woodland dominated by birches. It is Hermann who selects the district's postal name, Ardalion, as well as the yellow sign post that marks the spot. Later in the novel, Hermann chooses to take refuge in the French city of *Pignon*, where he hopes to meet his wife after she has secured the insurance money. Notably, both names, Ardalion and Pignon, are related to the male sexual organ. Referring to the work of Rabelais, Stephen Blackwell contends that *pignon* means *penis*, while Ardalion is a slang French term for the male organ (2002/2003, 145). The choice of these names is certainly purposeful. As Hermann waits for Lydia in Pignon, he becomes involved in a conversation with a doctor who is evidently a psychiatrist. The conversation quickly degenerates into a quarrel, almost as though the argument involves Freud and Nabokov. We should recall that, earlier in the narrative, the unshaven Hermann acknowledges his dislike of mirrors, noting that they reflect the image of a bearded stranger (DP 21). One wonders if the bearded stranger Hermann so dislikes is an oblique reference to the "Viennese quack," Freud. It does not seem coincidental that Hermann's memoir is peppered with references to phallic objects: a sausage with a pretzel, a yellow post, a gun barrel, a birch tree, and above all, a stick. At one point, the protagonist dismisses his wife as an uneducated dreamer who spends her time reading trashy novels and tabloids. He goes on to assert that, for Lydia, the word mystic is related to mist, mistake, and stick, although she has no clue about the nature of a mystic (23). As Stephen Suagee argues, Hermann is preoccupied, consciously and unconsciously, with phallic objects, and he records them compulsively, without interpretation.[3]

In his preference for Realism, Hermann apparently represents at least two distinguished figures, Freud and Marx, who were, in Nabokov's words, "fake thinkers" (SO 18). When Hermann emphasizes type, or resemblance, he appears to echo Freud, who was convinced of the universality of the Oedipus myth, applying it in his analysis of the human psyche. Yet, Hermann's outlook also overlaps with that of Marx, who insisted upon the equality of all human beings: an assertion implying that all people are alike. As a Marxist, Hermann supports a classless society and argues that art should have a social function. He regards philosophy as an invention of the privileged, along with religion and poetry (DP 75). A disciple of Freud, he also insists that he has a photographic memory (61). Although Freud (along with other psychotherapists) denied that humans had the capacity to recollect the past with such precision, Nabokov chooses to exaggerate his foil's reliance upon generalization. Significantly, Hermann's preoccupation with resemblance and generalization leads him to overlook critical details, especially the presence of Felix's walking stick in his car. Likewise, he fails to grasp Lydia's wordplay, in which she makes reference to the mysterious stick. Thus, in his haste to execute the perfect crime, he is guilty of a damning oversight. Throughout the novel, Hermann proves blind to a host of other phallic objects, even as he fastidiously records them, as though he were serving as a representative of Freud (or Marx). Periodically, he informs us that it is "time to go to my patient" (154), almost as though his routine were controlled by an artist of a higher order—Ardalion, the representative of Nabokov.

Hermann's most glaring error as an aspiring artist is his lack of attention to detail, a point that Julian W. Connolly makes in his analysis of the novel's original Russian-language version. The second chapter of the original version describes one of Ardalion's paintings as "raspberry-colored lilacs in a leaning vase" (2005, 138), which, in Russian, encapsulates the author's pen name, *Sirin*, placing it in "Nabokov's vase." At that point, Hermann is perplexed, since his pen begins to shake and dances away.[4] Connolly shrewdly observes that, "in reality it is not that his pen has 'danced away' (139) of its own accord, but rather that it has been seized by the hand of his creator, Vladimir Nabokov," and he concludes that "the genuine artist in the novel is not, of course, Hermann Karlovish, but Nabokov-Sirin" (138). This scene underscores Hermann's embarrassment as his memoir devolves into a diary. We must bear in mind, of course, that in Nabokov's literary world, memory and diaries are incompatible. For the author, recollections of the past only have enduring power if they are infused with the magic of memory. When people record what has happened to them in a diary, the interval between the event and the entry is generally quite short. Hence, the entry is devoid of the fantasy that enhances memories of the distant past. For Nabokov, the criminal as writer is willing to follow his memory's whims, as well as its seemingly arbitrary rules, for the creation of enduring art is dependent upon the magic of remembering. As noted, he contended that literature was born at the moment that a boy cried, "wolf, wolf," when there was no wolf: "between the wolf in the grass and wolf in the story, there is a shimmering go-between and that go-between, that prism, is the art of literature" (LL, 5). The criminal is therefore an inventor, a deceiver, a creator of fiction. Hence, when reviewing the chapters, the reader should try to parse out the author's voice from that of the various characters, including the narrator. In the tenth chapter, it becomes clear that several voices are blended together, producing a triple mimicry that calls to mind Hermann's dream.

Perhaps the most remarkable example of mimicry is reflected in the character of Felix. When he makes an appearance as Hermann's double, Freud, he simultaneously assumes the mask of his foe, Nabokov. A tramp from Czechoslovakia, Felix is a man of Hermann's age, lank, dirty, and possessed of a shabby knapsack. However, the knapsack contains a sausage and pretzel, both Freudian symbols of sex, as though the tramp were seeking to tempt Hermann's instincts, unconsciously. With his blurry eyes, dirty face, and crestfallen demeanor, Felix seems a perfect fool. Nevertheless, Hermann discerns in his features a faithful replica of his own—the image of his own corpse (DP 15). As noted, Hermann proves carelessly unaware of Felix's walking stick, which is inscribed with his *own name*, not Hermann's. The meaning of the stick depends largely on one's point of view. For Freudians, it might serve as a symbol of the male organ. For Nabokov, however, it represents the contingency that is bound to subvert the most perfectly conceived plan, the concept of unity, or the ideal of generalization. As Felix's blackened fingers clasp Hermann's silver pencil, the narrator observes that "a violet dangled from a buttonhole," a detail that symbolizes Nature, the sublime deceiver, the creator of the highest art, in Nabokov's view (DP 57). Accordingly, it is possible to view Felix as another facet of Ardalion. From this perspective, Felix's letters to Hermann, which feature the address of Ardalion, could be seen as *the self-addressed* letters to which Orlovius later refers.

In the end, Felix's flawless act of deception enables him to defeat Hermann. Throughout the narrative, the tramp deftly employs all of the tricks at his disposal: mysterious expressions, enigmatic behavior, provocative personal belongings, and, finally, the inscribed walking stick. Meanwhile, blinded by self-confidence, Hermann assumes the persona of a film director, aggressively instructing Felix on all of the details of his role. Hermann's proposal suggests that Felix will be paid to pass himself as Hermann (donning his clothes and driving his car), while Hermann is engaged in an illicit activity elsewhere. The seemingly malleable Felix proves skeptical, questioning whether the proposal is a "lie." At that point, he seems to be operating on a higher plane than Hermann, in terms of the art of deception.

Indeed, Felix has played his role as Freud so well that he deceives even Hermann, who fails in his effort to perform the role of Felix. In the tenth chapter, where several voices blend together, Hermann (as Felix) states: "I met a swell fellow who kept saying he was like me. Nonsense. He was not like me in the least" (176). Felix, his slayer (victim and victimizer are now reversed), sports a beard, like many doctors in Nabokov's fiction. Hermann, who now plays the role of Felix, struggles to grow a beard, not so much to hide from others as to conceal his visage from himself. Desperate to achieve the role of an artist by playing himself as Felix, he ultimately fails to deceive the police. Once again, his plot is not about the insurance money, for he aspires to the art of acting and deceiving: mimicry as theatricality. Yet, beyond the veil of voices (Hermann as Felix), the reader can discern the witty and playful voice of the author: "Russian author who lives in the neighborhood highly praises my style and vivid imagination" (179). Pointing to his banal choice of an insurance scam, Ardalion rejects Hermann as an artist. He goes on to criticize Hermann's blindness to the importance of the walking stick—the sparse remains of the ingredients of a classic recipe. Furthermore, Hermann's attempt to play the role of Felix proves disastrous, and it is incompatible with Felix's assumption of the role of Nabokov. The crucial fact that Hermann is not the double of Felix has serious consequences. His voice is

snatched by that of Felix, the slayer, and he ceases to serve as a representative of Freud, instead taking the position of Nabokov. Thus, it is Felix
who turns out to be the most accomplished deceiver. Not only is he the
most effective performer; he is also the best mimic. Guided by the patterns of Nature, his emblem becomes the violet that he has so jauntily
placed in his buttonhole.

Thanks to Felix's outstanding performance, the award for best deceiver eludes Hermann-Freud and goes instead to Ardalion-Nabokov, whose
combined voice soon emanates from behind Hermann's mask. While he
awaits Lydia at the hotel in *Pignon*, Hermann encounters a doctor who
takes his place at the head of the dinner table. Stout and businesslike,
with a goat's beard and watery blue eyes, the doctor describes an insu-
rance-related murder that has recently occurred in Germany. Recoiling
from the doctor's version of events, Felix-Nabokov shouts: "Stop, stop!
How dare you, what right have you got? Of all the insulting—No, I won't
stand it! How dare you—Of my land, of my people . . . be silent! Be
silent" (DP 184). It would appear that behind the mask of Hermann—
behind the mask of the criminal—Nabokov lustily berates the doctor,
almost as though he were an analyst dealing with a stubborn, uncooperative patient. He castigates him for the guilt he supposedly feels over his
latent homosexuality, which is linked to a primal scene in which he
watched as his parents engaged in sex.

This passage sheds light on what the author evidently regards as the
true crime: the needless slighting of a Russian aristocratic family, which
echoes the crime committed by Hermann-Freud, against Ardalion-Nabokov. As though he were begging for forgiveness over his offensive analysis, the doctor offers an apology: "there has been a mistake. You have
wrongly interpreted my meaning. I'd very much like—" (186). Yet, Nabokov's shouts angrily, once again: "Out you go!" On the surface level of
the narrative, the doctor points out Hermann's shortcomings, leading
Hermann to react angrily. Behind the mask of Hermann, however, we
can discern the voice of Nabokov, who cries out against the "Viennese
quack" and his disciples. Their humorous quarrel could be interpreted as
one that pits Felix-Freud against Felix-Nabokov. At one point, the latter
screams, "the things you are doing to me—It's beyond—You dare not
humiliate me and take revenge—," while the former responds, "only a
misunderstanding! . . . You've got your defects, and we've got ours"
(187–188, my abbreviation).

The concluding battle unfolds within the last chapter, when Hermann's defeat is signaled by the discovery of Felix's walking stick in
Hermann's automobile. Ultimately, there is no way for the detectives to
draw a neat connection between the poor man's walking stick and the
rich man's car—and in short order, the victim's identity is revealed. We
might ask ourselves why Nabokov chooses a stick as the instrument of
Hermann's downfall. A couple of possible reasons come to mind. First,

he may have intended the stick as a symbol of *details*, which hold no interest for Hermann, unlike Nabokov. Secondly, it could represent Felix's role in the author's strategy of mimicry. As a proxy of Freud, Felix would regard the stick as a symbol of the *male organ*. If, on the other hand, Felix were to serve as a stand-in for Nabokov, he would regard it as *contingency*, the surplus between "mist" and "mistake," as in Lydia's riddle. It might even represent the missing link, the forgotten experience in our memory and cognition that William James discerned. In James's view, memory and cognition flow like a stream. Our brains are bombarded with new experiences, even as we discard or forget earlier ones. In the end, Hermann's blind confidence in his plan is rooted in his belief that his memory is infallible. Nabokov, on the other hand, emphasizes the critical role of omission, chance, or *contingency* in cognition and memory. From his perspective, the stick is the kernel of the memoir, the unknown agent X that determines one's destiny. As Siggy Frank observes, Hermann is positioned to understand this only in the wake of his failure, as he rereads the story.[5]

Stephen Blackwell has argued that "the Attis myth represents both a part of Nabokov's punishment of Hermann, as well as the focal point of his indictment of Freudian interpretation through Hermann's worldview" (2002/2003, 147). On the whole, Blackwell's argument seems quite reasonable, but one might question his assumption that Nabokov used the carefully concealed myth of Attis and Cybele to entrap those given to Freudian interpretation, since Nabokov denied the universality of myths. Blackwell asserts that Nabokov may have read Freud before his arrival in Western Europe, noting that the first abridged Russian-language version of *The Interpretation of Dreams* appeared in 1904, while the journal *Psychotherapy* was established in Russia that same year. Blackwell went on to state that "in no other country was Freud's work translated as intensely as in Russia in the 1920s," entailing a note about V. M. Leibin's *Zigmund Freid* (Blackwell, 2002/2003, 130). Significantly, Freud's analysis of the so-called Wolf Man was published in 1918, just four years after the subject's sudden return to Russia. Although Freud regretted the fact that the case study ended abruptly, he nevertheless chose to publish it in unfinished form. It is therefore possible that Nabokov read it before, or shortly after, his exile from Russia. In any case, he employed the concept of "the Primal Scene" throughout much of his fiction.[6]

Notably, during his time at Cambridge, Nabokov witnessed the intelligentsia's overheated enthusiasm for psychoanalysis. He reacted strongly against such zeal, in much the same way he recoiled from popular support for Communism and Nazism. Joanna Trzeciak notes that "Nabokov's pre-revolutionary generation was far more strongly influenced by such psychological thinkers as Otto Weininger, Havelock Ellis, William James, and Richard Von Krafft-Ebing than by Freud"(2009, 56). Beyond these pivotal figures, however, Nabokov was especially influenced by two eminent Russian intellectuals, whose contributions he came to regard as part of his cultural inheritance. P. D. Ouspensky and Nicolas Evreinoff asserted that mimicry was essentially a human instinct in which we strive to be someone else, as though one were playing a role on stage. This led to the introduction of the term, *theatricality*.[7] They further contended that the instinct to mimic someone else (or something else) was so strong that it overshadowed the instinct for either sex or self-preservation, which were given priority by Freud. Indeed, for Ouspensky, the tendency towards decorativeness, the impulse to disguise and masquerade, were manifested in Nature. He noted that we all enjoy the opportunity to don mask and fancy dress, while taking the stage and posing as something else: a green leaf, a bit of moss, a shiny stone. In his conception of theatricality in Nature as mimicry, Evreinoff differed little from Ouspensky. As reflected in thousands of instances of masquerading within Nature, the theatrical principle to imitate a form different from oneself is delightful and ethical. Moreover, it is nowhere revealed more clearly than within the narrative arts.

> Equally theatrical is our literature. A novel is always a puppet-show of life, and writing is always equivalent to the staging of a play. In order to blow life into his heroes the writer has to transform himself into each one of them. He has to play mentally their roles, to wear their masks. Sometimes he virtually begins to forget himself behind these beings created by his imagination. (Evreinoff 2013, 60)

> The theatre is from beginning to end a lie, a deception, a premeditated lie and a prearranged deception. Yet, so charming is this lie, and the deception so miraculous, that if they didn't exist our world wouldn't be worth living in! (Evreinoff 2013, 144)

Yet, how closely was Nabokov's art, in terms of the strategy of mimicry, connected to the concept of *theatricality* set forth by these two Russian philosophers? It seems clear that, from the beginning of his literary career—as reflected in *The Eye, The Luzhin Defense,* and *Despair*—mimicry in the form of acting, deception, and transformation served as a powerful structural element. In the case of *The Eye,* for instance, the protagonist is driven to kill himself out of shame and depression. By chance, he survives, and he manages to distance himself from his predicament by assuming the roles of multiple actors on a stage. In order to confront the challenges of the world and regain his self-esteem, he assumes a wide variety of masks. He finds that pretending to be someone else is a delightful task that resembles the *childish* amusements of his youth. It enables him to transgress the boundary of self and assume the identities of beings that are more noble and ethical than he. Deception, acting, and the playing of games are essential, not only for the development of higher intelligence. They also enable one to confront the world as an indifferent spectator. Through intentional self-delusion, one can transform even devastating tragedies into light comedies (Evreinoff, 2013, 263). In short, the act of being childish, with all of its attendant joyfulness, is not only ethical but also therapeutic. Armed with this perspective, Nabokov was naturally drawn to mimic Freud, who interpreted childhood in the context of infantile sexuality, while employing memory as a tool to uncover trauma. A literary approach to mimicry was a crucial means for Nabokov to explore *theatric-therapy*, as opposed to Freudian psychotherapy, which relies upon myths and types.

In an effort to explain why Nabokov highlighted the "Viennese Delegation" in the forewords of the translations of his novels that appeared in the 1960s, Joanna Trzeciak notes that American ego-psychology of the 1950s featured a cookbook approach to Freudianism—"more a caricature than a fair rendering of Freud's ideas" (2009, 57). Indeed, ego-psychology read Freud reductively, mainly because of its overwhelming emphasis on therapy and psychoanalysis. During his lifetime, Freud expressed concern that his concepts would serve as the basis of stable disciplines. Since the case study was the experimental backbone of theoretical formulation, Freud was careful in his handling of them. He insisted that the primal scene of the Wolf Man was constructed through a process of transference, and he sought to retain the fictional, literary elements in what many scientists treated as an objective method. Carl Pletsch observes that Freud's case studies had more of a literary than a scientific character, and "what worried him was that hysteria was drawing him out of a recognizably scientific discourse into a sort of literary discourse" (1981, 105). Freud's liberation from a strict, rigid scientific approach was achieved largely by letting go of these concerns and entering into the realm of transference. Freud, for instance, did not accept the analyst's transference that had been influenced by the patient during the talking cure in the Dora case study, concluding that the failure of the treatment was brought about by Dora, who transferred her affects to Freud. Finally, he reached the evolutionary stage of transference during the Wolf Man case, placing it at the precious center of analysis. Over time, he came to realize that the analyst's rhetorical strategy was unavoidable, and that treatment was impossible without *transference* and *intersubjectivity*. Indeed, those two concepts would become the seeds of Lacan's formulation of analytic discourse. Lacan would react against ego-psychology, moving forward to a reinterpretation of Freud's unconscious.

In the case of the Wolf Man, Freud simultaneously explored the wolf dream and the memory of the butterfly. His analysis proceeded in a fragmentary manner, and he reached no conclusion, going so far as to note, in retrospect, that the *Primal Scene* could be a fabrication. As Pletsch observes, "by the time he published his analysis of the Wolf Man, the psychoanalytic movement was definitely established as a discipline," and Freud pursued no further case studies (1981, 116). He became concerned that his theories would take on the weight of orthodoxy. The discourse between an analyst and a patient was a practice, but it was likely to be turned into a discipline in the hands of fellow practitioners. In light of these developments, one factor should be considered when we examine Nabokov's understanding of Freud. Although he denied the validity of such theoretical formulas as dream analysis, myth, type, and Freudian sexuality, it is important to note that the characters who represent Freud's perspective in his fiction are largely doctors and therapists, that is, disciplined practitioners. Indeed, if we examine Freud's meta-psychology of the double, proposed in the contexts of infantile sexuality and the concept of narcissism, it becomes clear that he does not suggest a perfect resemblance as an ideal. On the contrary, he warns us that our erotic instinct tends to regard an erotic object as a perfect replica of ourselves. When elaborating the means to overcome this tendency, he developed such terms as auto-eroticism and primary narcissism.[8]

When we consider the extent to which Nabokov employed Freudian psychology as an artistic framework, it seems understandable that the English-language versions of his earlier works included forewords that criticized the "Viennese quack"—even after the spectacular success of *Lolita*. The topic of Freudian psychology had already saturated his work during his years of exile in Western Europe, exemplified by *Despair*, and he certainly would have been attentive to the U.S. public's obsession with ego-psychology in the 1960s. At the same time, however, it is likely that Nabokov wanted a new generation of readers to appreciate his work in the contexts of theatricality and anti-Freudianism, rather than focusing solely on the controversial issue of pedophilia, which had dominated critical treatments of *Lolita*. In light of both critical and popular responses to *Lolita*, Nabokov may have concluded that his strategy of mimicry was too deeply buried to be appreciated—perhaps even discerned—by critics or readers. As Joanna Trzeciak observed,

> His Freudian teasers not only serve as a protective shield, but also become structural devices that often function in the sexual psychology and motivation of his characters—so much so that his novels and self-translations do indeed come to rely on the very Freudian notions being discredited." (2009, 57–58)

In *Despair*, Nabokov engages in mimicry of psychotherapy in order to distract readers from his dual attack on Russian Communism and German Nazism: a risky enterprise at that particular time in history. In *Lolita*, Humbert's description of his love for the nymphet is laced with references to Freudian sexuality, which lends irony to his eventual defeat by the disguised Freudian, Quilty. In compensation for this defeat, however, Humbert achieves his longstanding dream to create an enduring work of art. Freud, after all, is not merely Nabokov's foil. He is an inseparable *other*, so deeply embedded in Nabokov's literature that it scarcely seems feasible in his absence. This phenomenon calls to mind Freud's essay,

"Instincts and their Vicissitudes," in which he formulates the dynamics between looking at and being looked upon—a theory that eventually served as the ground for Lacan's concept of the *gaze*. It would appear that Nabokov was constantly looking at Freud, with more than a touch of humor, while he simultaneously imagined Freud looking at him. This narrative device included more than a trace of *theatricality*, and it seems perfectly reasonable to assert that, in the absence of his dialogue with Freud, Nabokov's work would be deprived of much of its artistry.

NOTES

1. Regarding art, see Nabokov's National Book Award acceptance speech (April 1975, Montreux), pp. 16-17; about literature as a lie, see "Good Readers and Good Writers" in *Lectures on Literature*, pp. 1-6.

2. Ann Smock reads *Despair* in the context of Blanchot's concept of gaze, a fantasy in which regarding *the void* is desirable. Smock contends that we cannot tell whether Hermann is the ingenious criminal or the unfortunate victim, because his life is based on his own death. Life is based on the void, given that Felix is dead, although he is alive in Hermann. Hence, the act of being suicidal is very deceptive. Hermann is the victim of his own deception, and to be a man is to be a criminal. *Double Dealing*, 1985, pp. 3-69.

3. Stephen Suagee states that "we can never penetrate their tangled surface, simply because Hermann does not tell us enough." See p. 60 of the essay, "An Artist's Memory Beats all Other Kinds: An Essay on *Despair*," 1974, pp. 54-62.

4. See *Despair*, p. 32: "phallic tulips in a leaning vase."

5. Siggy Frank observes that the mishap involving the stick is an obvious oversight in the plot construction, which any reader, including Hermann, can discern upon rereading the story. See *Nabokov's Theatrical Imagination*, p. 153; Helen Oakley posits Humbert, Hermann, Kinbote, and Vans in the category of the unreliable narrator and notes that Hermann's narrative runs to eleven chapters, as opposed to his planned ten chapters. Thus, it has degenerated into a diary. See her essay, "Disturbing Design: Nabokov's Manipulation of the Detective Fiction Genre in *Pale Fire* and *Despair*," pp. 480-496.

6. For instance, see p. 94 in *Pale Fire*, where Kinbote introduces one stanza that Shade has crossed out lightly in the draft: "The future patient of the future quack / May find, all set for him, the Primal Scene."

7. P. D. Ouspensky composed *A New Model of the Universe* between 1912 and 1921, publishing it in 1931 through Alfred A. Knopf. The work was translated by R. R. Merton and reprinted by Dover Publications in 1997. Ouspensky defines mimicry as any imitation or copying by living forms, either of other living forms or of surrounding natural conditions; it is clearly manifested in the world of insects and plants. From page 271, he engages in criticism of Freud; Nicolas Evreinoff published *The Theatre in Life* in 1927 at Brentano's. It was reprinted in 2013. Evreinoff asserts that a time is coming when we will at last realize that there is as much of "theatre" in "nature" as there is of "nature" in "theatre." We are all essentially theatrical beings and the essence of all theatrical art is deception and transformation.

8. About autoeroticism, see *Three Essays on the Theory of Sexuality, Standard Edition* Vol. 7, 1905, pp. 135-243; about Primary Narcissism, see "On Narcissism: An Introduction." *Standard Edition* Vol. 14, 1914, pp. 73-102.

FIVE

Lolita

Nabokov's Memory War against Freud

In the history of twentieth-century literature, it would be difficult to locate a novelist who voices more antipathy toward psychoanalysis than Vladimir Nabokov. As Jeffrey Berman argues, "if Freud had not existed, Nabokov would have had to invent him" (1987, 213). Yet the Russian-born author's persistent antagonism toward Freud and Freudianism raises questions—even suspicions—about the source of his hostility. Was it the byproduct of a hidden motivation, one closely related to the writer's creative process? There is little doubt that reading the works of Nabokov and Freud side by side can be an unsettling experience, especially if one happens to be sympathetic toward both. Perhaps, as Berman suggests, Nabokov's precarious position as a middle-aged immigrant in an unfamiliar country compelled him to reject any established ideological milieu, while reacting against those systematic thinkers who embraced Freud as one of their own.[1] It must have been a singular challenge for a Russian refugee from the Bolshevik Revolution to compose fiction in the English language. Furthermore, American culture of the cold war period was antagonistic to the political situation in his homeland—a country that he dearly loved. Perhaps the personal conflict that arose because of his simultaneous love for his native land and hatred of its politics left him estranged from any social system or body of ideological generalizations. Still, a question remains: who would deliberately eschew systematic thought, especially if one was determined to become a "name" in the world?

Nabokov's fierce resistance to systematic thought appears to be rooted in many of his earlier experiences. As a consequence of the Bolshevik Revolution, he lost not only his country, language, and homeland but also his father and brothers, who perished in the political turmoil that came in its wake. His state of mind upon embarking on a new life in the United States is aptly reflected in his letters to Edmund Wilson; and Wilson's advice to him is revealing. Upon reviewing Nabokov's first work of fiction in the English language, *The Real Life of Sebastian Knight* (1941), Wilson recommended that the immigrant immerse himself in serious, moralistic novels that reflect an understanding of human society, such as those written by Henry James or William Faulkner: "You aren't good at this kind of subject, which involves questions of politics and social change, because you are totally uninterested in these matters and have never taken the trouble to understand them" (Karlinsky, 1979, 183). Stubbornly resistant to this advice, Nabokov insisted that a competent artist had no need to bother with society or politics—or, for that matter, even the concerns of "real people." Thus, he ranks Dostoevsky, Henry James, and T. S. Eliot rather low in his personal hierarchy of artists, while elevating Joyce, Kafka, Proust, and Bergson to his preferred literary models. It would not be an overstatement to suggest that Nabokov rejects any writer whose propensities are linked to the political, social, realistic, and ideological spheres.

Of those systematic thinkers he repudiates—who include Lenin, Marx, and Darwin—the name of Sigmund Freud surfaces repeatedly. Although Nabokov cites Freud, along with Marx, as only one member of an influential body of "fake thinkers and puffed-up poets"(SO 18), Geoffrey Green notes that Freud is "lurking behind all these doubles"(1988, 77). The difficulty, however, is that we know little about the degree to which Nabokov was familiar with Freud's work, and therefore we cannot determine which aspects of it he particularly disliked. It is not clear whether Nabokov disparaged Freud as a therapist, as a natural scientist who was influenced by Darwin, as a neuroscientist who devoted his life to investigating the mnemic apparatus and the human psyche, or as a precursor of the hermeneutic approach to reading texts. During a 1964 interview, Nabokov offered the following diatribe when questioned about his hostility toward Freud and American psychology: "Freudism and all it has tainted with its grotesque implications and methods appears to me to be one of the vilest deceits practiced by people on themselves and on others. I reject it utterly, along with a few other medieval items still adored by the ignorant, the conventional, or the very sick" (SO 23–24). Beyond these sporadic comments to interviewers, one also encounters numerous parodies of psychoanalysis throughout Nabokov's work. As Jenefer Shute contends, "Freud's presence has haunted the Nabokovian text," almost as if he were involved in a competition with Freud's narrative (1995, 413). Indeed, his most successful work, *Lolita* (1955), can be read as a mimic of psychoanalysis, an issue that will be discussed later in this chapter. Although the specter of Freud haunts many of Nabokov's interviews and literary works, it is also true that he rarely provides us with details that might shed light on his hostility toward the "Viennese quack"—an omission that has generated a great deal of scholarly controversy.

What is the origin of Nabokov's negative preoccupation with Freud, and what is the nature of his aversion? Is Nabokov's position fair to Freud? Bearing these questions in mind, this chapter will proceed in three steps. The first involves a survey of criticism dealing with Nabokov's hostility to Freud to determine if anything has been ignored or overlooked. Building on this survey, the second step will compare Freud's concept of screen memories to Nabokov's use of childhood memories, with the goal of showing to what degree they resemble one another. The third step will contrast Nabokov's art of memory, as it is reflected in his literary work, with Freud's system of remembering, which informs his analysis of the human psyche. The aim of this chapter as a whole is to show that Nabokov perceived Freud as a literary rival. This poet, who was also a scientist, engaged in a playful, even joyful, negation of Freud, a scientist who was also a poet.

THE REMAINS OF THE CRITICISM

It was L. R. Hiatt who first identified the structure of the Oedipus complex in *Lolita*, and he went on to present Nabokov as a cryptic Freudian. In his essay, "Nabokov's *Lolita*: A 'Freudian' Cryptic Crossword," Hiatt examines in detail the manner in which Nabokov follows the schema of ancient myth, despite his much-vaunted antipathy toward its appropriation by Freud: "he knowingly but surreptitiously endows Humbert with classical symptoms of the Oedipus complex"(1967, 361). The narrator's triangular relationship to Quilty, as father, and Lolita, as mother-surrogate, sustains the oedipal drama until the final act, "the slow, dreamy, joyful patricide" (361). Thus, Humbert is consciously unaware of Quilty's identity, even though he unconsciously knows he will be deprived of his lover by his father (366). Yet, in Hiatt's view, there is a disturbing element in this narrative, given that Quilty does not truly deserve Lolita (after all, he exploits her sexuality in a pornographic film). Therefore, the act of murdering Quilty does not precipitate the trauma associated with patricide. Indeed, it is justified by Humbert's sublimated love. While the morality of the two male characters is divergent, the aesthetic victory belongs not to the father but to the son. Nabokov, who openly denounces the application of symbols and allegories to the reading of literature, may have intentionally constructed a parody of the oedipal myth. Consequently, Hiatt's insightful discourse remains an important breakthrough, one that is especially relevant to John Ray's Preface. After reviewing this curious preface, one might ask, who is this editor, Ray, and why does the author need him?

Berman was the first critic whose empathy for these two literary "rivals" spurred him to discover important clues about the mysterious connections between Freud and Nabokov. He carefully investigated potential sources of Nabokov's antipathy toward Freud, examining interviews and literary works, while also drawing upon such topics as the Oedipus complex, unconscious motivation, dream interpretation, and biological drives. Attentive to Nabokov's parody of the talking cure as "a form of manipulation" or "mind-control" (217), Berman nevertheless claims him as a Freudian: "Despite his contempt for psychology as a discipline, Nabokov was a psychological novelist, whether or not he was parodying the subject" (220). Among Berman's insights, two are especially relevant here. First, he points out that Ray's position as a guarantor of "clinical authenticity" (222) is precisely what Nabokov seeks to parody. Berman suggests that Humbert's real target is Freud rather than Quilty, given that "Humbert's criticisms of psychoanalysis coincide exactly with Nabokov's position, and both use the identical parodic attack to demolish the foe" (224). Second, Berman notes that Nabokov takes issue with the biologizing of psychology: "For all its eroticism, *Lolita* remains curiously suspicious of the biological components of sexuality" (231).

Leland de la Durantaye viewed the complicated issue of Nabokov's ambivalence toward Freud from a somewhat different perspective—as "a particular problem," instead of as an instance of the oedipal triangle. Not only does Nabokov repudiate any totalitarian generalizations, including those of psychoanalysis, but he vehemently opposes the sacrifice of any of the singular details that serve as the compositional elements of life and art. Ironically, however, his condemnation of psychoanalysis is itself rather fragmentary, general, and abstract, and thus scarcely in keeping with his own aesthetic standard: it is "a final irony in Nabokov's attacks on Freud as prophet and promulgator of the general" that "in vilifying Freud, Nabokov followed only the most general lines of attack" (2005, 69). Implicitly, de la Durantaye provides us with two important clues to understanding the relationship between Nabokov and Freud. First, in the spirit of fair play, we must analyze the particularity of psychoanalysis (and not exclusively from a Nabokovian perspective) to determine which aspects aroused feelings of aversion in Nabokov, and whether or not those feelings are justifiable. Second, if Freud is indeed a "double" of Nabokov, we should be able to discern a resemblance—as well as a difference—between them.

A starting point for the latter discussion is the emphasis placed by both on the "remembering" associated with the primal scene or childhood memory. For Freud, uncovering repressed memories was integral to analytic work, while for Nabokov remembering was the pathway to a work of art, as reflected in his statement that imagination is a form of memory.[2] Significantly, in his fiction, there is no such thing as pure memory or unmediated reality, because the author's biography is always permeated by the retrospective eye; and the writing process exploits this state of affairs in a self-conscious manner. Consequently, Proust and Bergson were his favorite authors; and he advised his students not to explore the author's life when reading Proust because the narrator and the author resemble each other in various ways but are not identical. He notes that the work is neither an autobiography nor a historical account: "the narrator is not Proust the person, and the characters never existed except in the author's mind. Let us not, therefore, go into the author's life" (LL 208). Since the narrator is not *quite* Proust, even if he is the eyes and ears of the book, the reader should be attentive to a focal shift that "produces a rainbow edge" between author and narrator (210). By implication, however, this subtle advice confirms that, since a memoir is not an objective description of the past but an evocation of it, the author (Nabokov) and the narrator (Humbert) are inseparable in *Lolita*. In *Matter and Memory* (1912), Bergson generalizes the system of remembering, while Proust employs it for the purpose of metaphorical representation in his fiction. This invites the question: if Bergson's generalizations are congenial to Nabokov, why then is he so repelled by those of Freud? Freud, after all, advocates a similar theory, reflected in terms such as "transference," when he constructs the past.

In his ambitious work, *Freud and Nabokov*, Green highlights the degree to which the two men resemble each other, especially in their representation of childhood memories: "All of Nabokov's novels are open in this sense to a multitude of interpretive possibilities that are psychoanalytically resonant" (1988, 92). Throughout, Green treats fiction as the product of analysis, while interpreting psychology as the product of fiction. For all its merits, however, Green's work ultimately fails to provide a clear answer to the questions that inform this chapter: what is the motivation that lurks behind Nabokov's relentless attacks on Freud, and can Nabokov's position be described as justifiable? As Shute notes, Green's "very symmetry is the problem"—for both novelist and critic—"not its solution" (1995, 415). In an effort to defend Freud, Shute mainly attributes Nabokov's hostility toward psychoanalysis to the anxiety of influence. In other words, it reflects the territorial struggle waged by a strong-minded poet who does not wish to be influenced by a forerunner. This view seems plausible, given that the novelist's "tools" of memory and desire are consistent with Freud's masterplot. Green's parallel reading of the two rivals' works has narrowed down its scope to the realm of mnemic apparatuses. Yet both Green and Shute leave us with unanswered questions about the ways in which the two men differed, and why these differences elicited so much rage on the part of Nabokov.

THE REPRESENTATION OF CHILDHOOD

Freud's early work "Screen Memories" (1899) is essentially an autobiographical essay, though it takes the form of a dialogue involving an analyst and his patient. The essay focuses mainly on Freud's self-analysis for the cure of a phobia, but as Theodor Reik observes in *Listening with the Third Ear*, it also lays the groundwork for his lifelong preoccupations with remembering, the primal scene, displacement, repression, memory-traces and consciousness, and even the color yellow.[3] According to Freud's essay, one's earliest childhood memories are not genuine but are rather fabrications shaped by later experiences. Interestingly, Endel Tulving's recent scientific research indicates that infantile experiences are not preserved, given that this period precedes the development of self-knowledge, or autonoetic consciousness, a conclusion that supports Freud's concept of screen memories.[4] In his essay, Freud describes what we know now to be a recollection of his own childhood that derives not only from early experiences but also from incidents that occurred much later. Freud concludes, "It looks as though a memory-trace from childhood had here been translated back into a plastic and visual form at a later date—the date of the memory's arousal" (SE 3: 321). Thus, the original impression never entered into the subject's consciousness. On the contrary, the early memories are byproducts of later experiences, and their falsification was achieved by projecting the "repressed" memories of later years back to the patient's early childhood because "the recollection of the remote past is in itself facilitated by some pleasurable motive" (317).

Freud's closing remark that "the raw material of memory-traces out of which it was forged remains unknown to us in its original form" (SE 3: 322) invites comparison to Nabokov's brief poem, "Rain," of which I quote the second stanza. Many a tangled year of speed upon the roads of "the steeds of rain,"

> but they can never reach the last
> dip at the Bottom of the past
> because the sun is there. (PN 533)

Like Freud, Nabokov holds that the past cannot be restored without being transferred to later experiences. But while the former analyzes screen memories in terms of instincts (sexuality and hunger) that are constructed by the oedipal structure, the latter implies that childhood—"the Bottom of the past"—cannot be reached by the "steeds of rain" that carry our recollections, because it is blocked by the sun, the magic of fantasy.

More radically, Nabokov denies the validity of any kind of interpretation, particularly when it involves a matter of the real. In "Reply to My Critics," he disparages his detractors, including Edmund Wilson, as "commonsensical, artless, average" readers: "I do not believe in the old-fashioned, naïve, and musty method of human-interest criticism cham-pioned by Mr. Wilson that consists of removing the characters from an author's imaginary world to the imaginary, but generally far less plau-sible, world of the critic who then proceeds to examine these displaced characters as if they were 'real people'" (PN 321). This complaint is echoed in the voices of various characters in his fiction. It would not be too much to suggest that Nabokov's fictional works are metaphorical configurations of the idea of "the real," or that they serve as arenas for competition among imaginary characters on opposing sides of this issue. For instance, John Ray, who supposedly edited Humbert's memoir, intro-duces it as a "real" story, and regards the author's imaginary people as "real people" in the "real" world. Not only does he inform us that Lolita "died in childbed giving birth to a stillborn girl on Christmas Day 1952" (LO 6), but he also reads the fiction as a case history, predicting that "*Lolita* will become, no doubt, a classic in psychiatric circles" (LO 7). This puzzling editor, who urges us to consider the ethical impact and "general lesson" of the work of art in society, appears to function as a stand-in for naïve realists such as Wilson or Freud. Indeed, at the intradiegetic level of the narrative, Ray resembles the veiled character Quilty, who is thoroughly incompatible with Humbert: one is a successful writer, the other is not; one is Lolita's eternal lover, the other is a base criminal. In this sense, John M. Ingham's suggestion that Quilty represents Freud appears convincing: "he is the invasive psychoanalyst who subjects his patient to prurient interpretations" (2002, 41). Yet it seems more plausible that Humbert sets out to murder Quilty because of Nabokov's tendency to mock and parody "the real" rather than as a consequence of the au-thor's Oedipus complex (oriented by sex), as Ingham has suggested (44).

Nabokov is hostile to naïve realism and makes this perfectly apparent in his interviews and essays. At the same time, he weaves its ideas throughout his fiction, though in the form of parody. His first work of fiction in English, *The Real Life of Sebastian Knight*, is a parody of "the real" that is informed by the vision and voice of a narrator known simply as "V." While gathering materials on the life of his deceased brother Sebas-tian, a well-known writer, V gradually confides to the reader that these materials, far from being rooted in reality, are fabrications that are medi-ated not only by the originators but also by Sebastian himself. It becomes apparent that these storytellers are not discussing the undiluted past of V's late brother, but rather their own current desires. Ultimately, the biographer accepts that one's past cannot be restored as it was, given that the real is refracted at least three times. Unsurprisingly, Nabokov repudi-ates real people and the real past, no matter whether their existence is advocated by writers, critics, social scientists, or natural scientists. He denounces systematic thinkers as fakes, dismisses Dostoevsky as a third-rate writer, and argues that reality is "a very subjective affair" that is never to be entirely grasped, "an infinite succession of steps, levels of perception, false bottoms, and hence unquenchable, unattainable" (SO 11). Thus, for Nabokov, reality is not a fitting object of art. Instead, it should be the subject of an art that seeks to reveal how it is filtered by the mediators. One of these filtering tools, in his opinion, is the art of memory, because an author's attempt to remember his or her past is an act of creation—our psyche, in itself, is an act of imaginative composition. It follows that the nymphet can never be possessed by Humbert, who cannot reach the territory of childhood, while Quilty, a naïve realist, succeeds in possessing her, even though he does not deserve her.

Humbert acknowledges Quilty as his counterpart, observing that they share certain affinities of personality, genre, sense of humor, and mindset. They are both not only literate intellectuals but also cunning seducers. Indeed, they are collaborators in a play, and the two men are even described as "literary figures" at the murder scene: "it was a silent, soft, formless tussle on the part of the two literati" (LO 272). As doubles, however, they are not entirely compatible. Although corrupt, Quilty is well known and successful, and he ultimately steals Lolita away from Humbert, who is relegated to the role of the dejected lover. Perhaps the most conspicuous difference between the two pedophiles is that one focuses exclusively on Lolita's sexuality, while the other does not. Although Humbert is a disturbing figure, he idolizes Lolita, in much the same way that Dante worshipped Beatrice. During his first night with Lolita, Humbert outlines his purpose: "I am not concerned with so-called 'sex' at all. Anybody can imagine those elements of animality. A greater endeavor lures me on: to fix once and for all the perilous magic of nymphets" (LO 123). But what is "the perilous magic of nymphets," if it is not entirely about sex? We learn that, before his encounter with Lolita, Humbert was treated in a sanatorium for more than a year. Shrewdly concealing his true sexual predicament, Humbert enjoyed trifling with his psychiatrists. He cunningly led them to explore fabricated primal scenes and even to conclude that his breakdown resulted from the fact that he was "potentially homosexual" and "totally impotent" (LO 34). This passage that indicates Humbert's (and Nabokov's) interest in the nymphet is not motivated so much by sex as it is by a desire to mock what he considers to be the psychoanalyst's obsession with sex.

Always sensitive to Freud's interpretation of childhood as a time of nascent sexuality, Nabokov was repulsed by the symbols of dream analysis and their mythic implications.[5] In 1956, upon returning from a butterfly hunt in the Rockies, he wrote a letter to Wilson that features the following passage: "Incidentally, in one of his letters to Fliess, the Viennese Sage mentions a young patient who masturbated in the W.C. of an Interlaken hotel in a special contracted position so as to be able to glimpse (now comes the Viennese Sage's curative explanation) the Jungfrau" (Karlinsky, 1979, 300). As the editor, Simon Karlinsky, indicates in his note on the same page, Freud's letter to Fliess (dated December 9,

1899) proposed the concept of autoerotism, the childhood sexual experience that he deemed to be "the lowest of the sexual strata"(Masson 1985, 390). Freud contends that, while this earliest sexual experience gradually develops into an adult alloerotism, it does not entirely disappear but "continues to exist as an undercurrent." Therefore, one's ability to distinguish neurosis from paranoia depends on whether "a forward surge of the autoerotic current" emerges (390). Notably, Freud establishes infantile sexuality as the earliest stage of autoerotism and regards it as the source of the affectionate current (as opposed to the adult's sensual current) in his metapsychology, *Three Essays on the Theory of Sexuality* (1905), where he concludes that a mother's love has a crucial impact on her child's life after puberty.[6]

For Freud, the association of memories with dream interpretation is inseparable from an examination of early sexuality; and this style of systematic thinking, with its emphasis on sexuality, was evidently unbearable to Nabokov. In a particularly harsh tone, he dismisses Freud's interpretations of dreams as one of the greatest pieces of satanic nonsense imposed on a gullible public. He describes symbolism in dreams as a series of "traps set for Freudians" and deliberately mispronounces the term "Freudian slip" as Freudian "slippers," the whole time attacking Freud for his supposed lack of subtlety (Rowe, 1971, 109). Based on Nabokov's well-documented contempt for Freudian thought, and the central theme of his poem "Rain" — in which access to the past is impeded by the sunny place while the "steeds of rain" represents (Freudian) recollections — we might assume that *Lolita* is designed as the mimicry of infantile sexuality. In the intradiegetic narrative, Quilty, who steals Lolita from Humbert (only to turn around and exploit her as a sexual object), is eventually defeated by Humbert, who is then deprived of her and thus compelled to sublimate her in a palliative work of art. At the extradiegetic level, Ray is defeated by Nabokov, who turns him into a fictional character when he attaches an Afterword "on a book entitled *Lolita*." This aesthetic device ensures that the authorial voice will erase the editor's voice, presenting a completely different dimension of the book: "After doing my impersonation of suave John Ray, the character in *Lolita* who pens the Foreword, any comments coming straight from me may strike one — may strike me, in fact — as an impersonation of Vladimir Nabokov talking about his own book" (LO 282). Even while impersonating himself as a fictional character, however, Nabokov simultaneously achieves a subtle parody of the real, and of infantile sexuality, without abandoning his propensity for humor and comic gestures. For instance, the pistol Humbert uses to slay Quilty is described as a "Freudian symbol of the Ur-father's central forelimb" (LO 197).

Beneath this mimicry of Freudian sexuality, however, lurks a deep sorrow, one fueled by the tenacious, apparently unquenchable, longing for the past that informs Humbert's undying love for Lolita. Then, what indeed is the true nature of Humbert's past, his childhood—and what distinguishes it from classic Freudian lore? Is Freud's aim as a psychoanalyst simply to analyze dreams, equating them with a primal scene of autoerotism, which is ultimately the source of a cure? Despite Freud's suggestion, in "Screen Memories," that the primal scene is unreachable terrain—a contention that prompts Green to argue for a symmetry between the two literary rivals—a question lingers. In what ways did Nabokov's childhood differ from that of Freud, and how might those differences be connected to their respective concepts of the structure of memory?

DIFFERING CURES: THE BUTTERFLY IN NABOKOV AND FREUD

In the summer of 1953—as if to underscore his belief that every work of fiction is, in some way, an autobiography—Nabokov translated his memoir into Russian, while also composing *Lolita* and hunting for butterflies. Throughout his life, Nabokov often acknowledged that writing and butterfly hunting were the sole comforts of an enchanted poet who pined endlessly for his native land.[7] After catching his first butterfly at the age of seven, under the strict guidance of parents who strongly encouraged scientific pursuits, he gradually learned how to handle the creatures. It appears that the butterfly was yet another nymphet he dearly loved. Perhaps, the nymphet is a metaphoric representation of a childhood that was enriched by butterfly hunting—a childhood to which he obsessively returned in his memory.

Nabokov's childhood loomed large in his memory, as evidenced by his autobiography, *Speak, Memory,* and reflected in the voice of his character, Humbert: "my fancy was both Proustianized and Procrusteanized" (LO 241). Proust and Procrustes have in common their sensuality and arbitrariness: Marcel's memory was aroused by the taste of a madeleine, and Procrustes's violence lies in his coercive force. Likewise, the subject of childhood memories surfaces in an interview where Nabokov acknowledges that they are not recollections of a genuine reality:

> the more you love a memory, the stronger and stranger it is. I think it's natural that I have a more passionate affection for my old memories, the memories of my childhood, than I have for later ones, so that Cambridge in England or Cambridge in New England is less vivid in my mind and in my self than some kind of nook in the park on our country estate in Russia. (SO 12)

At the center of Nabokov's autobiography are memories of the North Russian landscape of boyhood, along with memories of his father, who encouraged not only his taste for the thrill of a great poem but also his love of scientific inquiry, as well as of his mother, whose grace and endurance he cherished, even revered. For Nabokov, memories of being surrounded by nature, along with the boundless affection of his parents, inspired deep feelings of nostalgia—"a hypertrophied sense of lost childhood, not sorrow for lost banknotes" (SM 73). As he wandered through alien locales under the skies of Europe and America, burdened by that hyperbolic fantasy, is there any chance he might have analyzed his childhood in terms of infantile sexuality, or the Oedipus complex? Given that his was a passionate and private fantasy, he resisted any generalizations that accorded with the myths and symbols of incest. Furthermore, his yearning for the native province, *Vyre*, cannot be the object of analysis by any systematic method, since the loss of his country constituted nothing less than the loss of what he most deeply loved: "Beneath the sky of my America to sigh for *one* locality in Russia" (SM 73). Determined to retain recollections of his childhood as the place blocked by the sun (like screen memories) in his mind, Nabokov firmly rejects the lure of curability: "I also suggest that the Freudian faith leads to dangerous ethical consequences, such as when a filthy murderer with the brain of a tapeworm is given a lighter sentence because his mother spanked him too much or too little—it works both ways" (SO 116). The only possible remedy lies in writing fiction and hunting butterflies. For Nabokov, there was to be no talking cure.

Accordingly, Nabokov attempted in *Lolita* to create a work of fiction that uses the Freudian cure as a springboard to demonstrate how "a nymphet's spell," the pure past, can be neither grasped nor generalized. Rejecting naïve realism, he sets out to challenge the old assumptions of morality and representation, displacing them with a unique style of puzzling, mischievous word play. Ultimately, a cure for his misery cannot be achieved through sex, which is merely "the ancilla of art," but rather through "the melancholy and very local palliative of articulate art" (LO 258). As Humbert's yearning for the nymphet intensifies, she becomes more cruel and deceptive. In this way, Lolita becomes less an object of sex than an incarnation of childhood, and the narrative engages the reader's sympathy as it moves relentlessly toward the final, poignant scene. At one point, while being pursued by the police, Humbert stops his car and listens to the noises emanating from below in "the streets of the transparent town." In the melodious sounds of children at play, he no longer hears Lolita's voice: "I knew that the hopelessly poignant thing was not Lolita's absence from my side, but the absence of her voice from that concord" (280). This is simultaneously a story about the beloved in Humbert's childhood, Annabel, a nymphet, who epitomizes how *Vyre* always functions "in a certain magic and fateful way" (16) in Nabokov's adult life. While recollecting his love for Annabel, Humbert designates as "nymphets" creatures between nine and fourteen, to evoke a magic for their bewitched travelers who may be twice or even several times older than them.

The mysterious and elusive magic of childhood is personified by characters who are themselves embodiments of the human psyche. Lolita is "a combination of naïveté and deception, of charm and vulgarity" (135). She possesses the tenderness of a dreamy child as well as the callous deceptiveness of a seductress who ultimately cheats Humbert. She is both the victim of two relentless pedophiles and a victimizer who incites one of them to murder. Likewise, Humbert presents the same unsettling duality. He appears to the reader as a cunning liar and a cruel seducer as he actively conceals his passion for Lolita from her mother and neighbors. Indeed, in many respects, Humbert is a monster. Despite his ugly nature, however, we cannot find it within ourselves to hate him as he struggles pathetically to protect Lolita's purity and render her beauty immortal. Overall, we are inclined to forgive him, particularly as the story develops, because he is resolute in his love for her. Hence, the traditional distinction between beast and beauty becomes redundant, for the contradictory and deceptive nature of the characters reflects the author's desire to overturn naïve representations of the human psyche—the kind that might be found in a fairy tale.

The contradictory, whimsical nature of the characters is further mirrored in the narrative itself. Not only does the story unfold within the memory of a narrator, reflecting that "such suffusions of swimming colors are not to be disdained by the artist in recollection" (240), but the elusive object of his desire also finds herself with an unattainable lover, a situation that provokes the sigh, "Oh, Mnemosyne, sweetest and most mischievous of muses!" (237). Moreover, the subject's deployment of memory is, in itself, an act of imagination, while the object is Mnemosyne, the muse of poetry as well as memory. The narrative is not so much a description of the past as an evocation of it. The story does not move consecutively, as is the case with realism; instead, it is rewritten numerous times, with puns and parodies—many inspired by familiar works of fiction—dispersed throughout. Nabokov's art is endlessly deceptive. Indeed, in the Nabokovian world art is at its finest when it is fantastically deceitful, whimsical, and complex. For Nabokov, the primary concern of art is not with society; instead, the focus is on the individual artist. Yet, for all this, Nabokov does not care for the slogan art for art's sake. For him, writing is simply a delightful act aimed at the retention of a personal past that is too elusive and complicated to be generalized. Art combines puzzling patterns where one thing is disguised as another, in the same way that a butterfly or caterpillar mimics its surroundings to camouflage itself.

Of the three components that make up a good writer—storytelling, teaching, and enchanting—Nabokov places the greatest emphasis on the role of the enchanter. His passion for both writing and butterfly hunting lead him to conclude that all art is deception and so is nature. Nabokov links literature to the dissimulation practiced throughout the natural world:

> Literature is invention. Fiction is fiction. To call a story a true story is an insult to both art and truth. Every great writer is a great deceiver, but so is that arch-cheat Nature. Nature always deceives. From the simple deception of propagation to the prodigiously sophisticated illusion of protective colors in butterflies or birds, there is in Nature a marvelous system of spells and wiles. The writer of fiction only follows Nature's lead. (LL 5)

The incomparable delight Nabokov finds in butterfly hunting is echoed precisely in the joy that he takes in producing a work of fiction. In short, nature and art share a common link with scientific particularity. Both are deceptive, contradictory, and contain a marvelous web concealed behind an attractive design. With his parents' encouragement, the young Nabokov learned how to catch a butterfly and to analyze its abundant and puzzling beauty. He notes in a 1969 interview that "not only do we collect butterflies, but we examine under the microscope their minuscule organs whose form helps to classify the creature more certainly than the color of its wings." Recognition of such differences produces "a feeling in which the scientific and the artistic sides join in an apex of sharp pleasure unknown to the man walking under trees he cannot even name" (Boyd and Pyle 2000, 671). His delight in nature is not inspired by the truth behind phenomena but by the magic of deception. His fascination with animal mimicry, for instance, stems not only from his interest in its protective aspect but also from his awareness that these mysterious processes go beyond the crude purpose of survival; he was even approached by Edmund Wilson's daughter to write a book on mimicry for Houghton Mifflin as Boyd remarks (2000, 13).

For Nabokov, to perceive the infinite elusiveness of reality does not guarantee that one can approach it, despite his statement that the glory of God is to hide a thing while the glory of man is to find it. On the contrary, he believes the intricate and concealed patterns of nature are too complex, too recalcitrant, to fall prey to human perception. He believes that "all reality is comparative reality," while each "-ism" is little more than a comparative notion; for any given reality is dependent not only on "a crude give-and-take of the senses" but also "various levels of information" as he stressed in *Lectures on Literature* (146). In the Nabokovian world, the human psyche, art, and science (represented by nature and the butterfly) are involved in a subtle partnership, for "all butterflies are beautiful and ugly at the same time—like human beings" (Boyd and Pyle 2000, 708). Nature and the human psyche go hand in hand, sharing the same spirit of enchantment in an endless game. Given his belief that the arts of deception and mimicry are practiced more beautifully by that other "V. N." (SO 153), Visible Nature, he demonstrates an unyielding preference for specific details over generalizations, for images over ideas, for obscure facts over concrete symbols. Yet we are tempted to ask: doesn't Nabokov generalize the concept of deception, in his own way?

Nabokov's tendency to connect literature and lepidoptera is evident in his 1970 interview with Alfred Appel, Jr., where he states that the fact "that in some cases the butterfly symbolizes something (e.g., Psyche) lies utterly outside my area of interest" (Boyd and Pyle, 2000, 675). Given his fascination with butterflies, is it likely that Nabokov had read Freud's case study of the Wolf Man? Underscoring the similarity between Nabokov and the Wolf Man, both of whom were scions of aristocratic families in czarist Russia, Ingham surmises that "both the interest in peasant girls and the butterfly phobia must have been especially interesting for Nabokov," while he reads *Lolita* as the displacement of the Wolf Man and Little Red Riding Hood.[8] Likewise, de la Durantaye perceives resemblances between Nabokov and the protagonist of Freud's clinical narrative in that both were wealthy and cultivated men who had been displaced by the Russian Revolution into European exile, and he speculates that "Nabokov *had* encountered the case of the Wolf-Man" since the case history was among the most famous ever published and Nabokov was much interested in this genre while composing *Lolita* (2005, 62). Unsurprisingly, Appel suggests in his edition of *Lolita* that Nabokov was familiar with Freud's case study on the Wolf Man.[9]

Nabokov himself repeats and renovates such crucial terms as "the primal scene" and "the primordial cave" in conjunction with "age four" and "parents' love life." He rejects completely the vulgar, shabby, medieval world of Freud, along with his quest for sexual symbols, with his analysis of a little baby's spying upon the sexual acts of its parents. We also encounter the trace of the Wolf Man in *Ada*: "poor speakers are obsessed with in familiar dreams (attributed by Dr. Froid of Signy-Mondieu-Mondieu to the dreamer's having read in infancy his adulterous parents' love letters)" (549). Significantly, Nabokov's longstanding interest in butterfly hunting is aptly conveyed in the following comment: "My entomological library in Montreux is smaller, in fact, than the heaps of butterfly books I had as a child" (SO 190). Thus, it would not be a bold leap to infer that Freud's characterization of a butterfly as the source of his patient's phobia would have struck Nabokov as outrageous, given his delight in the guidance he received from his parents surrounded by the magic of nature. This raises another question: is the Wolf Man's own primal scene really about sex, the butterfly as the mythic symbol of the psyche, or something else altogether?

Freud's case study, *From the History of an Infantile Neurosis* (1918), involves a patient burdened with an animal phobia that manifested itself in unsettling dream images, especially those of a wolf standing upright and a magnificent butterfly with striped yellow wings. Although Freud accepts "the distortion and refurbishing to which a person's own past is subjected when it is looked back upon from a later period" (SE 17: 9), he sets out to examine the patient's condition in the context of his relationships with his sister, who was intellectually superior to him; with his Nanya ("nanny"), who offered him unconditional love; and with his father, who usually sided with his sister against him. The patient, who failed to identify with his father, became in Freud's account a passive sexual object whose sadomasochistic tendencies were the byproduct of the guilt he felt over his homosexuality. Focusing on the patient's phobia toward animals, Freud approaches the primal scene, concluding that the wolves in the recurrent dream recall the position of his parents when he encountered them having sex at the age of one-and-a-half—"the man upright, and the woman bent down like an animal" (SE 17: 39). He adds that the trauma produced by this encounter surfaced as a deferred effect when the patient was four-and-a-half years old. Freud also speculates the patient's fear of castration may have impelled him to substitute the image of an animal for that of his father: "what the child observed was not copulation between his parents but copulation between animals, which he then displaced on to his parents, as though he had inferred that his parents did things in the same way" (57). One might question, however, why Freud would go on to suggest that the patient's obsession with a yellow, striped swallowtail butterfly is somehow related to his fear of wolves.

The primal scene that is reflected in the dream of wolves could easily have been inspired by illustrations in a children's picture book; it may also have been constructed from memories of later experiences, "gradually and laboriously from an aggregate of indications" (51). Furthermore, it is possible the scene was not rooted in an actual event; it could even have been a fantasy of the analyst himself (52). At this point, Freud requires evidence to support his premise, and he turns to the butterfly phobia, which offers concrete data based on the patient's memory. Freud argues in "Remembering, Repetition and Working-Through" (1914) that "we may say that the patient does not *remember* anything of what he has forgotten and repressed, but *acts* it out. He reproduces it not as a memory but as an action; he *repeats* it, without, of course, knowing that he is repeating it" (italics in original, SE 12:150).

In Russian, the word "butterfly" (*babushka*) means "granny" or "girl," and the patient's fear may have been inspired by the stick-like projections on the butterfly's wings, which could be perceived as symbolic genitals. Freud's conjecture then builds on the given name of the nursery-maid who was so fond of the patient: Grusha. He presents the image of a large pear with yellow stripes on its skin, observing that the word for "pear" in the patient's language was *grusha*. Linking the patient's butterfly phobia to the posture of the nursery-maid, who knelt on the floor when cleaning it, Freud concludes that the patient shows a compulsive passion for the assumed posture of his mother in the primal scene. Hence, Freud's analysis of the patient's butterfly phobia enables him to support his assumption that recollections of the past are carried forward through deferred *acts*. Notably, Freud emphasizes that the patient's fear of the butterfly reflected the compelling influence of the Grusha scene, "the first experience that he could really remember, and one which he had remembered without any conjectures or intervention on my part" (SE 17: 94). Freud contends that the Grusha scene illustrates, retrospectively, the primal scene that the patient presumably experienced when he was one-and-a-half years old. If indeed this is true, Freud's overriding concern in the case study of the Wolf Man is neither sex nor mythic symbols. Instead, he is focused on the *act* of remembering, a motive inconsistent with Nabokov's criticisms. Freud is ultimately seeking to prove his theory that the mnemic apparatus operates through deferred acts, with repetition and transference. The patient's butterfly phobia plays a crucial role in this process.

As Ernest Jones argues, Freud began his career as a scientist who was so rigorous in his research methods that, if he could not fully ascertain a result, he treated it as pointless. As a neuroscientist, Freud struggled to understand how it was possible "for neurons to be permanently altered from receiving an impression, and storing its traces and yet to receive fresh ones in just the same manner as before" (Jones 1981,1: 387). As Jones explains, "Freud's detailed exploration and description of the two sets of processes, something that had never before been even attempted" (398), received its fullest exposition in his unpublished *Project for a Scientific Psychology* (1895). By postulating that there are two classes of neurons, one permeable that are reached by external stimuli, and the other impermeable that store traces of those stimulations, he was able to access a more refined, yet simpler, model of the mind that he later argued found a counterpart in the "mystic writing-pad" (1925). He regards these two types of contact barriers as the explanation for the *mutually exclusive* relation between memory-traces and consciousness.

Nabokov evidently disagrees with Freud's use of the butterfly, along with the Grusha scene, to highlight the animal posture of *coitus a tergo*, mainly because he perceives the butterfly as an emblem of the deceptive and contradictory magic of nature. As I have argued, however, Freud's ultimate purpose in this analysis is not so much to shed light on sexuality as to examine the memory that emerges from contact between a sequence of traces and consciousness. In his analysis of the Wolf Man's animal phobia, he suggests that the cause of the neurosis could be the existence of those preliminary stages (SE 17: 120). The significance of early childhood would thus lie in the biological blow that is inevitably dealt to human narcissism. Freud, in tandem with his discovery of memory-traces as the mnemic apparatus of the unconscious, sets out to argue that we are human *nature*, while condemning the arrogance behind human attempts to conquer nature. As current scientific research on the brain attests, consciousness is an evolutionary achievement that enables humans to recall the past and anticipate the future. Only when connected to memory-traces can human consciousness reach a higher forms of cognition, with the capacity for desire and narrative. Tulving observes that, after the age of two years, a child begins to develop self-knowledge due to the evolution of "autonoetic consciousness," and this erases the earlier semantic memories through "infantile amnesia," which is precisely foreshadowed in the theory of screen memories Freud proposed almost a century ago.[10]

Given that Nabokov, with his emphasis on the magic of mimicry and deception, believes there is a symmetrical relationship between art and nature, he is inclined to push aside the theories of Darwin along with those of Freud:

> "Natural selection," in the Darwinian sense, could not explain the miraculous coincidence of imitative aspect and imitative behavior, nor could one appeal to the theory of "the struggle for life" when a protective device was carried to a point of mimetic subtlety, exuberance and luxury far in excess of a predator's power of appreciation. I discovered in nature the non-utilitarian delights that I sought in art. Both were a form of magic, both were a game of intricate enchantment and deception. (SM 125)

Nabokov dismisses Darwin's theory of natural selection as a utilitarian view of nature; and in response to interview questions, he places Darwin in the same category as Marx and Freud, condemning him as a systematizing and universalizing thinker. As we have seen, however, it would be more appropriate to suggest that Freud, as a scientist, was compelled to generalize a theory, while Nabokov, as a poet, was ultimately unable to avoid generalizing about the deceptive magic of the human psyche in its protean manifestations. Moreover, without the evolution of consciousness, it would have been impossible for Nabokov to produce fiction based on recollections of the past. Perhaps, if Freud had been Nabokov's contemporary, he would have answered the latter's criticisms by asserting that his job involved little more than the discovery of unconscious memory-traces, which contain the riddle of the human psyche that Nabokov was compelled to generalize in his own way.

NOTES

1. See Berman, p. 218. He considers the possibility that still-unknown personal experiences influenced Nabokov's thinking. In other words, his contempt for Freud may have been part of a larger reaction against despised German and Russian elements that he perceived to be the cause of his family's destruction. See Alan C. Elms, "Nabokov Contra Freud," pp. 42-44. He also observes that Nabokov's hostility to Freud had more complex and more personal origins (44).

2. In Nabokov's work, memory is often equated with imagination. In *Strong Opinions*, for instance, memory is one of many tools that an artist employs (12); the logic of artistic combination is to follow memory (32); both memory and imagination are a negation of time (78), and so on.

3. See Theodor Reik, *Listening with the Third Ear* (1948; New York: Farrar, Straus & Giroux, 1998). He argues that Freud's self-analysis is a very important stage in his career as an analyst: "There is always a second person there who observes the Me" (7). Thus, analysis was directed by Freud's fine ear for his inner voices (17, 19).

4. Endel Tulving, et al. "Toward a Theory of Episodic Memory: The Frontal Lobes and Autonoetic Consciousness," pp. 331-54. Tulving defines infantile amnesia as "the inability of adults to remember experiences from their first few years of life." See p. 345.

5. See Berman, p. 216. He observes that, during the remaining forty-five years of his writing career, Nabokov continued to satirize the Oedipus complex, unconscious motivation, dream interpretation, and biological drives.

6. S. Freud, *Three Essays on the Theory of Sexuality*, Standard Edition, Vol. 7, 125-243. He regards fore-pleasure as the same kind of pleasure that has already been produced, albeit on a smaller scale, through the infantile sexual instinct, whereas end-pleasure is something new that may be conditioned by circumstances that do not arise until puberty (210-11); what we call affection will eventually show its effects on the genital zones, so the mother plays a crucial role in teaching the infant how to love someone later in life (223).

7. See *Strong Opinions*, p. 3. In his interview of June 5, 1962, Nabokov mentions that "my pleasures are the most intense known to man: writing and butterfly hunting."

8. See "Primal Scene and Misreading in Nabokov's *Lolita*." According to Ingham, Nabokov's version of Victor X and his parody of "Little Red Riding Hood" displace the Wolf Man, while evoking Freud's narration that the Wolf Man's sister liked to frighten him by showing an illustration of the wolf in an edition of "Little Red Riding Hood" (2002, 35, 36, 38).

9. Alfred Jr. Appel, ed., *The Annotated Lolita*, by Vladimir Nabokov, 1991, p. 325. Appel calls attention in *Pale Fire* to Kinbote's notes to line 57, where Shade crossed out the following lines in the draft. "The light is good; the reading lamps, long-necked; / All doors have keys. Your modern architect / Is in collusion with psychoanalysts: When planning parents' bedrooms, he insists / On lockless doors so that, when looking back, / The future patient of the future quack / May find, all set for him, the Primal Scene." See also the traces of the Wolf Man in *Pale Fire*, pp. 32, 40, 60, 97, 103, 181-82.

10. Tulving et al. (1997) refer to the unique capacities of human consciousness as "autonoetic consciousness," and affirm its location to be in the most recently evolved portion of the brain (335).

SIX

Pale Fire

Analyze Me If You Can[1]

Toward the end of *Lolita*, as Humbert continues his fruitless search for the missing nymphet, he recalls an essay he once published in an academic journal. The essay, titled "Mimir and Memory," deals with "a theory of perceptual time based in the circulation of the blood," which depends upon "the mind's being conscious not only of matter but also of its own self" (LO 237). Significantly, the essay describes time as a continuous spanning of two points: the storable future and the stored past. Two aspects of Humbert's scholarly discourse seem especially relevant. First, his comments reflect the artistic evolution of the author (or narrator), while showcasing the ways in which this development parallels the natural phenomenon of *metamorphosis*, in which caterpillars emerge as butterflies. Secondly, they call to mind the systems of memory and cognition formulated in James's *The Principles of Psychology*, particularly the chapter titled "Perception of Time" (2010, 1: 403–405).

It is worth noting that James's theory of memory is not inconsistent with Freud's mnemic system, illustrated through an analogy featuring the two components of "the mystic writing-pad." Yet, Nabokov purposefully ignores Freud's theoretical exploration of memory and instead focuses on his tendency toward generalization, especially in the areas of sexuality, mythology, and symbolism, which Freud regarded as essential to a doctor's analysis of a patient. For Nabokov, the talking cure serves as a springboard to attack the Cartesian absolutism he perceived beneath the umbrella of Freudian sexuality. At the same time, his embrace of James's concept of the perception of time enables him to cope with the mischievous, playful, and deceptive elements of memory and cognition. In this regard, *Pale Fire* replicates a pattern found in many of his works.

When it appeared in 1962, critics regarded *Pale Fire* as an unusually complex novel that was open to a wide range of interpretations.[2] In a manner consistent with the organization of a scientific work, the novel comprises four parts: a foreword, a collection of four cantos composed by John Shade, commentaries on these poems by a critic called Charles Kinbote, and an index. The question posed by many readers is, "Who wrote the foreword, commentary, and index—Nabokov or Kinbote?" Indeed, the boundary between the author and protagonist is blurred from the outset, while the characters Shade and Kinbote not only resemble each other, but also remind us of someone else—Nabokov, himself. The textual complications of *Pale Fire* exceed those of *Lolita*, in which a psychiatrist edits Humbert's confession, while Nabokov subverts this confession through the addition of an afterword. *Pale Fire* features a complex series of camouflages and deceptions. At the beginning of the novel, the poet, Shade, is shot to death by an assassin who was actually targeting someone else, and his neighbor, Kinbote, seizes the opportunity to edit the dead man's poem. As the editor notes, however, all of the three main characters—the poet, the assassin, and the commentator—share a birthday, and we are left to conclude that they are facets of a single individual. We are ultimately left to resolve the dichotomy between Shade's reference to "*Man's life as commentary to abstruse unfinished poem*" (ll: 939–940) and Kinbote's observation that the assassin's journey was *synchronized with* Shade's composition of his poems. What are we to make of the apparent discrepancy in linear time—before and after—that reveals itself when examining the work of art and the critical commentaries inspired by it, which emerge almost simultaneously?

Any reasonable effort to resolve this problem must depend, to some extent, on James's concept of the perception of time, which suggests memories of the past are inseparable from perceptions of the present, in the same way that perceptions of the present depend upon stored memories of the past. Notably, James's model of memory and cognition is informed by a continuous spanning of two points—the stored past and the storable future—in a manner aptly reflected in Shade's poem and Kinbote's commentary. In this model, the past and the present do not conform to linear time. On the contrary, they are superimposed upon each other, even as we are *experiencing* them. For time exists only as *duration* in our perception, given that the present moment is too brief for us to truly grasp. Mary McCarthy's contention that "all genuine works contain pre-cognitions of other works or reminiscences of them" (1982, 134) is essentially correct, but her observation is nevertheless deceptive, given that time exists in dualistic form—in mechanical linear time and perceptive time, as though Freud's generalization were intertwined with Nabokov's insistence on the particular. However, since Nabokov adopts James's view of the dimension of *experience*, while at the same time attacking the idea of generalization prior to experience, it would appear that Kinbote's perspective (far more than Shade's) coincides with that of Nabokov.

In our perception, the world exists in a state of endless modification, or as James called it, the stream of thought. Things, people, and institutions are perceived amid the flux of constant change, for, as Heraclitus put it, we can never step into the same stream twice. Therefore, contrary to the Cartesian concept of generalization, our consciousness is inherently fictional, and its duration only compounds that fictional quality, moving inexorably in the direction of a fairy tale. Hence, James writes that "remoter dates are conceived, not perceived" (2010, 1: 436). Grounded upon the magic of memory and cognition, *Pale Fire* reflects a renovated form of *deception* that is the essence of mimicry and memory. In the same way that deceptive memory deepens amid the flow of time, this work of fiction becomes increasingly deceptive. The reader finds it more and more difficult to distinguish Freud from Nabokov, as the boundaries separating them are blurred, while their identities become almost interchangeable. If we are to understand Nabokov's strategy, we must be alert to the moment in which each character's metamorphosis occurs. At that point, we discern Nabokov's own voice emanating from a camouflaged character. To vanquish the ideology of resemblance, the author employs the tactic of resemblance, in which contingency—or chance—lurk in the background, only to expose crucial differences at a precise moment. Now, let us commence the game with the multifaceted Nabokov, in an effort to reveal his tactics. If we are able to address this challenge successfully, we may be in a position to ask the following question: "Isn't Freud's concept of *transference* similar to that of 'pale fire'?"

THE SHADOW OF RESEMBLANCE AS IN *TROMPE L'OEIL*

In the Foreword, Kinbote boastfully describes his friendship with his neighbor, Shade, a celebrated poet and professor. He then provides a detailed explanation of the circumstances that enabled him to edit Shade's unfinished poem. We learn that the poet had been murdered by Jack Grey, an escapee from an insane asylum who planned to shoot down one Judge Goldsworth, the man who had him committed. In short, the shooter mistakenly killed the poet, who happened to be walking toward the judge's house, and also bore a striking resemblance to the intended victim. This initial account of the murder will be complicated and undermined in Kinbote's subsequent commentary, where he describes the killer as one Jakob Gradus, a political assassin. This apparent discrepancy, along with others, sheds light on the author's intentions. We eventually learn that Kinbote, who rented the house of the absent Judge Goldsworth (interestingly, Nabokov also rented the house of a colleague who was on leave), engaged in an unsuccessful effort to save the poet. This thwarted act of heroism enables him to gain the trust of the poet's widow, Sybil, who supplies Kinbote with the manuscript of her husband's last poem. Against her wishes, Kinbote sets out to edit and annotate the poem, reinserting portions that describe the (fictional) kingdom of Zembla, which Shade had removed and Sybil hoped to suppress. Outraged, Sybil condemns Kinbote as "an elephantine tick; a king-sized botfly; a macaco worm; the monstrous parasite of a genius" (PF 171–172). Behind this verbal abuse we sense the voice of the author, who showed little patience for those who sought to attach themselves to accomplished artists.[3]

While Kinbote might be expected to treat the original manuscript with reverence, he instead takes liberties with it, reinserting excised passages and adding material of his own. Ultimately, his annotated and edited version of the poem is ten times longer than the original. Throughout the novel, Nabokov casts doubt on the objectivity (and veracity) of literary criticism. At the same time, *Pale Fire* can be read as comic mimicry of analytical discourse, in which the analyst projects his own experiences upon those of the patient. In a larger sense, we could interpret this peculiar work of art as an attempt to capture the arbitrary nature of reality, in line with James's contention that our perceptions are deeply informed by personal experiences. If indeed our thoughts and perceptions are overwhelmingly shaped by our experiences, it would be unavoidable for an author to transgress the boundaries of his characters, inserting his or her own views and drawing heavily on personal experience. In other words, characters are shadowed by the author's intentions, in one way or another and to varying degrees. At this point, it seems appropriate to explore the shadows of resemblance—and difference—within Nabokov's *trompe l'oeil*.

Resemblance

Shade's poem opens with the following line: "I was the shadow of the waxwing slain/ By the false azure in the windowpane" (ll. 1–2). The poem continues with a description of the manner in which the evening light and nighttime scenery are reflected upon the windowpane: a process in which interior and exterior appear to merge. Thus, the poem begins with a blurring of reality and reflection, along with a blurring of view and viewer. Indeed, the windowpane appears to symbolize our consciousness, the boundary between stored memory and the outside world, in the context of thinking and remembering. These opening lines signify that humans, as the subjects of memory, are little more than shadows that die and are reborn every moment. Yet, we are compelled to question the poet's capacity to predict his own future as a shadow—in essence, to foresee his own murder. Does this anachronism suggest a blurring between slayer and slain? Before addressing such questions, though, we should examine the circumstances leading up to Kinbote's acquisition of Shade's poem.

We learn that Shade was sixty-one years old when he died, leaving behind 999 lines of an unfinished poem. Kinbote, just forty-five years old when he transgresses the boundary between view and viewer (as well as model and mimic), adds the one-thousandth line, which is identical to the first at the end of commentary. We are informed that Shade had been troubled by insomnia and often used index cards to prepare for the composition of his poems. His forty-year marriage to Sybil had been a happy one, and he often referred to his wife as "my dark Vanessa," a reference to an exquisite, crimson-barred butterfly. He was particularly drawn to her during times when she was surrounded by Nature, including the trees and grass bordering their home. Interestingly, these qualities overlap with those generally associated with Nabokov—his insomnia, his reliance on index cards, his Lepidoptera, and his acute appreciation of Nature.

Yet, for all the acclaim he had received as a poet, Shade was preoccupied by unsettling memories of his deceased daughter, Hazel, whose homeliness prevented her from finding either friends or lovers. Shade was especially distressed by a school play in which his daughter was selected to play the role of Mother Time as "a bent charwoman with slop pail and broom" (II, 313). Interestingly, we discern in descriptions of Hazel telling traces of Kinbote, and even Nabokov himself, both of whom are solitary figures who fail to bond with colleagues and neighbors. Such isolated characters are commonplace in Nabokov's fiction. Notable examples include Smurov in *Eye*, Felix in *Despair*, Humbert in *Lolita*, as well as Aqua and Lucette in *Ada*. All of these characters are, to some degree, contained within the ghost of Hazel, who is the shadow of an exile. (Nabokov, of course, understood the nature of exile, given his experiences in Western Europe, the United States, and a Russia that stood on the brink of revolution.) In the course of Hazel's exile from life, she functions as an emblem of a lost childhood that is closely linked to fantasies of another world. In the case of Humbert, this attachment to a childhood fantasy world is expressed through his uncontrollable longing for the nymphet. In the case of Kinbote, the phenomenon is evident in his extreme identification with Zembla and its deposed king.

Significantly, as we pore over Shade's poem, we feel an urge to trace the author's shadow within his various characters. Indeed, as the cantos move forward, the shadow of Nabokov becomes more pronounced. It expresses itself in his characters' intentions, particularly their hostility to Freud. Before going further, however, let us examine the hidden message beyond Hazel's ghost. Notably, we learn that the tragic drowning of his daughter compelled Shade to meditate on the meaning of human existence. Swept away by the melancholy and tenderness of human life, he concluded that oblivion is an essential part of this phenomenon. He then determined that life itself is little more than a message scribbled in the dark. After all, who can deny that "our best yesterdays are now foul piles," while Shade himself might well reemerge as "a floweret, or a fat fly"? Inexorably drawn to the death that resides within life, he decides that one way out of such transience is to achieve immortality through art. Only through art can he insulate himself from the all-encompassing sorrow resulting from the loss of his child, which was compounded by his awareness of the "nothingness" of life. The tool required to grasp the fleeting moments of life is none other than the faculty of imagination, which plays a crucial role in our recollection of the past. Memory offers the magic of deception, and Shade poetically describes it as the *domestic ghost*. It has the power to focus him artistically, and he writes perceptively of "the shadow of the waxwing slain by feigned remoteness." So, the question is, "If our memory flows like a dream, how is it possible to interpret this dream by means of generalizing myths and symbols?" The poet rejects this possibility, writing, "For as we know from dreams it is so hard / To speak to our dear dead! They disregard / Our apprehension, queaziness and shame" (ll. 589–591).

Over time, Shade ceases to lament the limited mortal existence of his daughter and comes to appreciate her seeming gift for communicating through anagrams and riddles, one of which appears intended to warn him of his impending death. Gennady Barabtarlo suggests that the message delivered by the so-called barn ghost is a warning "not to go to Goldsworth's," which had been issued to Shade by his aunt's spirit (1993, 208).[4] Finally, we come across such lines as "Hurricane/Lolita swept from Florida to Maine" (ll. 679–680), which are bound to confuse the reader, while amusing the *rereader*. Such lines are closely associated with Hazel's ghost, the symbol of childhood memory, who is playful and mischievous, much like the nymphet in *Lolita*, the King in *Pale Fire*, and Annabel Lee in Poe's haunting poem. Such deceptive flourishes are a source of delight, but they also contribute to the evolution of a character, as Shade is gradually unmasked as Freud and, finally, as Nabokov, himself. If Lolita serves as the ghost of Annabel Lee, an object of overwhelming desire, Charles Kinbote, who believes he is a banished king, functions as the ghost of Hazel, an exile from the remote kingdom of Zembla. From this perspective, it does not seem surprising that Shade (as a proxy for Nabokov) raises questions about Dostoevsky and Freud in a four-line poetic passage: "Fra Karamazov, mumbling his inept / *All is allowed*, into some classed crept; / and to fulfill the fish wish of the womb, / A school of Freudians headed for the tomb" (ll. 641–644). Those four lines are apt to be overlooked by readers of a larger passage that focuses on a father's grief for his deceased daughter. However, if we read the lines carefully, in the context of Freud's analysis of the Russian novelist in "Dostoevsky and Parricide" (1928), it seems apparent that Nabokov has used Shade for his own purposes.

In his essay, Freud acknowledges that Dostoevsky was a great writer. While he may have been dissolute and neurotic, Dostoevsky was nevertheless a firm moralist. Indeed, the novelist was so sensitive to repressed instincts that he appears to have suffered from sadomasochistic drives, reflected in inveterate gambling, chronic debt, and occasional *fits* (the apparent product of *epilepsy*). Freud analyzed those symptoms in the context of repressed infantile sexuality arising from the Oedipus complex. According to Freud's analysis, the young Dostoevsky, in response to erotic feelings toward his mother, fantasized about murdering his father while, at the same time, fearing that his father would castrate him in revenge. In turn, he sought to compromise with reality by choosing to be a man like his father. For a creative figure like Dostoevsky, however, repressing this instinct proved too difficult. Hence, the continual return of these impulses spurred masochistic responses such as violent fits. For Dostoevsky, the composition of novels proved the only way out of an unresolved conflict between the competing impulses of parricide and abject guilt.

Similarly, Freud attributed the homosexual impulses of the Wolf Man to an internal conflict over whether to embrace the masculinity of his father (a move toward heterosexuality) or the femininity of his mother (a move toward homosexuality). Meanwhile, he places the parricide of Dostoevsky's Karamazov brothers in the context of the Greek tragedy of Oedipus, as well as the British tragedy of Hamlet, both of which involve the slaying of a father or paternal figure. In terms of chronological age, the accomplished Shade is old enough to be the father to Kinbote, a less elevated figure who views him with mixed feelings of envy, hatred, and admiration. Indeed, Kinbote's creation of Gradus reveals his impulse to function as a king-killer. At the same time, Shade's understated lines concerning the Karamazov brothers are closely related to two questions: "Is Kinbote truly a homosexual, or does he simply mimic one?" "Is sexuality the sole impulse that prompts Kinbote to imitate parricide?" All of these details seem to be elements of a larger plan that Nabokov assembled in order to mimic Freud, an issue I will return to later.

In our exploration of resemblance, we will next focus on the Nabokovian *primal scene*, contrasting it with its Freudian counterpart. It seems natural to begin with a reference to the poet's heart attack, which (like his periodic fits) brings about a "temporary death." At this point, the author's effort to manipulate the character becomes more evident. We learn that the date of Shade's heart attack, October 7, 1958, coincides with that of Kinbote's departure for America. While in a trance-like state, Shade spies a towering white fountain that flows in a strange and unfamiliar world. He also encounters examples of deception that occur in nature: "the reed becomes a bird, the knobby twig / An inchworm, and the cobra head, a big / Wickedly folded moth" (ll. 713–15). When he regains consciousness, Shade continues to replay this strange vision within his mind, especially the striking image of the white fountain, along with the fresh vision of biological mimicry.

During his recovery, he comes across a magazine article concerning a "Mrs. Z," who reportedly lost consciousness but recovered due to a surgeon's deft intervention. Upon regaining consciousness, the woman indicated that, during her unconscious state, she found herself in a remote landscape, wandering through a mysterious orchard. Shortly after catching a glimpse of a tall white fountain situated beyond the orchard, she suddenly awoke. Not surprisingly, Shade immediately identifies with the woman's experience: "our fountain was a signpost and a mark / Objectively enduring in the dark, / Strong as a bone, substantial as a tooth, / And almost vulgar in its robust truth!" (ll. 763–766). Notably, though, the story includes one misprint, which has enormous significance for Shade (the disguised Nabokov). According to the article, the woman did not encounter a fountain, but instead a *mountain*. Despite the seemingly minor nature of the typo, Shade understands that it radically changes the story: "Life Everlasting—based on a misprint!"(II, 803). Ultimately, he comes to recognize that resemblance or generalization is impossible, for contingency is the kernel of life. Is this not "the contrapuntal theme" of the Freudian primal scene?

> Just this: not text, but texture; not the dream
> But topsy-turvical coincidence,
> Not flimsy nonsense, but a web of sense.
> Yes ! It sufficed that I in life could find
> Some kind of link-and-bobolink, some kind
> Of correlated pattern in the game,
> Plexed artistry, and something of the same
> Pleasure in it as they who played it found.

(ll. 808–815)

This awakening enables Shade to grasp that the essence of the primal scene is contingency not resemblance, a mischievous game not sexuality, and a multiplied self not a stable identity. Indeed, this situation reminds us of Smurov, the protagonist of *Eye*, who not only sees himself as detached from the world, but also views a multiplied version of himself on stage following the experience of a temporary death. Significantly, the new vision of self that Shade secures (through Nabokov's manipulation) is not only theatrical but also artistic, so that he can "speak of evil as none has spoken before" (ll. 923–924).

It seems apparent that it is none other than Nabokov who dismisses Freud and Marx as "fake" thinkers, yet his voice is merged with that of the editor, Kinbote, who sets out to insert the story of Zembla into the commentary on Shade's poem.[5] We cannot help but ask, "Who is writing those lines, then?" Ultimately, as we move further into the poem and commentary, it becomes more difficult to identify the author, for three distinct voices are mingled together. Indeed, the poet, commentator, and author are barely distinguishable when Shade writes that "only through my art in terms of combinational delight . . . my darling is alive somewhere (my abbreviation, ll. 973–978). *My darling* could signify Hazel for the poet, the old Kingdom for Kinbote, and Vyra for Nabokov. Overall, they signify the essence of a lost childhood. Yet, if Kinbote represents author and the author manipulates Shade, what is the point of commentary, if it is not designed to help us differentiate three voices from among the resemblances?

Differences

The poem is written in heroic couplets, the dominant form of eighteenth-century Neoclassicism, the period of Samuel Johnson, in which human imagination and fantasy were restrained in favor of "objective" reason. Thus, formality and an idealized view of the world dominate Shade's poem, even though a metamorphosis occurs in its later passages. Shade comes across as decent and decidedly heterosexual. He is a widely admired poet who idealizes his wife and cherishes his family. His writing style makes an appeal to universality, while at the same time reflecting current social norms, along with the poet's willingness to be reined in by average people and institutions. In contrast, Kinbote's commentary is brimming with private fantasies, all of which are informed by cruelty, political confusion, contingency, and deception. Acutely aware of the difference, Kinbote claims that, in the absence of his notes, Shade's poem would lack genuine humanity. As Michael Seidel notes, the narrative supplement Kinbote provides takes a variety of forms, enriching a wide array of events, including the death of Shade as well as the primal scene (1984, 854). Unlike the exiled Kinbote, Shade is in perfect command of his native tongue, and he is able to tone down his language, eliminating all references to the Zemblan theme, which his wife sought to censor. Overall, the two literary men are a study in contrast. If one demonstrates a genuine affection for Sybil, the other shows a deceptive longing for Disa. Indeed, they represent different degrees of faith in Freud—and beyond that, differing forms of childhood memory.

Presumably, *Zembla* is supposed to remind the reader of Russia. Not only does its very name call to mind the word *resemblance*, but, like Russia, Zembla has apparently experienced a communist revolution, although Mary McCarthy and Alfred Appel differ somewhat on this issue.[6] For Alvin Kernan, the name Zembla is nothing less than a form of Semberland—a "land of resemblers" (1987, 113). It is a country from which Kinbote had been forced to escape in disguise (echoing the manner in which Nabokov departed from revolutionary Russia), as well as the site of a political system that reveres the ideal of resemblance, which Nabokov took pains to criticize in *Despair*. In certain ways, Nabokov's literary career appears to involve a relentless attack on the popular faith in resemblance, along with the public's reverence for Freudian generalization. We learn that, despite its benign rhetoric, Zembla's policies are informed by cruelty, cynicism, and materialism. The Zemblan government, for instance, has organized a secret band of assassins to murder fugitive members of the country's royal family.

Notably, the commentary opens with the departure from Zembla of would-be regicide Jakob Gradus, who is determined to track down the exiled monarch, Charles the Beloved. Gradus's journey is seamlessly integrated into the notes on Shade's original poem; and in an ironic twist, the assassin's mistaken shooting of the poet inextricably links poem and commentary, producing a unified work of art. Unlike the poet, who appeals to the images and sensations of our day-to-day lives, the commentator's text is characterized by the sensual imagery of an unfettered (decidedly lascivious) imagination. We learn that John and Sybil Shade were married for forty years, since they met when they were high-school students. Shade evidently viewed Sybil as an ideal woman, whom he associated with flowers, trees, and the natural landscape. He referred to her as "my dark Vanessa," in a tone reflecting respect and admiration. Shade often observed that the Old English name, Vanessa, translates as the Red Admirable, one of the few butterflies with which Kinbote became familiar during his formative years in the palace garden. In Zembla, Vanessa was known to have appeared at the moment of the king's death, and it seems significant that it makes an appearance shortly before Shade's murder. For the poet, dark Vanessa is an erotic object. For Kinbote, on the other hand, it represents Gradus, the killer. Yet, in a curious way, Vanessa also represents Kinbote himself, whose deceptiveness and playfulness call to mind the mimicry of a butterfly.

The profound differences between Kinbote and the poet are exemplified by Kinbote's curious devotion to the queen, Disa. While he was never particularly drawn to her during the time when they were together, she has come to dominate his dreams during their separation. In short, as a real object, Disa failed to excite his passion. Nevertheless, she has been elevated and idealized in Kinbote's memory, in much the same way that Sybil will be idealized in Shade's poem. Hence, Shade's poetic image of Sybil bears an interesting comparison to Kinbote's dream image of Disa. Yet, Disa's real-life affection for Kinbote consistently generated cold, indifferent responses from him. Only in exile—with Disa in France, and Kinbote in America—do their mutual feelings of attraction flourish. It is almost as though the author were reflecting on his own memories of his European exile. Kinbote observes that, without an appreciation of the strangeness of dreams as reality, "there is no sense in writing poems, or notes to poems, or anything at all" (PF 207). Significantly, Nabokov was quite proficient at this sort of longing in the absence of a lover, and he

had more than his share of painful regrets. In his view, a man is essentially a dreamer, and sex has little to do with this kind of longing in absence—a situation Nabokov explored in *The Luzhin Defense*. Interestingly,
when Kinbote requests that Shade attempt to describe this fleeting and
wistful dream in verses, the poet responds, rather pointedly, "how can
you know that all this intimate stuff about your rather appalling king is
true?" Kinbote, however, contends that "true art is above false honor"
(PF 214).

The two characters' differing opinions on Freud are paralleled by their
decidedly different approaches to love. When editing and commenting
on Shade's poem, Kinbote amplifies what appears to be a mild distaste
for Freud, transforming it into a bitter repudiation. He accomplishes this
by restoring deleted portions of the poem, while inserting his own edito-
rial comments. If we examine the lines Shade supposedly eliminated
from the unfinished draft of his poem, it becomes clear that Nabokov was
familiar with Freud's Wolf Man analysis: "Your modern architect / Is in
collusion with psychoanalysis: / When planning parents' bedrooms, he
insists / On lockless doors so that, when looking back,/ The future patient
of the future quack / May find, all set for him, the Primal Scene"(94). *The
Primal Scene* that Kinbote presents is one in which architectural and social
arrangements permit a child to freely spy on his parents during their
private moments. Well-versed on dream analysis, Kinbote disputes
Freud's suggestion that his patient's trauma is rooted in a childhood
incident in which he peered into his parents' room as they engaged in
intercourse—a situation hard to imagine in the highly compartmental-
ized environment of a Russian aristocratic home such as that in which the
Wolf Man was raised. As noted in the previous chapter, Freud conceived
of the primal scene and at the same time downplayed it, asserting that the
patient may have developed such a fantasy while reading children's
books dealing with animal stories. Ultimately, Kinbote's apparent obsession with the constructive reality of psychoanalysis may reflect an impulse to simultaneously imitate and repudiate Freud—not for the sake of
sexuality but for the sake of art. If so, it is not surprising to learn that he
spied on Shade's bedroom, almost as though he were mimicking the Wolf
Man, who purportedly spied on his parents. At the same time, this symp-
tomatic resemblance belies different causes and different solutions. For
Nabokov, the ultimate purpose behind any imitation of sexuality is to
move toward an artistic brand of immorality in which science and art
merge seamlessly.

Overall, sexuality and generalization surface as the most attractive
elements for Nabokov as he focuses on Freud as both model and target.
Sexuality is treated as a humorous, real, and essential ingredient of life
and literature, while generalization emerges as the target in a concerted
attack on totalitarianism. Throughout, Kinbote disguises himself as a
Freud prototype, only to undermine psychoanalysis with a series of jokes

and hidden meanings. As a professor at an American university, Kinbote delights in debunking the work of supposedly learned scholars: "the analytic teacher knows that the appetite of the lustful one knows no limit in his phantasies," so that "the little cap of red velvet in the German version of Little Red Riding Hood is a symbol of menstruation. Do those clowns really believe what they teach?" (PF 271).[7] As McCarthy noted, this comment stands in memorable contrast to Kinbote's decision, as he escapes from Zembla, to don a red cap and sweater, in order to disguise himself as an actor or a bird. Drawing upon Shade's fresh vision of natural mimicry, acquired when he was unconscious (ll. 710–715), McCarthy interprets the exiled king's red cap and sweater as the markings of a bird, placing them in the context of both "natural shams, so-called protective mimicry" and "the impersonation of an actor" (1982, 131). Substituting the "red cap running" for the "red hood riding," Kinbote cleverly conveys his impatience with the enthusiastic musings of psychoanalytic theory.

Yet, Kinbote expands his scope beyond infantile sexuality, moving on to targets such as Freudian homosexuality and the Oedipus complex, in each case employing exceptional cunning and subtle mimicry. Interestingly, he never touches upon the sexual lives of Shade's deceased parents, indicating their early deaths left the poet with no memories of them (PF 100). Accordingly, his own early childhood memories bear no connection to either the Oedipus complex or primal scene. His father's absent-mindedness was combined with a passion for mechanical things, and upon his death, Kinbote felt no erotic desire for his mother. He was largely content in his living arrangements with his mother and sister, unlike the situation of the Wolf Man, who was supposedly caught up in an Oedipus triangle involving his sister: "she did not seem to mind when he abandoned her for manlier pleasures" (109). Yet, an important question remains: "Is Kinbote (Charles the beloved) truly homosexual?" We are left to wonder if his passionate love-hate relationship with the poet stems from a thwarted homosexual impulse. This assumption is seemingly supported by the revelation that Kinbote had no sexual interest in his mother, sister, or indeed other women. Even his devotion to Disa is curiously devoid of any sexual feeling. Instead, he has engaged in adventures and games with his male roommate, a situation that leads the ever-intrusive countess to bribe an elderly psychiatrist, who in turn, seeks to persuade Kinbote that his engagement in sodomy contributed to his mother's death, and would continue to undermine his memories of her. While some critics conclude that Kinbote is a genuine homosexual, it is also possible that he mimics this lifestyle in order to misdirect the reader from his larger goal: to mimic Freud.

Early critics like Page Stegner have interpreted Kinbote as a vegetarian and homosexual intellectual (1966, 126), while Peter Welsen concluded that he is a psychotic whose condition resulted from repressed homosexuality. Adding the possibility of a persecution complex and highlighting the role of Shade as a father figure, Welsen closely adheres to a classical Freudian perspective. At the same time, however, he ponders the possibility that Kinbote's sexuality is camouflage designed to conceal another purpose: "In spite of his psychosis, Kinbote is highly intelligent, and his commentary is by no means the nonsensical product of a deranged mind but a most intricately structured sublimation of the unconscious conflicts of a creative paranoiac" (1989, 389). More recently, Steven Belletto (2006), among others, has read Kinbote's homosexuality as part of a politically charged homophobic narrative.[8] Meanwhile, in his essay, "Homophobia," Eric Naiman draws a parallel between reading Nabokov and experiencing homosexuality, a phenomenon that is curiously aggressive and submissive, all at once (2008, 139). In a position that dovetails with my own proposal, Tony Sharpe places homosexuality in the broader context of "a rising arc of illicit sexual behavior, from Humbert's nympholepsy, through Kinbote's pederasty, to Van and Ada's incest" in Nabokov's sexual orgy (1991, 79). Significantly, as Maurice Couturier notes, even though Nabokov purports to despise Freud's theory of the unconscious, he demonstrates remarkable creativity in his treatment of the issue of sexual identity, from *Lolita* to *Ada* (1999, 68). At the same time, Kinbote never describes any cause for his apparent homosexuality, and as Stephen Blackwell observes, there is no attempt to depict this lifestyle realistically (2009, 131).

Indeed, *Pale Fire* concludes with the exposure of the narrator, Botkin (an anagram of Kinbote), who is revealed to be "an old, happy, healthy, heterosexual Russian, a writer in exile" (PF 300–301). This puts the reader in mind of the conclusion of *Lolita*, in which Humbert declares that sex is merely an ancillary to art. It would appear that Kinbote's homosexuality is simply one of many Freudian masquerades that Nabokov employs to deceive his opponent and "win" the game. Viewed from this context, the similarities between Nabokov and Freud appear less significant. We should instead focus on the ways in which Nabokov *recreates* Freud for his own purposes. One of the author's most exceptional devices involves the manner in which Kinbote recasts the character of Gradus, who is transformed from an addled asylum escapee to a political assassin.

DURATION OF TIME OR DEATH IN MEMORY: GRADUS

Before investigating the issue of Gradus's identity, we should examine one further difference between the poem and commentary. As noted, the two literary men are diametrically opposed: one is a rational, orderly, and respected poet, while the other is a mad, eccentric, and devious editor. David Galef observes that "where Hazel's art [by the poet] is solipsistic, Kinbote's creation is megalomaniac" (1985, 426). This view gains strength when we consider that Kinbote has invented Gradus, the assassin who is determined to murder the king in exile. He goes so far as to suggest that his fear of the assassin motivated him to spy on Shade. There is no question that the seemingly invented Gradus plays a critical role in the linking of the two heuristic literary men in a single text, *Pale Fire*. The source of Kinbote's fantasy appears to have roots in the earlier experiences of Nabokov, who once remarked that a sad and distant kingdom appeared to have haunted his poetry and fiction since the 1920s (Johnson and Proffer, 1991, 75). Significantly, the more generic ghost of Hazel pales before that of King Charles, who is vividly drawn and firmly positioned on the ground of political turmoil. The regicide Zemblans are recalled as cruel and murderous: "those perilous nights in my country where at any moment, a company of jittery revolutionists might enter and hustle me off to a moonlit wall" (PF 96). In a sense, Gradus is the fearsome shadow of Kinbote's past and the present, and he may be the catalyst who determines the sort of writer he becomes.

We learn that Kinbote has been plagued by hallucinations since his dramatic escape from a prison in Revolutionary Zembla, which was made possible by forty of his followers. He retains clear memories of two of those followers: Odon, a palace actor who helped him to escape captivity by leading him to the outskirts of the country, and Oleg, a playmate and bedfellow who spurred the king's memory of a secret door *by chance*. In search of playthings, the prisoner, the king, found "in the back of the closet, a keyhole to which the same gilt key was found to fit" (125). *Thirty years ago*, with Oleg, he had entered that door and discovered a long underground thoroughfare: a memory that has become critical in the wake of the Revolution. To deceive the guard, however, the king had to don a red cap and red sweater, while Odon concealed him within a crowd of one hundred clowns. "Feigning a causal stroll," he arrived at a place he had once visited as a member of the royal family. Odon, as an actor, proves adept at disguising himself, too, alternately assuming the roles of an Extremist or Merman.

In his recollection of the escape, we can discern the essence of Nabokov's art. When we encounter the actor Odon, he secures the king's freedom by employing disguises. He shows an instinct to be someone else, creating a structure in which he can hide and multiply himself. Thomas Karshan calls attention to this *theatrical self* and quotes Winnicott as follows: "the urgent need to communicate and the still more urgent need not to be found" (2011, 105). On the other hand, the bedfellow Oleg is the playmate who inadvertently leads the king to discover the secret door and the underground tunnel. Notably, the key to freedom is discovered by chance, *contingency*, thereby undermining the routine searches of the Extremists. Finally, we encounter the most significant symbol of the king's exile in the image of the migratory butterfly: a resonant symbol for

Nabokov, given his wanderings through Europe and America. (In interviews, Nabokov would repeatedly compare himself to a butterfly.)

Throughout the novel, the butterfly is a constant motif. The Vanessa Atalanta that settles on Shade's sleeve at the time of his death is often referred to as "the Red Admirable," or "the Butterfly of doom." Notably, it made an appearance in Russia in 1881, at the time of the tsar's death. Like many migratory butterflies, it swept across the countryside, its coloring so vivid that Nabokov often struggled to describe it. Ultimately, his attempts to delineate the butterfly's beauty (like his attempts to reconstruct his lost homeland) struck him as *pale and false* (SO 136). Indeed, it is impossible to recapture the colors of our past since our consciousness is a blend of memory-traces, much *like a plum pudding in which the ingredients cannot be sorted out* (SO 192). The symbol of this elusive butterfly is consistently evoked. The barn ghost warns Shade that Kinbote is the Red Admirable, the butterfly of doom, who will be an attendant at the poet's death.[9] Yet, the actual killer is Gradus, so he, too, is associated with the butterfly. This leads us to question the identity of Gradus, but it becomes clear that the answer will not be straightforward. His identity is a jumble of contradictions, given that he is simultaneously a regicide, a mask of Kinbote, and a catalyst of contingency.

Critics differ widely in their interpretation of *Pale Fire*. Andrew Field, for instance, viewed Shade as the sole author of the narrative, on the basis of his sanity. Meanwhile, Page Stegner suggested that Kinbote was the author, since his voice appears closest to that of the author. Conversely, Brian Boyd emphasized the importance of Gradus, since his approach to Shade gradually intensifies the narrative power of Kinbote as a mask of the author (1997, 200). Notably, Gradus means "degree" in Russian. While his name is given as Jakob Gradus, he refers to himself by a variety of pseudonyms, including Jack Degree, Jacques de Grey, or James de Gray. Perhaps this plethora of names is meant to suggest the changeable nature of identity within the flow of time, in a manner similar to Kinbote's multiplying identities. We learn that Gradus has been trained by the *Shadows*, as the Extremists call themselves, to assassinate the royal fugitive. Selected from the most hardened of prisoners and conditioned to function as a Shadow of Marx, Gradus is ordered to murder the exiled king, Charles Kinbote. Like Hermann in *Despair*, Gradus functions as a Cartesian devil who does not believe in chance or games. We learn that Gradus's spoken French is mediocre, his English worse, and his German merely fair (PF 199). While awaiting further orders in Nice, he shows little capacity to amuse himself in his spare time. When his wife leaves him, he engages in a sexual relationship with his mother-in-law, who turns out to be committed to an asylum. After reminding us of the incest taboo, Kinbote points out that Gradus is a worshipper of general ideas (152), adding that Zembla is a dangerous fraud (177). Once again alluding to fraud-Freud, Nabokov, grinning from behind Kinbote's mask, repudiates every species of generalization, in favor of consciousness in process.

As noted, the three characters share a birthday, and they begin their activities at the same time. Gradus, the Red Admirable, appears to serve as the kernel of Kinbote's creative capacity to counteract Shade, motivating the poet to write and, at the same time, dispense with versification. He is an emblem of death in memory, *Memento mori*, a constructing force of fantasy, as represented in Proustian prose. Proustian fantasy is only possible through the recollection of the past, and the more remote the past happens to be, the more distorted our recollections. In the case of Gradus, we learn that his search for the king initially takes him to Paris, where he encounters a potential source in a hotel lobby, solely by chance. His decision to break into Disa's house in search of letters that feature the king's address takes him to New York. Interestingly, Gradus's path corresponds with Nabokov's own travels in exile. Here, we should examine two crucial narrative devices. First, Gradus evidently represents the amount of time, or the *duration*, of exile, from Russia, Europe, and America. As James observes, we can only perceive time as duration, and its length has a significant impact on our memory and cognition. Secondly, Gradus's control by the Extremists ends at a certain point, and he is seemingly controlled by someone else. As he approaches the king's place, his behavior becomes more obtuse. In addition, he suffers continual digestive problems, and his efforts to locate the king on campus are continually hindered by those he encounters. Finally, he fires upon the exiled king but hits the hapless poet instead, almost as if he were drunk.

What happened to him in the course of his travels? It seems apparent that the old Shadows have lost their influence over him, and their place has been taken by an unknown X. This figure is almost certainly Kinbote, the lunatic who imagines he was the king. Martine Hennard makes this point when he states, "*Pale Fire* presents an ironic variation on the author's favorite image of the metamorphosis of the larva into a butterfly as an emblem for literary achievement" (1994, 303). Like Felix in *Despair*, Gradus is transformed from a blind killer to an agent of contingency, interfered with by his creator, Kinbote/Botkin/Nabokov.

From Insect Mimicry to Cosmic Mimicry

Through his addition of the commentary, Kinbote not only supersedes Shade in terms of the volume of text, but also in authority over the narrative. Indeed, he undermines the primacy of the poem by adding the thousandth line, which is identical to the first line of the Cantos. As a result, the linear form of the poem is altered into that of a circle. Interestingly, this circular form is intricately linked to a scene from Shakespeare's *Timon of Athens*. An exile from the city, Timon lives as a hermit in the desert, where he concludes that all things of the world reflect a cosmic selfishness and thievery (Act IV, Scene 3): "The sun is a thief: she lures the sea and robs it; The moon is a thief: he steals his silvery light from the sun; The sea is a thief: it dissolves the moon" (80). Why does Kinbote choose to quote these lines in his commentary? In this triangle of thievery, we discern two distinctive positions, including a fireside poet (Shade) as the sun (acme), and a cosmopolitan scholar (Kinbote) as the moon (right), since the latter steals the light of the former. This prompts the question, "Who is the third (left), the sea?" As we have continually perceived Nabokov's voice emanating from behind the mask of Kinbote, it seems clear that the sea represents Nabokov, who dissolves the moon that robs the sun. In turn, the sun robs the sea, i.e., Shade steals Nabokov, or Nabokov permits him to use his voice ("my voice for his use"). We could regard this interplay of patterns as "the webs of sense," since it is clear that Shade has robbed the words from Nabokov. Rather than treating the three characters as three dimensions of one persistent presence, the author (or Shade, as some critics have asserted), it is possible to discern a dynamic circling of cosmic thievery.[10]

If we accept this structure, it becomes apparent that Shade, who is sixteen years older than Kinbote, plays the role of father to his son, Kinbote, calling to mind the model of the Oedipus complex. However, Nabokov has neatly transformed the relationship of father-mother-son into that of the sun-the moon-the sea—or Shade-Kinbote-Nabokov. The differences are important. First, the energy of this model does not depend on pan-sexuality, but instead, on cosmic stealing. Secondly, for Nabokov, the triangle does not take a solid form, but instead is reflected in an infinite circling: "In the spiral form, the circle, uncoiled, unwound has ceased to be vicious. It has been set free" (SM 275).

In this cosmic mimicry, the sea functions as the center of the circling. It is not only the entity that dissolves the moon that robbed the light of the sun, but it is also the origin of yet another cycle. In this context, we can appreciate Nabokov's contention that it makes little difference whether the narrator of the story is Shade or Kinbote, since the ultimate message resides in his claim of human memory (or art), in light of natural mimicry (like a dead-leaf butterfly). We are tempted to ask where Shade, too, is a butterfly. Kinbote/Gradus are compared to a migratory butterfly, the Vanessa. Shade, however, is not. In other words, Kinbote is a writer in exile, while Shade is not, and this difference affects their respective writing styles, memories, and approaches to fantasy. The writer in exile, as opposed to the poet living in his native land, is apt to be more imaginative—a position that Nabokov argued. Interestingly, this position was anticipated in James's concept of consciousness and time:

> To remember a thing as past, it is necessary that the notion of 'past' should be one of our 'ideas.' . . . To think a thing as past is to think it amongst the objects or in the direction of the objects which at the

present moment appear affected by this quality. This is the original of our notion of past time, upon which memory and history build their systems. (2010, 1:403, my abbreviation).

All consciousness is in the form of *time,* or that time is the form of feeling, the form of sensibility (2010, 1: 404).

Freud recognized that memories of the past are shaped by present experiences, given that consciousness and the memory-traces are mutually exclusive. Similarly, James observes that humans can never truly possess knowledge beyond that of the present moment. Differences exist only in the context of differing concerns. A doctor, for instance, might focus on the system of remembering, whereas a philosopher might concentrate on cognition. For Nabokov, as an artist, time is crucial to the production of culture and language. He notes that man possesses consciousness and time, while animals only have time. Significantly, time makes it possible for us to experience things infinitely, and as Donald Crosby argues in *The Philosophy of William James*, emotions contribute greatly to our systems of thought (2013, 6, 94). Indeed, we remember something far better when it is associated with powerful emotions, such as affection, hatred, or fear. The stronger the feeling, the greater the chance that we will have recurring images of an event. In truth, however, this image is the product of two layers of *superimposed* memory, which blend and reshape one another over the course of time, ensuring that our memory will be distorted and exaggerated.

In this context, the presence of the author is discontinuous, like a fleeting, evanescent shadow, and the work produced by an artist in exile becomes truly fantastic, as reflected in the case of Kinbote. James asserts that emotions or feelings are inseparable from thinking and judgment, thereby reinforcing their conviction and credibility. In addition, they are closely tied to the faith on which our lives depend, given that "we cannot live or think at all without some degree of faith" (Crosby, 2013, 95). An exile's longing for a time and place to which he can never return may transform him into a monster that imagines himself a king pursued by a killer. At the same time, it becomes evident that Shade's art, in the absence of this rich streak of magical madness, lacks humanity. The vestiges of past memory occupy his consciousness like pale fire, as he produces his commentary in the remote confines of a mountain cabin. Yet, this raises a question about the credibility of the primal scene, which may well be a fable constructed from distorted fragments of the distant past.

While Freud focuses on the system of memory when he seeks to interpret a patient's trauma, Nabokov concerns himself with consciousness and time. For both authors, memory involves a series of deceptive copies of an original experience. Overall, it constitutes a second event that has nothing to do with the initial event, except that it happens to resemble it. To help explain the subjective and ever-changing nature of memory and cognition, Freud introduced the concept of *transference* between the analyst and the patient. Nabokov, on the other hand, perceives this phenomenon as a product of the cosmic thievery of Nature. If we examine the act of mimicry in which the sea appears to dissolve the moon that has already robbed the sun of its light, we can discern the outlines of an analogy for the interaction of the main characters in *Pale Fire*. The sea functions as Nabokov, the author, while the moon represents Kinbote, one of the many disguises the author assumes. We could complete the analogy by identifying Shade with the sun.

Whatever the case, *Pale Fire* is a novel filled with flickering shadows. Notably, even Nabokov's interviews related to the work are puzzling, including his employment of the word, *Schadenfreude* (SO 220). He contends that the compound word characterizes his art, given that it literally means *hatred of Freud*. We are left to consider, though, whether this curious combination of "Shade" and "Freud" serves as yet another act of mimicry. Shade is a vestige whose murder is the product of feigned remoteness, that is, the childhood memory of Kinbote in exile. Even in his poetry, his authority begins to crumble before the influence of the unknown X, a butterfly in the process of transforming from a larva. As we seek to determine whether Shade is a mask of Freud or Nabokov, we discover that no clear border separates them, given that Shade assumes characteristics of both at different time. In short, the characters do not simply resemble the author and his perceived enemies. As Nabokov observes: "I am very careful to keep my characters beyond the limits of my own identity" (SO 13).

THE RIDDLE OF *SCHADENFREUDE*

In his commentary, Kinbote criticizes both Marx and Freud, contending that "the worst of two false doctrines is always that which is harder to eradicate." Shade responds: "No, Charlie, there are simpler criteria: Marxism needs a dictator, and a dictator needs a secret police, and that is the end of the world; but the Freudian, no matter how stupid, can still cast his vote at the poll, even if he is pleased to call it [smiling] *political pollination*" (PF 155–156). One could argue that Shade's opinion, in this case, overlaps with that of Nabokov, given his use of Freud within his literary work. As Peter Welsen observes, Nabokov "knows psychoanalysis, and, above all, he knows how to use it as an aesthetic device" (1989, 385). It is worth noting, however, that Nabokov's use of Freud is so subtle that, in some cases, Shade appears to serve as the proxy of Freud.

Before the barn ghost incident, a series of mysterious events take place at the poet's home. Since these incidents appear to be related to Sybil, the Shades decide to consult a psychiatrist, Dr. Sutton, despite the fact that they have reservations about him. Initially, Dr. Sutton's advice strikes them as preposterous. He contends that, if they shout at the ghost, it will disappear. As it turns out, his suggestion proves effective, and the ghost departs. In his introduction to this incident, Kinbote suggests that science and mysticism are not necessarily distinct approaches, since reason invariably leads us to the conclusion we wish to reach (PF 167). Evoking James's *will to believe*, Kinbote denies the claim that the Freudian talking cure operates within the realm of objectivity. Unlike Shade, the ghost of Hazel, given her preference for games and wordplay, rejects the talking cure and shouts, "why can't you leave people *alone*?" (192). If these examples are not enough to suggest that Shade periodically dons the mask of Freud—in opposition to Kinbote/Nabokov—we might consider another question.[11] Who is Judge Goldsworth, and how is he connected to the poet?

We learn that Kinbote has rented the house of a vacationing law professor, Judge Goldsworth, who had imprisoned many people and condemned others to death. While staying at the house, Kinbote discovers a scrapbook featuring short biographies of the criminals the judge had sentenced. In due course, he comes across the photograph of a homicidal maniac named Jack Grey, an escapee from the local mental institute who, as we later learn, is determined to avenge himself upon the barrister. In his commentary, Kinbote provides the murderer with a decidedly exotic background. An incarnation of the exile's fear of the assassin, Jack Grey, we are told, is actually Jakob Gradus, a foreigner and would-be regicide. In time, we secure two important pieces of information: Shade was killed because he closely resembled Judge Goldsworth, while at the same time, Kinbote persuaded the murderer to confess to "deceiving the police and nation by posing as Jack Grey, escapee from an asylum, who mistook Shade for the man who sent him there" (299). Nabokov implicitly criticizes the ideology of resemblance by exposing its innate contingency, as he did with Felix's stick in *Despair*. He also calls into question whether there is a substantial difference between personal revenge and political assassination—the sort of question that can only be posed by a character who is a madman.

Ultimately, Shade plays the role of the sacred poet who is sacrificed at the hands of two lunatics for no other reason than his resemblance to a judge who has made his share of enemies. In this regard, he functions as a shadow of Freud, one who is gradually deprived of his authority by the shadow of Nabokov. At the same time, Judge Goldworth serves as the shell (house) of the kernel (tenant). We learn that the judge declared Jack Grey insane and committed him to an asylum, in much the same way that a psychiatrist commits a troubled individual to an institution. As Donald Morton observes, "Kinbote confesses that it was his fear of death that actually led him to the obsessive interest in John Shade" (1974, 121). Is it possible to conclude that Judge Goldsworth, like Shade, is merely a disguised Freud—a model for the mimic, Nabokov? Perhaps the assumption of disguises offered the only way for Nabokov to sublimate his fear of Death and channel it into a creative work of art, enabling him, like Gradus, to climb Mount Parnasos.

Kinbote asserts that we can never truly grasp the nature of God, given that we know Him only by what He is not. He is not despair. He is not *terror*. His presence as the absolute cause, the Universal Mind, is reflected in the cosmic mimicry of Nature. As this cycle plays out, Shade robs the spirit of Nabokov, while Kinbote robs the light of Shade. Perhaps it is poetic justice that, in the end, Nabokov's battle against Freud does not involve an appeal to reason so much as an appeal to readers to enjoy the game.[12] It makes little difference whether Shade's murder was a political assassination or an act of personal revenge. Ultimately, he is the victim of "the topsy-turvical coincidence" that Shade perceived while in an unconscious state. For Nabokov, this dreamlike encounter is the *Primal Scene*, for Shade's near-death experience reveals to him that God is not equivalent to terror. Nor is God to be experienced in the context of a linear system of cause and effect. Instead, God is revealed through an endless cycle of imitation and deceit, which is designed for delight and amusement. Nabokov's anti-Darwinian perspective is suggested in the very nature of Shade's death, given that a distinguished poet's life is extinguished by an apparent lunatic. This outcome flies in the face of Darwin's view, since a superior organism has been destroyed by one who is obviously inferior.

Only if we accept Nabokov's view of Nature as a boundless of display of sensual beauty (as opposed to a slaughterhouse of natural selection) can we grasp the significance of Nabokov's mad characters, Humbert and Kinbote. In *Lolita*, as Humbert and Quilty struggle in the minutes leading up to Quilty's murder, we encounter these mystifying lines: "I rolled over him. We rolled over me. They rolled over him. We rolled over us" (LO 272). Similarly, in *Pale Fire*, just moments after Shade is murdered and Kinbote is saved by a gardener (actually a disguised author), "the armed gardener and the battered killer were smoking side by side on the steps." (295). What can all this mean? In the case of *Lolita*, the string of pronouns—I, him, we, they—points to the various disguises donned by the characters, as they mimic Freud and Nabokov at different points in the author's topsy-turvy narrative. Meanwhile, in *Pale Fire*, the gardener and the killer also assume disguises that represent the author and his enemies. They smoke together after a game in which Nabokov wins and Schadenfreude loses, or vice versa, given that we are always on the verge of a new cycle. They, like we, are merely actors on a stage.

NOTES

1. Copyright © 2011 by Johns Hopkins University Press. This chapter was first published as an article in *American Imago* 68.1 (2011), 67–91. Reprinted with permission by Johns Hopkins University Press.

2. Pekka Tammi notices that *Pale Fire* is one of the most complex novels ever written: "Not counting reviews, there are more than eighty studies" (1995, 572). Tammi's intuition of the novel is particularly crucial to my exploration, that is, the distinctive Nabokovian handling of the internal links between the embedded levels of fiction, which reverse the standard narrative hierarchy.

3. For instance, James Ramey, in his "Parasitism and *Pale Fire*'s Camouflage," points out that Kinbote resembles the botfly living in mammals in a number of ways—most of all, deceptive and parasitic reproduction of himself (2004, 189). Its anagram, Botkin, is an American professor who had once been a Russian one.

4. In his note, Kinbote said that he does not know what those spellings mean (188). Gennady Barabtarlo solves the riddle of barn ghost by drawing upon Vanessa *atalants*: "pada **ATALAN**e pad no**T** ogo old w**A**r**TALAN** / Ther t**A**le feur far r**A**n'**T LANT** t**A**l told."(1993, 207).

5. Those lines from 936 to 940 ("Now I plough / Old Zembla's fields where my gray stubble grows, / And slaves make hay between my mouth and nose") imply that the poet is a mask of editor, or editor puts a mask of poet who is ultimately a mirror of Freud. In Nabokov's fiction, Freud usually appears as a bearded doctor. See also Alvin Kernan: Kinbote "is now in hiding disguised as a bearded teacher in this obscure American college town" (1987, 108).

6. According to McCarthy, "there is an actual Nova Zembla, a group of islands in the Artic Ocean, north of Archangel. The name is derived from the Russian Novaya Zemlya, which means 'new land' (1982, 129). Alfred Appel also mentioned that Nabokov's great grandfather explored and mapped Nova Zembla where Nabokov River is named after him (1967, 25). Nabokov's own remarks from *Strong Opinions* (1973) would be helpful to link Zembla to Russia: "I am always there"(18); the hiding place of the crown jewels, *Kobatana*, but not tell to the Russians (92).

7. See also Kinbote's comment that American novelists and members of United English Department are soaked in literary talent, Freudian fancies, and ignoble heterosexual lust than all the rest of the world (PF 228).

8. Steven Belletto (2006, 755-780) remarks that "with the story of Zembla and its Revolution, Kinbote is not only inverting the homophobia of Cold War American culture, he is also reproducing a narrative that legitimates anti-Communist fears of subversion" (767). Significantly observable is his note that Nabokov and Freud should be studied in the way he uses Freud (776).

9. About Nabokov's remarks on butterflies in his interviews, see *Strong Opinions*, 136, 170, 192. About color of pale gray, see also Timothy F. Flower's "The Scientific Art of Nabokov's *Pale Fire*." He remarks that "the Vanessa Atalanta wears Kinbote's colors but has a grayish underside" (1975, 223-233). Amy Reading also points out that Nabokov's characters are galley slaves, that his room is filled with people wearing his own mask, and that he was delighted with insect look-alikes as a scientist (2006, 81).

10. In this regard, Marilyn Edelstein observes one undeniable human presence in the novel as the author himself and three main characters can be seen as constituting one aspect of a whole human self (1982, 214).

11. See *Pale Fire*, p. 187: "the ever-sagacious Dr. Sutton affirmed—on what authority I cannot tell—that cases in which the same person was again involved in the same type of outbreaks after a lapse of six years were practically unknown." Another examples of Kinbote's distaste of Freud: "Doctor is far too dull to have such wit," or "All bearded Zemblans resembled one another," and so on.

12. Nabokov confirms that if our life is the complex artistry of mimicry and deception, then understanding and order can only be obtained by our imagination to participate in the game. We can hear the voice of the author's mother from Kinbote's saying

that "a good Zemblan Christian is taught that true faith is not there to supply pictures or maps, but that it should quietly content itself with a warm haze of pleasurable anticipation" (PF 219).

SEVEN

Ada

In Opposition to the Incest Taboo

Vladimir Nabokov was seventy years old when he published *Ada, or Ardor: A Family Chronicle*, a novel whose ninety-two-year-old narrator, Dr. Ivan ("Van") Veen, presents a rambling, dreamlike memoir that casually transgresses the boundary between fantasy and objective reality. Some of the novel's most memorable passages describe the narrator's lifelong love for his soul mate, Ada Veen. As the title suggests, however, the novel also provides an historical overview of the Veen family, which features some of Nabokov's most painterly and evocative prose. Veen's idiosyncratic memoir opens in the late-nineteenth century in Anti-terra, or Demonia, a world closely intertwined with Terra. As though it were intended to reflect the elderly narrator's fantastic impressions of the past, the world he describes differs substantially from that of the present, even if its geography is somewhat familiar. In Van Veen's world, Russia has been conquered centuries earlier by the barbarian Tartars, while America is essentially a patchwork of Russian, English, and French colonies: a situation that draws humorously from the author's experiences in those countries. The peculiarity of the settings Veen describes is heightened by the introduction of unusual names and titles, such as "Lord Goal," the apparent ruler of France. The writer Borges becomes "Osberg," and T. S. Eliot emerges as a Jewish businessman.

As usual, Nabokov takes gleeful pleasure in providing alternative names for Freud and prominent advocates of his ideas. Hence, the universe we are invited to explore is largely divorced from the objective world in which we live, and at times, we sense it is the creation of an elderly man in the throes of dementia. The story subtly combines the narrator's inner world and the external order with which we are all acquainted. The narrative is divided into five distinct parts, which deal, respectively, with the themes of childhood, separation, climax (or metamorphosis), perceptual time, and the emergence of a new ethics. The sections move from events in the remote past to those that are relatively recent, and the length of these sections becomes progressively shorter—the final and fifth part being the most concise. Significantly, the length of the various sections appears to reflect the elderly narrator's obsession with his childhood, as well as his declining capacity to recall more recent events.

For most readers, *Ada* presents a challenge, as it is far removed from a conventional chronological narrative of past events. The novel does not focus on an external, objective world. Instead, it describes a perceptual world that is linked to *perceptual time*. The primary challenge of reading *Ada* stems from the fact that the narrator's declining mental powers ensure that his recollection of events will be organized in *relatively* chronological order. Indeed, throughout the narrative, the border separating past events from present-day commentary is difficult to discern. Nevertheless, we should be attentive to its presence, for it enables us to appreciate the characterization and the narrative's metamorphosis. Since the narrator is a ninety-two-year-old man, his recollection of events in the distant past frequently takes on the characteristics of a fairy tale, even though his memories are subject to Ada's corrections throughout the first part of the novel. Yet, the challenges presented by *Ada* do not end there. The narrative is fraught with riddles and deceptions, and the reader is buffeted with stand-ins for Freud and Nabokov.[1] The author was no stranger to such idiosyncrasies, of course. In his foreword to the 1965 English-language version of *The Eye*, released four years before *Ada*, Nabokov amusingly describes his work as "mythproof," adding that "Freudians flutter around them avidly, approach with itching oviducts, stop, sniff, and recoil" (1990, iii).

Overall, *Ada* is a novel characterized by intertwining, or *chiasm*. This interweaving occurs not only between the past and the present, but also among various characters: Van and Ada (vaniada), Ada and Lucette (adalucinda), and even Aqua and Marina (aquamarina). These interweaving relationships ultimately encompass Freud and Nabokov, as well. Significantly, each of these intertwined pairs can be interpreted as the reflection of an obsessive form of sibling-incest, not unlike that which exists between Van and Ada. This relationship also appears to extend to the pairing of Terra and Anti-terra, which seems to reflect an intertwining of linear and perceptual time. Naturally, we are inclined to question how these incestuous pairs function in the contexts of Nabokov's concept of mimicry and Freudian sexuality. As in other works, Nabokov sets out to imitate *incestuous love*, only to subvert the *incest taboo*, along with the sexual triangle of the Oedipus complex. Positioning our lives in the context of a dream, as they are informed by deceptive memory and cognition, *Ada* continually questions the viability of the Freudian approach to dream interpretation, while employing playful anagrams, e.g., *insect, incest,* and *nicest,* that reflect the essence of the author's art and imaginative life.

CHILDHOOD IS NOT AN OBJECT OF SEXUALITY

Significantly, through his interpretation of dreams, Freud spotlights the human instincts that are repressed by social mores in order to determine the cause of a patient's trauma. He contends that instinctive pleasures cannot be eliminated through such prohibitions, for they return in variously disguised forms. These disguised forms include the dream image, the product of a compromise between the pleasure principle and reality principle. When setting out to cure a patient's mental disorder or illness, Freud relied heavily on talking, which enabled him to determine the content of the patient's dreams and his or her memories of the past. Given its arbitrary nature, dream analysis became a subject of controversy among contemporary academics and practitioners. Critics and supporters alike noted that Freud, in his quest for a buried instinctive pattern, turned to mythology, history, and literature, which led to his formulation of the Oedipus complex. He contended that a child's affection for his mother inspires a desire to kill his father, although this desire is repressed because of the child's fear that his father will castrate him: the source of the so-called *incest taboo.* The problem is, the child never abandons his affection for his mother, but instead, directs it to a woman who resembles his mother. Postulating erotic desire as the basic component of repressed emotions, Freud developed this assumption into broader fields of the humanities and science. For instance, in his *Three Essays on the Theory of Sexuality* (1905), Freud classifies our desires into the affective current of childhood and the sensual current of adulthood, while indicating that the ideal approach to love involves a dynamic compromise between the two currents. This secondary process of libido-projection, from the mother to the sexual object, enables Freud to explain why we are capable of hating someone we also dearly love. Indeed, there is no one like our mother, and therefore, our frustrated affection and desire for attachment becomes the source of discontent and hatred.

When we compare Freud's view of childhood in psychoanalysis to that of Nabokov in his art, we should be attentive to two elements: different content and different periods. Freud's stage of the unconscious, or childhood, refers to the period of development before the age of three or four. In the case of Nabokov, however, this stage refers to the period before he was compelled to leave his native country—especially his beloved *Vyre*—as a result of the Revolution. The place and time from which he was exiled is the cradle of a primal scene that he revisits continuously through his fiction. Notably, in *Ada*, when Van contends that Ada's sixteenth birthday marks the end of childhood (AD 179), he describes the period beforehand as one marked by freedom, happiness, and naïveté. This view could not be further removed from the general, mythical, and objective perspective offered by the theory of infantile sexuality. Furthermore, in the novel, childhood is symbolized by Ardis Hall, the library in Ladore County in which Van and Ada—at ages fourteen and twelve, respectively—meet and fall in love, sharing wholesome and innocent experiences. We learn that the library's owner is Ada's father, Dan, although we are quickly informed that he is not her biological father. Indeed, the prelude to the sibling's tragic love story is a tangled family history informed by incest, scheming, and lust. The family's tragedy, as well as that of the two siblings, is inextricably linked to a quote from Tolstoy's *Anna Karenina* in inverted form "All happy families are more or less dissimilar; all unhappy ones are more or less alike" (3).

When the family's saga opens, Demon Veen, a Manhattan banker, is obsessed with an actress named Marina and begs her to abandon her career and marry him. When Marina rejects his proposition, Demon instead marries her weak-willed sister, Aqua, driven by a combination of malice, pity, and incestuous pleasure. This development lays the groundwork for an increasingly complex network of family relationships. While the protagonist, Van, is widely believed to be the son of Demon and Aqua, he is actually the product of a liaison involving Demon and Marina. Amid the unraveling of their doomed marriage, Demon chooses to deceive Aqua, replacing her dead infant son with Marina's baby. If Aqua is unaware of this development, Van senses from an early age that he is not her biological child. Meanwhile, Marina marries Demon's brother, Daniel, an art dealer, and they raise two daughters, Ada and Lucette. Given that Daniel's romantic life is uncomplicated, Marina chooses, even after their marriage, to conceal the fact that she was sexually involved with Demon and bore him a son. Consequently, when Van and Ada meet, they believe they are cousins, not siblings. Not surprisingly, the Veen family history that Van presents in his memoir suggests that the couple's tragedy is the result of generations of recklessness; and Ada, who occasionally corrects Van's narrative, is moved to comment, "Awkward, Reword!" (9). As Barton Jonson observes, the sibling incest in *Ada* draws on examples found in three distinct cultures: the Russian Pushkin, the French Chateaubriand, and the English Byron. Interestingly, these are all cultures that Nabokov experienced personally, and the novel appears to advocate a spirit of rebellion against the prohibitions of the fatherland.[2]

When Van visits Ardis Hall, an extravagantly beautiful country house at the edge of a largely Russian village, he notices that Marina pronounces Ada in the Russian manner, with two deep, dark *a*'s, making it sound rather like *ardor*. Apparently, the title of the novel, *Ada or Ardor*, draws on Nabokov's own experience as an exile whose second language was superimposed upon his native Russian: a phenomenon critics have described as *Amerussia*.[3] In any event, Van is taken with Ada, who loves to invent games and declares that she is obsessed with everything that crawls. He describes her larvarium as the real marvel of Ardis Manor, and he notes that she dreams of one day becoming a scientist and establishing an institute devoted to fritillary larvae. Indeed, she is fascinated by the moth's shocking metamorphosis, as well as the sheer variety and inventiveness of insect mimicry. Smitten with Ada, Van sees her plain Irish nose as a miniature version of his own; he will later recall that her languid, pale gray beauty resembled the delicate wings of an insect.

> Many decades later Van remembered having much admired the lovely, naked, shiny, gaudily spotted and streaked sharkmoth caterpillars, as poisonous as the mullein flowers clustering around them, and the flat larva of a local catocalid whose gray knobs and lilac plaques mimicked the knots and lichens of the twig to which it clung so closely as to practically lock with it... (AD 55)

What is the nature of Van's attraction to Ada, anyway? We sense that, in his youth, he is too enthralled with her physical beauty to pay much attention to insect mimicry as aesthetic empathy. Years later, however, he can virtually taste this phenomenon, in a manner that calls to mind the involuntary memories recorded in the works of Proust. As William James observes, memories that are inscribed within the body persists as *habit*, unlike voluntary memories. Hence, in the same way that Proust involuntarily recalls the taste of a piece of cake that is served with tea, Van recollects his childhood as a fairy tale that is saturated with physical things, natural things, and sensual feelings. His memories do not follow the template of an antiquated myth; instead, they are structured around private sensations, like those recorded in Ada's entomological entries. At one point, she describes the pleasant, silky sensation of stroking an insect's smooth body, that is, until an irritated caterpillar (its face resembling the lens of a folding camera) shoots a stream of liquid in her direction. Commenting on such distant memories, Ada writes, "*even* I did not quite assimilate," adding, "What a hoaxer, that old V. V.!" (56). One is inclined to ask, who is Ada, and what does she represent?

Ada as the Mask of Nabokov

In *Ada*, the pattern of incest that unfolds takes on a unique, peculiarly private form. Ada appears to represent the author's concept of reality as a synonym for natural science, or insect mimicry. Van, meanwhile, serves as a crucial supplement to Ada: an element required to bring Nabokov's work of art to fruition. Interestingly, Van's childhood memories are often corrected by Ada, which suggests that they are so deeply intertwined that they practically form a single entity (109). Indeed, Roy Swanson suggests that the siblings are intended to represent one person, Nabokov. Swanson supports this position by referring to several significant details. He notes that, in Russian, Ada means "hell," or "Hades," while Van (Ivan) is the Russian equivalent of "John." Thus, it appears that *Vaniada* is a reference to John Shade, the mask of the American Nabokov, who dreamt of a Russian childhood while ensconced at an American college (1975, 79). From this perspective, Ada appears to function as a ghost who encapsulates the essence of the author's thoughts and impressions, which are shaped by his childhood.

In Van's case, this childhood is spent at Ardis Hall, which serves as an emblem of the natural sciences, though it later takes on elements of the humanities, as well. Despite her ghostly nature, Ada is more real than a flesh-and-blood person for the novel's ninety-two-year-old narrator. Instances of deception in Van's narrative are plentiful, and extreme, given that the period of time involved exceeds the relative handful of years separating the nymphet, Lolita, from Humbert. Ada serves as Van's *pale amorette*, the boundless vista of flowering orchards and vineyards in which he delighted before the prohibition of the father (fatherland): an obvious reference to the Revolution. During his exile, though, Van is free to engage in a fantasy dialogue and debate that even expresses itself in manuscript corrections. In short, Ada serves as his muse, Mynemosyne, and he is compelled to ask, "My sister, do you still recall / The castle, The Ladore, and all?" (AD 141).

For Van, the tragedy of separation, along with the haunting of the pale ghost, begins when he is eighteen, just four years after his initial meeting with Ada. On the evening of a devastating barn fire, the pair engages in intercourse for the first time, following years of foreplay. During that time, they attempted to deceive others by mimicking insects and playing games. Both engaged in the invention of codes, riddles, and anagrams in order to conceal their affection for one another. Their behavior had become still more cautious after the discovery of birth certificates that had been hidden away in an attic. Van's depiction of this momentous discovery is so vague, so understated, that the reader cannot be blamed for failing to grasp its significance on a first reading of the novel: "My love, my love, as if you don't know! We'll manage, perhaps, to wear our masks always, till dee do us part" (263). But they shall never be able to marry, because Demon is more conventional in his own way than even the law. Van's father, Demon, who represents the incest taboo, also appears to symbolize the Russian government, from which the author is compelled to escape, never to return.

While mimicking the sexuality of incest, the narrator subtly reveals his state of mind when he flees his homeland, Terra the Fair, which has devolved into a nation of therapists. Afterward, Ada plays the role of Van's pale and deceptive mistress, engaging in a series of sexual adventures that include a lesbian affair. Ultimately, the oppressive nature of the incest taboo leads Van to invent an alternative universe, in which the ghost of Terra (and of Ada) remains within him as a hopeless fantasy, even as he lives on in Anti-terra. The incest taboo, which had been the cause of his exile, becomes the source of a new form of art and memory. Hence, in *Ada*, sexuality is merely ancillary to art, in much the same way it is in *Lolita*.

As the story progresses, the incestuous couple move along divergent paths. Van leaves for America to study philosophy and psychiatry, while Ada abandons her plants and worms, along with her dream of becoming a biologist. She throws over the orchids and mushrooms and violets she once cherished in order to pursue a career on the stage. In a sense, this is appropriate, for acting is yet another form of mimicry, a yielding to an instinct to be someone (or something) else, to conceal oneself in another form. Significantly, Nabokov himself sought to disguise himself by adopting the surname, *Sirin,* while producing fiction in politically tumultuous Berlin. Given the author's penchant for deception and disguises, his writing has much in common with Ada's performances on the stage. Interestingly, Van draws a parallel between writing and acting when he observes that when he acts in a good play, he feels authored and passed by the board of censors (426). Apparently, without the creation of art, life for Vaniada is meaningless, the void.

If we consider the novel from the perspective of Nabokov's apparent obsession with Russia, the sweet land of his birth, the title could be reconfigured as *Ada or adoration*, and the novel could also be seen to encompass all of Russian culture, not merely the author's embellished childhood memories. Since images, like memories, are fluid and subject to change, it is possible to view Ada as an emblem of *science*, a complement to Van's representation of art. In an apparent reaction against his father, Van boldly asserts that he and Ada have more in common than ordinary lovers or siblings: they are really inseparable. Given their access to the library, they have become self-educated individuals, and as residents of a free country, they have learned the names of the various insects, flowers, and birds that inhabit Terra before the advent of the incest taboo, i.e., before the Revolution. David Field, employing Edward O. Wilson's term, *consilience,* places the incest in *Ada* within the context of a merging of science and art, eschewing an overtly sexual interpretation: "science thus resembles poetry because both involve imaginative creations and deal with elusive and dynamic reality" (1986, 330).

Meanwhile, Stephen Blackwell contends that, beyond exploring the ways in which a scientific and artistic temperament may coexist within a single individual, we need to question whether science and art emanate from a common core within an author of genius.[4] Answering this question might take us closer to the point at which insect mimicry and deceptive memory merge. As James argues, thinking and feeling do not stand firmly apart from each other when the subject fails to establish an absolute distance from the object. Moreover, in the incestuous relationship between science and art, dreams converge with reality. For Nabokov, the incest taboo is the absolute condition for epistemology, in the same way that it serves as a rationale for certain forms of art. The author goes on to assert that, in sharp contrast to the claims of Freudian sexuality, childhood is actually the source of play, inventiveness, and deceptive mimicry, which are intertwined with all of the human vagaries and contingencies that occur later on. In the absence of this process, no history or art would be possible. As illustrated in the tragedy of Lucette, we cannot rely on a perfect solution or generalization. This is especially true when we consider that the mimicry that informs innocent Terra already contains the seeds of tragic contingency. We might ask whether there is any other means by which Van can seek to avert Lucette's tragic ending.

LUCETTE AS THE HIGHLIGHT OF THE PLOT

It is important to note that, while sibling incest may serve as an emblem of the author's art, the novel's focal point is Van, not Ada. Throughout *Ada*, Van functions as the narrator-protagonist, whose development is critical to the plot, while Ada is simply an object, endlessly transformed in the context of Van's memories. From a metaphorical perspective, if Van were to symbolize consciousness, Ada would represent the memory-traces, or materiality. After all, she configures herself as physical, *horribly physical*. In an especially revealing interview, Nabokov acknowledged his distaste for the character of Van Veen: he suspects that Van Veen, having less control over his imagination than the author himself, invented in his indulgent old age many images of his youth (SO, 121). While the characters of Van and Ada may appear to merge inseparably into a single individual that represents the author's art, they do not overlap precisely. Van appears to be much closer to Freud than Nabokov, and he manifests an overflowing sexuality, before and after his exile. Ada, on the other hand, possesses a more liberal approach to sexuality, reflected in a tolerance for homosexuality and incest. This is the product of her firsthand knowledge of inbreeding within the natural world, as well as her grounding in the natural sciences.

Meanwhile, Van is fiercely heterosexual and tends to treat Ada as a sexual object. Fiercely jealous of her real and imagined male lovers, he even threatens to kill them. While he may be a lover of liberty, his commitment to freedom falls short of Ada's. Moreover, they appear to disagree on the typology of mimicry, as Dieter E. Zimmer notes, with Ada standing firmly on the side of Nabokov. Thus, she recoils when Van violently exclaims, in response to her protests: "Accursed? Accursed? It was . . . professor Nabonidus . . . " (AD 158, my abbreviation). Zimmer interprets her response as follows: "If she shares her author's [Van's] thinking on the matter, she would rather call it blessed" (2002, 56). Notably, in his memories of childhood, Van focuses on the issue of sexuality, prompting Ada to ask, "I wonder, Van, why you are doing your best to transform our poetical and unique past into a dirty farce?" (120). While both of them consent to the fact that *think* and *dream* in French are not really different, Ada associates the word *douceur* with the rhythm of prose, while Van associates it with bodily tenderness.

In time, we learn that Van's field of research is *Terrology*, the theory of therapy—a branch of psychiatry. Although Dr. Veen may have been a diligent student of case histories, he nevertheless seems incapable of analyzing Ada's identity, or his mysterious passion for her. Only in the throes of dementia does he acknowledge that she is "a complex system of subtle bridges which the senses traverse—laughing, embraced, throwing flowers in the air—between membrane and brain, and which always was and is a form of memory, even at the moment of its perception" (221). What gives rise to this dramatically altered perspective, which is duly reflected in the metamorphosis of his narrative?

Dr. Van Veen as the Mask of Freud

Following his separation from Ada as a consequence of the law of the father, Van goes on to publish various scholarly works whose names appear throughout Part Two. On the one hand, Van appears to mimic Freudian sexuality, while on the other, he competes fiercely with his rivals, including Ada's numerous boyfriends, who occasionally appear to be disguised representatives of Freud. During a long period that includes travel, study, teaching, and writing, Van struggles to drive away Ada's lovers, but to no avail. As it turns out, the rules regarding incest in Terra are also in place on dismal Anti-terra. (At this point, we should bear in mind that American college students were infatuated by Freud in the 1950s, at the time Nabokov was teaching at Cornell). The view that Van adopts an essentially Freudian mask is supported by critics such as Liana Ashenden, who notes that Ada's obsession with insects is paralleled by Van's focus on their sexual connotations. He takes note of the position beetles adopt when copulating, and during a sexual encounter with Ada in Manhattan, he makes violent love to her from behind, an expression of his rage upon learning of Ada's fiancé from Lucette (Ashenden, 2000/2001, 136). Indeed, Van draws much of his sexual imagery from the natural world, as reflected in a joke he makes regarding oral sex that refers to the habits of the Swallowtail butterfly. The orchid is yet another recurrent symbol of sexuality throughout the novel, as Brian Boyd observes in his "Annotations to *Ada*," where he notes that the flower's name derives from the Greek word for testicle. Boyd also draws attention to Van's mimicking of insects, drawing an analogy between Van's masturbation

over an image of Ada who was painting orchids and the pseudo-copula-
tion of male insects (2000, 66). However, we must question whether these
sexual connotations have anything to do with Freudian sexuality.

Nabokov presents Van's sexual interests as a clue to the reader that he
is attacking Freud by mimicking the brand of sexuality described in such
landmark works as "From the History of an Infantile Neurosis" (1918),
also known as the Wolf Man case study, and "Leonardo Da Vinci and a
Memory of his Childhood" (1910), in which Freud infers a reference to
oral sex from Leonardo's childhood memory of an eagle's tail beating
against his open mouth. In the former work, Freud draws a parallel between the Wolf Man's dream of wolves and his fearful memory of the
butterfly to construct a primal scene in which the patient, as a one-and-a-
half-year-old child, observed his parents engaging in *coitus a tergo*. Acknowledging that his case study was incomplete, Freud contended that
the patient's memories could be fully constructed if he were compelled to
reveal subsequent fantasies to an analyst. Yet, he took pains to qualify his
analysis, adding that "perhaps what the child observed was not copulation between his parents but copulation between animals, which he then
displaced on to his parents" (SE, 17: 57). As noted, the Freudian *primal
scene* is a frequent object of ridicule in Nabokov's fiction, and *Ada* certainly follows this pattern. By drawing repeated parallels between Van's sexual propensities and detailed descriptions of copulation in the natural
world, the author seeks to undermine the primal scene and expose it as a
travesty.

Ultimately, Van's careless attitude toward Lucette contributes to her
suicide, which occurs after she is forced to confront Van's obsession with
Ada. The tragedy of Lucette's suicide, as well as Van's moral responsibility for this outcome, can be viewed in the context of the protagonist's
Freudian mask: an issue discussed by critics. For instance, in *Nabokov's
Ada: the Place of Consciousness*, Boyd argues that, beneath the surface, the
novel is a study of irrevocable human limitations. In his view, Nabokov
deals seriously with the issue of Lucette's suicide, and he is attentive to
the demonic side of Van and Ada, as well as their cold indifference to
their sister and their lack of sensitivity to her needs (2001, 113, 116). He
notes that, early in the novel, when they engage in games of mimicry,
Van and Ada are amused by Lucette, a naïve girl who has no idea what
they are doing.

Given the exclusivity of their relationship, Lucette feels alienated from
her cousin and sister. The more subtle the alienation, the more she desires
to be an object of their affection. We are told that she appears to lurk
behind every screen and tries to imitate the pair's activities. Van evidently takes pleasure in deceiving Lucette, stroking her fondly in Ada's presence, as he simultaneously kisses Ada. The trouble arises when Van's
careless attachments produce sexual excitement. When Ada senses this,
she poses a question regarding Lucette: "She excites you, confess?" (214).

While Ada and Van may look back regretfully on those summer days, there is little doubt that their deceptive activities stirred within Lucette deep emotions for Van—feelings that remain strong until her death.[5] Can they be redeemed for their mistreatment of Lucette, and to what degree should Van be held responsible for her suicide?

At one point, Lucette confesses her love to Van and also reveals the fact that her sister, Ada, had introduced her to certain sexual techniques, adding "we interweaved like serpents and sobbed like pumas" (375). While the scene underscores the similarities between the two sisters, it also sheds light on the universal traits of an unhappy family, and as the story progresses, a clear pattern emerges. Aqua and Lucette have been unintentionally victimized by their own sisters, Marina and Ada: a fact that is underscored by the appearance of the anagrams, *aquamarina* and *adalucinda*. Perhaps the most conspicuous quality that Aqua and Lucette share is their total ignorance of deception and mimicry. We should recall that Aqua was deceived by Marina and Demon, for she remains convinced that Van is her son. Meanwhile, Lucette seems oblivious to the incestuous relationship that develops between Van and Ada. Spurned by Van and Ada, she comments plaintively, "you two *can't* tell me why exactly you want to get rid of me" (229). Devoid of any knowledge of disguise or contingency, Aqua and Lucette are victims of deceptive reality. They are relegated to Demonia, a planet of dismal Anti-terra on which there is no room to stand. Demonia, we are told, is the land of pale ghosts—painful memories of the past that are shadowed by thoughts and feelings of the present.

Unlike Ada, Van, and Demon, Aqua and Lucette are stark *realists* who are unaware of the ghosts that dance within our minds. Significantly, it is Marina's foolish rejection of Demon that leads him to marry her sister, although he, in turn, travels and shares pleasure with Marina, going so far as to admit he is jealous of her lover. Much of the unhappiness of the Veen extended family owes to the sexual antics of the parents, and this behavior will inform the tragedies of both Vaniada and Lucette. Is there a way to subvert this destructive pattern? An examination of the characters in conflict—those representing Freud and those representing Nabokov— could provide answers.

A natural place to start is with the protagonist/narrator, Van, whose formative years stand in sharp contrast to the outlines of the Freudian Oedipus complex. Van admires his father, and he has little regard for his actress mother, Marina. We learn that, unlike her daughter, Ada, Marina has no special talent for mimicry, and Van finds her irredeemably dull, essentially a dummy in human disguise while lacking in the *third sight* of individual, magically detailed imagination. Ada does not hold a particularly high opinion of her mother, either. When they meet for tea, and Marina casually mentions that Dostoevsky enjoyed his tea with raspberry syrup, Ada responds irreverently, "Pah!" Overall, she seems bored and perplexed by her mother's behavior. Meanwhile, Marina is clueless about the relationship that has arisen between Ada and Van. Convinced Van loves Lucette, she fails to grasp the relevance of the siblings' long conversations on subjects like botany and biology, and she cannot fathom their endless riddles. Van's distaste for Marina is nowhere more evident than a passage in which he describes her unimaginative approach to the magic of memory: she pondered that one's past must be put in order and should be retouched and retaken by "wipes" and "inserts" (253). Marina comes off as a naïve realist whose views are in conflict with James's stream of thought, or memories in process. Given her resemblance to Lolita's mother, Charlotte, we can assume that Marina stands on the side of Nabokov's foe, Freud. If this is so, can we deduce anything about Lucette's approach to memory?

We know that Lucette is the favored child of Marina, an inverted image of Dolores in *Lolita*. She stubbornly clings to her past in Terra and, after a certain point, she refuses to even enter Anti-terra. Lucette proves to be humorless, has little time for ghosts, and lacks the capacity for playful mimicry. Tellingly, she treats every playful thing in a literal manner, a trait reflected in her comment that Bergson is solely for a very young man or very unhappy man. While Lucette proves a skillful imitator and enjoys mimicking Ada's affection for Van, she never truly changes as a real object for love. During the scene in which Lucette delivers Ada's letter to Van, which reveals Ada's plan to marry the wealthy Andrey Vinelander, Van responds as though performing Hamlet on the stage, relegating Lucette to the role of Ophelia, rather than that of the Queen. Meanwhile, Ada dons the mask of Nabokov and emerges as an editor of Van's writing. The pair are not always on the same page, however. In a particularly humorous passage, Van uses a magnifying glass for deciphering the details of his patients' drawings, and Ada uses the same magnifying glass to examine the pattern of a hammock. Throughout the novel, Ada expresses concern about Van's vulnerability to Lucette, who is armed with physical beauty and a fierce determination to court Van. At times, Nabokov adopts the role of stage manager in his efforts to guide Van, who operates within the limited sphere of a Freudian psychiatrist: "Pause (about fifteen minutes to go to the end of the act)" (384). The tension escalates as Van enters his final struggle with Lucette, which, to some extent, functions as a match involving Nabokov and Freud. Not surprisingly, Ada/Nabokov seeks to support Van, going so far as to coach him.

Ultimately, Lucette confesses to Van her dream to relive the old days, when the three of them—Van, Ada, and Lucette—formed a triangular relationship. In her desperation to secure a commitment from Van, she even tries to bargain with him: "You marry me. You get my Ardis. We live there, you write there. I keep melting into the background, never bothering you. We invite Ada—alone, of course—to stay for a while on *her* estate." If Van initially seems open to this proposal, he points out that "the only trouble is: she will never come" (466). What Van is actually saying is that the past, their shared childhood (the ghost in Anti-terra), can never be restored. For him, the happiness of his childhood exists only in fantasy, and given the passage of time, his memories of that childhood have taken on the characteristics of fiction. Faithful to the script provided by Ada/Nabokov, Van fails to respond to Lucette's proposal. Crucially, unlike Lucette, he does not regard memory as an object through which to recover eroticism; instead, he views it as a form of art. Furthermore, Van seeks to avoid the mistakes of his parents. He has no desire to marry Lucette as a surrogate for her sister, Ada, and he does not want Ada's child to be disguised as Lucette's.

Given that the story unfolds not in Terra, but in Anti-terra, Tolstoy's maxim regarding unhappy families should perhaps be inverted: All happy families are more or less dissimilar; all unhappy ones are more or less alike.[6] Throughout the novel, Nabokov relentlessly criticizes resemblance, a stark Realism as he did with Zembla in *Pale Fire* and Hermann in *Despair*. In doing so, of course, he seeks to challenge Freudian generalization, which is reflected in the naïve ideology of Terra and the doomed desire of Lucette to recapture her youth. Distracted by Ada's appearance in a film, at the moment he seems about to succumb to Lucette's charms, Van successfully resists the fatal error of generalization. However, his choice has other implications that we need to discuss.

While Aqua and Lucette have no place to stand on Anti-terra, it would be wrong to assume that their characters overlap. Indeed, Van and Ada will later reflect mournfully on Lucette's fidelity, physical beauty, and futile desire to relive her youth. She was, after all, an integral part of their youthful experiences. While she was desperately lonely and received little comfort from Van, she remained committed to rekindling the joy of their shared youth. This leads us to question why it is that people find it so difficult to let go of a past that is irretrievable. This impulse is clearly evident in Humbert's undying love for Lolita, as well as Van and Ada's longing for their shared past at Ardis Hall. Shaken by Lucette's suicide, Van understands how agonizing and how absurd it is to put all one's soul into one physical fancy, and he realizes that his plight closely resembled Lucette's. In the case of *Lolita*, Humbert mourns the loss of childhood, but he also responds to the nymphet's repudiation by struggling to survive as an artist. Ultimately, he sublimates the loss of childhood into the creation of an immortal work of art, *Lolita*. Van appears to believe that this sort of option may be available to Lucette. After all, he has endured his own sense of loss by immersing himself in fantasies of Ada, who remains a child in his mind. Hence, the fatal words exchanged by Lucette and Van on the night before her suicide—"Can I come now?"/ "I am not alone" (491)—appear to have a dual meaning. Van's response to Lucette is a lie that is intended to avoid destroying his cousin's life over a momentary pleasure. For Nabokov, however, his response rings true.

Van as the Mask of Nabokov

Lucette's suicide is a devastating blow to Van, not only because of his affection for her, but also because of his sympathy for human limitations, especially in the context of Anti-terra. Dana Dragunoiu observes that Lucette's death is "an unavoidable consequence of living on Anti-terra" (2005, 316), and Van makes a similar observation in a letter to Ada: "In other more deeply moral worlds than this pellet of muck, there might exist restraints, principles, transcendental consolations, and even a certain pride in making happy someone one does not really love; but on this planet Lucettes are doomed" (AD 498). Ultimately, there is no way to repeat the past, and we must detour it by turning persistent ghosts into a work of art. In this sense, Lucette functions as Nabokov's gift to Van, since she forces him to taste the bitter contingency of life. Stephen Blackwell argues that, despite Van's professional interest in mental illness, he has few insights into human suffering. Consequently, as a psychologist, he has little understanding of his patients, including Lucette (2009, 107).

His moment of metamorphosis comes as he watches a dead and dry hummingbird moth lie on the window ledge of the lavatory, which prompts him to observe that symbols do not exist in dreams or in the life in between. In the next instant, he is "shot dead from behind" and moves into his next stage of existence (AD 510). Doffing his Freudian mask, Van refuses to offer any explanations for mental illness, including Marina's delusions. When Dorothy asks, "how does your school of psychiatry explain that kind of conflict?" Van declares, "I don't attend school any longer" (519). Largely as a result of Ada/Nabokov's remarkable mimicry, he can barely resist his selfish quest for sex, and he eventually abandons his work as a therapist. In this sense, Part Three functions as the climax of *Ada*, as Van is able to remove the mask of Freud and function as the avatar of Nabokov. This interpretation can be supported by examining the ways in which Van's outlook evolves in the wake of his transformation. These developments will be analyzed in the context of what appears to be an intertwining of Freud with Nabokov.

INTERWEAVING FREUD WITH NABOKOV

As with Joyce's *Finnegans Wake*, we can sense the presence of the author's experiences beneath each sentence uttered by the narrator and characters, as though to confirm that the novel is not about society, but the author himself. When Van comments that Kinston University had "a first-rate madhouse as well as a famous Department of Terrapy" (AD 365), we can discern a residue of Nabokov's distaste for the wild popularity of Freud at Cambridge University, and we can make sense of the puns: *Terrapy* and *theraphy*, as well as Terra and terrapists. Part Two, in particular, is filled with puns, allusions, and riddles, as well as disguises that are more subtle than in other parts of the novel. Nabokov takes pleasure in the introduction of numerous characters, some of whom play the role of Freud, while others are representatives of the author himself. This gives rise to sweeping and complex webs of deception. While the dialogue is more accessible than the idiosyncratic language in Joyce's work, it is clear that the memory of the ninety-two-year-old narrator is confused, distorted, and displaced.

Words and sentences pop up here and there, seemingly at random. The reader is prompted to question the author's motivation for introducing such extravagant deceptions. One possible explanation is that this part of the novel deals with Van's devastating banishment from Ardis Hall as a result of the incest taboo. (This section may have drawn inspiration from the author's years of exile in Western Europe.) Since Part Three serves as the climax, in which the narrative metamorphosis occurs, Part Two must set the stage for the upcoming battle between two literary rivals. Naturally, this portion of the novel is rife with instances of camouflage and deception, and even the author seems to find it difficult to watch as his unarmed warrior attempts to meet these challenges. This discomfort leads to interference in Van's narrative, and we will discuss some of the author's amusing tactics, in the pre-metamorphosis period.

Before the Metamorphosis: Authorial Interference in the Narrative

In one of the novel's amusing interludes, a therapist who treats Aqua at an asylum attributes her delusion to popular fantasies that draw upon old myths: "A Dr. Froid, one of the administerial centaurs, who may have been an émigré brother with a passport-changed name of the Dr. Froit of Signy-Mondieu-Mondieu in the Ardennes, or more likely, the same man, because they both came from Vienne" (27). Nabokov is clearly having fun here, since the name of Sigmund Freud has been variously distorted as "Froid," "Froit of Signy-Mondieu-Mondieu," "Dr. Sig Heiler," or simply "Siggy" or "Sig," etc. Interestingly, "Mondieu-Mondieu" translates into English as either "My God" or "Good Heavens." As Claude Mouchard notes, "Signy" means "signify," while "Heiler" includes the root, "Heil," which indicates a balance between medical rescue and spiritual salvation (1984, 130). We can infer from this string of puns that the author is taking aim at academics who worship Freud as a god, while also criticizing those who covet a god's authority and concepts, only to subvert them by mimicking that god.

As it turns out, Siggy, as a resident of Terra, is as ignorant of human deception and fantasy as Aqua and Lucette proved to be. Under Sig's advice, Demon orders Van to end his relationship with Ada: "if you marry her, I will disinherit you." Thus, his father's prohibition marks Van's separation from Ada (Russia) and the beginning of his life in Demonia, or Anti-terra. There, Van, as a mimic of Freudian erotomania, is destined to chase Ada, who in turn, pretends to be an obscene girl. Nevertheless, Van resists Sig's influence by defying the Oedipus complex. He continues to respect his father and honors his Russian heritage, even as he disregards his mother, Marina. Ultimately, Van characterizes those who tend to generalize as "all clowns and clods." He recognizes that Sig fails to take into account individual vagaries, without which art cannot exist. Art is the product of whims, and that is the sweetest revenge for all the detractions that hampered his life's work. During this unhappy period, a series of crude showmen surround Ada, including Dr. Fizbishop, or Doc Fitz, a pretentious vulgarian, and the fashionable Dr. F. S. Fraser, a psychotechnician. Van madly pursues Ada's lovers, much like the frenzied Humbert, who chased—and earlier, was chased by—the elusive Quilty. In this sense, Van can be seen as an elderly Humbert who struggles with senility.

To remember is to dream, especially as one approaches old age. Hence, the younger author seeks excuses to interfere in the rambling narrative of his elderly protagonist. Initially, he is disguised as David Van Veen, a famous architect who is born into a wealthy family headed by one Eric. His architecture features idiosyncrasies that are described as the greatest grief's greatest remedy. Art redeems not only politics, but also the ultra-utilitarian boxes of brick of El Freud. We learn that David Van Veen's new mansion resembles a renovated farmhouse or "a converted convent on a small offshore island with such miraculous effect that one could not distinguish the arabesque from the arbutus, ardor from art, the sore from the rose" (351). Only the guests (readers) and guards (critics) who were acquainted with the pleasant tactics of mimicry possess keys. Evoking *Finnegans Wake,* and alluding to Freud's interpretation of dreams, the narrator imposes one condition that was initially suggested by Eric: his mansion should open at nightfall and close at sunrise. As we move beyond a veil of puns and deceptions, we set out to identify the disguises of the author and those of Freud.

Van is clearly not a reliable narrator, given that he wears the mask of Freud before his ordeal with Lucette. Under these circumstances, Nabokov's intervention in the person of Narrator I *seems* unsurprising. At one point, the narrator describes a visit to the country house of a wealthy acquaintance, whose "charming" twelve-year-old daughters are named Ala, Lola, and Lalage. Following this obvious reference to *Lolita,* the narrator adds that he cannot name it though his reader insists he had mentioned it somewhere before. Ultimately, Narrator I presents a view of dreams that is at odds with that of the "Viennese quack": "a random sequence of scenes, trivial or tragic, viatic or static, fantastic or familiar, featuring more or less plausible events patched up with grotesque details, and recasting dead people in new settings" (359). After providing this definition, he goes on to ridicule a systematic approach to dream analysis, noting sarcastically that, even if a patient is under the influence of hypnosis, dreams cannot produce any semblance of morality or symbol or allegory or Greek myth, "unless, naturally, the dreamer is a Greek or a mythicist" (363). Any doubts about Nabokov's allegiances in this debate are settled by his comments in a 1969 interview: "I—or whatever impersonates me—is obviously on Van's side in the account of his anti-Vienna lecture on dreams" (SO 123). As though he were attempting to support Van in his brewing conflict with Freud, Narrator I (Nabokov) presents the following lecture:

> Now the mistake—the lewd, ludicrous and vulgar mistake of the Signy-Mondieu analysts consists in their regarding a real object, a pompon, say, or pumpkin (actually seen in a dream by the patient) as a significant abstraction of the real object, as a bumpkin's bonbon or one-half of the bust if you see what I mean (scattered giggles). There can be no emblem or parable in a village idiot's hallucinations or in last night's dream of any of us in this hall. In those random visions nothing . . . can be construed as allowing itself to be deciphered by a witch doctor who can then cure a madman or give comfort to a killer by laying the blame on a too fond, too fiendish or too indifferent parent . . . (laughter and applause). (AD 363–364, my abbreviation)

It is unclear, though, whether his master's lecture will enable Van to deal effectively with Lucette, and his ultimate failure contributes to her suicide. Hence, he learns a brutal lesson that facilitates his emergence as Nabokov's double.

After Metamorphosis: Art as Natural Science

In sharp contrast to the complicated, slippery style of Part Two, the reader finds that Part Four is relatively straightforward, given that it is much closer to academic prose. Upon his awakening, Van denounces Freudian sexuality, along with the primal scene. Indeed, he jokingly refers to the primal scene as the philistine's post-coital cigarette, while comparing it to "the dreamer's having read in infancy his adulterous parent's love letters" (549). Furthermore, Van engages in lengthy meditations on memory, thinking, and, above all, *perceptual* time, adopting the perspective of both a philosopher and psychologist. He roundly rejects the established pairing of space-time, which is based on linear Time, noting that a stretch of Time is more difficult to perceive than a stretch of Space. Furthermore, he rejects the mechanical concept of Time that compares it to a running stream, for he contends that Time runs over a wide variety of landscapes, including snow-lined mountains, treacherous cliffs, and wind-swept valleys (539), depending on the intensity of our emotional state.

Perceptual Time is *experienced* Time, paralyzed by emotion or expanded by the workings of the human will. It bears closer resemblance to William James's concept of Time, with its strong links to emotion, than to Proust's involuntary memory, which is inscribed within the body. For James, time is essentially linked to consciousness, or cognitive acts, which are blended with our memories of the past. He observes that "knowledge of some other part of the stream, past or future, near or remote, is always mixed in with our knowledge of the present thing" (2010, 1: 404). Thus, time is measured as the duration of perceptual consciousness, and its length depends largely on our intensity of feeling at the moment of perception. In short, all consciousness exists in the form of Time, and that time is an integral part of our feelings and stored memories—all of the creative forces within our mind.

Given that the passage of time is an invention of our mind, it is a purely imaginational product, having little to do with immediate external objects. In relation to experiences that are stored in our mind, Time is only perceived *in the rear view*, as images and *ghosts*. Hence, our emphasis should not be on the physiological process of becoming, but rather on the psychological process of making *oneself* in order to bring the totality of what one *has been* in proportion to one's emotional intensity. Since experiences of the present are inscribed upon memories of the past, knowledge is basically an impression that is superimposed on past memories. Hence, the Present can be understood as the constant building up of the Past, which gives rise to the illusion of thought, though it has little to do with the reality of the immediate past or immediate future. Indeed, Time can only be viewed retrospectively within the context of either the past or future, for the present is superimposed upon the past at the very moment that we perceive it. As Van's narrative indicates, "Our modest Present is, then, the time span that one is directly and actually aware of, with the lingering freshness of the Past still perceived as part of the nowness" (AD 550). Time is rhythm, not the recurrent beats of a rhythm. It is the gap between two such beats, which Nabokov referred to as *the tender interval*, and James called *the glow-worm spark* that illuminates "the point it immediately covered, but leaving all beyond in total darkness" (2010, 1: 404). Once again, a reference to James will help us to unpack Van's concept of Time:

> Crudely and popularly we divide the course of time into past, present, and the future; but strictly speaking, there is no present; it is composed of past and future divided by an indivisible point or instant. That instant, or time-point, is the strict *present*. What we call, loosely, the present, is an empirical portion of the course of time, containing at least a minimum of consciousness, in which the instant of change is the present time-point. . . . If we take this as the present time-point, it is

clear that the minimum of feeling contains two portions—a sub-feeling that goes and a sub-feeling that comes. One is remembered, the other imagined. The limits of both are indefinite at beginning and end of the minimum, and ready to melt into other minima, proceeding from other stimuli. (James's abbreviation, 2010, 1: 404–05)

James's concept of consciousness in relation to Time is echoed in Van's view on life and love. He contends that time does not consist of a triptych, but instead comprises two panels: the Past, which is ever-existing within the mind, and the Present, to which the mind provides duration and, therefore, reality. Meanwhile, the future exists as a *not-yet* that may never come to fruition (AD 560). These panels are exceptionally thin and subtle, for the past involves the storage of time and cannot be revisited in chronological order. The present is a tender interval, a soft hollow, while the future is not an item of Time. On the contrary, it is an image developed in the context of desire that our mind produces in order to live in the present. Closely related to a mirage in the desert, reality is ultimately a fragile and vulnerable commodity. As our life is full of deception, like "a generous chaos," we might ask whether life is worth living. Yet, Nabokov suggests that we can transform our meager lives into something magical by filling that *soft hollow* with our imagination.

Our imagination, of course, is a form of memory, as well as a work of art. After all, the human imagination is required to taste the Past and to create the Future. In this sense, Ada is the ultimate representative of *Art*, for she insists that "if there were no future, then one had the right of making up a future, and in that case one's very own future did exist, insofar as one existed oneself" (585). Examples of this approach to memory are found throughout the novel. For instance, in his old age, Van observes that he is bored less often than he was in childhood, while also acknowledging that time passes by more quickly than it did in his youth. Hence, the format of his memoir changes in response to the passage of time. For Van, childhood memories are the most precious, since they resonate throughout his life, and it takes the largest part of the entire narrative. Meanwhile, his hopes for the future contract over time. It is worth noting, however, that the issue of Time was not entirely insignificant to Freud.

While Freud did not appear overly concerned with the concept of Time, as either a psychologist or a doctor, he nevertheless began his career as a neuroscientist, and he consistently developed scientific approaches to examine the process of remembering, as reflected in his fine analogy of memory in which he compares it to the mystic writing-pad. When treating his patients' symptoms, he focused on repression and the unconscious in order to identify the cause of their trauma. As a doctor, he did not attend much on the philosophical concepts of consciousness, cognition, and Time. Significantly, however, Freud provides an interesting passage regarding his own concept of Time. As noted earlier, Freud's mystic writing-pad consists of three layers: the celluloid protective cover, the waxed paper (consciousness) on which something can be written, and the wax slab (memory-traces) that preserves traces of the writing. While the waxed paper is attached to the slab, its bottom rests on the slab without being affixed to it. Thus, in this simple device, Freud discerned an ideal analogy for our mnemic apparatus, which involves two separate but interrelated components.

Freud argues that our consciousness, in order to preserve unlimited receptive capacity, passes short-term memory over to the neurons on which permanent traces are inscribed. In the mutually exclusive relationship between consciousness and the memory-traces, the former must periodically attach and detach from the latter. Given the non-excitability of consciousness, perceptual Time becomes complicated and illusive, and Freud suggests that "this discontinuous method of functioning of the system, *Pcpt.-Cs.* lies at the bottom of the origin of the concept of time" (SE 19: 231). We may assume that this brief moment of non-excitability is the void that exists between two beats, which Van (as a representative of Nabokov) refers to as the *tender interval* or *soft hollow*. In addition, we could associate this soft hollow with the tender Ada, who originates as a ghost that is the object of fantasy. I will consider this assumption in connection with the riddle of *adalucinda*.

Time as Pain: adalucinda

As noted, Brian Boyd, who views Lucette as the center of the novel, interprets *Ada* as the narrator's tortured quest for redemption: six decades after his indifference to Lucette, he contributes to her suicide (1991, 554). Support for Boyd's view can be found in Part Five of the novel, in which the elderly narrator deals with Time as *Pain*. At this point, the reader is encouraged to view the anagram of V*aniada* (AD 583) as a form of Time and memory: an interpretation consistent with the novel's style, given that Van and Ada attempt a joint work that is intended to bring about a merging of art and science. Meanwhile, the anagram *adalucinda* appears to refer to Time as pain and regret. Throughout, Ada represents the ghost of childhood, art, or the inseparable materiality of Van's memory. Only after he is free to live with Ada does Van come to regret his shoddy treatment of Lucette, an emotional response that is echoed in Ada's comment: "Oh, Van, oh Van, we did not love her enough." In response, Van asks, "Was it time for the morphine?" (586).

Overall, the novel illustrates that we cannot touch or grasp the present, because at the moment we attempt to do so, it has already become part of the past. It exists as a void, a soft hollow that is filled with longing for the past or hopes for the future. As suggested in Van's amusing lecture on dreams, our grasp of the real object is impossible, for it is constantly deferred as regret or pain. Thus, when Van is enthralled with Ada and the beauty of Ardis Hall, he is incapable of perceiving Lucette's thwarted love and emotional pain. He becomes aware of her dire situation only when it is too late for him to address it. As Van reflects, life is so deceptive that our hopes can no more bring to fruition the Future than our regrets can change the Past. Indeed, time can only be viewed in retrospect. At the moment Van is reunited with Ada (who appears to serve as an emblem of Europe, or Russia, for Nabokov), he loses contact with the ghost of Ada, who is replaced by the ghost of Lucette (an apparent emblem of America). For Van, the pain of this recognition is overwhelming, because Lucette is gone, and he is nearing the end of his life.

Notably, in a letter penned to Dan Lacy in 1973, Nabokov describes his plan to compose *Speak, America*, which he frames as a continuation of his *Speak, Memory*—although the project would never be realized (SL, 508). His apparent longing for America also surfaced in numerous interviews: "I feel very nostalgic about America and as soon as I muster the necessary energy I shall return there for good" (SO 56).[7] During his time in America, the ghost that haunted Nabokov was that of his childhood in Russia and his exile in Western Europe. Yet, when he left America and returned to Europe, Switzerland, America soon emerged as a ghost: a place to which he could no longer return, as he proclaims that Lucette's tragic destiny constitutes one of the highlights of this book. Similarly, in *Ada*, Van rejects Lucette not only because he remains in love with Ada, but also because Lucette appears not as a veiled image but instead as a real object. Ultimately, Van concludes that Terra and Anti-terra do not exist separately, but rather as two components within one dimension of reality, thereby serving as a contingency of generalization, or resemblance. More than anything else, Terra exists within us as a contingency of Anti-terra.

Following Van's banishment from Ardis Hall, he comes to despise Terra as a bastion of generalization, whose worst manifestations include Russian communism and German Nazism. Van is subsequently exiled to Anti-terra, a world of memory that could also be described as an anachronistic world of perception. These terms can be grasped more easily if they are related to the concept of time. For instance, if Terra-Time is equated with linear time, Antiterra-Time can be viewed as perceptual time, an observation that Van makes in Part Four. Interestingly, before his metamorphosis, he repudiates Terra's ideology as the instrument of "cosmic propaganda," or the product of the brutal Tartars of Russia. However, after his transformation, he comes to accept Terra as a contingency of Anti-terra. As Michael Seidel argues, Anti-terra is conceived as a personal dimension, "which is why it exists aesthetically" (1987, 242), whereas Terra belongs to the realm of the formal dimension of generalization. Indeed, at one point, Van states that "sick minds identified the notion of a Terra planet with that of another world and this 'Other

World' got confused not only with the 'Next World' but with the Real World in us and beyond us" (AD 20).

Van's passion for meaningful intercommunication between Terra the Fair and the dismal Anti-terra finds its parallel in the apparent intertwining of Freud and Nabokov throughout the novel. Is it possible that Nabokov, in his subversive imitation of Freudian sexuality (particularly the Oedipus complex), positions Freud as an intimate foe, an inseparable contingency of his own psyche? Notably, while his protagonist, Van, rejects the unconscious, he does so with a violence that betrays his furtive attraction to it. For Van, Freudians serve simultaneously as an object of contempt and admiration. Indeed, as Claude Mouchard observes, Nabokov's challenge to Freudians, especially in his preface, is "almost an obligatory rite of passage" (1984, 131). In this amusing anti-Signy ritual, scientific approaches to mimicry and memory are merged into an aesthetic form, while Nabokov turns his intimate foe, Freud, into the lynchpin of his art. He does so with a rich humor that reflects his celebratory view of the possibilities of the human imagination.

NOTES

1. Mary Ellmann contends "that teasing of the reader which was sufficient in *Pale Fire* is now excessive" (1982, 208).

2. Barton Jonson introduces a new family tree that reflects a prevalence of incest. For instance, Dolly is Demon's true father, just as Marina is Van's real mother, and so on (1986, 224-255).

3. George Steiner argues that the novel's cross-cultural elements are composed of three different languages (1970); Alfred Appel, Jr., regards *Amerussia* as the merging of Lucette and Ada (1970, 167); Susan Elizabeth Sweeney observes that, in *Ada*, the two worlds of Kinbote's Zembla and Shade's New Wye have been merged into one, *Amerussia* (1994, 332).

4. See Stephen H. Blackwell, "The Poetics of Science in, and around, Nabokov's *The Gift*" (2003): "we need to begin to address how it is that the scientific temperament and the artistic are mixed in one individual. A still greater challenge is the question of how the scientific (that is, objective, descriptive) and artistic (subjective, creative) expressions of Nabokov's genius in fact emanate from a common core" (244).

5. Alfred Appel, Jr., contends that we are witnesses to Ada's and Van's role in Lucette's self-destruction (1970, 181).

6. The actual opening sentence of *Anna Karenina* goes as follows: "Happy families are all alike; every unhappy family is unhappy in its own way."

7. In 1964, Nabokov participated in two interviews in which he remarked that he possessed the same fertile nostalgia in regard to America, his new country, as he evolved for Russia, his old one, "in the first post-revolution years of West-European expatriation" (SO 49). As Susan Elizabeth Sweeney notes, Nabokov claimed repeatedly that he was happier in America with his best readers than in any other country, and he was *an American writer* (1994, 333).

Conclusion

Nabokov enjoyed writing fiction every bit as much as he enjoyed butter-fly hunting, since they share a common element of deception. It is, there-fore, no coincidence that his work focuses so consistently on his memo-ries of childhood, which drift into the realms of fantasy and fiction. His passion for chasing the butterfly reflected its personal significance as an emblem of the subtle yet intricate mimicry that enlivens a sophisticated consciousness. Repudiating a strictly utilitarian view of biological mimic-ry, along with a totalistic perception of the past and time, Nabokov em-ploys literary devices of deception, drawing upon psychology and biolo-gy, i.e., memory and mimicry. Accordingly, his art appears to unfold in an arena in which the humanities are devoted to natural phenomena, while biology seeks to demonstrate the imaginative capacity of the hu-man mind.

As he strove to produce art that was experimental in nature, the de-gree of deception in his work gradually increased, doing so in proportion to his advancing years. It is, after all, widely recognized that one's memo-ry becomes blurred and complicated over time, with the superimposition of later experiences upon earlier ones. Consequently, as Nabokov's work developed, it involved more extravagant forms of mimicry. This seems quite natural, given that his fiction was a reflection of his mind. De la Durantaye's claim that Nabokov was "a creature in a deceptive creation and a creator of deceptive creations" is, in this sense, readily apparent (2007, 156). Nabokov, through his work, sheds light on human beings in the contexts of both natural phenomena (mimicry) and material con-sciousness (deceptive memory). While it may be true that one's creative force becomes enfeebled over time, it also expands in accordance with the development of consciousness, given that memory is, in itself, a work of art.

In my readings of Nabokov's work, I have identified the author's incremental progress in the direction of complexity. Hence, *The Luzhin Defense* is less challenging than his next novel, *Despair*. In the latter, the deceptive strategy of mimicry has been integrated carefully into what appears to be a well-organized plot featuring plausible characterizations; and one can only hope that my analysis reflects my appreciation of the work's rich humor. Nevertheless, his third novel, *Lolita*, represents the zenith of his literary career, especially in terms of his masterful mimicry of Freud. Throughout the novel, the author engages in a game of hide-

and-seek with the reader, while employing carefully nuanced levels of deception. Hence, for ordinary readers, *Lolita* functions as a literary masterpiece that explores the vagaries of love, while more sophisticated readers recognize it as something altogether different: a groundbreaking work in which the author presents *art as science*.

In *Pale Fire*, Nabokov's approach to composition becomes more intricate and complex as his memory grows more pale and, in certain ways, larger. Indeed, the author's unfettered imagination encompasses much of the world, stretching from Russia, through Europe, to America. As the novel alternates between verse and prose, with a narrative forged by the competing voices of a poet and a mad critic, the game of hide-and-seek proves more arduous. Admittedly, in my effort to analyze this mysterious novel, I struggled to untangle the densely interwoven significations to get to the point, i.e., the manner in which the characters imitate either Freud or Nabokov. The modes of disguise adopted by the poet and commentator are less tangible—and far less consistent—than in the cases of either Humbert or Quilty, in *Lolita*, and the density of the deception is more profound. Moreover, the duration of Kinbote's memory is longer than that of Humbert, given that he is described as older, and it takes on more fictional elements. As William James observes, the remote past is not so much perceived as madly conceived. If, however, it seems unlikely that Nabokov could produce a deception based on memory and mimicry that exceeds the pale memory of *Pale Fire*, he nevertheless manages to do so. Approaching his seventies, the author immerses himself in the character of Van, the ninety-two-year-old narrator of *Ada, or Ardor*, who suffers from weak memory.

The challenge that the author assumes in *Ada* takes the form of a pseudo-philosophical pamphlet in which his artistic sensibility stretches across national boundaries to encompass the material world. In some ways, the novel echoes the final stage of Joyce's creative evolution, *Finnegans Wake*. There is much that is familiar, however. As usual, Nabokov mimics the Freudian incest taboo, in a manner that is clearly subversive. That being said, the work focuses on the expanded consciousness of an elderly man in terms of his relationship with the world. Nabokov, then a resident of Switzerland, appears to ruefully reflect on his years in America, regretting that he did not fully appreciate the experience at the time. These feelings lend weight to Van's poignant feelings of regret over the loss of Lucette, which surface in the wake of his reunion with Ada. Overall, the novel suggests that we tend to love that which turns out to be unreachable, which is absent; and this may be Nabokov's parting sentiment. It is important to add, however, that given the distortions and deceptions that shape the narrative, *Ada* is largely resistant to any straightforward analysis.

As noted, Nabokov, in interview after interview, eagerly denounced Freud, in a manner that suggested he was enjoying himself. At the same time, he appeared to be operating out of a sense of artistic duty. Significantly, Freud does seem to play an almost collaborative role in Nabokov's art: a situation underscored in *Lolita*, when we learn that a play in which Lolita appears has been co-authored by Humbert and Quilty. However, the role that Freud plays in Nabokov's work is so deeply embedded within the narrative that it transcends the surface level of words and sentences, as shown in my analysis of five of his major novels. In *The Luzhin Defense*, for instance, dreams serve as reality for a protagonist who sustains his life with a series of chess matches, while reflecting on vague memories of the past. In *Despair*, the Freudian symbol of the *stick* emerges as a contingency, while in *Lolita*, infantile sexuality is mimicked, only to be transcended by an artist seeking the brand of immortality that is achieved only through art. Likewise, homosexuality in *Pale Fire* and the incest taboo in *Ada* are closely related to the strategy of resemblance with a difference. In short, we find the repetition of a similar strategy throughout Nabokov's various works of fiction. Could it be that he is unconsciously generalizing as an artistic device? Whatever the case, it is crucial to remember that Nabokov, as a mimic, functions as a poet who is also a scientist, while his model, Freud, operates as a scientist who is also a poet. What both writers have in common is that they are gifted humorists, and Nabokov himself acknowledged that he admired Freud as a great comic writer.[1] In *Gift*, he appears to celebrate wit and humor as the essence of mimicry, while positioning it as a central feature of his art. Yet, while he evidently takes pleasure in art for its own sake, Nabokov also views it as a formidable vehicle for the repudiation of all forms of totality.

NOTE

1. In a televised French interview (*Aphostrophes*), Nabokov acknowledged, "I admire Freud greatly as a comic writer." See de la Durantaye's *Style Is Matter*, p. 118.

References

THE PRIMARY SOURCES: VLADIMIR NABOKOV

Nabokov, Vladimir. *Ada, or Ardor* (1969). New York: Vintage International, 1990.
———. *Bend Sinister* (1947). New York: McGraw-Hill paperback edition, 1974.
———. *Despair* (1965, 1966). New York: Vintage International, 1989.
———. *The Eye* (1965, 1990). New York: Vintage International, 1990.
———. *The Gift.* New York: G.P. Putnam's Sons. 1963.
———. *King, Queen, Knave* (1968). New York: McGraw-Hill Book Company, 1981.
———. *Lectures on Literature* (1980). Edited by Fredson Bowers. New York: A Harvest/HBJ Book, 1982.
———. *Lolita* (1955). New York: Berkley Medallion Books, 1966.
———. *Lolita: A Screenplay* (1974). New York: Vintage International, 1997.
———. *The Luzhin Defense* (1964). New York: Vintage International, 1990.
———. *The Real Life of Sebastian Knight* (1941). New York: New Directions, 1959.
———. *Pale Fire* (1962). New York: Vintage International, 1989.
———. *Strong Opinions.* New York: Vintage International, 1973.
———. *Speak, Memory: An Autobiography Revisited.* New York: Vintage International, 1989.
———. *Vladimir Nabokov: Selected Letters 1940–1977.* Edited by Dmitri Nabokov & Matthew J. Bruccoli. New York: A Harvest/HBJ Book, 1989.
———. "Rain." *The Portable Nabokov.* Edited by Page Stegner. New York: Penguin Books. 1968, 533.
———. "Reply to My Critics." *The Portable Nabokov.* Edited by Page Stegner. New York: Penguin Books. 1968, 300–24.
———. "Signs and Symbols." *Nabokov's Dozen: A Collection of Thirteen Stories.* New York: Anchor Press/Doubleday, 1984, 67–74.
———. "Cloud, Castle, Lake." *Nabokov's Dozen: A Collection of Thirteen Stories.* New York: Anchor Press/Doubleday, 1984, 113–123.
———. "Scenes from the Life of a Double Monster." *Nabokov's Dozen: A Collection of the Thirteen Stories,* 1984, 165–175.
———. "Nabokov's Dreams." *The New Yorker,* Mar 29, Vol. 75.5, 1999, 87–88.
———. "National Book Award Acceptance Speech" (April 1975, Montreux.) *The Nabokovian* 13 (1984): 16–17.

INTERVIEWS

January 30, 1966 with Robert Hughes at Switzerland, *The New York Times* on the Web. http://www.nytimes.com/books/97/03/02/lifetimes/nab-v-freud.html
Gold, Herbert. "Interview with Vladimir Nabokov." Ed. Ellen Pifer. *Vladimir Nabokov's Lolita: a Casebook.* New York: Oxford University Press, 2003, 195–206.

SIGMUND FREUD

Freud, Sigmund. "Project for a Scientific Psychology." The *Standard Edition of the Complete Psychological Works of Sigmund Freud*. Edited & Translated by James Strachey. New York: Norton, Vol. 1, 281–397. 1950 [1895].

———. "Screen Memories." *Standard Edition*, Vol. 3, 301–22.

———. *The Interpretation of Dreams. Standard Edition*. Vols. 4 & 5, 1–621.

———. *Three Essays on the Theory of Sexuality. Standard Edition*. Vol. 7, 125–243.

———. "Jokes and their Relation to the Unconsciousness." *Standard Edition*. Vol. 8, 3–237.

———. "Creative Writers and Day-Dreaming." *Standard Edition*. Vol. 9, 141–153.

———. "Leonardo Da Vinci and a Memory of his Childhood." *Standard Edition*. Vol. 11, 59–137.

———. "Remembering, Repeating, and Working-Through." *Standard Edition*. Vol. 12, 145–156.

———. "On Narcissism: An Introduction." *Standard Edition*. Vol. 14, 67–104.

———. "Instincts and their Vicissitudes." *Standard Edition*. Vol. 14, 109–140.

———. "A Difficulty in the Path of Psychoanalysis." *Standard Edition*. Vol. 17, 137–44.

———. "From the History of an Infantile Neurosis." *Standard Edition*. Vol. 17, 3–123.

———. "A Note upon the 'Mystic writing-Pad'." *Standard Edition*. Vol. 19, 225–32.

———. "Humour." *Standard Edition*. Vol. 21, 160–166.

———. "Dostoevsky and Parricide." *Standard Edition*, Vol. 21, 173–194.

———. *The Complete Letters of Sigmund Freud to Wilhelm Fliess 1887–1904*. Edited & Translated by Jeffrey M. Masson. Cambridge, Mass.: Harvard University Press, 1985.

THE SECONDARY SOURCES

Alexander, Victoria N. "Nabokov, Teleology, and Insect Mimicry." *Nabokov Studies* 7 (2002/2003): 177–213.

Alexandrov, Vladimir E. "A Note on Nabokov's Anti-Darwinism; or, Why Apes Feed on Butterflies in *The Gift*." *Freedom and Responsibility in Russian Literature*. Evanston: Northwestern University Press, 1994, 239–44.

Andrews, David. "Varieties of Determinism: Nabokov among Rorty, Freud, and Sartre." *Nabokov Studies* 6 (2000/2001): 1–33.

Appel, Alfred. Jr. "Nabokov's Puppet Show-ll." *New Republic*. Vol. 156 (21 Jan. 1967), 25–32.

———. "*Ada* described." *Nabokov: Criticism, Reminiscences, Translations, and Tributes*. Eds. Alfred Appel, Jr. & Charles Newman. New York: Simon and Schuster, 1970, 160–186.

Appel, Alfred Jr., ed. *The Annotated Lolita* by Vladimir Nabokov. New York: Penguin Books, 2000.

Ashenden, Liana. "*Ada*'s Erotic Entomology." *Nabokov Studies* 6 (2000/2001): 129–148.

Barabtarlo, Gennady. *Aerial View: Essays on Nabokov's Art and Metaphysics*. New York: Peter Lang Publishing, 1993.

Belletto, Steven. "The Zemblan who came in from the cold, or Nabokov's *Pale Fire*, Chance and the Cold War." *ELH* 73 (2006): 755–780.

Berenbaum, May. "Blue Book Value." *Science*. Vol. 290, no. 5489, 6 Oct. 2000, 57–58.

Bergson, Henri. *Matter and Memory*. Translated by Nancy Margaret Paul & W. Scott Palmer. New York: Dover Publisher (1912), 2004.

Berman, Jeffrey. "Nabokov and the Viennese Witch Doctor." *The Talking Cure: Literary Representations of Psychoanalysis*. New York: New York University Press, 1985, 1987, 211–238.

Bhabha, Homi. *The Location of Culture*. London: Routledge, 1994.

Blackwell, Stephen H. *The Quill and the Scalpel: Nabokov's Art and the Worlds of Science*. Columbus: The Ohio State University Press, 2009.

———. "The Poetics of Science in and around Nabokov's *The Gift*." *The Russian Review* 62 (2003): 243–261.

———. "Nabokov's Wiener-schnitzel Dreams: *Despair* and Anti-Freudian Poetics." *Nabokov Studies* 7 (2002/2003): 129–150.

Borden, Richard C. "Nabokov's Travesties of Childhood Nostalgia." *Nabokov Studies* 2 (1995): 104–134.

Boyd, Brian. "*Ada*." *The Garland Companion to Vladimir Nabokov*. Edited by Vladimir E. Alexandrov. New York: Garland Publishing, 1995, 3–18.

———. "Annotations to *Ada*: 16: Part 1 Chapter 16." *Nabokovian* 45 (Fall 2000): 54–76.

———. *Nabokov's Ada: the Place of Consciousness*. New Zealand: Cybereditions, 2001.

———. "Nabokov, Literature, Lepidoptera." Boyd and Pyle 2000, 1–31.

———. "Pale Fire." *Nabokov at Cornell*. Edited by Gavriel Shapiro. Ithaca: Cornell University Press, 2003, 78–90.

———. "Shade and Shape in *Pale Fire*." *Nabokov Studies* 4 (1997): 173–224.

———. *Vladimir Nabokov: The American Years*. Princeton: Princeton University Press, 1991.

———. *Vladimir Nabokov: The Russian Years*. Princeton: Princeton University Press, 1990.

Boyd, Brian and Robert M. Pyle, eds. *Nabokov's Butterflies: Unpublished and Uncollected Writings*. Translated by Dmitri Nabokov. Boston: Beacon Press, 2000.

Bruss, Elizabeth W. "Vladimir Nabokov: Illusions of Reality and the Reality of Illusions." *Modern Critical Views: Vladimir Nabokov*. Edited by Harold Bloom. New York: Chelsea House, 1967, 1987, 27–64.

Bruss, Paul. *Victims: Textual Strategies in Recent American Fiction*. New Jersey: Associated University Press, 1981.

Cameron, Laura and John Forrester. "Tansley's Psychoanalytic Network: an Episode out of the Early History of Psychoanalysis in England." *Psychoanalysis and History* 2.2 (2000): 189–256.

Casey, M. A. *Meaninglessness: The Solutions of Nietzsche, Freud, and Rorty*. New York: Lexington Books, 2002.

Connolly, Julian W. "The Major Russian Novels." *The Cambridge Companion to Nabokov*. Edited by Julian W. Connolly. Cambridge: Cambridge University Press, 2005. 135–150.

Couturier, Maurice. "The near-tyranny of the author: *Pale Fire*." *Nabokov and his Fiction: New Perspectives*. Edited by Julian W. Connolly. Cambridge: Cambridge University Press, 1999, 54–72.

Crosby, Donald A. *The Philosophy of William James*. New York: Rowman & Littlefield Publishers, 2013.

Damasio, Antonio. *Descartes' Error: Emotion, Reason, and the Human Brain*. New York: Penguin Books, 1994.

De la Durantaye, Leland. "Vladimir Nabokov and Sigmund Freud, or a Particular Problem." *American Imago* 62.1 (2005): 59–73.

———. *Style Is Matter: The Moral Art of Vladimir Nabokov*. Ithaca: Cornell University Press, 2007.

———. "Artistic Selection: Science and Art in Vladimir Nabokov." *Transitional Nabokov*. Edited by Will Norman & Duncan White. Oxford: Peter Lang, 2009, 55–66.

Detweiler, Robert. "Games and Play in Modern American Fiction." *Contemporary Literature* 17 (1976): 44–62.

Dragunoiu, Dana. "Vladimir Nabokov's *Ada*: Art, Deception, Ethics." *Contemporary Literature* 46.2 (2005): 311–339.

Edelman, Gerald M. *Wider than the Sky: the phenomenal gift of consciousness*. New Haven: Yale University Press, 2004.

Edelstein, Marilyn. "*Pale Fire*: The Art of Consciousness." *Nabokov's Fifth Arc*. Edited by J. E. Rivers & Charles Nicol. Austin: University of Texas Press, 1982, 213–223.

Ellmann, Mary. "Mary Ellmann in *Yale Review*, Oct. 1969, 118–19." *Nabokov: The Critical Heritage*. Edited by Norman Page. London: Routledge, 1982, 207–208.

Elms, Alan C. "Nabokov contra Freud." *The Nabokovian* 13 (1984): 42–44.

———. "Cloud, Castle, Claustrum: Nabokov as a Freudian in spite of himself." *Russian Literature and Psychoanalysis*. Edited by Daniel Rancour-Laferriere. Amsterdam: J. Benjamins Pub. Co., 1989, 353–379.

Evreinoff, Nicolas. *The Theatre in Life*. Edited & Translated by Alexander I. Nazaroff. New York: Brentano's, 1927. Reprint: Mansfield Centre, Conn.: Martino Publishing, 2013.

Field, Andrew. *Nabokov: His Life in Art*. Boston: Little Brown, 1967.

Field, David. "Fluid Worlds: Lem's *Solaris* and Nabokov's *Ada*." *Science-Fiction Studies* 13 (1986): 329–344.

Flower, Timothy F. "The Scientific Art of Nabokov's *Pale Fire*." *Criticism: a Quarterly for Literature and the Arts*. 17.3 (1975): 223–233.

Forbes, Peter. *Dazzled and Deceived: Mimicry and Camouflage*. New Haven: Yale University Press, 2009.

Forrester, John. "Freud in Cambridge." *Critical Quarterly* 46.2 (2004): 1–26.

Forrester, John and Laura Cameron. "Tansley's Psychoanalytic Network: An Episode out of the Early History of Psychoanalysis in England." *Psychoanalysis and History* 2.2 (2000): 189–256.

Fowler, Douglas. *Reading Nabokov*. Ithaca: Cornell University Press, 1974.

Frank, Siggy. *Nabokov's Theatrical Imagination*. Cambridge: Cambridge University Press, 2012.

Fulford, Robert. "Deceit, Parody and the Furtive Pleasures of Art." *Queen's Quarterly* 119/1 (2012): 59–68.

Galef, David. "The Self-Annihilating Artists of *Pale Fire*." *Twentieth Century Literature* 31.4 (1985): 421–437.

Glynn, Michael. "'The word is not a shadow. The word is a thing'—Nabokov as Anti-symbolist." *European Journal of American Culture* 25.1 (2006): 3–30.

Gould, Stephen Jay. "No Science without Fancy, No Art without Facts: The Lepidoptery of Vladimir Nabokov." *Vera's Butterflies*. Sarah Funke et. al. New York: Glenn Horowitz Bookseller, 1999, 29–53.

Green, Geoffrey. *Freud and Nabokov*. Lincoln: University of Nebraska Press, 1988.

———. "Splitting of the Ego: Freudian doubles, Nabokovian doubles." *Russian Literature and Psychoanalysis*. Edited by Daniel Rancour-Laferriere. Amsterdam: J. Benjamins Pub. Co., 1989, 369–379.

Grishakova, Marina. "On Some Semiotic Models in Vladimir Nabokov's Fiction." *Interliteraria* 8 (2003): 291–306.

Guerard, Albert J. "Notes on the Rhetoric of Anti-realist Fiction." *Triquarterly* 30 (1974): 3–50.

Heidegger, Martin. *What is Called Thinking?* Translated by J. Glenn Gray. New York: Perennial, 1976, 2004.

Hennard, Martine. "Playing a Game of Worlds in Nabokov's *Pale Fire*." *Modern Fiction Studies* 40.2 (summer 1994): 299–317.

Hiatt, L. R. "Nabokov's *Lolita*: A "Freudian" Cryptic Crossword." *American Imago* 24.4 (1967): 360–70.

Ingham, John M. "Primal Scene and Misreading in Nabokov's *Lolita*." *American Imago* 59 (2002): 27–52.

James, William. *The Principles of Psychology*." Vol. 1 & 2. New York: Digireads, 2010. Print.

———. "Does 'Consciousness' Exist? *Journal of Philosophy, Psychology, and Scientific Methods* 1 (1904): 477–491.

Johnson, Barton D. "The Labyrinth of Incest in Nabokov's *Ada*." *Comparative Literature* 38.3 (1986): 224–255.

———. "Sources of Nabokov's *Despair*." *Nabokov at Cornell*. Edited by Gavriel Shapiro. Ithaca: Cornell University Press, 2003, 10–19.

Johnson, Barton D. and Ellendea Proffer. "Interview with Véra Nabokov and Dmitri Nabokov." *Russian Literature and Triquarterly* 24 (1991): 73–85.

Johnson, Kurt. "Recognizing Vladimir Nabokov's Legacy in Science: Where We Are Today: Where We Go from Here." *Nabokov Studies* 6 (2000/2001): 149–161.

Johnson, Kurt and Steve Coates. *Nabokov's Blues: The Scientific Odyssey of a Literary Genius.* New York: McGraw-Hill, 1999.

Jones, Ernest. *The Life and Work of Sigmund Freud. Vol. 1.* New York: Basic Books, 1953, 1981.

Kandel, Erick R. *The Age of Insight.* New York: Random House, 2012.

Karlinsky, Simon, ed. *The Nabokov-Wilson Letters.* New York: Harper and Row, 1979.

Karshan, Thomas. *Vladimir Nabokov and the Art of Play.* Oxford: Oxford University Press, 2011.

Kernan, Alvin B. "Reading Zemblan: The Audience Disappears in *Pale Fire.*" *Vladimir Nabokov.* Ed. Harold Bloom. New York: Chelsea House Publishers, 1987, 101–125.

Kilbourn, R. J. A. "*Ada* in Chiasmus: Chiasmus in *Ada.*" *Nabokov Studies* 5 (1998/1999): 129–143.

Kleisner, Karel and Anton Markoš. "Semetic rings: towards the new concept of mimetic resemblances." *Theory in Biosciences* 123 (2005): 209–222.

Kuzmanovich, Zoran. "'Splendid Insincerity' as 'Utmost Truthfulness': Nabokov and the Claims of the Real." *Nabokov's World. Vol. 1: The Shape of Nabokov's World.* New York: Palgrave, 2002, 26–46.

Lacan, Jacques. *The Fundamental Concepts of Psychoanalysis. The Seminar of Jacques Lacan, Book XI.* Edited by J-A. Miller. Translated by Alan Sheridan. New York: Norton, 1981.

Lee, L. L. *Vladimir Nabokov.* Boston: Twayne Publishers, 1976.

Livak, Leonid. "Vladimir Nabokov's Apprenticeship in Andre Gide's Science of Illumination. *Comparative Literature* 54.3 (2002): 197–213.

Lyons, John O. "*Pale Fire* and the Fine Art of Annotation." *Wisconsin Studies in Contemporary Literature* 8.2 (1967): 242–249.

Maran, Timo. "Semiotic Interpretations of Biological Mimicry." *Semiotica* 167–1/4 (2007): 223–248.

McCaffery, Larry. *The Metafictional Muse.* Pittsburgh: University of Pittsburgh Press, 1982.

McCarthy, Mary. "*Pale Fire.*" *Nabokov: The Critical Heritage.* Edited by Norman Page. London: Routledge, 1982, 124–136.

Metzger, Sabine. "Beyond the Pleasure Principle: Nabokov's *Homo Poeticus.*" *Nabokovian* 62 (2009): 2–25.

Moraru, Christian. "Time, Writing, and Ecstasy in *Speak, Memory*: Dramatizing the Proustian Project." *Nabokov Studies* 2 (1995): 173–90.

Morton, Donald E. *Vladimir Nabokov.* New York: Frederick Unger Publishing Co., 1974.

Mouchard, Claude. "Doctor Froid." *Critical Essays on Vladimir Nabokov.* Edited by Phyllis A. Roth. Boston: G. K. Hall Publishers. 1984, 130–134.

Naiman, Eric. "Litland: The Allegorical Poetics of *The Defense.*" *Nabokov Studies* 5 (1998/1999): 1–46.

———. "Homophobia (On Sexual Orientation and Reading Nabokov)." *Representations* 101 (2008): 116–143.

Nepomnyashchy, Catharine T. "King, Queen, Sui-mate: Nabokov's *Defense* against Freud's 'Uncanny.'" *Intertexts* 12.1/2 (2008): 7–24.

Nicol, Charles. "*Ada* or Disorder." *Nabokov's Fifth Arc.* Edited by J. E. Rivers and Charles Nicol. Austin: University of Texas Press, 1982, 230–241.

Oakley, Helen. "Disturbing Design: Nabokov's Manipulation of the Detective Fiction Genre in *Pale Fire* and *Despair.*" *Journal of Popular Culture* 36 (2003): 480–496.

Ouspensky, P. D. *A New Model of the Universe.* Translated by R. R. Merton, New York: Dover Publications, 1997 (orig. New York: Alfred A. Knopf, 1931).

Pletsch, Carl. "Freud's Case Studies." *Partisan Review* 1 (1981): 101–118.

Ramey, James. "Parasitism and *Pale Fire*'s Camouflage." *Comparative Literature Studies* 41.2 (2004): 185–212.

Rea, John. Entry on NABOKOV-L. March 22, 2000.

Reading, Amy. "Vulgarity's Ironist: New Criticism, Midcult, and Nabokov's *Pale Fire*." *Arizona Quarterly* 62.2 (2006): 77–97.

Reik, Theodor. *Listening with the Third Ear*. New York: Farrar, Straus, and Giroux, 1948, 1975, 1998.

Ritland, David B. and Lincoln P. Brower. "The viceroy butterfly is not a batesian mimic." *Nature* Vol. 350 (April 1991): 497–498.

Rivers, J. E. "Proust, Nabokov, and *Ada*." *French-American Review* 1.3 (1977): 173–197.

Rorty, Richard. "The Barber of Kasbeam: Nabokov on Cruelty." In *Contingency, Irony, and Solidarity*. Cambridge: Cambridge University Press, 1989, 141–168.

———. "Freud and Moral Reflection." In *Essays on Heidegger and Others: Philosophical Papers*. Vol. 2. Cambridge: Cambridge University Press, 1991, 143–163.

Rowe, William Woodin. *Nabokov's Deceptive World*. New York: New York University Press, 1971.

Schacter, Daniel L. *Searching for Memory: the Brain, the Mind, and the Past*. New York: Basic Books, 1996.

Schiff, Stacy. *Vera*. New York: The Modern Library, 1999.

Schuetz, Alfred. "William James's Concept of the Stream of Thought Phenomenologically Interpreted." *Philosophy and Phenomenological Research* 1.4 (1941): 442–452.

Seidel, Michael. "*Pale Fire* and the Art of the Narrative Supplement." *ELH* 51.4 (1984): 837–855.

———. "Stereoscope: Nabokov's *Ada* and *Pale Fire*." *Vladimir Nabokov*. Edited by Harold Bloom. New York: Chelsea House Publishers, 1987, 235–257.

Sharpe, Tony. *Vladimir Nabokov*. London: Edward Arnold, 1991.

Shevrin, Howard. "A Psychoanalytic View of Memory in the Light of Recent Cognitive and Neuroscience Research." *Neuropsychoanalysis* 4 (2002): 131–139.

Shute, Jenefer. "Nabokov and Freud." *The Garland Companion to Vladimir Nabokov*. Edited by Vladimir E. Alexandrov. New York: Garland Publishing Inc., 1995, 412–420.

Sicker, Philip. "Practicing Nostalgia: Time and Memory in Nabokov's Early Russian Fiction." *Studies in Twentieth Century Literature* 11.2 (1987): 253–270.

Singer, Jefferson A. and Peter Salovey. *The Remembered Self: Emotion and Memory in Personality*. New York: The Free Press, 1993.

Smock, Ann. *Double Dealing*. Lincoln: University of Nebraska Press, 1985.

Steiner, George. "Extraterritorial." *Nabokov: Criticism, Reminiscences, Translations, and Tributes*. Edited by Alfred Appel, Jr. and Charles Newman. New York: Simon and Schuster, 1970, 119–127.

Stegner, Page. *Escape into Aesthetics: The Art of Vladimir Nabokov*. London: Eyre and Spottiswoode, 1966.

Stuart, Dabney. *Nabokov. The Dimensions of Parody*. Baton Rouge: Louisiana State University Press, 1978.

Straumann, Barbara. *Figurations of Exile in Hitchcock and Nabokov*. Edinburgh: Edinburgh University Press, 2008.

Suagee, Stephen. "An Artist's Memory Beats all Other Kinds: An Essay on *Despair*." *A Book of Things about Vladimir Nabokov*. Edited by Carl Proffer. Ann Arbor, Mich.: Ardis, 1974, 54–62.

Swanson, Roy A. "Nabokov's *Ada* as Science Fiction." *Science-Fiction Studies* 2.1 (1975): 76–88.

Sweeney, Susan Elizabeth. "'April in Arizona': Nabokov as an American Writer." *American Literary History* 6.2 (1994): 325–335.

Tammi, Pekka. "*Pale Fire*." *The Garland Companion to Vladimir Nabokov*. Edited by Vladimir E. Alexandrov. New York: Garland Publishers, 1995, 571–586.

Toker, Leona. *The Mystery of Literary Structures*. Ithaca: Cornell University Press, 1989.

Trzeciak, Joanna. "Viennese Waltz: Freud in Nabokov's *Despair.*" *Comparative Literature* 61.1 (2009): 53–68.

Tucker, Brian. *Reading Riddles: Rhetorics of Obscurity from Romanticism to Freud.* Lanham: Bucknell University Press, 2011.

Tulving, Endel, et al. "Toward a Theory of Episodic Memory: The Frontal Lobes and Autonoetic Consciousness." *Psychological Bulletin* 121 (1997): 331–54.

Turner, John R. G. "Mimicry: the Paratability Spectrum and its Consequences." *Biology of Butterflies.* Edited by R. I. Vane-Wright and P. R. Ackery. London: Academic Press, 1984, 141–161.

Updike, John. "Van Loves Ada, Ada Loves Van." *The New Yorker.* Aug. 2, 1969, 67–75.

Vane-Wright. R. I. "On the Definition of Mimicry." *Biological Journal of the Linnean Society* 13 (1980): 1–6.

———. "A case of self-deception" *Nature* (11 April, 1991) Vol. 350, 460–461.

Welsen, Peter. "Charles Kinbote's Psychosis—a Key to Vladimir Nabokov's *Pale Fire.*" *Russian Literature and Psychoanalysis.* Amsterdam: J. Benjamins Pub. Co., 1989, 381–400.

Wickler, Wolfgang. *Mimicry in Plants and Animals.* Translated by R. D. Martin. New York: McGraw-Hill Book Co., 1968.

———. "Mimicry." *The New Encyclopedia Britannica.* 15th ed. Vol. 24, 1998, 109–116.

Wood, Michael. *The Magician's Doubts: Nabokov and the Risks of Fiction.* Princeton: Princeton University Press, 1994.

Zaleski, Philip. "Nabokov's Blue Period." *Harvard Megazine* 86.6 (1986): 34–38.

Zimmer, Dieter E. "Mimicry in Nature and Art." *Nabokov's World: The Shape of Nabokov's World.* Vol. 1. Edited by Jane Grayson, Arnold McMillin, and Priscilla Meyer. New York: Palgrave, 2002, 47–57.

Index

About the Author

Teckyoung Kwon is a professor, literary critic, and noted authority on psychoanalytic theory in the Republic of Korea. She has been the recipient of numerous fellowships, including the National Research Foundation of Korea's "Fellow of Excellence Scholar in Humanities" (2012–2017). A prominent academic leader, Dr. Kwon has served as president of the American Fiction Association of Korea (2005–2007), as well as the American Studies Association of Korea (2009). Her Korean-language publications include numerous books, such as *What Is Post-Modernism?* (1990), *How to Read Fiction* (1995), *Writing in the Multicultural Age* (1997, winner of the Kim Hwan-tae Critic Award), and *Bio-Humanity* (2014). Dr. Kwon's various journal articles on literary theory, psychoanalysis, and fiction include "Materiality of Remembering," *New Literary History* 41.1 (2010); "Nabokov's Memory War against Freud," *American Imago* 68.1 (2011); and "Love as an Act of Dissimulation in 'The Beast in the Jungle,'" *Henry James Review* 36 (2015). Since completing her doctoral studies in the United States, she has served as a professor of English at Kyung Hee University in Seoul.